#1 *New York Times* bestselling author
Debbie Macomber

"Popular romance writer Debbie Macomber has a gift for evoking the emotions that are at the heart of the genre's popularity." —*Publishers Weekly*

"It's clear that Debbie Macomber cares deeply about her fully realized characters and their families, friends and loves, along with their hopes and dreams. She also makes her readers care about them."
—*Bookreporter.com*

"Debbie Macomber is one of the most reliable, versatile romance writers around." —*Milwaukee Journal Sentinel*

"Readers won't be able to get enough of Macomber's gentle storytelling." —*RT Book Reviews*

"Bestselling Macomber...sure has a way of pleasing readers." —*Booklist*

"It's impossible not to cheer for Macomber's characters.... When it comes to creating a special place and memorable, honorable characters, nobody does it better than Macomber." —*BookPage*

"Macomber is a master storyteller."
—*Times Record News*

DEBBIE MACOMBER

An Unexpected Love

The Man You'll Marry and *Bride on the Loose*

/// MIRA

/II MIRA™

ISBN-13: 978-0-7783-6857-1

An Unexpected Love

Recycling programs
for this product may
not exist in your area.

The Man You'll Marry
First published in 1992. This edition published in 2025.

Bride on the Loose
First published in 1992. This edition published in 2025.

Mira
22 Adelaide St. West, 41st Floor
Toronto, Ontario M5H 4E3, Canada
MIRABooks.com

Printed in U.S.A.

Also available from Debbie Macomber and MIRA

CONTENTS

THE MAN YOU'LL MARRY

One

Jill Morrison caught her breath as she stared excitedly out the airplane window. Seattle and everything familiar was quickly shrinking from view. She settled back and sighed with pure satisfaction.

This first-class seat was an unexpected gift from the airline. The booking agent had made a mistake and Jill turned out to be the beneficiary. Not a bad way to start a long-awaited vacation.

She glanced, not for the first time, at the man sitting beside her. He looked like the stereotypical businessman, typing industriously on a laptop, his brow furrowed with concentration. She couldn't tell exactly what he was doing, but noticed several columns of figures. He paused, and something must have troubled him, because he reached for a calculator in his briefcase and punched out a series of numbers. When he'd finished, he returned to his computer. He seemed impatient and restless, as though he begrudged the travel time. Not a good sign, in Jill's opinion, since the flight to Honolulu was scheduled to take five hours.

He wasn't the talkative sort, either. In her enthusi-

asm before takeoff, Jill had made a couple of attempts at light conversation, but both tries had met with minimal responses, followed by cool silence.

Great. She was stuck sitting next to this grouch for the beginning of a vacation she'd been planning for nearly two years. A vacation that Jill and her best friend, Shelly Hansen, had once dreamed of taking together. Only Shelly wasn't Shelly Hansen anymore. Her former college roommate was married now. For an entire month Shelly Hansen had been Shelly Brady.

Even after all this time, Jill had problems taking it in. For as long as Jill had known Shelly, her friend had been adamant about making her career as a producer of DVDs her highest priority. She'd vowed that men and relationships would always remain a distant second in her busy life. For years Jill had watched Shelly discourage attention from the opposite sex. From college onward, Shelly had carefully avoided any hint of commitment.

Then it had happened. Shelly met Mark Brady and the unexpected became a reality. To Shelly's way of thinking, her mother's great-aunt Millicent—known to everyone in the family as Aunt Milly—was directly responsible for her present happiness. She'd met her tax-accountant husband immediately after the elderly woman had mailed Shelly a "magic" wedding dress. The same dress Milly had worn herself more than sixty years earlier.

Both Shelly and Jill had insisted there was no such thing as magic, especially associated with a wedding dress. Magic belonged to wands or fairy godmothers, not wedding dresses. To fairy tales, not real life. They'd scoffed at the ridiculous story that went along with the

gown. Both refused to believe what Aunt Milly had written in her letter; no one in her right mind, they told each other, could possibly take the sweet old woman seriously. *Marry the next man you meet?* Preposterous.

Personally, Jill had found the whole story amusing. Shelly hadn't been laughing though. Shelly, being Shelly, had overreacted, fretting and worrying, wondering if there wasn't some small chance that Milly could be right. Shelly hadn't *wanted* her to be right, but there it was—the dress arrived one day, and the next she'd fallen into Mark Brady's arms.

Literally.

The rest, as they say, is history and Jill wasn't laughing anymore. Shelly and Mark had been married in June and to all appearances were blissfully happy.

Four weeks after the wedding, Jill was flying off to Hawaii. Not the best month to visit the tropics, perhaps, but that couldn't be helped. Her budget was limited and July offered the most value for her money.

Her seatmate leaned back and sighed deeply, pinching the bridge of his nose. Whatever problem he'd encountered earlier had persisted, Jill guessed. She must have been correct, because no more than ten seconds later, he reached for his calculator again. Jill had the impression this man never stopped working; even during their meal he continued his calculations. Not a moment of their flight time was wasted. If he wasn't studying papers from his briefcase, he was typing more columns of figures into his computer.

An hour passed. A couple of times, almost against her will, she found herself watching him. Although she assumed he was somewhere in his mid-thirties, he seemed older. No, she decided, not older, but...expe-

rienced. His face managed to be pleasing to the eye despite his rugged, uneven features. She wondered fleetingly how he'd assess *her* appearance. Except he hadn't looked at her once. He seemed totally unaware that there was anyone in the seat next to him. His eyes were gray, she'd noted earlier, the color of polished steel. There was nothing soft about him.

This was obviously a man who had it all—hand-tailored suits, Italian leather shoes, gold pen and watch. She'd bet even his plastic was gold! No doubt he lived the way he flew—first class. He was the type who had all the answers, too. The type of man who didn't question his own attitudes and beliefs....

He reminded Jill of her father, long dead, long grieved. He, too, had been an influential businessman who'd held success in the palm of his hand. Adam Morrison had fought off middle age on a gym floor. Energy was his trademark and death was an eternity away. Only it was just around the corner, and he hadn't known it.

Ironic that she should be sitting next to him thirteen years after his death. Not her father, but someone so much like him it was all Jill could do not to ask when he'd last seen his family.

He must have felt her scrutiny, because he suddenly turned and stared at her. Jill blushed guiltily, bowing her head over her book, reading it with exaggerated fervor.

"Did you like what you saw?" he asked her boldly.

"I—I don't know what you mean," she said in a small voice, moving the paperback close to her face.

For the first time since he'd taken the seat next to her, the stranger grinned. It was an odd smile, off center and unpracticed, as if he didn't often find anything to smile about.

The remainder of the flight was uneventful. Jill held her breath during the descent, until the tires bumped down on the runway in Honolulu. She wished again that Shelly was taking this trip, too. With or without her best friend, though, Jill intended to have the time of her life. She had seven glorious days to laze in the sun. Seven days to shop to her heart's content and to go sightseeing and to swim and relax and eat glorious meals.

For months Jill had dreamed of the wonders she would see and experience. Tranquil villages, orchid plantations—oh, how she loved orchids. At night, she'd stroll along lava-strewn beaches and by day there'd be canyons to explore, tumbling waterfalls and smoldering volcanoes. Hawaii was going to be a grand adventure, Jill felt sure of it.

The man beside her was on his feet the instant their plane came to a standstill. He removed his carry-on bag from the storage compartment above the seat with an efficiency that told her he was a seasoned traveler. The smiling flight attendant handed him a garment bag as he strode off the plane.

Jill followed him, watching for directions to the baggage pickup. Her seatmate's steps were crisp and purposeful. It didn't surprise her; this was a man on the go, always in a rush to get somewhere. Meet someone. Make a deal. No time to stop and smell the orchids for her friend the grouch.

Jill lost sight of him when she purchased a lei at a concession stand. She draped the lovely garland of orchids around her neck and fingered the delicate flowers, marveling at their beauty.

Once again the reminder that adventures awaited her on this tropical island moved full sail across her

heart. She wasn't the fanciful sort, nor did she possess an extravagant imagination. Not like Shelly. Yet Jill felt something deep inside her stir to life....

Shelly had become a real believer in magic, Jill mused, smiling as she bought herself a slice of fresh pineapple. For that matter, even she—ever the practical one—found herself a tiny bit susceptible to the claims of a charmed wedding dress. Just a tiny bit, though.

Jill's pulse quickened the way it did whenever she thought about what had happened between Shelly and Mark. It was simply the most romantic thing she'd ever known.

Romance had scurried past Jill several times. Currently she was dating Ralph, a computer programmer, but it was more for companionship than romance, although he'd been hinting for several months that they should start "getting serious." Jill assumed he meant marriage. Ralph was nice, and so far Jill had been able to dissuade him from discussing the future of their relationship. She didn't want to hurt his feelings, but she just wasn't interested in marrying him.

However, Jill fully intended to marry someday. There'd never been any question of that. The only question was *who*. She'd dated frequently in college, but there hadn't been anyone special. Then, when she'd been hired as a pharmacist for PayRite, a drugstore chain with several outlets in the Pacific Northwest, the opportunities to meet eligible men had dwindled dramatically.

Prospects weren't exactly crowding the horizon, but Jill had given up worrying about it. She'd done a fair job of pushing the thought of a husband and family

to the far reaches of her mind—until she'd made one small mistake.

She'd tried on Aunt Milly's wedding dress.

Shelly had hung the infamous dress in the very back of her closet. Out of sight, out of mind—only it hadn't worked that way. Not a minute passed that Shelly wasn't keenly aware of the dress and its alleged powers.

On impulse, Jill had tried it on herself. To this day she didn't know what had prompted her to slip into the beautiful hand-sewn wedding dress. It was so elegant, so beautiful, with row upon row of pearls and delicate lace layered over satin.

That it fit as though it had been specifically designed for her had been as much of a surprise to Shelly as it had to Jill. Shelly had seemed almost giddy with relief, insisting her aunt had made a mistake and the dress was actually meant for Jill. But by that time, Shelly had already met Mark....

No, Aunt Milly hadn't made a mistake—the wedding dress had been meant for Shelly all along. Her marriage to Mark proved it. And really, she'd have to attribute Shelly's meeting and marrying Mark to the power of suggestion, the power of expectation—not to *magic*. She shook her head and hurried off to retrieve her luggage.

Then she headed outside, intent on grabbing a taxi. As the driver loaded her bags, she stood for a moment, savoring the warm breeze, enjoying the first sounds and sights of Hawaii. She couldn't wait to get to her hotel. Through a friend who was a travel agent, Jill had been able to book a room in one of the most exclusive places on Oahu at a ridiculously low rate.

The hotel was everything the brochure had promised

and more. Jill had to pinch herself when she got to her room. The first thing she did was walk to the sliding-glass doors that led to the lanai, a balcony overlooking the swimming-pool area. Beyond that, the Pacific Ocean thundered against the sandy shore. The sight was mesmerizing, the beauty so keen, it brought tears of appreciation to Jill's eyes.

She tipped the bellhop, who'd brought up her luggage, and returned to the view. If she never went beyond this room, Jill would have been satisfied. She stood at the railing, the breeze riffling her long hair.

The hotel was U-shaped, and something—a movement, a figure—caught her eye. A man. Jill glanced across the swimming pool, across the tiki-hut roof of the bar until her gaze found what she was seeking. The grouch. In a lanai directly opposite hers. At least she thought so. He wore the same dark suit as the man with whom she'd spent five of the most uncommunicative hours of her life.

Jill didn't know what prompted her, but she waved. After a moment, he waved back. He stepped farther out onto the lanai and she knew beyond a doubt. Their rooms were in different sections of the hotel, but they were on the same floor, their lanais facing each other.

He held a cell phone to his ear, but slowly lowered it.

For several minutes they simply stared at each other. After what seemed like an embarrassingly long time, Jill tried to pull herself away and found she couldn't. Unsure why, unsure what had attracted her attention to the man in the first place, unsure of everything, Jill looked away.

A knock at the door distracted her.

"Yes?" she asked, opening her door. A bellhop in

a crisp white uniform stood before her with a large wrapped box.

"This arrived by special courier for you earlier today, Ms. Morrison," he explained politely.

When he'd gone, Jill studied the package, reading the Seattle postmark and the unfamiliar block printing. She carried it to the bed, still puzzled. She had no idea who would be mailing her anything from home. Especially since she'd only left that morning.

Sitting on the edge of the bed, she unwrapped the package and lifted the lid. Her hands froze. Her heart froze. Her breath jammed in her throat. When she was able to move again, she inhaled sharply and closed her eyes.

It was Aunt Milly's wedding dress.

A letter rested on top of the tissue-wrapped dress. With trembling hands, Jill reached for it.

Dearest Jill,
Trust me, I know exactly what you're feeling. I remember my own emotions when I opened this very box and found Aunt Milly's wedding dress staring up at me. As you know, my first instinct was to run and hide. Instead I was fortunate enough to find Mark and fall in love.

I suppose you're wondering why I'm mailing this dress to you in Hawaii. Why didn't I just give it to you before you left Seattle? Good question, and if I had a reasonable answer I'd be more than happy to share it.

One thing I've learned these past few months is that there's precious little logic when it comes to understanding any of this—love, fate, the magic

within Aunt Milly's wedding dress. Take my advice and don't even try to make sense of it.

I suppose I should tell you why I'm giving you the dress. I was sitting at the table one morning last week, with my first cup of coffee. I wasn't fully awake yet. My eyes were closed. Suddenly you were in my mind, standing waist-deep in blue-green water. There was a waterfall behind you and lush, beautiful plants all around. It had to be Hawaii. You looked happier than I can ever remember seeing you.

There was a man with you, and I wish I could describe him. Unfortunately, he was in shadow. Read into that whatever you will. There was a look about you, a look I've only seen once before—the day you tried on the wedding gown. You were radiant.

I talked to Mark about it, and he seemed to feel the same way I did—that the dress was meant for you. I phoned Aunt Milly and told her. She said by all means to make you its next recipient.

I should probably have given you the dress then, but something held me back. Nothing I can put into words, but a feeling that it would be too soon. So I'm sending it to you now.

My wish for you, Jill, is that you find someone to love. Someone as wonderful as Mark. Of the two of us, you've always been the sensible one. You believed in logic and common sense. But you also believed in love, long before I did. I was the skeptic there. Something tells me the man you'll marry is just as cynical as I once was. You're

going to have to teach him about love, the same
way Mark's taught me.

Call me as soon as you get back. I'll be waiting to hear what happens. In my heart I already
know it's going to be wonderful.

Love,
Shelly

Jill read the letter twice. Her pulse quickened as her
eyes lifted and involuntarily returned to the lanai directly across from her own.

The frantic pace of her heart slowed to normal.

The grouch was gone.

Jill recalled Aunt Milly's letter to Shelly. "When you
receive this dress," she'd written, "the first man you
meet is the man you'll marry."

So it wasn't the grouch, it was someone else. Not that
she really believed in any of this. Still, her knees went
unaccountably weak with relief.

After unpacking her clothes, Jill showered and lay
down for a few minutes. She hadn't intended to fall
asleep, but when she awoke, a rosy dusk had settled.
Flickering fires from the bamboo poles that surrounded
the pool sent shadows dancing on her walls.

She'd seen him, Jill realized. While she slept. Her
hero, her predestined husband. But try as she might, she
couldn't bring him into clear focus. Naturally it was her
imagination. Fanciful thinking. Dreams gone wild. Jill
reminded herself stoutly that she didn't believe in the
power of the wedding dress any more than she believed
in the Easter Bunny. But it was nice to fantasize now
and then, to pretend.

Unquestionably, there was a certain amount of antici-

pation created by the delivery of the wedding dress and
Shelly's letter. But unlike her friend, Jill didn't expect
anything to come of this. Jill's feet were firmly planted
on the ground. She wasn't as whimsical as Shelly, nor
was she as easily influenced.

True, at twenty-eight, Jill was more than ready to
marry and settle down. She knew she wanted children
eventually, too. But when it came to finding the man of
her dreams, she'd prefer to do it the old trial-and-error
way. She didn't need a magic wedding dress guiding
her toward him!

Initially, Shelly had had many of the same thoughts
herself, Jill remembered, but she'd married the first man
she'd met after the dress arrived.

The first man you meet. She was thinking about that
while she changed into a light cotton dress and sandals.
She was still thinking about it as she rode the elevator
down to the lobby to have a look around.

There must have been something in the air. Maybe it
was because she was on vacation and feeling free of her
usual routines and restraints; Jill didn't know. But for
some reason she found herself glancing around, wondering which man it might be.

The hotel was full of possibilities. A distinguished
gentleman sauntered past. An ambassador perhaps? Or
a politician? Hmm, that might be nice.

Nah, she countered silently, laughing at herself. She
wasn't interested in politics. Furthermore she didn't see
herself as an ambassador's wife. She'd probably say
the wrong thing to the wrong person and inadvertently
cause an international incident.

A guy who looked like a rock star strolled her way
next. Now, there was an interesting prospect, although

Jill had a minor problem picturing herself married to a man who wore his hair longer than she did. He was cute, though. A definite possibility—*if* she took Shelly's letter seriously.

A doctor would be ideal, Jill decided. With her medical background, they were sure to have a lot in common. She scanned the lobby area, searching for someone who looked as if he'd feel at home with a stethoscope around his neck.

No luck. Nor, for that matter, did she seem to be generating any interest herself. She might as well be invisible. So much for that! These speculations were all in fun anyway....

Swallowing an urge to laugh, she headed out the back of the hotel toward the pristine beach. A lazy evening stroll among swaying palms sounded just the thing.

She walked toward the ocean, removed her shoes and held them by the straps as she wandered ankle-deep into the delightfully warm water. She wasn't paying much attention to where she was going, thinking, instead, about her hopes for a family of her own. Thinking about the few truly happy memories she had of her father. The Christmas when she was five and a camping trip two years later. A picnic, once. But by the time she was eight, his success had overtaken him. It wasn't that he didn't love her or her mother, she supposed, but—

"I wouldn't go out much farther if I were you," a deep male voice called from behind her.

Jill's pulse soared at the unexpectedness of the intrusion. She saw the silhouette of a man leaning against a palm tree. In the darkness she couldn't make out his features, yet he seemed vaguely familiar.

"I won't," she said, trying to see who'd spoken. Whoever it was stayed stubbornly in the shadows of the tree.

From the distance Jill noted that he had the physique of an athlete. She happened to appreciate wide, powerful shoulders on a man. She stepped closer, attempting to get a better look at him without being obvious. Although his features remained hidden, his chin was tilted at a confident angle.

She'd always found confidence an appealing trait in a man....

"I wondered if you were planning to go swimming at night. Only a fool would do that."

Jill bristled. She had no intention of swimming. For one thing, she wasn't dressed for it. Before she could defend herself, however, he continued, "You look like one of those helpless romantics who can't resist testing the water. Let me guess—this is your first visit to the islands?"

Jill nodded. She'd ventured far enough onto the beach to actually see him now. Her heart sank—no wonder he'd seemed familiar. No wonder he was insulting. For the second time in a twenty-four-hour period she'd happened upon the grouch.

"I don't suppose you took time to eat dinner, either."

"I...had something earlier. On the plane." That had been one of the benefits of her unexpected move to first class.

"I was there, remember?" He snickered softly. "Plastic food."

Jill didn't agree—she'd enjoyed it—but she wasn't going to argue. "I don't know what concern it is of yours," she said.

"None," he admitted, shrugging.

"Then my going without dinner shouldn't bother you." She bristled again at the intense way he was studying her. His mouth had twisted into a faint smile, and he seemed amused by her.

"Thank you for your advice," she said stiffly, turning away from him and heading back toward the water.

"You're not wearing your lei."

Jill's fingers automatically went to her neck as she stopped. She'd left it in her room when she changed clothes.

"Allow me." He stepped forward, removed the one from his own neck and draped it around hers. Since this was her first visit to the islands, Jill didn't know if giving someone a lei had any symbolism attached to it. She didn't really want that kind of connection with him. Just in case.

"Thank you." She hoped she sounded adequately grateful.

"I might have saved your life, you know."

That was a ridiculous comment. "How?"

"You could've drowned."

Jill couldn't help it. She laughed. "Not very likely. I had no intention of swimming."

"You can't trust the tides here. Even this close to shore, the waves are capable of jerking your feet right out from under you. You might easily have been swept out to sea."

"That's absurd."

"Perhaps," he agreed, amicably enough. "But I was hoping you'd realize you're in my debt."

Ah, now they were getting somewhere. This man wasn't given to generosity. She'd bet a month's wages that he'd initiated the conversation for his own purposes.

He'd had plenty of time on their flight from Seattle to advise her about swimming.

No, he was after something.

"What is it you want?" she asked bluntly.

He grinned that cocky, unused smile of his and nodded. Apparently this was high praise of her finely honed intuitive skills.

"Nothing much. I was hoping you'd attend a small business dinner with me."

"Tonight?"

He nodded again. "You did mention you hadn't eaten."

"Yes, but…"

"It'll only take an hour or so of your time." He sounded impatient, as if he'd expected her to agree to his scheme without question.

"I don't even know who you are. Why would I want to attend a dinner party with you? I'm Jill Morrison, by the way."

"Jordan Wilcox," he said abruptly. "All right, if you must know, I need a woman to come with me so I won't be forced to offend someone I can't afford to alienate."

"Then don't."

"He's not the one I'm worried about. It's his daughter. She's apparently set her sights on me and doesn't seem capable of taking a hint."

"Well, then, it sounds as though you've got yourself a problem." Privately Jill wondered at the woman's taste.

He frowned, shoving his hands into the pockets of his dinner jacket. He'd changed clothes, too, but he hadn't substituted something more casual for his business suit. Quite the reverse. But then, that shouldn't have sur-

prised her. It was always business, never pleasure, with people like him.

"I don't know what it is about you women," he said plaintively. "Can't you tell when a man's not interested?"

"Not always." Jill was beginning to feel a bit smug. She swung her shoes at her side. "In other words, you need me as a bodyguard."

Clearly he didn't approve of her terminology, but he let it pass. "Something like that."

"Do I have to pretend to be madly in love with you?"

"Good heavens, no."

Jill hesitated. "I'm not sure I brought anything appropriate to wear."

He reached inside his pocket and pulled out a thick wad of cash. He peeled away several hundred-dollar bills and stuffed them in her hand. "Buy yourself something. The shop in the hotel's still open."

Two

"I'll pay for the dress myself," Jill insisted for the tenth time. She couldn't believe she'd agreed to attend this dinner party with Jordan Wilcox. Not only didn't she know the man, she didn't even like him.

"I'll pay for the dress," he said, also for the tenth time. "It's the least I can do."

They were in the ultraexpensive dress shop located off the hotel lobby. Jill was shifting judiciously through the rack of evening gowns. Most were outrageously overpriced. She found a simple one she thought might flatter her petite build, ran her hand down the sleeve until she reached the white tag, then sighed. The price was higher than any of the others. Grumbling under her breath, she dropped the sleeve and continued her search.

Jordan glanced impatiently at his watch. "What's wrong with this one?" He held up an elegant cocktail dress. It was made of dark green silk, with a draped bodice and a slim skirt. Lovely indeed, but hardly worth a week's salary.

"Nothing's wrong with it," she answered absently as she flipped through the row of dresses.

"Then buy it."

Jill glared at him. "I can't afford eight hundred dollars for a dress I'll probably wear once."

"I can," he returned from between clenched teeth.

"I *won't* allow you to pay for my dress."

"The party's in thirty minutes," he reminded her sharply.

"All right, all right."

He sighed with relief and put out a hand for the dress. Jill stopped him.

"Obviously nothing here is going to work. I'll check what I brought with me. Maybe what I have is more suitable than I thought."

Groaning, he followed her to the elevator. "Wait in the hall," she said as she unlocked her door. She wasn't about to let a strange man into her room. She stood by the closet and rooted through the few dresses she'd unpacked that afternoon. The only suitable one was an antique-white sleeveless dress with large gold buttons down the front. It wasn't exactly what one would wear to an elegant dinner party, but it was passable.

She raced to the door and held it up for Jordan. "Will this do?"

The poor man looked exasperated. "How do I know?"

Leaving the door open, Jill ran back to her closet. "The only other dress I have is Aunt Milly's wedding gown," she muttered.

"You packed a wedding dress?" His gray eyes lit up with amusement. It seemed an effort not to laugh out loud. "You apparently have high hopes for this vacation."

"I didn't bring it with me," she informed him primly,

sorry she'd even mentioned it. "A friend had it delivered."

"You're getting married?"

"No. I— Oh, I don't have time to explain."

Jordan eyed her as if he had plenty of questions, but wasn't sure he wanted to ask them.

"Wear the one you showed me, then," he said testily. "I'm sure it'll be fine."

"All right, I will." By now Jill regretted agreeing to attend the dinner party. "I'll be ready in five minutes." She closed the door again, but not before she got a glimpse of the surprised look on Jordan's face. It wasn't until she'd slipped out of her sundress that she realized he probably wasn't accustomed to women who left him waiting in the hallway while they changed clothes.

Although she knew Jordan was impatient, Jill took an extra few minutes to freshen her makeup and run a brush through her shoulder-length brown hair. Using a gold clip, she pinned it up in a simple chignon. Despite herself, she couldn't help feeling excited about this small adventure. There was no telling whom she might meet tonight.

Drawing in a deep breath to calm herself, she smoothed the skirt of her dress, then walked slowly to the door. Jordan was waiting for her, his back against the opposite wall. He straightened when she appeared.

"Do I look okay?"

His gaze narrowed assessingly. His scrutiny made Jill uncomfortable, and she held herself stiffly. At last he nodded.

"You look fine," was all he said.

Jill heaved a sigh of relief, returned to her room to retrieve her purse and then joined Jordan.

The dinner party, as he'd explained earlier, was in a private room in one of the hotel's restaurants. Jordan led the way to the elevator, his pace urgent.

"You'd better tell me what you want me to do," she said.

"Do?" he repeated with a frown. "Just do whatever you women do to let one another know a certain man is off-limits, and make sure Suzi understands." He hesitated. "Only do it without fawning all over me."

"I wouldn't dream of it," Jill said, gazing up at him in mock adoration and fluttering her lashes.

Jordan's frown deepened. "None of that, either."

"Of what?"

"That thing with the eyes." He motioned with his hand, looking annoyed.

"Should I know something about who's attending the party?"

"Not really," he said impatiently.

"What about you?" He shot her a puzzled look, and Jill elaborated. "If I'm your date, it makes sense I'd know who you are—something beyond your name, I mean—and what you do."

"I suppose it does." He buried his hands in his pockets. "I'm the CEO for a large development company based in Seattle. Simply put, we develop projects, gather together the financing, arrange for the construction, and then once the project's completed, we sell."

"That sounds interesting." If you thrived on tension and pressure, that is.

"It can be," was his only response. He looked her over once more, but his glance revealed neither approval nor reproach.

"I didn't like you when we first met." Jill wasn't

sure why she felt obliged to tell him this. In fact, she still didn't like him, although she had to admit he was a very attractive man indeed. "When I sat next to you during the flight, I thought you were very unfriendly," she continued.

"I take it your opinion of me hasn't changed?" He cocked one brow with the question, as if to suggest her answer wouldn't trouble him one way or the other.

Jill ignored him. "You don't like women very much, do you?"

"They have their uses."

He said it in such a belittling, negative way that Jill felt a flash of hot color invade her cheeks. She turned to look at him, feeling almost sorry for a man who had everything yet seemed so empty inside. "What's made you so cynical?"

He glanced at her again, a bit scornfully. "Life."

Jill didn't know what to make of that response, but luckily the elevator arrived just then.

"Is there anything else I should know before we get there?" she asked once they were inside. Her role, Jill understood, was to protect him from an associate's daughter. She had no idea how she was supposed to manage that, but she'd think of something when the time came.

"Nothing important." He paused, frowning. "I'm afraid the two of us might arouse some curiosity, though."

"Why's that?"

"I don't generally associate with…innocents."

"Innocents?" He made her sound like one of the preschool crowd. No one she'd ever known could in-

sult her with less effort. "I am over twenty-one, in case you didn't realize it."

He laughed outright at that, and Jill stiffened, regretting—probably not for the last time—that she'd actually agreed to this.

"I think you're wonderful, too," she said sarcastically.

"So you told me before."

The elevator arrived at the top floor of the hotel, where the restaurant was located. Jordan spoke briefly to the maître d', who led them to the dinner party.

Jill glanced around the simple, elegant room, and her heart did a tiny somersault. All the guests were executive types, the men in dark suits, the women in sophisticated dresses that could all have been bought at the little boutique downstairs. Everyone had an aura of prosperity and power.

Jill's breath came in shallow gasps. She was miles out of her league. These people had money, real money, whereas she'd spent months just saving for this vacation. Her money was invested in panty hose and frozen dinners, not property and office towers and massive stock portfolios.

Jordan must have felt her unease, because he turned to her and smiled briefly. "You'll be fine."

It astonished Jill that three little words from him could give her an immeasurable boost of confidence. She smiled and drew herself up as tall as her five-foot-three-inch frame would allow.

Waiters carried trays of delicate hors d'oeuvres and narrow etched-glass flutes filled with sparkling, golden champagne. Jill reached for a glass and took her first

sip, widening her eyes in surprise. Never had she tasted anything better.

"This is excellent."

"It should be, at three hundred dollars a bottle."

Before Jill could comment, an older, distinguished-looking gentleman detached himself from a younger colleague and made his way across the room toward them. He looked close to sixty, but could have stepped off the pages of *Gentlemen's Quarterly*.

"Jordan," he said in a hearty voice, extending his hand, "I'm delighted you could make it."

"I am, too."

"I trust your flight was uneventful."

Jordan's gaze briefly met Jill's. "It was fine. I'd like you to meet Jill Morrison. Jill, Dean Lundquist."

"Hello," she said pleasantly, giving him her hand.

"Delighted," Dean said again, turning to smile at her. He held her hand considerably longer than good manners required. Jill had the impression she was being carefully inspected and did her utmost to appear composed.

Finally, he released her and nodded toward the entrance. "If you'll both excuse me for a moment, Nicholson's just arrived."

"Of course," Jordan agreed politely.

Jill waited until Dean Lundquist was out of earshot. Then she leaned toward Jordan and whispered, "Suzi's dad?"

Jordan made a wry face. "Smart girl."

Not really, since few other men would have had cause to inspect her so closely, but Jill didn't discount the compliment. She wasn't likely to receive that many, at least not from Jordan.

"Who was that standing with him?" She inclined her head in the direction of a tall, good-looking young man. Something about him didn't seem quite right. Nothing she could put her finger on, but it was a feeling she couldn't shake.

"That's Dean Junior," Jordan explained.

Jill noticed the way Jordan's mouth thinned and the thoughtful, preoccupied look that came into his eyes. "He's being groomed by Daddy to take my place."

"Junior?" Jill studied the younger man a second time. "I don't think you'll have much of a problem."

"Why's that?"

She shrugged, not sure why she felt so confident of that. "I can't picture you losing at anything."

His gaze swept her warmly. "I have no intention of giving Junior the opportunity, but I'm going to have a real fight on my hands soon."

"Just a minute," Jill said. "If Suzi is Dean Senior's daughter, then wouldn't a marriage between you two secure your position?" It wouldn't exactly be a love match, but she couldn't envision Jordan marrying for something as commonplace as love.

Jordan gave her a quick, unreadable look. "It'd help, but unfortunately I'm not the marrying kind."

Jill had guessed as much. She doubted there was time in his busy schedule for love or commitment, just for work, work, work. Complete one project and start another. She knew the pattern.

Jill couldn't imagine falling in love with someone like Jordan. And she couldn't picture Jordan in love at all. As he'd said, he wasn't the marrying kind.

"Jordan." A woman's shrill voice sent a chill up Jill's spine as a beautiful blonde hurried past her and straight

into Jordan's unsuspecting arms, locking him in a tight embrace.

"This must be Suzi," Jill said conversationally from behind the woman who was squeezing Jordan for all she was worth.

Jordan's irate eyes found hers. "Do something!" he mouthed.

Jill was enjoying the scene far too much to interrupt Suzi's passionate greeting. While Jordan was occupied, Jill took an hors d'oeuvre from a nearby silver platter. Whatever it was tasted divine, and she automatically reached for two more. She hadn't recognized how hungry she was. Not until she was on her third cracker did she realize she was sampling caviar.

"Oh, darling, I didn't think you'd ever get here," Suzi said breathlessly. Her pretty blue eyes filled with something close to hero worship as she gazed up at Jordan. "Whatever took you so long? Didn't you know I'd been waiting hours and hours for you?"

"Suzi," Jordan said stiffly, disentangling himself from the blonde's embrace. He straightened the cuffs of his shirt. "I'd like you to meet Jill Morrison, my date. Jill, this is Suzi Lundquist."

"Hello," Jill said before helping herself to yet another cracker. Jordan's look told her this was not the time to discover a taste for Russian caviar.

Suzi's big blue eyes widened incredulously. She really was lovely, but one glimpse and Jill understood Jordan's reluctance. Suzi was very young, early twenties at most, and terribly vulnerable. She had to admire his tactic of putting the girl off without being unnecessarily rude.

Jordan had made Dean Lundquist's daughter sound

like a vamp. Jill disagreed. Suzi might be a vamp-in-training, but right now she was only young and head-strong.

"You're Jordan's date?" Suzi asked, fluttering her incredible lashes—which were almost long enough to cause a draft, Jill decided.

She smiled and nodded. "We're very good friends, aren't we, Jordan?" She slipped her arm in his and looked up at him, ever so sweetly.

"But I thought—I hoped..." Suzi turned to Jordan, who'd edged himself closer to Jill, draping his arm across her shoulders as though they'd been an item for quite some time.

"Yes?"

Suzi glanced from Jordan to Jill and then back to Jordan. Tears brimmed in her bright blue eyes. "I thought there was something special between us...."

"I'm sorry, Suzi," he said gently.

"But Daddy seemed to think..." She left the rest un-said as she slowly backed away. After three short steps, she turned and dashed out of the room. Jill popped an-other cracker in her mouth.

Several people were looking in their direction, al-though Jordan seemed unaware of it. Jill, however, keenly felt the interested glances. Not exactly a com-fortable feeling, especially when one's mouth was full of caviar.

After an awkward moment, conversation resumed, and Jill was able to swallow. "That was dreadful," she muttered. "I feel sorry for the poor girl."

"Frankly, so do I. But she'll get over it." He turned toward Jill. "A lot of help *you* were," he grumbled. "You

were stuffing down crackers like there was no tomorrow."

"This is the first time I've tasted caviar. I didn't know it was so good."

"I didn't bring you along to appraise the hors d'oeuvres."

"I served my purpose," Jill countered. "But I'm not happy about it. She's not a bad kid."

"Believe me," Jordan insisted, his face tightening, "she *will* get over it. She'll pout for a while, but in the end she'll realize we did her a favor."

"I still don't like it."

Now that her mission was accomplished, Jill felt free to examine the room. She wandered around a bit, sipping her champagne. The young man playing the piano caught her attention. He was good. Very good. After five years of lessons herself, Jill knew talent when she heard it. She walked over to the baby grand to compliment the pianist, and they chatted briefly about music until she saw Jordan looking for her. Jill excused herself; their meal was about to be served.

Dinner was delicious. Jill was seated beside Jordan, who was busy carrying on a conversation with a stately-looking gentleman on his other side. The man on her right, a distinguished gentleman in his mid-sixties, introduced himself as Andrew Howard. Although he didn't acknowledge it in so many words, Jill knew he was the president of Howard Pharmaceuticals, now retired. Jill pointed out that PayRite Pharmacy, where she worked, carried a number of his company's medications, and the two of them were quickly engaged in a lengthy conversation. By the time dessert was served Jill felt as comfortable with Mr. Howard as if she'd known him all her life.

Following a glass of brandy, Jordan seemed ready to leave.

"Thank you so much," she told Mr. Howard as she slid back her chair. "I enjoyed our conversation immensely."

He stood with her and clasped her hand warmly. "I did, too. If you don't mind, I'd like to keep in touch."

Jill smiled. "I'd enjoy that. And thank you for the invitation."

Then she and Jordan exchanged good-nights with her dinner companion and headed for the elevator. Jordan didn't speak until they were inside.

"What was all that with Howard?"

"Nothing. He invited me out to see his home. Apparently it's something of a showplace."

"He's a bit old for you, don't you think?"

Jill gave him an incredulous look. "Don't be ridiculous. He assumed you and I knew each other. He just wanted me to feel welcome." She didn't mention that Jordan had spent the entire dinner talking with a business associate. He seemed to have all but forgotten she was with him.

"Howard invited you to his home?"

"Us, actually. You can make your excuses if you want, but I'd really like to take him up on his offer."

"Andrew Howard and my father were good friends. My father passed away several years back, and Howard likes to keep track of the projects I'm involved with. He's gone in on the occasional deal."

"He's a sweet man. Did you know he lost his only son to cancer? It's the reason his company's done so much in the field of cancer research. His son's death changed his life."

"I had no idea." Jordan was obviously astounded that he'd known Andrew Howard for so many years and hadn't realized he'd lost a child. "You learned this over dinner?"

"Good grief, dinner lasted nearly two hours." She sighed deeply and pressed her hands to her stomach. "I'm stuffed. I'll never sleep unless I walk off some of this food."

"It would've helped if you hadn't eaten half the hors d'oeuvres all by yourself."

Jill decided to ignore that comment.

"Do you mind if I join you?" Jordan surprised her by asking.

"Not in the least, as long as you promise not to make any more remarks about hors d'oeuvres. *Or* lecture me about the dangers of swimming at night."

Jordan grinned. "You've got yourself a deal."

They walked through the lobby and out of the hotel toward the beach. The surf thundered against the shore, slapping the sand, then retreating. Jill found the rhythmic sounds relaxing.

"What sort of project do you have planned for Hawaii?" she asked after a few minutes.

"A shopping complex."

Although he'd answered her question, his expression was preoccupied. "Why the frown?" she asked.

He shot a quick glance her way. "The Lundquists seem to have some sort of hidden agenda," he said.

"You said Daddy's grooming Junior to take your place," Jill prompted.

"It looks like I'm headed for a proxy fight, which is an expensive and costly proposition for everyone in-

volved. For now, I have the controlling interest, but by no means do I have control."

"This trip to Hawaii?"

"Is strictly business. I just wish I knew what's going on behind my back."

"Good luck with it." This was a world far removed from Jill's.

"Thanks." He grinned and suddenly seemed to leave his worries behind.

They strolled for several minutes in companionable silence. The breeze was warm, the moon full and bright, and the rhythm of the ocean waves went on and on.

"I suppose I should go back," Jill said reluctantly. She had a full day planned, beginning first thing in the morning, and although she didn't feel the least bit tired, she knew she should get some sleep.

"Me, too."

They altered their meandering course in the direction of the hotel, their shoes sinking into the moist sand.

"Thanks for your help with Suzi Lundquist."

"Anytime. Just say the word and I'll be there, especially if there's caviar involved." She felt guilty, however, about the young and vulnerable Suzi. Jordan had been gentle with her; nevertheless, Jill's sympathy went out to the girl. "I feel kind of bad for Suzi."

Jordan sighed. "The girl just won't take no for an answer."

"Do you?"

"What do you mean?"

Jill stopped a moment to collect her thoughts. "I don't understand finance, but it seems to me that you'd never get anywhere if you quit at the first stumbling block. Suzi takes after her father and brother. She saw what

she wanted and went after it. Rather an admirable trait, I guess. I suspect you haven't seen the last of her."

"Probably not, but I won't be here for more than a few days. I should be able to avoid her during that time."

"Good luck," she said again. She hesitated when they reached the pathway, bordered by vivid flowering shrubs, that led to the huge lighted swimming pool.

Jordan grinned. "I have a feeling I'm going to need it."

The night couldn't have been more perfect. It seemed such a shame to waste these romantic moments, but Jill finally forced herself to murmur good-night.

"Here," Jordan said just as she did.

Jill was startled when he presented her with a single lavender orchid. "What's this for?"

"In appreciation for all your help."

"Actually, I should be the one thanking you. I had a wonderful evening." It sure beat sitting in front of her television and ordering dinner from room service, which was what she'd planned. She held the flower under her nose and breathed in its delicate scent.

"Enjoy your stay in Hawaii."

"Thank you, I will." Her itinerary was full nearly every day. "I might even see you...around the hotel."

"Don't count on it. I'm headed back to Seattle in two days."

"Goodbye, then."

"Goodbye."

Neither moved. Jill didn't understand why. They'd said their good-nights—there seemed nothing left to say. It was time to leave. Time for her to return to her room and sleep off the effects of an exceptionally long day.

She made a decisive movement, but before she could

turn away, his hand at her shoulder stopped her. Jill's troubled eyes met his. "Jordan?"

He caught her chin, his touch light but firm.

"Yes?" she whispered, her heart in her throat.

"Nothing." He dropped his hand.

Jill was about to turn away again when he stepped toward her, took her by the shoulders and kissed her. Jill had certainly been kissed before, and the experience had always been pleasant, if a bit predictable.

Not this time.

Exciting, unfamiliar sensations raced through her. Jordan's mouth caressed hers with practiced ease while his hands roved her back, moving slowly, confidently.

Jill was breathless and weak when he finally broke away. He stared down at her with a perplexed look, as if he'd shocked himself by kissing her. As if he didn't know what had come over him.

Jill didn't know, either. There was a sinking feeling in the pit of her stomach, and then she remembered something Shelly had told her—the overwhelming sensation she'd experienced the first time Mark had kissed her. From that moment on, Shelly had known her fate was sealed.

Jill had never felt anything that even came close to what she'd just felt in Jordan's arms. Was it possible? *Could* there be something magical about Aunt Milly's wedding dress? Jill didn't know. She didn't want to find out, either.

"Jill?"

"Oh, no," she moaned as she looked up at him.

"Oh, no," Jordan echoed, apparently amused. "I'll admit women have reacted when I've kissed them, but no one's ever said that."

She barely heard him.

"What's wrong?"

"The dress…" Jill stopped herself in time.

"What dress?"

Jill knew she wasn't making any sense. The whole thing was ridiculous. Unbelievable.

"What dress?" he repeated.

"You wouldn't understand." She had no intention of explaining it to him. She could just imagine what someone like Jordan Wilcox would say when he heard about Aunt Milly's wedding dress.

Three

Jill glared at Jordan. He had no idea how devastating she'd found his kiss. And the worst of it was, *she* had no idea why she was feeling this way.

"Jill?" he said, eyeing her suspiciously. "What does my kissing you have to do with a dress?"

She squeezed her eyes shut, then opened them. "It doesn't have anything to do with it," she blurted without thinking, then quickly corrected herself. "It's got everything to do with it." She knew she was overreacting, but she couldn't seem to help herself. All he'd done was kiss her! There was no reason to behave like a fool. She had a good excuse, however. It had been a long and unusual day compounded by Shelly's letter and the arrival of the wedding dress. Who *wouldn't* be flustered? Who wouldn't be confused—especially in light of Shelly's experience?

"You're not being too clear," Jordan told her.

"I know. I'm sorry."

"What dress are you talking about?" he asked patiently. "Could you explain yourself?"

Jill didn't see how that was possible. Jordan wouldn't

understand. Not only that, he was cynical and scornful. The man who placed power and profit above all else would laugh at something as absurd as the story about the wedding dress.

She drew in an unsteady breath. "There's nothing I can say."

"Was my kiss so repugnant to you?" It didn't appear that he was going to graciously drop the matter, not when his male ego was on the line.

Forcing her voice to sound carefree, Jill placed a hand on his shoulder and looked him square in the eye. "I'd think a man of your experience would be accustomed to having women crumple at his feet."

"Don't be ridiculous." His habitual frown snapped into place.

"I'm not," she said. Best to keep Jordan in the dark, otherwise he might misread her intentions. Besides, he wouldn't be any more enthusiastic about a romance between them than she was. "The kiss was very nice," she admitted grudgingly.

"And that's bad?" He rubbed a frustrated hand along his blunt, determined-looking jaw. "Perhaps you'll feel better once you're back in your room."

Jill nodded eagerly. "Thank you. For dinner," she added, remembering her manners.

"Thank you for joining me. It was…a pleasure meeting you."

"You, too."

"I probably won't see you again."

"That's right," she agreed resolutely. No reason to tempt fate. She was beginning to like him and that could be dangerous. "You'll be gone in a couple of days, won't

you? I'm here for the week." She retreated a couple of steps. "Have a safe trip home, and don't work too hard."

They parted then, but before she walked into the hotel, Jill turned back to see Jordan strolling in the opposite direction, away from her.

Jill awoke late the following morning. It was rare for her to sleep past eight-thirty, even on weekends. The tour bus wasn't scheduled to leave the hotel until ten, so she took her time showering and dressing. Breakfast consisted of coffee, an English muffin and slices of fresh pineapple, which she ate leisurely on her lanai, savoring the morning sunlight.

Out of curiosity, she glanced over at Jordan's room to see if the drapes were open. They were. From what she could discern, he was sitting at a table near the window, talking on his phone and working with his computer.

Business. Business. Business.

The man lived and breathed it, just like her father had. And, in the end, it had killed him.

Dismissing Jordan from her thoughts, she collected her purse and hurried down to the lobby, where she was meeting the tour group.

The sightseeing expedition proved excellent. Jill visited Pearl Harbor and the U.S.S. *Arizona* memorial and a huge shopping mall, returning to the hotel by three o'clock.

Her room was cool and inviting. Jill took a few minutes to examine the souvenirs she'd purchased, a shell lei and several colorful T-shirts. Then, with a good portion of the day still left to enjoy, she decided to spend the remaining afternoon hours lazing around the pool. Once again she glanced over at Jordan's room, her ac-

tion almost involuntary. And once again she saw that he was on the phone. Jill wondered if he'd been talking since morning.

Changing into her bathing suit, a modest one-piece in a—what else—Hawaiian print, she carried her beach bag, complete with three different kinds of sunscreen, down to the swimming pool. With a large straw hat perched on her head and sunglasses protecting her eyes, she stretched out on a chaise longue to absorb the sun.

She hadn't been there more than fifteen minutes when a waiter approached carrying a dome-covered platter and a glass of champagne. "Ms. Morrison?"

"Yes?" Jill sat up abruptly, knocking her hat askew. "I… I didn't order anything," she said uncertainly as she reached up to straighten her hat.

"This was sent compliments of Mr. Wilcox."

"Oh." Jill wasn't sure what to say. She twisted around and, shading her eyes with her hand, looked up. Jordan was standing on his lanai. She waved, and he returned the gesture.

"If that will be all?" the waiter murmured, stepping away.

"Yes… Oh, just a moment." Jill scrambled in her beach bag for a tip, which she handed to the young man. He smiled his appreciation.

Curious, she balanced the glass of champagne as she lifted the lid—and nearly laughed out loud. Inside was a large array of crackers topped with caviar. She glanced up at Jordan a second time and blew him a kiss.

Something must have distracted him then. He turned away, and when Jill saw him again a few minutes later, he was pacing the lanai, phone in hand. She was convinced he'd completely forgotten about her. It was

ironic, she mused, and really rather sad; here he was in paradise and he'd hardly ventured beyond his hotel room.

Jill drank her champagne and savored a few of the caviar-laden crackers, then decided she couldn't stand his attitude a minute longer. Packing up her things, she looped the towel around her neck and picked up the platter in one hand, her beach bag in the other. After that, she headed back inside the hotel. She knew she was breaking her promise to herself by seeking him out, but she couldn't stop herself.

Muttering under her breath, she took the elevator up to Jordan's floor, calculated which room was his and knocked boldly on the door.

A long moment passed before the door finally opened. Jordan, still talking on his phone, gestured her inside. He didn't so much as pause in his conversation, tossing dollar figures around as casually as other people talked about the weather.

Jill sat on the edge of his bed and crossed her legs, swinging her foot impatiently as Jordan strode back and forth across the carpet, seemingly oblivious to her presence.

"Listen, Rick, something's come up," he said, darting a look in her direction. "Give me a call in five minutes. Sure, sure, no problem. Five minutes. See if you can contact Raymond, get these numbers to him and call me back." He disconnected the line without a word of farewell, then glanced at Jill.

"Hello," he said.

"Hi," she returned, holding out the platter to offer him an hors d'oeuvre.

"No, thanks."

She took one herself and chewed it slowly. She could almost feel his irritation.

"Something I can do for you?"

"Yes," she stated calmly. "Sit down a minute."

"Sit down?"

She nodded, motioning toward the table. "I have a story to tell you."

"A story?" He didn't seem particularly charmed by the idea.

"Yes, and I promise it won't take longer than five minutes," she added pointedly.

He was obviously relieved that she intended to keep this short. "Go on."

"As I've mentioned before, I don't know a lot about the world of high finance. But I'm well aware that time has skyrocketed in value. I also realize that the value of any commodity depends on its availability."

"Does this story have a point?"

"Actually I haven't got to the story yet, but I will soon," she announced cheerfully.

"Can you do it in—" he paused to check his watch "—two and a half minutes?"

"I'll hurry," she promised, and drew a deep breath. "I was nine when my mother signed me up for piano lessons. I could hardly wait. The other kids dreaded having to practice, but not me. From the time I was in kindergarten, I loved to pound away at the old upright in our living room. My heart and soul went into making music. It was probably no coincidence that one of the first pieces I learned was 'Heart and Soul.' I hammered out those notes like machine-gun blasts. I over-emphasized each crescendo, cherished each lingering note. Van Cliburn couldn't have finished a piece with

more pizzazz than I did. My hands would fly into the air, then flutter gently to my lap."

"I noticed you standing by the piano at the dinner party. Are you a musician?"

"Nope. For all my theatrical talents, I had one serious shortcoming. I could never master the caesura—the rest."

"The rest?"

"You know, that little zigzag thingamajig on sheet music that instructs the player to do nothing."

"Nothing," he repeated slowly.

"My impatience was a disappointment to my mother. I'm sure I frustrated my piano teacher no end. As hard as she tried, she couldn't make me understand that music was always sweeter and more compelling after a rest."

"I see." His hands were buried deep in his pockets as he studied her.

If Jordan was as much like her father as she suspected, she doubted he really did understand. But she'd told him what she'd come to say. Mission accomplished. There wasn't any other reason to stay, so she got briskly to her feet and scooped up her beach bag.

"That's it?"

"That's it. Thank you for the caviar. It was a delightful surprise." With that she moved toward the door. "Just remember what I said about the rest," she said, glancing over her shoulder.

The phone pealed sharply and Jill grimaced. "Goodbye," she mouthed, grasping the doorknob.

The phone rang again. "Goodbye." Jordan hesitated. "Jill?"

"Yes?" The way he said her name seemed so urgent.

She whirled around, hope surging in her heart. Perhaps he didn't intend to answer the phone!

It rang a third time, and Jordan's eyes, dark gray, smoky with indecision, traveled from Jill to the telephone.

"Yes?" she repeated.

"Nothing," he said harshly, reaching for the phone. "Thanks for the story."

"You're welcome." With nothing left to say, Jill walked out of his room and closed the door. Even before the lock slid into place she heard Jordan rhyming off lists of figures.

Her room felt less welcoming than when she'd returned earlier. Jill slipped out of her swimsuit and showered. She was vain enough to check her reflection in the mirror, hoping to have enhanced the slight tan she'd managed to achieve between Seattle's infamous June cloudbursts. It didn't look as though her sojourn in the tropics had done anything but add a not-so-fetching touch of pink across her shoulders.

She dressed in a thick terry robe supplied by the hotel and had just wrapped a towel around her wet hair when her phone rang.

"Hello," she said breathlessly, sinking onto her bed. Her stomach knotted with anticipation.

"Jill Morrison?"

"Yes." It wasn't Jordan. But the voice sounded vaguely familiar, although she couldn't immediately place it.

"Andrew Howard. I sat next to you at the dinner party last night."

"Yes, of course." Her voice rose with pleasure. She'd

thoroughly enjoyed her chat with the older man. "How are you?"

He chuckled. "I'm fine. I tried to phone earlier, but you were out and I didn't leave a message."

"I went on a tour this morning."

"Ah, that explains it. I realize it's rather short notice, but are you free for dinner tonight?"

Jill didn't hesitate. "Yes, I am."

"Good, good. Could you join me around eight?"

"Eight would be perfect." Normally Jill dined much earlier, but she wasn't hungry yet, thanks to an expensive snack, compliments of Jordan Wilcox.

"Wonderful." Mr. Howard seemed genuinely pleased. "I'll have a car waiting for you and Wilcox out front at seven-thirty."

And Wilcox. She'd almost missed the words. So Jordan had accepted Mr. Howard's invitation. Perhaps she'd been too critical; perhaps he'd understood the point of her story, after all, and was willing to put business aside for one evening. Perhaps he was as eager to spend time with her as she was with him.

"I wondered if you'd be here," Jordan announced when they met in the lobby at the appointed time. He didn't exactly greet her with open enthusiasm, but Jill comforted herself with the observation that Jordan wasn't one to reveal his emotions.

"I wouldn't miss this for the world," he added. That was when she remembered he was hoping to interest the older man in his shopping-mall project. Dinner, for Jordan, would be a golden opportunity to conduct business, elicit Mr. Howard's support and gain the financial backing he needed for the project.

Jill couldn't help feeling disappointed. "I'll do my best not to interrupt your sales pitch," she said sarcastically.

"My sales pitch?" he echoed, then grinned, apparently amused by her assumption. "You don't have to worry. Howard doesn't want in on this project, which is fine. He just likes to keep tabs on me, especially since Dad died. He seems to think I need a mentor, or at least some kind of paternal adviser."

"Do you?"

Jordan shrugged. "There've been one or two occasions when I've appreciated his wisdom. I don't need him holding my hand, but I have sometimes looked to him for advice."

Remembering her dinner conversation with the older man, Jill said, "In some ways, Mr. Howard must think of you as a son."

"I doubt that." Jordan scowled. "I've known him all this time and not once did he ever mention he'd lost a son."

"It was almost thirty years ago, and as I told you, it's the reason his company's done so much cancer research. Howard Pharmaceuticals makes several of the leading cancer-fighting drugs." When Andrew Howard had told her about his son's death, a tear had come to his eye. Although Jeff Howard had succumbed to childhood leukemia a long time ago, his father still grieved. Andrew had become a widower a few years later, and he'd never fully recovered from the double blow. Jill was deeply touched by his story. During their conversation, she'd shared a little of the pain she'd felt at her own father's death, something she rarely did, even with her mother or her closest friend.

"What shocks me," Jordan continued, "is that I've worked on different projects with him over the years. We've also kept in touch socially. And not once, *not once,* did he mention a son."

"Perhaps there was never a reason."

Jordan dismissed that idea with a shake of his head.

"Mr. Howard's a sweet man. I really like him," Jill asserted.

"Sweet? Andrew Howard?" Jordan grinned, his eyes bright with humor. "I've known alligators with more agreeable personalities."

"Apparently there's more to your friend than you realized."

"My friend," Jordan repeated. "Funny, I'd always thought of him as my father's friend, not mine. But you're right—he *is* my friend and— Oh, here's the car." With a hand on her arm, he escorted her outside.

A tall, uniformed driver stepped from the long white limousine. "Ms. Morrison and Mr. Wilcox?" he asked crisply.

Jordan nodded, and the chauffeur ceremoniously opened the back door for them. Soon they were heading out of the city toward the island's opposite coast.

"Do you still play the piano?" Jordan asked unexpectedly.

"Every so often, when the mood strikes me," Jill told him a bit ruefully. "Not as much as I'd like."

"I take it you still haven't conquered the caesura?"

"Not yet, but I'm learning." She wasn't sure what had prompted his question, then decided to ask one of her own. "What about you? Do you think you might be interested in learning to play the piano?"

Jordan shook his head adamantly. "Unfortunately, I've never had much interest in that sort of thing."

Jill sighed and looked away.

Nearly thirty minutes passed before they reached Andrew Howard's oceanside estate. Jill suspected it was the longest Jordan had gone without a business conversation since he'd registered at the hotel.

Her heart pounded as they approached the beautifully landscaped grounds. A security guard pushed a button that opened a huge wrought-iron gate. They drove down a private road, nearly a mile long and bordered on each side by rolling green lawns and tropical flower beds. At the end stood a sprawling stone house.

No sooner had the car stopped than Mr. Howard hurried out of the house, grinning broadly.

"Welcome, welcome!" He greeted them expansively, holding out his arms to Jill.

In a spontaneous display of affection, she hugged him and kissed his cheek. "Thank you so much for inviting us."

"The pleasure's all mine. Come inside. Everything's ready and waiting." After exchanging a hearty handshake with Jordan, Mr. Howard led the way into his home.

Jill had been impressed with the outside, but the beauty of the interior overwhelmed her. The entry was tiled in white marble and illuminated by a sparkling crystal chandelier. Huge crystal vases of vivid pink and purple hibiscus added color and life. From there, Mr. Howard escorted them into a massive living room with floor-to-ceiling windows that overlooked the Pacific. Frothing waves crashed against the shore, bathed in the fire of an island sunset.

"This is so lovely," Jill breathed in awe.

"I knew you'd appreciate it." Mr. Howard reached for a bell, which he rang once. Almost immediately the housekeeper appeared, carrying a tray of glasses and bottles of white and red wine, sherry and assorted aperitifs.

They were sipping their drinks when the same woman reappeared. "Mr. Wilcox, there's a phone call for you."

It was all Jill could do not to gnash her teeth. The man was never free, the phone cord wrapped around his neck more tightly than a hangman's noose.

"Excuse me, please," Jordan said as he left the room, his step brisk.

Jill looked away, refusing to watch him go.

"How do you feel about that young man?" Mr. Howard asked bluntly when Jordan was gone.

"We met only recently. I—I don't have any feelings for him one way or the other."

"Well, then, what do you think of him?"

Jill stared down at her wine. "He works too hard."

Sighing, the old man nodded and rubbed his eyes. "He reminds me of myself more than thirty years ago. Sometimes I'd like to take him by the shoulders and shake some sense into him, but I doubt it'd do much good. That boy's too stubborn to listen. Unfortunately, he's a lot like his father."

Knowing so little of Jordan and his background, Jill was eager to learn what she could. At the same time, a saner part of her insisted she was better off not hearing this. The more she knew, the greater her chances of caring.

Nevertheless, Jill found herself asking curiously, "What made Jordan the way he is?"

"To begin with, his parents divorced when he was young. It was a sad situation." Andrew leaned forward and clasped his wineglass with both hands. "It was plain as the nose on your face that James and Donna Wilcox were in love. But, somehow, bitterness replaced the love, and their son became a weapon they used against each other."

"Oh, how sad." Just as she'd feared, Jill felt herself sympathizing with Jordan.

"They both married other people, and Jordan seemed to remind his parents of their earlier unhappiness. He was sent to the best boarding schools, but there was precious little love in his life. Before he died, James tried to build a relationship with his son, but…" He shrugged. "And to the best of my knowledge his mother hasn't seen him since he was a teenager. I'm afraid he's had very little experience of real love, the kind that gives life meaning. Oh, there've been women, plenty of them, but never one who could teach him how to love and bring joy into his life—until now." He paused and looked pointedly at Jill.

"As I said before, I've only known Jordan for a short time."

"Be patient with him," Mr. Howard continued, as though Jill hadn't spoken. "Jordan's talented, don't get me wrong—the boy's got a way of pulling a deal together that amazes just about everyone—but there are times when he seems to forget about human values, like compassion. And the ability to enjoy what you have."

Jill wasn't sure how to respond.

"Frankly, I was beginning to lose faith in him," Mr. Howard said, grinning sheepishly. "He can be hard and unforgiving. You've given me the first ray of hope."

Jill took a big swallow of wine.

"He needs you. Your warmth, your gentleness, your love."

Jill wanted to weep with frustration. Andrew Howard was telling her exactly what she didn't want to hear. "I think you're mistaken," she murmured.

He chuckled. "I doubt that, but I'm an old man, so indulge me, will you?"

"Of course, but—"

"There's a reason you've come into his life," he said, gazing intently at her. "A very important reason." Andrew closed his eyes. "I feel this more profoundly than I've felt anything in a long while. He needs you, Jill."

"No... I'm sure he doesn't." Jill realized she was beginning to sound desperate, but she couldn't help it.

The old man's eyes opened slowly and he smiled. "And I'm just as sure he does." He would have continued, but Jordan returned to the room then.

From the marinated-shrimp appetizer to the home-made mango-and-pineapple ice cream, dinner was one of the most delectable, elegant meals Jill had ever tasted. They lingered over coffee, followed by a glass of smooth brandy. By the end of the evening, Jill felt mellow and warm, a dangerous sensation. Jordan had been wonderful company—witty, charming, fun. He seemed more relaxed, too. Apparently the phone call had brought good news; it was the only thing to which she could attribute his cheerfulness.

"I can't thank you enough," she told Andrew when the limousine arrived to drive her and Jordan back to the hotel. "It was a lovely evening."

The older man hugged Jill and whispered close to her ear, "Remember what I said." Breaking away, he

extended his hand, gripping Jordan's elbow. "It was good of you to come."

"I'll be in touch soon," Jordan promised.

"I'll look forward to hearing from you. Let me know what happens with this shopping-mall project."

"I will," Jordan said.

The car was cool and inviting in the warm night. Before she realized it, Jill found her head resting on Jordan's broad shoulder. "Oh, sorry," she mumbled through a yawn.

"Are you sleepy?"

She smiled softly to herself, too tired to fight the power of attraction—and exhaustion. "Maybe a little. Wine makes me sleepy."

Jordan pressed her head against his shoulder and held her there. His hand gently stroked her hair. "Do you mind telling me what went on between you and Howard while I was on the phone?"

Jill went stock-still. "Uh, nothing. What makes you ask?" She decided it was best to pretend she didn't know what he was talking about.

"Then why was Howard wearing a silly grin every time he looked at me?" Jordan demanded.

"I—I don't know. You'll have to ask him." She tried to straighten, but Jordan wouldn't allow it. After a moment she gave up, too relaxed to put up much of a struggle.

"I swear there was a twinkle in his eye from the moment I returned after my phone call. It was like I'd been left out of a joke."

"I'm sure you're wrong."

Jordan seemed to ponder that. "I doubt it," he said.

"Hmm." She felt sleepy, and leaning against Jordan was strangely comforting.

"I've been thinking about what you said this afternoon," he told her a few minutes later. His mouth was against her ear, and although she might have been mistaken, she thought his lips lightly brushed her cheek.

"My sad but true tale," she whispered on the end of another yawn.

"About your trouble with the musical rest."

"Ah, yes, the rest."

"I'm flying back to Seattle tomorrow," Jordan said abruptly.

Jill nodded, feeling inexplicably sad, then surprised by the intensity of her reaction. With Jordan in Seattle, they wouldn't be bumping into each other at every turn. Wouldn't be arguing, bantering—or kissing. With Jordan in Seattle, she wouldn't confuse him with the legacy behind Aunt Milly's dress. "Well… I hope you have a good flight."

"I have a meeting Tuesday morning. It would be impossible to cancel at this late date, but I was able to change my flight."

"You changed your flight?" Jill prayed he wouldn't hear the breathless catch in her voice.

"I don't have to be at the airport until evening."

"When?" It shouldn't make any difference to her, yet she found herself wanting to know. Needing to know.

"Eight."

Jill was much too dazed to calculate the time difference, but she knew it meant he'd arrive in Seattle in the early morning. He'd be exhausted. Not exactly the best way to show up at a high-powered meeting.

"I was thinking," Jordan continued. "I've been to

Hawaii a number of times but other than meetings or dinner engagements, I haven't seen much of the islands. I've never explored them."

"That's a pity," she said, meaning it.

"And," he went on, "it seemed to me that sightseeing wouldn't be nearly as much fun alone."

"I enjoyed myself this morning." Her effort to refute him was feeble at best.

His fingers were entwined in her hair. "Will you come with me, Jill?" he asked, his voice a husky whisper. "Share the day with me. Let's discover Hawaii together."

Four

"I can't" was Jill's immediate response. She'd already lowered her guard—enough to be snuggling in his arms. So much for her resolve not to get involved with Jordan Wilcox, she thought with dismay. So much for steering a wide course around the man.

"Why not?" Jordan asked with the directness she'd come to expect from him.

"I've...m-made plans," she stammered. Even now, she could feel herself weakening. With his arm around her and her head nestled against his shoulder it was difficult to refuse him.

"Cancel them."

How arrogant of him to assume she should abandon her plans because the almighty businessman was willing to grant her some of his valuable time.

"I'm afraid I can't do that," she answered coolly, her determination reinforced. She'd already paid for the rental car as part of her vacation package, she rationalized, and she wasn't about to let that money go to waste.

"Why not?" He sounded surprised.

Isn't being with him what you really want? The ques-

tion stole into her mind, and Jill wanted to scream out her response. A resounding NO. Jordan Wilcox frightened her. It was all too easy to envision them together, strolling hand in hand along sun-drenched beaches. He'd kissed her that first time, that only time, on the beach, and the memory stubbornly refused to go away.

"Jill?"

At the softness in his voice, she involuntarily raised her eyes to his. Jill hadn't expected to see tenderness in Jordan, but she did now, and it was nearly her undoing. Her feelings for him were changing, and she found herself more strongly attracted than ever. She remembered when she'd first seen him, the way she'd been convinced there was nothing gentle in him. He'd seemed so hard, so untouchable. Yet, right now, at this very moment, he'd made himself vulnerable to her. *For* her.

"You're trembling," he said, running his hands down her arms. "What's wrong?"

"Nothing," she denied quickly, breathlessly. "I'm…a little tired. It's been a long day."

"That's what you said last night when I kissed you. Remember? You started mumbling some nonsense about a dress, then you went stiff as a board on me."

"Nothing's wrong," she insisted, breaking away from him. She straightened and lowered her hand to her skirt, smoothing away imaginary creases.

"I don't buy that, Jill. Something's bothering you."

She wished he hadn't mentioned the dress, because it brought to mind, uninvited and unwanted, Aunt Milly's wedding dress, which was hanging in her hotel-room closet.

"You'd be shaking, too, if you knew the things I did," she exclaimed, instantly regretting the impulse.

"What are you afraid of?"

She stared out the window, then slowly her lower lip began to quiver with the effort to restrain her laughter. She was actually frightened of a silly dress! She wasn't afraid to fall in love; she just didn't want it to be with Jordan.

"For a woman who drags a wedding dress on vacation with her, you're not doing very much to encourage romance."

"I did not bring that dress with me!"

"It was in the room when you arrived? Someone left it behind?"

"Not exactly. Shelly did. She, uh, enjoys a good laugh. She mailed it to me."

"It never occurred to me that you might be engaged," he said slowly. "You're not, are you?"

"No." But according to her friend, she soon would be.

"Who's Shelly?"

"My best friend," Jill explained, "or at least she used to be." Then, impulsively, her heart racing, she added, "Listen, Jordan, I think you have a lot of potential in the husband category, but I can't fall in love with you. I just can't."

A stunned silence followed her announcement.

He cocked his eyebrows. "Aren't you taking a bit too much for granted here? I asked you to explore the island with me, not bear my children."

She'd done it again, blurted out something totally illogical. Worse, she couldn't make herself stop. Children were a subject near and dear to her heart.

"That's another thing," she wailed. "I bet you don't even like children. No, I can't go with you tomorrow. Please don't ask me to…because it's so hard to say no."

It must be the wine, Jill decided; she was saying far more than she should.

Jordan relaxed against the leather upholstery and crossed his long legs. "All right, if you'd rather not go, I'm certainly not going to force you."

His easy acceptance astonished her. She glanced at him out of the corner of her eye, feeling almost disappointed that he wasn't trying to persuade her.

Something was drastically, dangerously wrong with her. She was beginning to like Jordan, really like him. Yet she couldn't allow this attraction to continue. She couldn't allow herself to fall in love with a man so much like her father. Because she knew what that meant, what kind of life it led to, what kind of unhappiness it caused.

When the limousine stopped in front of the hotel, it was all Jill could do to wait for the chauffeur to climb out of the driver's seat, walk around the car and open the door for her.

She hurried inside the lobby, needing to breathe in the fresh air of reason. Wait for sanity to catch up with her heart.

She reached the elevators and pushed the button, holding her thumb in place, hoping that would hurry it along.

"Next time, keep your little anecdotes to yourself," Jordan said sharply from behind her. Then he walked leisurely across the lobby.

Keep her little anecdotes to herself? The temptation to rush after him and demand an explanation was strong, but Jill made herself resist it.

Not until she was in the elevator did she understand. This entire discussion had arisen because she'd told him her story about the caesura and her lack of musi-

cal talent. And now he was turning her own disclosure against her! Righteous anger began to build in her heart.

But by the time Jill was in her room and ready for bed, she felt wretched. Jordan had asked her to spend a day with him, and she'd reacted as if he'd insulted her.

The way she'd gone on and on about his potential as a husband was bad enough, but then she'd dragged the subject of children into their conversation. That mortified her even more. The wine could be blamed for only so much.

She cringed, too, as she recalled what Andrew Howard had said, the faith he'd placed in her. Jordan needed her, he'd said, apparently convinced that Jordan would never experience love if she didn't teach him. She hated disappointing Andrew, and yet…and yet…

It didn't surprise Jill that she slept poorly. By morning she wasn't feeling any enthusiasm at all about picking up her rental car or sightseeing on the north shore.

She reviewed the room-service menu, ordered coffee and toast, then stared at the phone for several minutes before conceding there was one thing she still had to do. Anxious to get it over with, Jill rang through to Jordan's room.

"Hello," he answered gruffly on the first ring. He was definitely a man who never ventured far from his phone.

"Hello," she said with uncharacteristic meekness. "I'm…calling to apologize."

"Are you sorry enough to change your mind and spend the day with me?"

Jill hesitated. "I've already paid for a rental car."

"Great, then I won't need to get one."

Jill closed her eyes. She knew what she was going to say, had known it the night before. In the same heart-

beat, she realized she'd regret it later. "Yes," she whispered. "If you still want me to join you, I'll meet you in the lobby in half an hour."

"Twenty minutes."

She groaned. "Fine, twenty minutes, then."

Despite her misgivings, Jill's spirits lifted immediately. "One day won't hurt anything," she said out loud. What could possibly happen in so short a time? Certainly nothing earth-shattering. Nothing of consequence.

Who was she kidding? Not herself, Jill admitted.

She thought she understood why moths ventured close to the fire, enticed by the light and the warmth. Against her will, Jordan was drawing her dangerously close. She knew even as she came nearer that she was going to get burned. And yet she didn't walk away.

He was waiting for her when she stepped out of the elevator and into the lobby. He stood there grinning, his look almost boyish. This was the first time she'd seen him without a business suit. Instead, he wore white slacks and a pale blue shirt with the sleeves rolled up.

"You ready?" he asked, taking her beach bag from her.

"One question." Her heart was pounding because she had no right to ask.

"Sure." His eyes held hers.

"Your cell phone—do you have it?"

Jordan nodded and pulled a tiny phone from his shirt pocket.

Jill stared at it for a moment, feeling the tension work its way down her back. Jordan's cell phone reminded her of the pager her father had always carried. Always. All family outings, which were few and far between,

had been subject to outside interference. Early in life, Jill had received a clear message: business was more important to her father than she was. In fact, almost everything had seemed more significant than spending time with the people who loved him.

Jordan must have read the look in her eyes because he said, "I'll leave it in my room," and then promptly strolled to the elevator. Stunned, Jill watched as he stepped inside. Bit by bit, her muscles began to relax.

While he was gone, Jill filled out the paperwork for the rental car. She was waiting outside by the economy model when Jordan appeared. He paused, staring at it with narrowed eyes as if he wasn't sure the car would make it to the end of the street, let alone around the island.

"I'm on a limited budget," Jill explained, hiding a smile. The car suited her petite frame perfectly, but for a man of Jordan's stature it was like…like stuffing a rag doll inside a pickle jar, Jill thought, enjoying the whimsical comparison.

"You're positive this thing runs?" he muttered under his breath as he climbed into the driver's seat. His long legs were cramped below the steering wheel, his head practically touching the roof.

Jill nodded. She remembered reading that this particular model got exceptionally good gas mileage—but then it should, with an engine only a little bigger than a lawnmower's.

To prove her right, the car roared to life with a flick of the key.

"Where are we going?" Jill asked once they'd merged with the flow of traffic on the busy thoroughfare by the hotel.

"The airport."

"The airport?" she repeated, struggling to hide her disappointment. "I thought your flight didn't leave until eight."

"Mine doesn't, but ours takes off in half an hour."

"Ours?" What about the sugarcane fields and watching the workers harvest pineapple? Surely he didn't intend for them to miss that. "Where is this plane taking us?"

"Hawaii," he announced casually. "The island of. Do you know how to scuba dive?"

"No." Her voice was oddly breathless and high-pitched. She might have spent the past twenty-odd years in Seattle—practically surrounded by water—but she wasn't all that comfortable *under* it.

"How about snorkeling?"

"Ah…" She jerked her thumb over her shoulder. "There are pineapple fields on the other side of this island. I assumed you'd want to see those."

"Another visit, perhaps. I'd like to try my hand at marlin fishing, too, but we don't have enough time today."

"Snorkeling," Jill said as though she'd never heard the word before. "Well…it might be fun." In her guidebook Jill remembered reading about green beaches of crushed olivine crystals and black sands of soft lava. These were sights she couldn't expect to find anywhere else. However, she wasn't sure she wanted to view them through a rubber mask.

A small private plane was ready for them when they arrived at Honolulu Airport. The pilot, who apparently knew Jordan, greeted them cordially. After brief introductions and a few minutes' chat, they were on their way.

Another car, considerably larger than the one Jill had

rented, was waiting for them on the island of Hawaii. A large, white wicker picnic basket sat in the middle of the backseat.

"I hope you're hungry."

"Not yet."

"You will be," Jordan promised.

He drove for half an hour or so, until they reached a deserted inlet with a magnificent waterfall. He parked the car, then got out and opened the trunk. Inside was everything they'd need for snorkeling in the crystal-clear aquamarine waters.

Never having done this before, Jill was uncertain of the procedure. Jordan patiently answered her questions and waded into the water with her. He paused when they were waist-deep, gave her detailed instructions, then clasped her hand. His touch lent her confidence, and soon she was investigating an undersea world of breathtaking beauty. Swimming out of the inlet, they came upon a reef, with colorful fish slipping in and out of white coral caverns. After what seemed like only minutes, Jordan steered them back toward the inlet and shore.

"I don't think I've ever seen anything more beautiful," she breathed, pushing the mask from her face.

"I don't think I have, either," he agreed as they emerged from the water.

While Jill ran a comb through her hair and put on a shirt to protect her shoulders from the sun, Jordan brought out their lunch.

He spread the blanket in the shade of a palm tree. Jill knelt down beside him and opened the basket. Inside were generous crab-salad sandwiches, fresh slices of papaya and pineapple and thick chocolate-chip cook-

ies. She removed two cold cans of soda and handed one to Jordan.

They ate, then napped with a cool, gentle breeze whisking over them.

Jill awoke before Jordan. He was asleep on his back with his hand thrown carelessly across his face, shading his eyes from the glare of the sun. His features were more relaxed than she'd ever seen them. Jill studied him for several minutes, her heart aching for the man she'd loved so long ago. Her father. The man she'd never really had a chance to know. In some ways, Jordan was so much like her father it pained her to be with him, and at the same time it thrilled her. Not only because in learning about Jordan she was discovering a part of her past, of herself, but because she'd rarely felt so *alive* in anyone's company.

As she recognized this truth, a heaviness settled over her. She didn't *want* to fall in love with him. She was so afraid her life would mirror her mother's. Elaine Morrison had grown embittered. She'd been a young woman when her husband died, but she'd never remarried; instead she'd closed herself off, not wanting to risk the kind of pain that loving Jill's father had brought her.

Sitting up, Jill shoved her now-dry hair away from her face. She wrapped her arms around her bent legs and pressed her forehead to her knees, gulping in breath after breath.

"Jill?" His voice was soft. Husky.

"You shouldn't have left your pager behind, after all," she told him, her voice tight. "Or your phone." Without them, he was a handsome, compelling man who appealed to all her senses. Without them, she was defenseless against his charm.

"Why not?"

"Because I like you too much."

"That's a problem?"

"Yes!" she cried. "Don't you understand?"

"Obviously not," he said with such tenderness she wanted to jump to her feet and yell at him to stop. "Maybe you'd better explain it to me," he added.

"I can't," she whispered, keeping her head lowered. "You'd never believe me. I don't blame you—I wouldn't believe me, either."

Jordan frowned. "Does this have something to do with your reaction the first time I kissed you?"

"The only time!"

"That's about to change."

Her head shot up at the casual way in which he said it, as though kissing her was a foregone conclusion.

He was right.

His kiss was gentle. Jill resisted, unwilling to give him her heart, knowing what became of women who loved men like this. Men like Jordan Wilcox.

Their kiss now was much more potent than that first night. His touch somehow transcended the sensual. Jill could think of no other words to describe it. His fingers brushed her temple. His lips moved across her face, grazing her chin, her cheek, her eyes. She moaned, not from pleasure, but from fear, from a pain that reached deep inside her.

"Oh, no…"

"It's happening again, isn't it?" he whispered.

She nodded. "Can you feel it?"

"Yes. I did the other time, too."

Her eyes drifted slowly open. "I can't love you."

"So you've told me. More than once."

"It isn't personal." She tried to break free without being obvious about it, but Jordan held her firmly in his embrace.

"Tell me what's upsetting you so much."

"I can't." Looking into the distance, she focused on the smoky-blue outline of a mountain. Anything to avoid gazing at Jordan.

"You're involved with someone else, aren't you?"

It would be so easy to lie to him. To tell him about Ralph as though the friendship they shared was one of blazing passion, but she found she couldn't do it.

"No," she wailed, "but I wish I was."

"Why?" he demanded gruffly.

"What about you?" she countered. "Why did you seek out my company? Why'd you ask me to attend the dinner party with you? Surely there was someone else, someone more suitable."

"I'll admit that kissing you is a…unique experience," he confessed.

"But I've been rude."

"Actually, more amusing than rude."

"But why?" she asked again. "What is it about me that interests you? We're about as different as two people can get. We're strangers—strangers with nothing in common."

Jordan was frowning, his eyes revealing his own lack of understanding. "I don't know."

"See what I mean?" She spoke as if it were the jury's final decree. "The whole thing is a farce. You kiss me and…and I feel a certain…feeling."

"So do I. And it's something I can't explain. But I've seen electrical storms that unleash less energy than we did when we kissed."

Suddenly Jill found it nearly impossible to breathe. Jordan couldn't be affected by the wedding dress and its so-called magic—could he? Jill swore the minute she arrived in Seattle she was returning it to Shelly and Mark. She wasn't taking any chances.

"You remind me of my father," Jill said, refusing to meet his eyes. Even talking about Adam Morrison was painful to her. "He was always in a hurry to get somewhere, to meet someone, to make a deal. We took a family vacation when I was ten. My dad, my mom and me. We saw California in one day, Disneyland in an hour. Do you get the picture?" She didn't wait for a response. "He died of a heart attack when I was fifteen. We were wealthy by a lot of people's standards, and after his death my mother didn't have to work. We had no financial worries at all. And yet we would've been happier with far less money if it meant my father was still alive."

An awkward moment passed. When Jordan didn't comment, Jill glanced at him. "You don't have anything to say?"

"Not really, other than to point out that I'm not your father."

"But you're exactly like him! I recognized it the first minute I saw you." She leaped to her feet, grabbed her towel and crammed it into her beach bag.

Jordan reluctantly stood, and while she shook the sand off the blanket and folded it, he loaded their snorkeling gear into the trunk of the car.

They were both quiet during the drive back to the airport, the silence strained and unnatural. A couple of times, Jill looked in Jordan's direction. The hardness

was back. The tightness in his jaw, the harsh, almost grim expression…

Jill could well imagine what he'd be like in a board meeting. No wonder he didn't seem too concerned about the threat of a takeover. He would withstand that, and a whole lot more, in the years to come. But at what price? Power demanded sacrifice; prestige didn't come cheap. There was a cost, and Jill could only speculate what it would be for Jordan. His health? His happiness?

She found it intolerable to think about. Words burned in her heart. Words of caution. Words of appeal, but he wouldn't listen to her any more than her father had heeded her mother's tearful pleas.

As the airport came into view, Jill knew she couldn't let their day end on such an unhappy note. "I did have a wonderful time. Thank you."

"Mmm," he replied, his gaze focused on the road ahead.

Jill stared at him. "That's it?"

"What else do you want me to say?" His voice was crisp and emotionless.

"Like, I don't know, that you enjoyed yourself, too."

"It was interesting."

"Interesting?" Jill repeated.

They'd had a marvelous adventure! Not only that, he'd actually *relaxed*. The lines of fatigue around his eyes were gone. She'd bet a month's wages that this was the first afternoon nap he'd had in years. Possibly decades. It was probably the longest stretch of time he'd been away from a telephone in his adult life.

And all he'd say was that their day had been "interesting"?

"What about the kissing?" she demanded. "Was *that* interesting?"

"Very."

Jill seethed silently. "It was…interesting for me, too."

"So you said."

Jill tucked a long strand of hair behind her ear. "I was only being honest with you."

"I admit it was a fresh approach. Do you generally discuss marriage and children with a man on a first date?"

Color exploded in her cheeks, and she looked uncomfortably away. "No, but you were different…and it wasn't an approach."

"Excuse me, that's right, you were being honest." The cold sarcasm in his voice kept her from even trying to explain.

They'd almost reached the airport when she spoke again. "Would you do me one small favor?" She nearly choked on the pride she had to swallow.

"What?"

"Would you… The next time you see Mr. Howard, would you tell him something for me? Would you tell him I'm sorry?" He'd be disappointed in her, but Jill couldn't risk her own happiness because a dear man with a romantic heart believed she was Jordan Wilcox's one chance at finding love.

Jordan stopped the car abruptly and turned to glare at her. "You want me to apologize to Howard?"

"Please."

"Sorry," he said without a pause. "You'll have to do that yourself."

Five

Four days later, Jill stepped off the plane at Sea-Tac Airport in Seattle. Her skin glowed with a golden tan, accentuated by the bold pink flower print of her new sundress. She hadn't expected anyone to meet her, but was pleasantly surprised to see Shelly and Mark. Shelly waved excitedly when she located Jill in the baggage claim area.

"Welcome home," Shelly said as she rushed forward, exuberantly throwing her arms around Jill. "How was Hawaii? My goodness, your tan is gorgeous. You must've spent *hours* in the sun."

"Hawaii was wonderful." A slight exaggeration. She'd hardly slept since Jordan's departure.

"Tell me everything," Shelly insisted, taking Jill's hands. "I'm dying to find out who you met after we mailed you the wedding dress."

"Honey," Mark chided gently, "give her a chance to breathe."

"Are you with someone?" Shelly asked, looking around expectantly. "I mean, you know, you're not married, are you?"

"I'm not even close to being married," Jill informed her friend dryly.

Mark took charge of the beach bag Jill had brought home with her, stuffed full of souvenirs and everything she couldn't fit into her suitcase. She removed one of the three leis she was wearing and looped it around Shelly's neck. "Here, my gift to you."

"Oh, Jill, it's beautiful. Thank you," Shelly said, fingering the fragrant lei of pink orchids. As they walked toward the appropriate carousel, Shelly slipped her arm through Jill's. "I can't wait a second longer. Tell me what happened after the dress arrived. I want to hear every detail."

Jill had been dreading this moment, but she hadn't thought she'd face it quite so soon. "I'm afraid I'm going to have to return the dress."

Shelly stared at her as if she hadn't heard correctly. "Pardon?"

"I didn't meet anyone."

"You mean to tell me you spent seven days in Hawaii and you didn't speak to a single man?" Shelly asked incredulously.

"Not exactly."

"Aha! So there was someone."

Jill tried not to groan. "Sort of."

Shelly smiled, sliding one arm around her husband's waist. "The plot thickens."

"I met him briefly the first day. Actually I don't think he counts...."

"Why wouldn't he count?" Shelly asked.

"We sat next to each other on the plane, so technically we met *before* I got the wedding dress. I'm sure he's not the one." Jill had decided to play along with her

friend's theory, pretend to take it more seriously than she did. Logical objections, like this mistake in timing, *should* convince Shelly—but probably wouldn't.

"In fact," she continued, "I've been thinking about that dress lately, and I'm convinced you and your aunt Milly are wrong—it's not for me. It never was."

"But it fit you. Remember?"

Jill didn't need to be reminded. "That was a fluke. I'm sure if I were to try it on now, it wouldn't."

"Then try it on! Prove me wrong."

"Here?" Jill laughed.

"When you get home. Right now, just tell me about this guy you met. You keep trying to avoid the subject."

"There's nothing to tell," Jill insisted, sorry she'd said anything. She'd tried for the past few days to push every thought of Jordan from her mind, with little success. He'd haunted her remaining time on the islands, refusing to leave her alone. If she did sleep, he invaded her dreams.

"Start with his name," Shelly said. "Surely you know his name."

"Jordan Wilcox, but—"

"Jordan Wilcox," Mark repeated. "He doesn't happen to be a developer, does he?"

"He does something along those lines."

Mark released a low whistle. "He's one of the big boys."

"Big boys," Shelly echoed disparagingly. "Be more specific. Do you mean he's tall?"

"No." Mark's smiling eyes briefly met Jill's. "Although he is. I mean he's a well-known corporate giant. I've met him a few times. If I understand it correctly, he puts together commercial projects, finds backers for

them, works with the designer and the builders, and when the project's complete, he sells. He's made millions in the last few years."

"He was in Hawaii to put together financial backing for a shopping mall," Jill explained.

"Well," Shelly said, eyeing her closely, "what did you think of him?"

"What was there to think? I sat next to him on the plane and we stayed in the same hotel, but that was about it." It was best not to mention the other incidents; Shelly would put far too much stock in a couple of dinners and a day on the beach. Heaven help Jill if Shelly ever found out they'd exchanged a few kisses!

"I'm sure he's the one," Shelly announced gleefully. Her eyes fairly sparkled with delight. "I can *feel* it. He's our man."

"No, he isn't," Jill argued, knowing it was futile, yet compelled to try. "I already told you—I met him *before* the dress arrived. Besides, we have absolutely nothing in common."

"Do Mark and I?" Shelly glanced lovingly at her husband. "And I'm crazy about him."

At first, Jill had wondered what Mark, a tax consultant with orderly habits and a closetful of suits, could possibly have in common with her zany, creative, unconventional friend. The answer was simple. Nothing. But that hadn't stopped them from falling in love. Jill couldn't be in the same room with them without sensing the powerful attraction they felt for each other.

However, there was little similarity between Shelly's marriage to Mark and Jill's relationship with Jordan. What she'd learned from her father's life—and death— was the value of balance. Although her career mattered

to her, it didn't define her life or occupy every minute of her time.

"In this case I think Jill might be right," Mark said, his voice thoughtful.

"He's the one," Shelly said for the second time.

"I've met him," Mark went on to say. "He's cold and unemotional. If he does have a heart, it was frozen a long time ago."

"So?" Ever optimistic, Shelly refused to listen. "Jill's perfect for him, then. She's warm and gentle and caring."

At the moment Jill didn't feel any of those things. Listening to Mark describe Jordan, she had to fight the urge to defend him, to tell them what Andrew Howard had told her. Yes, Jordan was everything Mark said, but there was another side to him, one Jill had briefly encountered. One that was so appealing it had frightened her into running away, which was exactly what she'd done that day on the beach. He'd kissed her and she'd known immediately, intuitively, that she'd never be the same. But knowing it didn't alter her resolve. She couldn't love him because the price would be too high. He would give her all the things she craved, but eventually she'd end up like her mother, lonely and bitter.

"I just can't imagine Jordan Wilcox married," Mark concluded.

"I can," Shelly interrupted with unflinching enthusiasm. "To Jill."

"Shelly," Mark said, grinning indulgently, "listen to reason."

"When has falling in love ever been reasonable?" She fired the question at her husband, who merely shrugged,

then turned back to Jill. "Did you tell him about Aunt Milly's wedding dress?"

"Good heavens, no!"

"All the better. I'll bet you really threw the guy for a loop. Was he on this flight?"

"No, he returned four days ago."

"Four days ago?" Shelly asked suspiciously. "There's something you're not telling us. Come on, Jill, fess up. You did a whole lot more than sit next to him on the plane. And Mark and I want to know what."

"Uh…" Jill was tired from the flight and her resistance was low. Under normal circumstances she would've sidestepped the issue. "It isn't like it sounds," she said weakly. "We talked, that's all."

"Did you kiss?" The question came out in a soft whisper. "The first time Mark kissed me was when I knew. If you and Jordan kissed, there wouldn't be any doubt in your mind. You'd know."

Sooner or later Shelly would worm it out of her. By telling the truth now, Jill thought she might be able to avoid a lengthy inquisition later. "All right, fine. We did kiss. A couple of times."

Even Mark seemed surprised by that.

"See?" Shelly cried triumphantly. "And what happened?"

Jill heaved an exaggerated sigh. "Nothing. I want to return the wedding dress."

"Sorry," Shelly said, her eyes flashing with excitement, "it's nonreturnable."

"I don't plan on ever seeing him again," Jill said adamantly. She'd more or less told Jordan that, too. He was in full agreement; he wanted nothing to do with her, either. "I insist you take back the wedding dress," Jill

said. Shelly and Mark's eyes met. Slowly they smiled, as if sharing a private joke.

But in Jill's opinion, there was nothing to smile about.

The first person Jill called when she got home was her mother. Their conversation was friendly, and she was relieved to find Elaine less vague and self-absorbed than she'd been recently. Jill told a few anecdotes, described the island and the hotel, but avoided telling her mother about Jordan.

She was strangely reluctant to call Ralph, even though she knew he was waiting to hear from her. He was terribly nice, but unfortunately she found him…a bit dull. She put off calling; two days later, he called her, leaving a message.

They'd kissed a few times, and the kisses were pleasant enough, but for her there wasn't any spark. When Jordan took her in his arms it felt like a forest fire compared to the placid warmth she experienced with Ralph.

Jordan. Forgetting him hadn't become any easier. Jill had assumed that once she was home, surrounded by everything that was familiar and comfortable, she'd be able to put their brief interlude behind her.

It hadn't happened.

Wednesday afternoon, Jill returned home from work, put water on for tea and began reading the paper. Normally she didn't glance at the financial section. She wasn't sure why she did now. Skimming the headlines, she idly folded back the page—and saw Jordan's name. It seemed to leap out at her.

Jill's heart slowed, then vaulted into action as she read the article. He'd done it. The paper was report-

ing Jordan's latest coup. His company had reached an agreement with a land-management outfit in Hawaii, and construction on the shopping mall would begin within the next three months.

He must be pleased. Although he hadn't said much, Jill knew Jordan had wanted this project to fly. A hundred questions bombarded her. Had he heard from Andrew Howard? Had the older man joined forces with Jordan, after all? Had he asked Jordan about her, and if so, what had Jordan told him?

Jill had thought of writing Mr. Howard a note, but she didn't have his address. She didn't have Jordan's, either; however, it was a simple matter of checking the internet for his company's address.

Before she could determine the wisdom of her actions, she scribbled a few lines of congratulation, addressed the envelope, and the next morning, mailed the card. She had no idea if it would even reach him.

Two days later when Jill came home from work, she noticed a long luxury car parked in front of her apartment building. Other than giving it an inquisitive glance, she didn't pay any attention. She was shuffling through her purse, searching for her keys, when she heard someone approach from behind.

She turned her head to see—and nearly dropped her purse. It was Jordan. He looked very much as he had the first time she'd met him. Cynical and hard. Detached and unemotional. His smoky gray eyes scanned her, but there was nothing to indicate that he was glad to see her, or if he'd spared her a moment's thought since they'd parted. Nothing but cool indifference.

"Hello, Jill."

She was so flustered that the newspaper, which she'd

tucked under her arm, fell to the floor. Stooping, she retrieved it, then clutched it against her chest as she straightened. "Jordan."

"I got your note."

"I—I wanted you to know how happy I was for you." He was staring pointedly at her door.

"Um, would you like to come inside?" she asked, unlatching the door with fumbling fingers. "I'll make some tea if you like. Or coffee…" She hadn't expected this, nor was she emotionally prepared for seeing him. She'd figured he'd read the card and then drop it in his wastebasket.

"Tea sounds fine."

"I'll just be a minute," she said as she hurried into the kitchen. Her heart was rampaging, pounding against her ribs. "Make yourself at home," she called out, holding the teakettle under the faucet.

"You have a nice place," he said, standing in the doorway between the kitchen and the living room.

"Thank you. I've lived here for three years." She didn't know why she'd told him that. It didn't matter to him how long she'd lived there.

"Why'd you send me the card?" he asked while she was setting out cups and saucers.

She didn't feel comfortable using her everyday mugs; she had a couple of lovely china cups her mother had given her and decided on those instead. She paused at his question, frowning slightly. "To congratulate you."

"The *real* reason."

"That was the real reason. This shopping mall was important to you and I was happy to read that everything came together. I knew you worked hard to make it happen. That was the only reason I sent you the note."

Her cheeks heated at his implication. He seemed to believe something she hadn't intended—or had she?

"Andrew Howard decided to invest in the project at the last minute. It was his support that made the difference."

Jill nodded. "I was hoping he would."

"I have you to thank for that."

Nothing in his expression suggested he was grateful for any assistance she might unwittingly have given him. His features remained cold and hard. The man who'd spent that day on the beach with her wasn't the harsh, unrelenting businessman who stood before her now.

"If I played any part in Mr. Howard's decision, I'm sure it was small."

"He seemed quite taken with you."

"I was quite taken with him, too."

A flicker of emotion passed through Jordan's eyes, one so fleeting, so transitory, she was sure she'd imagined it.

"I'd like to thank you, if you'd let me," he said.

She was dropping tea bags into her best ceramic teapot. "Thank me? You already have."

"I was thinking more along the lines of dinner."

Jill's first thought was that she didn't have anything appropriate to wear. Not to an elegant restaurant, and of course she couldn't imagine Jordan dining anywhere else. He wasn't the kind of man who ate in a burger joint.

"Unless you already have plans…"

He was offering her an escape, and his eyes seemed to challenge her to take it.

"No," she said, almost gasping. Jill wasn't sure why

she accepted so readily, why she didn't even consider declining. "I don't have anything planned for tonight."

"Is there a particular place you'd like to go?"

She shook her head. "You choose."

Jill felt suddenly light-headed with happiness and anticipation. Trying to keep her voice steady, she added, "I'll need to change clothes, but that shouldn't take long."

He looked at her skirt and blouse as if he hadn't noticed them before. "You look fine just the way you are," he said, dismissing her concern.

The kettle whistled and Jill removed it from the burner, pouring the scalding water into the teapot. "This should steep for a few minutes." She backed out of the kitchen, irrationally fearing that he'd disappear if she let him out of her sight.

She chose the same outfit she'd worn on the trip home—the Hawaiian print shirt with the hot pink flowers. Narrow black pants set it off nicely, as did the shell lei she'd purchased the first day she'd gone touring. Then she freshened her makeup and brushed her hair.

Jordan had poured the tea and was adding sugar to his cup when she entered the kitchen. His gaze didn't waver or change in any way, yet she could tell he liked her choice.

The phone rang. Jill darted a look at it, willing it to stop. She sighed and went over to check call display.

Shelly.

"Hello, Shelly." She hoped her voice didn't convey her lack of enthusiasm.

"How are you? I haven't heard a word from you since you got home. Are you all right? I've been worried.

You generally phone once or twice a week, and it's not like you to—"

"I'm fine."

"You're sure?"

"Positive."

"You seem preoccupied. Am I catching you at a bad time? Is Ralph there? Maybe he'll take the hint and go home. Honestly, Jill, I don't know why you continue to see that guy. I mean, he's nice, but he's about as romantic as mold."

"Uh, I have company."

"Company," Shelly echoed. "Who? No, let me guess. Jordan Wilcox!"

"You got it."

"Talk to you later. Bye." The drone of the disconnected line sounded in her ear so fast that Jill was left holding the receiver for several seconds before she realized her friend had hung up.

No sooner had Jill replaced it than the phone rang again. She looked at call display, cast an apologetic glance toward Jordan and snatched up the receiver. "Hello, Shelly."

"I want it understood that you're to give me a full report later."

"Shelly!"

"And don't you dare try to return that wedding dress. He's the one, Jill. Quit fighting it. I'll let you go now, but just remember, I want details, so be prepared." She hung up as quickly as she had the first time.

"That was my best friend."

"Shelly?"

"She's married to Mark Brady." Jill waited, wondering if Jordan would recognize the name.

"Mark Brady." He spoke slowly, as though saying it aloud would jar his memory. "Is Mark a tax consultant? I seem to recall hearing something about him not long ago. Isn't he the head of his own firm?"

"That's Mark." Jill nearly told him how Shelly and Mark had met, but stopped herself just in time. Jordan knew about the wedding dress—though not, of course, its significance—because Jill had inadvertently let it slip that first night.

"And Mark's married to your best friend?"

"That's right." She took a sip of her tea. "When I said I'd met you, Mark knew who you were right away."

"So you mentioned me." He seemed pleasantly surprised.

He could have no idea how much he'd been in her thoughts during the past two weeks. She'd tried, heaven knew she'd tried, to push every memory of him from her mind. But it hadn't worked. She couldn't explain it, but somehow nothing was the same anymore.

"You ready?" he asked after a moment.

Jill nodded and carried their empty cups to the sink. Then Jordan led her to his car, opening the door and ushering her inside. When he joined her, he pulled out his ever-present cell phone...and turned it off.

"You don't need to do that on my account," she told him.

"I'm not," he said, his smile tight, almost a grimace. "I'm doing it for me." With that he started the engine.

Jill had no idea where they were going. He took the freeway and headed north, exiting into the downtown area of Seattle. There were any number of four-star restaurants within a five-block area. Jill was curious, but she didn't ask. She'd know soon enough.

When Jordan drove into the underground garage of a luxury skyscraper, Jill was momentarily surprised. But then, several of the office complexes housed world-class restaurants.

"I didn't know there was a restaurant here," she said conversationally.

"There isn't."

"Oh."

"I live in the penthouse."

"Oh."

"Unless you object?"

"No...no, that's fine."

"I phoned earlier and asked my cook to prepare dinner for two."

"You have a cook?" Oddly, that fact astounded her, although she supposed it shouldn't have, considering his wealth.

He smiled, his first genuine smile since he'd shown up at her door. "You're easily impressed."

He talked as though *everyone* employed a cook, and Jill couldn't help laughing.

They rode a private elevator thirty floors up to the penthouse suite. The view of Puget Sound that greeted Jill as the doors glided open was breathtaking.

"This is beautiful," she whispered, stepping out. She followed him through his living room, past a white leather sectional sofa and a glass-and-chrome coffee table that held a small abstract sculpture. She wasn't too knowledgeable when it came to works of art, but this looked valuable.

"That's a Davis Stanford piece," Jordan said matter-of-factly.

Jill nodded, hoping he wouldn't guess how ignorant she was.

"White wine?"

"Please." Jill couldn't take her eyes off the view. The waterways of Puget Sound were dotted with white-and-green ferries. The islands—Bainbridge, Whidbey and Vashon—were jewellike against the backdrop of the Olympic Mountains.

"Nothing like Hawaii, is it?" Jordan asked as he handed her a long-stemmed wineglass.

"No, but just as beautiful in its own way."

"I'm going back to Oahu next week."

"So soon?" Jill was envious.

"It's another short trip. Two or three days at most."

"Perhaps you'll get a chance to go snorkeling again."

Jordan shook his head. "I won't have time for any underwater adventures this trip," he told her.

Jill perched on the edge of the sofa, staring down at her wine. "I don't think I'll ever be able to separate you from my time in Oahu," she said softly. "The rest of my week seemed so…empty."

"I know what you mean."

Her heartbeat quickened as his gaze strayed to her mouth. He sat beside her and removed the wine goblet from her unresisting hand. Next his fingers curved around her neck, ever so lightly, brushing aside her hair. His eyes held hers as if he expected resistance. Then slowly, giving her ample opportunity to pull away if she wished, he lowered his mouth to hers.

Jill moaned in anticipation, instinctively moving closer. Common sense shouted in alarm, but she refused to listen. Just once she wanted to know what it was like to be kissed with real passion—to be cherished

by a man. Just once she wanted to know what it meant to be adored. Her heart filled with delirious joy. Her hands slid up his chest to his shoulders as she clung to him. He kissed her again, small, nibbling kisses, as though he was afraid of frightening her with the strength of his need. But he must have sensed her receptiveness, because he deepened the kiss.

Suddenly it came to her. The same thing that had happened to Shelly was now happening to her. The phenomenon Aunt Milly had experienced sixty-five years earlier was coming to pass a third time.

The wedding dress.

Abruptly, she broke off the kiss. Panting, she sprang to her feet. Her eyes were wide and incredulous as she gazed down at a surprised Jordan.

"It's you!" she cried. "It really is you."

Six

"What do you mean, it's me?" Jordan demanded. When she didn't answer, he asked, "What's wrong, Jill?"

"Everything," she cried, shaking her head.

"I hurt you?"

"No," she whispered, "no." She sobbed quietly as she wrung her hands. "I don't know what to do."

"Why do you have to do anything?"

"Because…oh, you wouldn't understand." Worse, she couldn't tell him. Every time he looked at her, she became more and more convinced that Shelly had been right. Jordan Wilcox was her future.

But she *couldn't* fall in love with him, because she knew what would happen to her if she did—she'd become like her mother, lonely, bitter and unhappy. If she was going to marry, she wanted a man who was safe and sensible. A man like… Ralph. Yet the thought of spending the rest of her life with Ralph produced an even deeper sense of discontent.

"I'm not an unreasonable man," Jordan said. Then

he added, "Well, generally I'm not. If there's a problem you can tell me."

"It's not supposed to be a problem. According to Shelly and her aunt Milly, it's a blessing. I know I'm talking in riddles, but…there's no way you'd understand!"

"Try me."

"I can't. I'm sorry, I just can't."

"But it has something to do with my kissing you?"

She stared at him blankly. "No. Yes."

"You seem rather uncertain about this. Perhaps we should try it again…."

"That isn't necessary." But even as she spoke, Jordan was reaching for her, pulling her onto his lap. Jill willingly surrendered to his embrace, greeting his kiss with a muffled groan of welcome, a sigh of defeat. His arms held her close, and not for the first time, Jill was stunned by the effect he had on her. It left her feeling both unnerved and overwhelmed.

"Better?" he asked in a remarkably steady voice.

Unable to answer, Jill closed her eyes, then nodded. Better, yes. And worse. Every time he touched her, it confirmed what she feared most.

"I thought so." He seemed reassured, but that did nothing to comfort Jill. For weeks she'd played a silly game of denial. They'd met, and from that moment on, nothing had been the same.

She didn't, couldn't, believe in the power of the wedding dress; she scoffed at the implausibility of its legend. Yet even Mr. Howard, who'd never heard of Aunt Milly or her dress, had felt compelled to explain Jordan's past to her, had seen Jill as his future.

She'd spent only three days with Jordan, but she

knew more about him than she knew about Ralph, whom she'd been dating for months. Their day on the beach and the dinner with Andrew Howard had given her insights into Jordan's personality. Since then Jill had found it more difficult to accept what she saw on the surface—the detached, cynical male. The man who wore his I-don't-give-a-damn attitude like an elaborate mask.

Perhaps she understood him because he was so much like her father. Adam Morrison had lived for the excitement, the risks, of the big deal. He poured his life's blood into each business transaction because he'd never really acknowledged the importance of family, emotion, human values.

Jordan wouldn't, either.

Dinner was a strained affair, although Jordan made several efforts to lighten the mood. As he drove her home, Jill sensed that he wanted to say something more. Whatever it was, he left unsaid.

"Have a safe trip," she told him when he escorted her to her door. Her heart was pounding, not with excitement, but with trepidation, wondering if he planned to kiss her again.

"I'll call you when I get back," he told her. And that was all.

"I have a special fondness for this place," Shelly said as she slipped into a chair opposite Jill. They were meeting for lunch at Patrick's, a restaurant in the mall where Jill's branch of PayRite was located. Typically, she was ten minutes late. Marriage to Mark, who was habitually prompt, hadn't improved Shelly's tardiness. Jill

often wondered how they managed to keep their love so strong when they were so different.

Patrick's had played a minor role in Shelly's romance with Mark. Jill recalled the Saturday she'd met her there for lunch, and how amused she'd been at Shelly's crazy story of receiving the infamous wedding dress.

The way Jill felt now—frantic, frightened, confused—was exactly the way Shelly had felt then.

"So tell me everything," Shelly said breathlessly.

"Jordan stopped by. We had dinner. He left this morning on a business trip," she explained dispassionately. "There isn't much to tell."

Shelly's hand closed around her water glass, her eyes connecting with Jill's. "Do you remember when I first met Mark?"

"I'm not likely to forget," Jill said, smiling despite her present mood.

"Anytime you or my mother or anyone else asked me about Mark, I always said there wasn't anything to tell. Remember?"

"Yes." Jill thought of how Shelly's face would become expressionless, her tone abrupt, whenever anyone mentioned Mark's name.

"Well, when I told you nothing was happening, I was stretching the truth," Shelly continued. "There was plenty going on, but nothing I felt I could share. Even with you." She raised her eyebrows. "You, my friend, have the same look I did then. A lot has taken place between you and Jordan. So much that you're frightened out of your wits. Trust me, I know."

"He kissed me again," Jill admitted.

"It was better than before?"

"Worse!"

Shelly apparently found Jill's answer humorous. She tried to hide her smile behind the menu, then lowered it to say, "Don't count on your feelings becoming any less complicated. They won't."

"He's going to be away for a few days. Thank goodness, because it gives me time to think."

"Oh, Jill," Shelly said with a sympathetic sigh, "I wish there was something I could say to help you. Why are you fighting this so hard?" She grinned sheepishly. "I fought it, too. Be smart, just accept it. Love isn't really all that terrifying once you let go of your doubts."

"Instead of talking about Jordan, why don't we order lunch?" Jill suggested a little curtly. "I'm starved."

"Me, too."

The waitress arrived at their table a moment later, and Jill ordered the split-pea soup and a turkey sandwich.

"Wait a minute," Shelly interrupted, motioning toward the waitress. She turned to Jill. "You don't even *like* split-pea soup. You never order it." She gave Jill an odd look, then turned back to the waitress. "She'll have the clam chowder."

"Shelly!"

The waitress wrote down the order quickly, as though she feared an argument was about to erupt.

"You're more upset than I realized," Shelly said when they were alone. "Ordering split-pea soup—I can't believe it."

"It's soup, Shelly, not nuclear waste." Her friend definitely had a tendency to overreact. It drove Jill crazy, but it was the very thing that made Shelly so endearing.

"I'm going to call Jordan Wilcox myself," Shelly announced suddenly.

"You're going to *what?*" It was all Jill could do to remain in her seat.

"You heard me."

"Shelly, no! I absolutely forbid you to discuss me with Jordan. How would you have felt if I'd called Mark?"

Shelly frowned. "I'd have been furious."

"I will be, too, if you say so much as one word to Jordan about me."

Shelly paused, her eyes wide with concern. "But I'm afraid you're going to mess this up."

Nothing to fear there—Jill already had. She reached for a package of rye crisps from the bread basket, and Shelly frowned again. That was when she remembered she wasn't any fonder of rye crisps than she was of split-pea soup.

"Promise me you'll stay out of it," Jill pleaded. "Please."

"All right," Shelly muttered. "Just don't do anything stupid."

"This is a pleasant surprise," Jill's mother said as she opened the front door. Elaine Morrison was in her late fifties, slim and attractive.

"I thought I'd bring over your gift from Hawaii," Jill said, following her mother into the kitchen, where Elaine poured them each a glass of iced tea. Jill set the box of chocolate-covered macadamia nuts on the counter.

"I'm glad your vacation went so well."

Jill pulled out a bar stool and sat at the counter, trying to look relaxed when she was anything but. "I met someone while I was in Hawaii."

Her mother paused, then smiled. "I thought you might have."

"What makes you say that?"

"Oh, there's a certain look about you. Now tell me how you met, what he's like, where he's from and what he does for a living."

Jill laughed at the rapid-fire questions.

Elaine added slices of lemon to their tea and started across the kitchen, a new excitement in her step. Finally, after all these years, her mother was beginning to overcome the bitterness her husband's obsession with business had created. She was finally coming to terms not only with his death but with her grief over his neglect.

Jill was relieved and delighted by the signs of her mother's recovery, but she had to say, "Frankly, Mom, I don't think you'll like him."

Her mother looked surprised. "Why ever not?"

Jill didn't hesitate. "Because he reminds me of Daddy."

Her mother's face contorted with shock, and tears sprang to her eyes. "Jill, no! For the love of heaven, no."

"I've been giving some thought to your suggestion," Jill said to Ralph a few hours later. Her nerves were in turmoil. The clam chowder sat like a dead weight in the pit of her stomach, and her mother's dire warnings had shaken her badly.

Ralph wasn't tall and strikingly handsome like Jordan, but he was a comfortable sort of man. He made a person feel at ease. In fact, his laid-back manner was a blessed relief after the high-stress, high-energy hours she'd spent with Jordan, few though they were.

Jordan Wilcox could pull together a deal for an apart-

ment complex before Ralph stepped out of the shower in the morning. Ralph's idea of an exhilarating evening was doing the newspaper crossword puzzle.

Everything about Jordan was complex. Everything about Ralph was uncomplicated; he was a straightforward, honest man who'd be a good husband and a loving father.

"Are you saying what I think you're saying?" Ralph prompted when she didn't immediately continue.

Jill held her water glass. "You said something not long ago about the two of us giving serious consideration to making our relationship permanent and…and I wanted you to know I was… I've been giving some thought to that."

Ralph didn't reveal any emotion. He put down his hamburger, looked at her and asked casually, "Why now?"

"Uh… I'm going to be twenty-nine soon." She managed to sound calm, although she felt anything but.

She was the biggest coward who ever lived. But what else could she do? Her mother had become nearly hysterical when Jill had told her about Jordan. Her own heart was filled with trepidation. On the one hand, there was Shelly, so confident Jordan was the man for Jill. On the other was her mother, adamant that Jill would be forever sorry if she got involved with a workaholic.

Jill was trapped in the middle, frightened and unsure.

Ralph relaxed against the red vinyl upholstery. The diner was his favorite place to eat, and he took her there every time they dined out. "So you think we should consider marriage?"

It was the subject Jill had been leading up to all evening, yet when Ralph posed the question directly, she

hesitated. If only Jordan hadn't kissed her. If only he hadn't held her in his arms. And if only she hadn't spoken to her mother…

"I missed you while you were away," Ralph said, his gaze holding hers.

Jill knew this was about as close to romance as she was likely to get from Ralph. Romance was his weakest suit, dependability and steadiness his strongest. Ralph would always be there by his wife's side. He'd make the kind of father who played catch in the backyard with his son. The kind of father who'd bring his wife and daughter pretty corsages on Easter morning. He was a rock, a fortress of permanence. She wished she could fall in love with him.

Jordan might have a talent for making millions, but all the money in the world couldn't buy happiness.

"I missed you, too," Jill said softly. She'd thought of Ralph, had wondered about him. A few times, anyway. Hadn't she mailed him a postcard? Hadn't she brought him a book on volcanoes?

"I'm glad to hear that," Ralph said. Then, clearing his throat, he asked, "Jill Morrison, will you do me the honor of becoming my wife?"

The question was out now, ready for her to answer. A proposal was what she'd been hinting at all evening. Now that Ralph had asked, Jill wasn't sure what she felt. Relief? No, it wasn't even close to that. Pleasure? Yes—in a way. But not a throw-open-the-windows-and-shout kind of joy.

Joy. The word hit her like an unexpected punch. Joy was what she'd experienced the first time Jordan had taken her in his arms. A free-flowing joy and the promise of so much more.

The promise she was rejecting.

Ralph might not be the love of her life, but he'd care for her and devote his life to her. It was enough.

"Jill?"

She tried to smile, tried to look happy and excited. Ralph deserved that much. "Yes," she whispered, stretching her hand across the table. "Yes, I'll marry you."

"What do you mean you're engaged to marry Ralph?" Shelly demanded. Her voice had risen to such a high pitch that Jill held the receiver away from her ear.

"He asked me tonight and I've accepted."

"You can't *do* that!" her friend shrieked.

"Of course I can."

"What about Jordan?" Shelly asked next.

"I'd already decided not to see him again." Jill was able to keep her composure, although it wasn't easy.

"If marrying Ralph is typical of your decisions, then I'd like to suggest you talk to a mental-health professional."

Jill laughed despite herself. Her decision had been based on maintaining her sanity, not destroying it.

"I don't know what's so funny. I can't believe you'd do something like this! What about Aunt Milly's wedding dress? Doesn't that mean anything to you? Don't you care that Mark, Aunt Milly and I all felt the dress should go to you? You can't ignore it. Something dreadful might happen."

"Don't be ridiculous."

"I'm not," Shelly said resolutely. "You can't reject the man destiny has chosen for you without consequences." Shelly's voice was solemn.

"You don't know that Jordan's the man," Jill said with far more conviction than she was feeling. "We both realize a wedding dress can't dictate who I'll marry. The choice is mine—and I've chosen Ralph."

"You're honestly choosing Ralph over Jordan?" The question had an incredulous quality.

"Yes."

There was a moment's silence.

"You're scared," Shelly went on, "frightened half out of your wits because of everything you feel. I know, because I went through the same thing. Jill, please, think about this before you do something you'll regret for the rest of your life."

"I have thought about it," she insisted. She'd thought of little else since her last encounter with Jordan. Since her talk with Shelly. Since her visit to her mother's. She'd carefully weighed her options. Marrying Ralph seemed the best course.

"You have no intention of changing your mind, do you?" Shelly cried. "Do you expect me to stand by and do *nothing* while you ruin your life?"

"I'm not ruining my life. Don't be absurd." Her voice grew hard. "Naturally I'll return your aunt Milly's wedding dress and—"

"No," Shelly groaned. "Here, talk to Mark."

"Jill?" Mark came on the line. "What's the problem?"

Jill didn't want to repeat everything. She was tired and it was late and all she wanted to do was go to bed. Escape for the next eight hours and then face the world again. Jill hadn't intended to tell Shelly and Mark her news quite so soon, but there'd been a telephone message from them when she got home. She'd decided she might as well let Shelly know about her decision. Jill

wasn't sure what kind of reaction she'd expected from her friends, but certainly not this.

"Just a minute," Mark said next. "Shelly's trying to tell me something."

Although Shelly had given the phone to her husband, Jill could hear her friend's frantic words as clearly as if she still held the receiver. Shelly was pleading with Mark to talk some sense into Jill, begging him to try because she hadn't been able to change Jill's mind.

"Mark," Jill called, but apparently he didn't hear her. "Mark," she tried again, louder this time.

"I'm sorry, Jill," he said politely, "but Shelly's upset, and I'm having a hard time figuring out just what the problem is. All I can make out is that you've decided not to see Jordan Wilcox again."

"I'm marrying Ralph Emery, and I don't think he'd take kindly to my dating Jordan."

Mark chuckled. "No, I don't suppose he would. Frankly, I believe the decision is yours, and yours alone. I know Jordan, I've talked to him a couple of times and I share your concerns. I can't picture him married."

"He's already married," Jill stated unemotionally, "to his job. A wife would only get in the way."

"That's probably true. What about Ralph—have I met him?"

"I don't think so," Jill returned stiffly. "He's a very nice man. Honest and hardworking. Shelly seems to think he's dull, and perhaps he is in some ways, but he...cares for me. It isn't a great love match, but we're both aware of that."

"Shelly thinks I'm dull, too, but that didn't stop her from marrying me."

Mark was so calm, so reassuring. He was exactly

what Jill needed. She was so grateful she felt close to tears. "I want to do the right thing," she said, gulping in a quick breath. Her voice wavered and she bit her lower lip, blinking rapidly.

"It's difficult knowing what's right sometimes, isn't it?" Mark said quietly. "I remember how I felt the first time I met Shelly. Here was this completely bizarre woman announcing to everyone who'd listen that she refused to marry me. I hadn't even asked—didn't even know her name. Then we stumbled on each other a second time and a third, and finally I learned about Aunt Milly's wedding dress."

"What did you think when she told you?"

"That it was the most ridiculous thing I'd ever heard."

"I did, too. I still do." She wanted a husband, *but not Jordan.*

"I'm sure you'll make the right decision," Mark said confidently.

"I am, too. Thanks, Mark, I really appreciate talking to you." The more she grew to know her friend's husband, the more Jill realized how perfectly they suited each other. Mark brought balance into Shelly's life, and she'd infused his with her warmth and wit. If only she, Jill, could have met someone like Mark.

No sooner had she hung up the phone than there was a loud knock on her door. Since it was late, close to eleven, Jill was surprised.

Peering through the peephole, she gasped and drew away. Jordan Wilcox.

"I thought you were in Hawaii," she said as she opened the door.

"I was." His eyes scanned her hungrily. "This morn-

ing I had the most incredible feeling something was wrong. I tried to call, but there wasn't any answer."

"I...was out for most of the day."

He took her by the shoulders and then, before she could protest, pulled her into his arms.

"Jordan?" She'd never seen him like this, didn't understand why he seemed so disturbed.

"I just couldn't shake the feeling something was wrong with you."

"I'm fine."

"I know," he said, inhaling deeply. "Thank God you're safe."

Seven

"Of course I'm safe," Jill said, still feeling bewildered. Jordan's arms were tight around her and he buried his head in the curve of her neck, his breathing hard.

"I've never experienced anything like this before," he said, loosening his hold. His hands caressed the length of her arms as he moved back one small step. He studied her, his gaze intimate and tender. "I hope it never happens to me again." Taking her hand, he led her to the sofa.

"You're not making any sense."

"I know." He momentarily closed his eyes, then gave a deep sigh. He raised her fingers to his lips and gently kissed the back of her hand.

"It was the most unbelievable thing," he continued with a shrug. "I awoke with this feeling of impending doom. At first I tried to ignore it. But as the day wore on I couldn't shake it. All I knew was that it had something to do with you.

"I thought if I talked to you I could assure myself that nothing was wrong and this feeling would go away. Only I couldn't get hold of you."

"I was out most of the day," she repeated unnecessarily.

Jordan rubbed a hand down his face. "I tried to phone you at home and I couldn't get an answer. I don't know your cell number. So I panicked. I booked the next flight to Seattle."

"What about your business in Hawaii?"

"I canceled one meeting and left what I could with an assistant. Everything's taken care of." He sighed once more and sagged against the back of her sofa. "I could do with a cup of coffee."

"Of course." Jill immediately stood and hurried into the kitchen, starting the coffee and assembling cups and saucers in a matter of minutes. She was arranging everything on a tray when Jordan stepped up behind her.

He slid his arms around her waist and kissed the side of her neck. "I don't know what's happening between us."

"I'm...not sure anything is."

Jordan chuckled softly, the sound a gentle caress against her skin. "I'm beginning to think you've cast a spell over me."

Jill froze. *Spell* and *magic* were words she'd rather not hear. Even the smallest hint that the wedding dress was affecting him wouldn't change what she'd done. She'd made her decision. The dress was packed away in the box Shelly had mailed her, ready to be returned.

"I've never experienced anything like this," Jordan said again, sounding almost uncertain.

Jill should have been shocked. Jordan Wilcox had probably never felt confused or doubtful about anything in his adult life. She speculated that his emotions had

been buried so deep, hidden by pride for so long, that he barely recognized them anymore.

"I think I'm falling in love with you."

Jill closed her eyes. She didn't want to hear this, didn't want to deal with a declaration of love. Not now. Not when she'd settled everything in her own mind. Not when she'd reconciled herself to never seeing him again.

"That's not true," Jordan countered, turning her around and into his arms. "I can't live without you. I've known that from the first moment we kissed."

"Oh, no…"

His amused laughter filled her small kitchen. "You said the same thing that night. Remember?" The smile faded as he gazed at her upturned face. His eyes, so gray and intense, seemed to sear her with a look of such power it was all Jill could do not to cry out and break off his embrace. She glanced away, chewing nervously on her lower lip, willing him to free her, willing him to leave.

His hands cupped her face, his thumbs stroking her cheeks. "You feel it, too, don't you?" he whispered. "You have from the very first. Neither one of us can deny it."

She meant to tell him then, to blurt out that she was engaged to Ralph, but she wasn't given the chance. Before she could utter a word, before she could even begin to explain, Jordan captured her mouth with his own.

His lips were hard and desperate as they claimed possession of hers, firing her senses to life. She moaned, not from pleasure, although that was keen, but from regret.

Ralph had kissed her that night, too. Jill had tried to reassure herself their marriage would work. She'd put

her heart and her soul into their good-night kiss and hadn't felt even a fraction of what she did with Jordan.

It was so unfair, so wrong. She was marrying *Ralph,* she reminded herself. But her heart, her foolish, romantic heart, refused to listen.

Nothing Jordan could say was going to change her plans, she decided, trying to think of Ralph and the commitment they'd made to each other a few hours earlier.

If only Jordan would stop kissing her. *Oh, please stop,* she begged silently as frustration brought burning tears to her eyes. If only he'd leave, walk out of her life forever so she could start forgetting.

But she had to push him out of her arms before she could push him out of her life. Yet here she was clinging to him, her arms curved around his neck. And she was holding on as though her very existence depended on it.

Jordan obviously felt none of her hesitation, none of her doubts, and soon, far too soon, Jill was returning his kisses with equal fervor. Raw emotion overwhelmed her until she was so weak she slumped against him, needing his support to remain upright. Her breath came in shallow gasps as his lips trembled against hers.

"Oh, Jill," he breathed, his voice a husky caress. "The things you do to me. I've frightened you, haven't I?"

"No." He had, but for none of the reasons he knew. She was terrified by the things he made her feel. Terrified by the rush of need and love that crowded her heart.

She hid her face in his shoulder, wanting to escape his embrace even as she submerged herself in it.

"I never knew love could be like this," Jordan said hoarsely. "I've never been in love, never experienced it

before you." He rested his jaw alongside her cheek in a gesture of tenderness that moved her deeply.

Jill swallowed and blinked through a wall of tears. "Please…" She had to say something, had to let him know before he spoke again, before he convinced her to love him. She'd set her mind, her will, everything within her, to resist him and found she couldn't.

"I realize we haven't known each other long," Jordan was saying. "Yet it seems as if you've always been part of my life, always will be."

"No…"

"Yes," he countered softly, his lips grazing the side of her face. "I want to marry you, Jill. Soon. The sooner the better. I need you in my life. I need you to teach me so many things. Loving me isn't going to be easy, but—"

"No!" Abruptly she broke away from him. "Please, no." She buried her face in her hands and began to sob.

"Jill, what is it?" He tried to comfort her, tried to bring her back into his embrace, but she wouldn't let him.

"I can't marry you." The words, born of frustration and anger, were meant to be shouted, but by the time they passed her lips they were barely audible.

"Can't marry me?" Jordan repeated as though he was sure he'd misunderstood. "Why not?"

"Because…" Saying it became a nearly impossible task, but she forced herself. "Because… I'm already engaged."

She saw and felt his shock. His eyes narrowed with pain and disbelief as the color drained from his face.

"You're making it up."

"No, it's true." She held herself stiff, braced for the backlash her words would bring.

"When?" he demanded.

She heaved in a breath and squared her shoulders. "Tonight."

A shudder went through him as his eyes, dark and haunting, raked her face. Jill's throat muscles constricted at his tortured look, and she couldn't speak.

It took Jordan a moment to compose himself. But he did so with remarkable dexterity. All emotion fled from his face. For a breathless moment he just stared at her.

"I'm sure," he said finally, without any outward hint of regret, "that whoever it is will make you a far better husband than I would have."

"His name is Ralph."

Jordan grimaced, but quickly rearranged his features into a cool mask. "I wish you and… Ralph every happiness."

With that, he turned and walked out of her life. Just as she'd wanted him to…

Early the next morning, after an almost sleepless night, Jill put the infamous wedding dress in her car and drove directly to Shelly and Mark's. The curtains were open so she assumed they were up and about. Even if they weren't, she didn't care.

Keeping the wedding dress a second longer was intolerable. The sooner she was rid of it, the sooner her life would return to normal.

Jill locked her car and carried the box to the Bradys' front door. Her steps were impatient. If Shelly wasn't home, Jill swore she'd leave the wedding gown on the front steps rather than take it back to her apartment.

A few minutes passed before the door opened. Shelly stood on the other side, dressed in a long robe, her hair in disarray and one hand covering her mouth to hide a huge yawn.

"I got you out of bed?" That much was obvious, but Jill was in no state for intelligent conversation.

"I was awake," Shelly said, yawning again. "Mark had to go into the office early, but I couldn't make myself get up." She gestured Jill inside. "Come on in. I'm sure Mark made a pot of coffee. He knows I need a cup first thing in the morning."

Jill set the box down on the sofa and followed Shelly into the kitchen. Clearly her friend wasn't fully awake yet, so Jill walked over to the cupboards and collected two mugs, filling each with coffee, then bringing them to the table where Shelly was sitting.

"Oh, thanks," she mumbled. "I'm impossible until I've had my first cup."

"I seem to remember that from our college days."

"Right," Shelly said, managing a half smile. "You know all my faults. Can you believe Mark loves me in spite of the fact that I can't cook, can't tolerate mornings and am totally disorganized?"

Having seen the love in Mark's eyes when he looked at his wife, Jill could well believe it. "Yes."

"I'm glad you're here," Shelly said, resting her head on her arm, which was stretched across the kitchen table.

"You are?" It was apparent that Shelly hadn't guessed the reason for this unexpected visit, hadn't realized Jill was returning the wedding dress. Half-asleep as she was, she obviously hadn't noticed the box.

"Yes, I'm *delighted* you're here," Shelly said as her

eyes drifted shut. "Mark and I had a long talk about you and Ralph. He seems to think I'm overreacting to this engagement thing. But you aren't going to marry Ralph—you know it and I know it. This engagement is a farce, even if you don't recognize that yet. Getting Ralph to propose is the only way you can deal with what's happening between you and Jordan. But you'd never go through with it. You're too honest. You won't let yourself cheat Ralph—because if you marry him, that's exactly what you'll be doing."

"He knows I'm not in love with him."

"I'm sure he does, but I'm also sure he believes that in time you'll feel differently. What he doesn't understand is that you're already in love with someone else."

A few hours earlier, Jill would have adamantly denied loving Jordan, but she couldn't any longer. Her heart burned with the intensity of her feelings. Still, it didn't change anything, didn't alter the path she'd chosen.

"Ralph doesn't know about Jordan, does he?"

"No," Jill said reluctantly. If she was forced to, she'd tell Ralph about him. Difficult as it was to admit, Shelly was right about one thing. Jill would never be able to marry Ralph unless she was completely honest with him.

Shelly straightened and took her first sip of coffee. It seemed to revive her somewhat. "I should apologize for what I said last night. I didn't mean to offend you."

"You didn't," Jill was quick to tell her.

"You frightened me."

"Why?"

"I was afraid for you, afraid you were going to ruin

your life. I don't think I could stand idly by and let you do it."

"I fully intend to marry Ralph." Jill didn't know for whose benefit she was saying this—Shelly's or her own. The doubts were back, but she did her best to ignore them.

"Oh, I believe you intend to marry Ralph...now," Shelly said, "but when the time comes, I don't think it's going to happen. Neither does Mark."

"That isn't what he said when we talked." Mark had been the cool voice of reason in their impassioned discussion the night before. He'd reassured her and comforted her, and for that Jill would always be grateful.

"What he said," Shelly explained between yawns, "was that he was sure you'd make the right decision. And he is. I was, too, after he calmed me down."

"I've made my choice. There's no turning back now."

"You'll change your mind."

"Perhaps. I don't know. All I know is that I agreed to marry Ralph." No matter how hard she tried, she couldn't keep the breathless catch from her voice.

Shelly heard it, and her eyes slowly opened. "What happened?" Her gaze sharply assessed Jill, who tried not to say or do anything that would give her away.

"Tell me," she said when Jill hesitated. "You know I'll get it out of you one way or another."

Jill sighed. Hiding the truth was pointless. "Jordan came by late last night."

"I thought you said he was in Hawaii."

"He was."

"Then what was he doing at your place?"

"He said he had a feeling there was something wrong—and he flew home."

"There *is* something wrong!" Shelly cried. "You're engaged to the wrong man."

Unexpectedly, Jill felt defeated. She'd hardly slept the night before, and the tears she'd managed to suppress refused to be held back any longer. They brimmed in her eyes, spilling onto her cheeks, cool against her flushed skin.

"I'm not *engaged* to the wrong man," she said once she was able to speak coherently. "I happen to *love* the wrong one."

"If you're in love with Jordan," Shelly said, "and I believe you are, then why in heaven's name would you even consider marrying Ralph?"

It was too difficult to explain. Rather than make the effort, she merely shook her head and stood, almost toppling her chair in her eagerness to escape.

"Jill." Shelly stood, too.

"I have to go now...."

"Jill, what's wrong? My goodness, I've never seen you like this. Tell me."

Jill shook her head again and hurried into the living room. "I brought back the wedding dress. Thank your aunt Milly for me, but I can't...wear it."

"You brought back the dress?" Shelly sounded as though she was about to break into tears herself. "Oh, Jill, I wish you hadn't."

Jill didn't stay around to argue. She rushed out the front door and to her car. Her destination wasn't clear until she reached Ralph's apartment. She hadn't planned to go there and wasn't sure what had directed her there. For several minutes she sat outside, collecting her thoughts—and gathering her courage.

When she'd composed herself, blown her nose and

dried her eyes, she walked to his front door and rang the doorbell. Ralph answered, looking pleased to see her.

"Good morning. You're out and about early. I was just getting ready to leave for work."

She forced a smile. "Have you got a minute?"

He nodded. "Come on in." He paused and seemed to remember that they were now an engaged couple. He leaned forward and lightly brushed his lips across her cheek.

"I should have phoned first."

"No. I was just thinking that this afternoon might be a good time for us to look at engagement rings."

Jill guiltily dropped her gaze and her voice trembled. "That's very sweet." She could barely say the words she had to say. "I should explain...the reason I'm here—"

Ralph motioned her toward a chair. "Please, sit down."

Jill was grateful because she didn't know how much longer her legs would support her. Everything seemed so much more difficult in the light of day. She'd been so confident before, so sure she and Ralph could make a life together. Now she felt as though she were walking around in a heavy fog. Nothing was clear, and confusion greeted her at every turn.

She took a deep breath. "There's something I need to explain."

"Go ahead." Ralph sat comfortably across from her.

She was so close to the edge of the chair she was in danger of slipping off. "It's only fair you should know." She hesitated, thinking he might say something, but when he didn't, she continued, "I met a man in Hawaii."

He nodded gravely. "I thought you must have."

His intuition surprised her. "His name... Oh, it

doesn't matter what his name is. We went out a couple of times."

"Are you in love with him?" Ralph asked outright.

"Yes," Jill whispered slowly. It hurt to admit, and for a moment she dared not look at Ralph.

"It doesn't seem like a lot of time to be falling in love with a man. You were only gone a week."

Jill didn't tell him Jordan was in Hawaii only three days. Nor did she mention the two brief times she'd seen him since. There was no reason to analyze the relationship. It was over. She'd made certain of that when she told him she was marrying Ralph. She'd never hear from Jordan again.

"Love happens like that sometimes," was all she could say.

"If you're so in love with this other guy, then why did you agree to marry me?"

"Because I'm scared and, oh, Ralph, I'm sorry. I should never have involved you in this. You're a wonderful man and I care for you, I really do. You've been a good friend and I've enjoyed our times together, but I realized this morning that I can't marry you."

For a moment he said nothing, then he reached for her hand and held it gently between his own. "You don't need to feel so guilty about it."

"Yes, I do." She was practically drowning in guilt.

"Don't. It took me about two minutes to realize something was troubling you last night. You surprised me completely when you started talking about getting married."

"I surprised you?"

"To be honest, I assumed you were about to tell me you'd met someone else and wouldn't be seeing me

anymore. I've known for a long time that you're not in love with me."

"But I believed that would've changed," Jill said almost desperately.

"That's what I figured, too."

"You're steady and dependable, and I need that in my life," she said, although the rationale sounded poor even to her own ears. True, if she married Ralph she wouldn't have the love match she'd always dreamed about, but she'd told herself that love was highly overrated. She'd decided she could live without love, live without passion—until Jordan showed up on her doorstep. And this morning, Shelly had told her what she already knew. She couldn't marry Ralph.

"You're here because you want to call off the engagement, aren't you?" Ralph asked.

Miserably, Jill nodded. "I didn't mean to hurt you. That's the last thing I want."

"You haven't," he said pragmatically. "I figured you'd call things off sooner or later."

"You did?"

He grinned sheepishly. "You going to marry this other man?"

Jill shrugged. "I don't know."

"If you do…"

"Yes?" Jill reluctantly raised her eyes to his.

"If you do, would you consider subletting your apartment to me? Your place is at least twice as big as mine, and your rent's lower."

Despite everything, Jill started to laugh. Leave it to Ralph, ever practical, ever sensible, to brush off a broken engagement and ask about subletting her apartment.

* * *

The week that followed was one of the worst of Jill's life. She awoke every morning feeling as though she hadn't slept. She was depressed and lonely. Several times she found herself close to tears for no apparent reason. She'd be reading a prescription and the words would blur and misery would grip her heart with such intensity she'd be forced to swallow a sob.

"Jill," her supervisor called early Friday afternoon, walking into the back room where she was taking her lunch break. "There's someone out front who wants to talk to you."

It was unusual for anyone to visit her at work. She immediately feared it was Jordan, but quickly dismissed that concern. She knew him too well. She was out of his life. The instant she'd told him she was engaged to Ralph, he'd cut her out, surgically removed all feeling for her. It was as if she no longer existed for him.

But as she'd been so often lately, Jill was wrong. Jordan stood there waiting for her. His gaze was as hard as flint. Something flickered briefly in the smoky-gray depths, but whatever emotion he felt at seeing her was too fleeting for Jill to identify.

She'd had far less practice at hiding her own feelings, and right now, they were wreaking havoc with her pulse. With great effort she managed to remain outwardly composed. "You wanted to speak to me?"

A nerve twitched in his jaw. "You might be more comfortable if we spoke elsewhere," he said stiffly.

Jill glanced at her watch. She had only fifteen minutes of her lunch break left. Time enough, she was sure, for whatever Jordan intended. "All right."

Wordlessly, he walked out of the drugstore, obvi-

ously expecting her to follow, which she did. He paused beside his car, then turned to face her. A cool, disinterested smile slanted his mouth.

"Yes?" she said after an awkward moment. She folded her arms defensively around her middle.

"I need you to explain something."

She nodded. "I'll try."

"Your friend Shelly Brady was in to see me this morning."

Jill groaned. She hadn't talked to Shelly since the morning she'd dropped off the wedding dress. Her friend had phoned several times and left messages, but Jill hadn't had either the energy or the patience to return the calls.

"How she managed to get past security and my two assistants is beyond me."

It was a nightmare come true. "What did she say?" As if Jill needed to know.

"She rambled on about how you were making the worst mistake of your life and how I'd be an even bigger fool if I let you. But, you know, if you prefer to marry Roger, then that's your prerogative."

"His name is Ralph," she corrected.

"It doesn't make any difference to me."

"I didn't think it would," she said, keeping her gaze lowered to the black asphalt of the parking lot.

"Then she started telling me this ridiculous story about a legend behind a certain wedding dress."

Jill's eyes closed in frustration. "It's a bunch of nonsense."

"It certainly didn't make too much sense, especially the part about the dress fitting her and her marrying Mark. But she insisted the dress also fits you."

"Don't take Shelly seriously. She seems to put a lot of credence in that dress. Personally, I think the whole thing's a fluke. You don't need to worry about it."

"*Then* she told me an equally ridiculous tale about a vision she had of you in Hawaii and how happy you looked. It didn't make any more sense than the rest."

"Don't worry," she said again. "Shelly means well, but she doesn't understand. The wedding dress is beautiful, but it isn't meant for me. The whole thing is ridiculous—you said so yourself, and I agree with you."

"That's what I thought—at first. A magic wedding dress is about as believable as a talking rabbit. I don't have any interest in that kind of fantasy."

"Then why are you here?"

"Because I remembered something. You had a wedding dress with you in Hawaii. When I asked you about it, you said a friend had mailed it to you. Then, this morning, Shelly arrived and told me why she'd sent you the dress. She told me the story of her aunt Milly and how she'd met her husband. She also said Milly had mailed the dress to her and she'd fallen into Mark Brady's arms."

"Did she leave anything out?" Jill asked sarcastically.

He ignored her question. "In the end I phoned Mark and asked him about it. I don't know Brady well, but I assumed he'd be able to explain the situation a little more rationally."

"Shelly does tend to get a bit dramatic."

"That's putting it mildly."

"I just wish she hadn't said anything to you."

"I imagine you do," he remarked dryly.

"What did Mark say?"

"We talked for several minutes. By this time Shelly

was weeping and nearly hysterical, convinced she was saving us both from a fate worse than death. Mark was kind enough to inject a bit of sanity into the discussion. What it boiled down to is this."

"What?" Jill wasn't purposely being obtuse.

"Me confronting you. I'm here to ask you about Aunt Milly's wedding dress."

He could ask her whatever he wanted, but she didn't have any answers.

"Jill?"

She heaved a sigh. "I returned the dress to Shelly."

"She explained that, too. Said you'd brought it back the morning after my visit."

"It wasn't meant for me."

"Not true, according to Shelly...and Mark." He remained standing where he was, unwilling to divulge his own feelings. "So you're going to go ahead and marry Roger."

"Ralph."

"Whoever," Jordan snapped.

"No!" she shouted, furious with him, furious with Shelly and Mark, too.

A moment of shocked silence followed her announcement. Several feet separated Jill from Jordan, and although neither of them moved, they suddenly seemed much closer.

"I knew that," he said.

"How could you possibly know?" Jill hadn't told anyone yet. Not Shelly and certainly not Jordan.

"Because you're marrying me."

Eight

All of Jill's defenses came tumbling down. She'd known they would from the moment she'd walked out of the lunchroom and confronted him. Known in the very depths of her soul that he'd eventually have his way. She didn't have the strength to fight him anymore.

He must have sensed her acquiescence because he moved toward her, pausing just short of taking her in his arms. "You will marry me, won't you?" The words were gentle yet insistent, brooking no argument.

Jill nodded. "I don't want...don't *want* to love you."

"I know." He reached for her then, drawing her into his embrace as though he were comforting a child.

It should have eased her mind that settling into his arms felt more natural than anything she'd done in the past week. A feeling of welcome. A feeling of rightness. And yet there was fear.

"You're going to break my heart," she whispered.

"Not if I can help it."

"Why do you want to marry me?" The answer evaded her. A man like Jordan could have his pick of women. He had wealth and prestige and a dozen other

attributes that attracted far more sophisticated and beautiful women than Jill.

The air between them seemed to pulse for a long moment before Jordan answered. "I've done some thinking about that myself. You're intelligent. Insightful. You feel things deeply and you're sensitive to the needs of others." He traced a finger along the line of her jaw, his touch light. "You're passionate about the people you love."

She should've been reassured that he seemed to know her so well after such a short acquaintance, but she wasn't. Because she knew that for a time she'd be a pleasant distraction. Their marriage would be like a toy to him. Then gradually, as the newness wore off, she'd be put on a shelf to look pretty and brought down when it suited his purposes. His life, his love, his personality, would be consumed by the drive to succeed, just the way her father's had been. Everything else would fade into the background, eventually to disappear. Love. Family. Commitment. Everything that was important to her would ultimately mean nothing to him.

"I want us to marry soon," Jordan whispered.

"I—I was hoping for a long engagement."

Jordan's eyes were adamant. "I've waited too long already."

Jill didn't understand what he meant, but she didn't question him. She knew Jordan was an impatient man. When he wanted something, he went after it with relentless determination. Now he wanted *her*—and heaven help her, she wanted him.

"A bride should be happy," he said, tucking his hand under her chin and raising her face to his. "Why the tears?"

How could she possibly explain? She loved him, although she'd fought it with everything she had. She'd been willing, for a time, to consider marrying Ralph in her effort to drive Jordan from her life. Yet even then she'd known it was useless and of course so had Ralph. Nothing could save her. Her heart had been on a collision course with Jordan's from the moment she'd been assigned the seat next to his on the flight to Hawaii.

"I'll be happy," she murmured, silently adding *for a while*.

"So will I," Jordan said, his chest expanding with a breath and then a sigh that seemed to come all the way from his soul.

The small private wedding took place three weeks later in Hawaii at the home of Andrew Howard. Shelly was Jill's matron of honor and Mark stood up for Jordan. Elaine Morrison was there, too, weeping through the entire ceremony. But these weren't tears of joy. Her mother, like Jill, recognized Jordan's type and feared what it meant for her daughter's life, her happiness.

"Jill," Elaine had pleaded with her earlier that morning, before the wedding. "Are you sure this is what you want?"

Jill had nearly laughed aloud. With all her heart, with all her being, she longed to be Jordan's wife. And yet, if the opportunity had availed itself, she would've backed out of the marriage.

"He needs me." Repeatedly over the past few weeks, Jill had been reminded how much Jordan did need her. He didn't realize it himself, of course, not on a conscious level, but something deep inside him had acknowledged his need. And in her own way, Jill needed him.

Andrew Howard had seen that they belonged together. He'd been the first one to point it out to Jill. From the time Jordan was a child, his life had been devoid of love. As an adult he'd closed himself off from emotion; he'd refused to allow himself to become vulnerable. That he should experience something as powerful as love for her in so short a time was close to a miracle. But then, Jill was becoming accustomed to miracles.

"All I want is your happiness," her mother had gone on to say, her eyes, so like Jill's, blurred with tears. "You're my only child. I don't want you to make the same mistakes I did."

Could loving someone ever be a mistake? Jill wondered. Her mother had loved her father, sacrificed herself for him even though, as the years went on, he'd barely seemed to reciprocate her love. And when he died prematurely, without warning, she'd become lost and miserable.

Jill knew she loved Jordan enough to put aside her fears, to bind herself in a relationship that might ultimately cause her pain. But she vowed she wouldn't lose her own identity. She wouldn't, couldn't, let Jordan's personality swallow her own.

He hadn't understood that in the beginning, despite her attempts to explain it. To him, Jill's desire to continue working after their marriage seemed utterly foolish. For what purpose? he'd asked. She didn't need the income; he'd made certain of that, lavishing her with gifts and more money than she could possibly spend. Her insistence on continuing her job resulted in their first real argument. But in the end Jordan had reluctantly agreed.

Andrew Howard had gone to a great deal of trouble to arrange their wedding, warming Jill's heart with his generosity. She'd come to understand that the older man looked upon Jordan as the son he'd lost. He was more than a mentor, far more than a friend. He was the only real family Jordan had—until now.

Flowers filled every room of Andrew's oceanfront home, their fragrance sweet in the summer air. An archway of orange blossoms stood outside on the lush green lawn that overlooked the roaring ocean. A small reception and dinner were to follow. Tables laid with white linen tablecloths were placed around the patio.

The warm wind whispered over Jill as Andrew Howard came to escort her into the sunshine where Jordan was waiting. Andrew paused when he saw her, his eyes vivid with appreciation. "I've never had a daughter," he said softly, "but if I did, I'd want her to be just like you."

Tears of love and gratitude gathered in her eyes. Her mother, fussing about Jill, arranged the long, flowing train of the dress, then slowly straightened. "He's right," Elaine said, stepping back to examine Jill. "You've never looked more beautiful."

It was the dress, Jill thought. The dress and its magic. She ran her glove along the bodice with its Venetian lace and row upon row of delicate pearls. The high collar was adorned with pearls, too, each one sewn on by hand. The skirt flared from her waist, the hem accentuated with a flounce of lace and wide satin ribbons.

Andrew Howard stood beside her mother as the minister asked Jordan and Jill to repeat their vows. Jill's gaze met Jordan's as she made her promises. Her voice, although low, was steady and confident. Jordan's eyes held hers with a look of warmth, of tenderness.

A magic wedding dress? The scenario seemed implausible. Yet here they were, standing before God, their family and friends, declaring their love for each other.

"You look so beautiful," Shelly told Jill shortly after the ceremony. "Even more beautiful than the day you first tried on the dress."

"My hair wasn't done and I didn't have on much makeup and I—"

"No," Shelly interrupted, squeezing Jill's fingers, "it's more than that. You hadn't met Jordan yet. It's complete now."

"What is?"

"Everything," Shelly explained with characteristic ambiguity. "Aunt Milly's wedding dress, you and Jordan. Oh, Jill," she whispered, her eyes brimming with tears, "you're going to be so happy."

Jill wanted to believe that—how she wanted to believe it!—but she was afraid. So afraid of what the future held for her and Jordan.

"I know what you're thinking," Shelly said, dabbing her eyes. "I loved Mark when I married him. I'd loved him for months, but deep down I wondered how long a marriage between us could last. We're totally different."

Jill smiled to herself. Shelly was right; she and Mark *were* different, but they were perfectly matched, balancing each other's strengths and weaknesses.

"I was sure my lack of domestic skills would drive Mark crazy, and at the same time I thought the way he organizes everything would kill our relationship. Did you know that man makes lists of lists? Even before I walked to the altar, I was worried this marriage was doomed."

"It's been all right, though, hasn't it?"

Shelly smiled. "It's been so easy—love does that, you know. Love takes something that's difficult and makes it feel so effortless. You'll understand what I mean in a few months."

Unfortunately Jill shared little of her friend's confidence. She was delighted that things had worked out between Shelly and Mark, but she didn't expect that kind of happiness for her and Jordan.

"When you think about it, it's not all that surprising," Shelly had gone on to say. "Take Aunt Milly and Uncle John for example. She's educated and idealistic, and John, bless his heart, was a realist and a mechanic with a grade-school education. Yet he was so proud of her. He loved her until the day he died."

"Mark will always love you, too," Jill said, smoothing the satin of the wedding dress.

"Jordan feels the same way about you."

Jill's heart stopped. It hit her then, for perhaps the first time—Jordan loved her. His love had guided Jill through her uncertainty. It had helped her understand what had led her to this point, helped her look past her mother's tears and her own doubts.

The small reception and dinner held immediately after the ceremony featured a light, elegant meal and a festive atmosphere. Jill met several of Jordan's business associates, who seemed both surprised and pleased for them. Even the Lundquists put in a jovial appearance, although Suzi was absent.

When it came time for them to leave, Jill kissed Andrew Howard's cheek and thanked him once more. "Everything's been wonderful."

"I lost my only son," he reminded her, his eyes momentarily aged and sad. "For years I've hungered for

a family. After my wife died, and even before, I shut myself away, locked in my grief, and watched the world go on without me."

"You're being too hard on yourself," Jill told him. "Your work—"

"True enough," he said, cutting her off. "For a while I was able to bury myself in my company, but two years ago I realized I'd wasted too much of my life struggling with this grief. Soon afterward I decided to retire." His gaze wandered away from Jill and toward her mother, and he smiled. "I think the time might be right for me to make other changes, take the next step. What do you think, my dear?"

Jill smiled, too. Her mother needed someone like Andrew. Someone to teach her that love didn't always mean pain.

"I'd forgotten what it was like to be young," he said, now smiling easily. "I've known Jordan nearly all his life. I've watched him build a name for himself and admired his cunning. He's good, Jill. But he's a man without a family, and I suspect I see a lot of myself in him. The thought of him growing old and disillusioned with life troubled me. I want him to avoid the mistakes I made."

Funny how her mother had said basically the same thing to Jill a few hours earlier. "There are certain mistakes we each have to make," Jill returned softly. "It's the only way we seem to learn, painful as it is."

"How smart you are," Andrew said, chuckling. "Much too clever for your years."

"I love him." Somehow it was important Mr. Howard know that. "I have no idea whether my love will make a lot of difference, but…"

"Ah, that's where you're wrong. It will change him. Love does that, my dear, and he needs you so badly."

"How can you be sure I'll have any influence over Jordan's life? I'm marrying him because I love him, but I don't expect anything to change."

"It will. Just wait and see."

"How do you know that?"

His smile came slowly, transforming his face, brightening his eyes and relaxing his mouth. "Because," he said, clasping her hand in his own, "because it once changed my life, and I'm hopeful that it will again." He glanced at her mother as he spoke, and Jill leaned over to give him another quick kiss.

"Good luck," she whispered.

"Jill," Jordan called then, approaching her. "Are you ready?"

She looked at her husband of less than two hours and nodded. He was referring to their honeymoon trip, but she...she was thinking about their lives together.

"Hmm," Jill murmured as the first light of dawn crept into their hotel room. She yawned widely, covering her mouth with both hands.

"Good morning, wife," Jordan said, kissing her ear.

"Good morning, husband."

"Did you sleep well?"

Eyes closed, she nodded.

"Me, too."

"I was exhausted," Jill told him, smiling shyly.

"No wonder."

Although her eyes remained closed, Jill knew Jordan was smiling. Her introduction to the physical aspect of their marriage had been incredible, wonderful. Jordan

was a patient and gentle lover. Jill had felt understandably nervous, but he'd been tender and reassuring.

"I didn't know it could be so good," she said, snuggling in her husband's arms.

"I didn't, either," he surprised her by saying. His lips were in her hair, his hands exploring her skin. "It's enough to make a husband think about wasting the morning in bed."

"Wasting?" Jill teased, a smile lifting the corners of her mouth. "Surely I misunderstood you. The Jordan Wilcox I've met wouldn't know how to waste time."

"It all has to do with the musical rest," he said seductively. "The all-important caesura. Who would ever have guessed something so small could change a man's entire life?" He kissed her with a hunger that moved her, then made love to her with a need that humbled her.

It was noon before they left the hotel room and one o'clock when they returned.

"Jordan," Jill said, blushing when he reached for her, "it's the middle of the day."

"So?"

"So...it's indecent."

"Really?" But as he spoke, he was lowering his mouth to hers. The kiss was intoxicating, and any resistance Jill might have felt vanished like ice in the sun.

She rested her palms against his shoulders as he kissed her again and again.

Unable to stop herself, Jill moaned softly.

Dragging his mouth from hers, he trailed kisses down the side of her neck. "There's that sightseeing trip you wanted to take," he reminded her. "To see the pineapple and sugarcane fields."

"It's not important. We could see them another time," she said breathlessly.

"That's not what you claimed earlier."

"I was just thinking…" She didn't get the opportunity to finish. Jordan's kiss absorbed her words and scattered the thought.

"What did you think?"

"That married people should occasionally be willing to change their plans," she managed to say.

Jordan chuckled, and lifting her gently into his arms, carried her to the bed. "I'm beginning to think married life is going to agree with me." His mouth found hers and gentleness gave way to urgency.

Five days later, when Jordan and Jill returned to the mainland, their honeymoon over, Jill was so deeply in love with her husband she wondered why she'd ever hesitated, why she'd fought so hard against marrying him.

The first person she called when they arrived at the penthouse was Shelly. Jordan had arranged to have her things moved there while they were away. Ralph lived at her previous apartment now and was elated with the extra space.

"Have you got time to meet an old friend for lunch?" Jill asked without preamble.

"Jill!" Shelly cried. "When did you get back?"

"About an hour ago." Although he hadn't said as much, she knew Jordan was dying to get to his office. "I thought I'd steal away for a few minutes and meet you."

"I'd love to see you. Just name the time and place."

Jill did, then kissed Jordan on the cheek while he was talking to his assistant on the phone in his study.

He broke away, covered the mouthpiece with his hand and gave her a surprised look. "Where are you headed?"

"Out for lunch. You don't mind, do you?"

"No." But he didn't sound all that sure.

"I thought you'd want to go to the office," she said.

"I do." He wrapped his arm around her waist, bringing her close to his side.

"I know, so I thought I'd meet Shelly."

He grinned, kissed her lightly and resumed his telephone conversation as though she'd already left. Jill lingered at the door, waiting for the elevator. Part of her longed to stay with him, to hold on to the happiness before it escaped, before it was dispersed by everyday tensions and demands.

"Well," Shelly said a half hour later as she slid into the restaurant booth across from Jill, "how are the newlyweds?"

"Wonderful."

"I thought you'd be more tanned."

Jill blushed; Shelly laughed and reached for her napkin. "It was the same with Mark and me. I swear, we didn't leave that hotel room for three days."

"We made several short trips," Jill said, but she didn't elaborate on exactly how short their sightseeing ventures had been.

"Married life certainly seems to agree with you."

"It's only been a week," Jill reminded her friend. "That's hardly time enough to tell."

"I knew after the first week," Shelly said confidently, her face animated by a smile. "I figured if Mark and I survived the honeymoon, our marriage had a chance. Mark wanted to honeymoon at Niagara Falls, remember?"

"And you suggested a rafting trip through the Grand Canyon." Jill smiled at the memory. Mark preferred tradition, while Shelly craved adventure, but in the end, they'd learned what she and Jordan had already discovered. All that mattered was their marriage, their love for each other.

"We couldn't agree," Shelly continued. "I was seriously worried about it. If we were at odds over a honeymoon site, then what on earth would happen when it came to dealing with the really important issues?"

Jill understood what Shelly meant. She loved Jordan; of that there could be no doubt. Now she had to place her trust in their love, hope it was strong enough to withstand day-to-day reality. She was still fearful, but ready to fight for her marriage, to keep it safe.

Suddenly Shelly set aside the menu, pressed her hand against her stomach and slowly exhaled.

"Shell, what's wrong?"

Shelly briefly closed her eyes. "Nothing bad. I just can't stand to read about food."

"About food?" That made no sense to Jill.

"I'm two months pregnant."

"Shelly!" Jill was so excited she nearly toppled her water glass. "Why didn't you say something sooner? Good grief, I'm your best friend—I'd think you'd want me to know."

"I do, but I couldn't tell you until I knew for sure, could I?"

"You just found out?"

"Not exactly." Shelly reached for a small packet of soda crackers, tore away the cellophane wrapper and munched on one. "I found out before your wedding, but I didn't want to say anything then."

Jill appreciated Shelly's considerateness, her wish not to compete with Jill's important day.

"Actually, it was Mark who told me. Imagine a husband explaining the facts of life to his wife. I'm such a scatterbrain, I made a mistake. I miscalculated and didn't even know it."

As far as Jill was concerned, this baby certainly wasn't a mistake, and from Shelly's happy glow, her friend felt the same way.

"I was afraid Mark might be upset. Naturally we'd talked about starting a family, but neither of us planned to have it happen so soon."

"He wasn't upset, though, was he?" Jill would've been shocked if Mark had been anything but thrilled.

"Not in the least. When he first told me what he suspected, I just laughed." She shook her head in mock consternation. "You'd think I'd know better than to question a man who sleeps with his daily planner by his side!"

"I'm thrilled for you."

"Now that I've adjusted to it, I can't wait. I'm looking forward to decorating the nursery and wearing maternity clothes and *everything*."

After the waitress had taken their order, Jill leaned back against the banquette cushion. "It happened just like you said it would," she said.

"What did?"

"Loving Jordan." Jill felt a little shy talking so openly about something so intimate. Although she and Jordan were married and deeply in love with each other, they never spoke of their feelings. Jordan was still uncomfortable with expressing emotion. But he didn't need to tell Jill he loved her, not when he went about proving

it every way he knew how. She'd never pressured him, never demanded the words.

"The day we were married you told me love makes the difficult things seem effortless. Remember?"

Ever confident, Shelly grinned. "You're going to be so happy…" She paused, swallowed and reached for her napkin, dabbing her eyes. "I get so emotional these days, I can't believe it. The other night I found myself crying at a stupid television commercial."

"You? Seattle's drama queen? Impossible," Jill teased.

Shelly shook her head ruefully. "Yes, me." She began to laugh, and Jill joined in.

Laughter came easily since her marriage; it was all the happiness in her heart brimming over, spilling out. She'd never felt so carefree or laughed at so many silly things before.

When Jill returned from lunch two hours later, Jordan was gone. Exhausted from the flight and the excitement of the past week, she crawled into bed and slept, not waking until it was dark.

Rolling onto her back, she stretched luxuriously under the weight of the blanket and smiled, musing how thoughtful it was of Jordan to let her sleep.

She kicked aside the blanket and searched blindly for her shoes. Yawning, she walked into the living room, surprised to find it dark.

"Jordan?" she called.

She was greeted by silence.

Turning on the lights, Jill was shocked to discover it was after nine. Jordan must still be at the office, she supposed, her stomach knotting. Could it be happening so soon? Could he have grown tired of her already?

No sooner had the thought formed than the elevator

doors opened and Jordan appeared. She didn't fly into his arms, although that was her first instinct.

"Hello," she greeted him, a bit coolly.

He was loosening his tie. "What time is it?"

"Nine-fifteen. Are you hungry?"

He paused, as though he needed to think about it. "Yeah, I guess I am. Sorry I didn't call. I didn't have a clue it was this late."

"That's okay," she muttered, although it really wasn't.

He followed her into the kitchen and slid his arms around her waist while she investigated the contents of the refrigerator.

"It won't be like this every night," he said, his words sounding very much like a promise her father had once made to her mother.

"I know," Jill said, desperately hoping that was true.

She couldn't sleep that night. Perhaps it was the long nap she'd taken in the middle of the afternoon; at least that was what she tried to tell herself. More likely, though, it was the gnawing fear that Jordan's love for her was already faltering. She tried to push the doubts aside, tried to convince herself she was overreacting. He'd been away from his office for a week. There must have been all kinds of important issues that required his attention. Was she expecting too much?

In the morning, she promised herself, she'd talk to him about it. But when she awoke, Jordan had left for the office.

Frowning, she dressed and wandered into the kitchen for a cup of coffee.

"Morning." Jordan's cook, Mrs. Murphy, a middle-aged woman with lively blue eyes and a wide smile,

greeted her. Jill smiled back, although her cheerfulness felt a little strained.

"Hello, Mrs. Murphy, it's nice to see you again," she said, helping herself to coffee. "Uh, what time did Jordan leave this morning?"

"Early," the cook said with a disappointed sigh. "I was thinking Mr. Wilcox would stop working so hard once he was married. He hasn't even been home from his honeymoon twenty-four hours and he's already at the office at the crack of dawn."

Jill hated to disillusion the woman, but this wasn't Jordan's first trip to the office. "I'll see what I can do about giving him some incentive to stay home," Jill said, savoring her coffee.

Mrs. Murphy chuckled. "I'm glad to hear it. That man works too many hours. I've been telling my George that Mr. Wilcox needs a wife to keep him home at night."

"I'll do my best," Jill said, but she had the distinct feeling her efforts would make little difference. Checking her watch, she quickly drank the rest of her coffee and hurried into the bedroom to shower.

Within half an hour she was dressed and ready for work.

"Mrs. Murphy," she told the cook, "I'll be at work— PayRite Pharmacy—if Jordan happens to call. Tell him I'll be home shortly after five." Jill wished she'd had the chance to talk to him herself; she knew he was going to be tied up in meetings and conference calls, so she was reluctant to interrupt. Still, she was more than a little distressed that within a week of their wedding she was communicating with her husband through a third party.

Despite everything, Jill enjoyed her day, which was

busier than usual. The pharmacy staff took her out for a celebration lunch, and dozens of customers came by to wish her well. Many of the people whose prescriptions she filled regularly had become friends. In light of how her married life was working out, Jill was thankful she'd decided to keep her job.

By five she was eager to get home, eager to share her day with Jordan and hear about his. She was met by the aroma of cheese, tomato sauce and garlic, and followed it into the kitchen, where she found Mrs. Murphy untying her apron.

"Whatever you're cooking smells absolutely delicious."

"It's my lasagna. Mr. Wilcox's favorite."

Jill opened the oven door and peeked inside. She was famished. "Did Jordan phone?" she asked, her voice rising on a note of longing.

"About fifteen minutes ago. I told him you'd be home a bit after five."

No sooner were the words out than the phone rang. Jill saw Jordan's office number on call display and answered immediately.

"This is Brian Macauley, Mr. Wilcox's assistant," a crisp male voice informed her. "He's asked that I let you know he won't be home for dinner."

Nine

"Jill."

Her name seemed to come from a long way off. Someone was calling her, but she could barely hear.

"Sweetheart." The voice was louder now.

She snuggled into the warmth, ignoring the persistent sound. After hours and hours of forcing herself to stay awake, she'd finally given up and succumbed to the sweet seduction of sleep.

"Honey, if you don't wake up, you'll get a crick in your neck."

"Jordan?" Her eyes instantly flew open, and she saw her husband kneeling on the carpet beside her chair. She straightened, throwing her arms around his neck. "Oh, Jordan," she whispered, "I'm so glad you're home."

"With this kind of reception, I'll have to stay away more often."

Jill decided to ignore that comment. "What time is it?"

"Late" was all he said.

She kissed him, needing him, savoring the feel of his arms around her. He looked dreadful. He hadn't been

home for dinner in well over a week and spent all hours of the day and night at his office.

Although she'd asked him several times, Jordan's only explanation was that a project he'd been working on had developed problems. *A project.* For this he was willing to send both their lives into tumult; for this he was willing to place their marriage at risk. The upheaval had all but ruined the memory of their brief idyllic honeymoon. They'd been back in Seattle for two weeks now, and Jill hadn't been allotted a single uninterrupted hour of Jordan's time.

"Are you hungry?" She doubted he'd eaten a decent meal in days.

He shook his head, then rubbed his face wearily. "I'm more tired than anything."

"How much longer is this going to continue?" she asked, keeping her voice as steady as she could. She'd gone into this marriage with her eyes wide open. From the moment she'd met Jordan, she'd known how stiff the competition would be, how demanding his way of life was. She'd always known it would be difficult to keep their marriage intact. But she'd figured their love would hold the edge for at least the first couple of years.

Unfortunately she'd figured wrong. If anything, she'd underestimated the strength of his obsession with business and success. Jordan loved her; he might rarely have told her that, but Jill didn't need the words. What she did need was some of his time, his attention.

"I've hardly seen you all week," she reminded him. "You're gone before I wake up in the mornings. Heaven only knows what time you get home at night."

"It won't be much longer," Jordan said stiffly, standing. "I promise."

"Would it be so terrible if this project folded?"

"Yes," he returned emphatically.

"One failure isn't the end of the world, you know."

Jordan smiled wryly, and his condescension angered her.

"It's true," she said. "Did I ever tell you about trying out for the lead in the high-school play during my senior year?"

Jordan frowned. "No, but is this another story like the one about your piano-playing?"

Jill tucked her legs under her and rested one elbow on the chair arm. "A little."

Jordan sank down on the leather sofa across from her, leaned his head back and closed his eyes. "In that case, why don't you move directly to the point and skip the story?"

He wasn't being rude, Jill told herself, only practical. He was exhausted and in desperate need of rest. He didn't have the energy to wade through her mournful tale in search of a moral.

"All right," she agreed amicably enough. "You've probably already guessed I didn't get the lead. But I'd been so sure I would. I'd played major roles in several plays. In fact, I'd gotten every part I'd ever tried out for. Not only didn't I get this part, I wasn't even in the play, and darn it all, even now I think I would've done a good job of playing Helen Keller."

He grinned. "I'm sure you would have, too."

"What I learned from that experience was not to fear failure. I survived not playing Helen Keller, and later, in college, when I was awarded a wonderful role, it heightened my appreciation of that success." When

Jordan didn't immediately respond, she added, "Do you understand what I'm saying or are you asleep?"

His eyes were still closed but his mouth lifted in a gentle smile. "I was just mulling over the sad history of your musical and acting careers."

Jill smiled, too. "I know it sounds ludicrous, but failure liberated me. My heart and soul went into my audition for that role, and when I lost, I felt I could never act again. It took me a long time to regain my confidence, to be willing to hazard another rejection, but eventually I was the stronger for it. When I decided to try out for a play in my freshman year of college, I felt as though I was somehow protected, because failure wasn't going to rock me the way it had earlier."

"So you wanted to be an actress?"

"No, I'm not much good at waiting tables."

Jordan didn't immediately catch her joke, but when he did, he laughed out loud.

"You know what they say about hindsight being twenty-twenty? In this case it's true. If failure hadn't taught me to appreciate success when I got it, I might have fallen into a nasty trap."

"What was that?"

"Thinking I deserved it, believing I was so talented, so gifted, so good that I'd never lose."

Jordan fell silent. Jill waited a moment, then said, "Mr. Howard told me something…about the shopping-mall project. I didn't say anything to you at the time because…well, because I wasn't sure he wanted me to."

She had Jordan's full attention now.

He straightened, his eyes searching hers. "What did he say?"

"He hasn't often gone in on construction projects with you, has he?"

"Only a handful of times."

"There's a reason for that."

"Oh?"

"You've never failed."

Jordan's head came up sharply. "I beg your pardon?"

Jill knew he found such thinking preposterous. If anything, his successes should have been an inducement to his financial supporters.

"Mr. Howard explained that he doesn't like to deal with a man until he's been devastated financially at least once."

"That makes no sense," Jordan returned irritably.

"Perhaps not. Since my experience in the financial world is limited to paying my bills, I wouldn't know," Jill admitted.

"Who's going to lend money to someone who's failed?"

"Apparently Andrew Howard," Jill said with a grin. "He told me the man who's lost everything is much more careful the next time around."

"I didn't realize you and Howard talked business."

"We didn't." She did her best to appear nonchalant. "Mostly we discussed you."

This didn't please Jordan, either. "I'd prefer to think I owe my success to hard work, determination and foresight. I certainly wouldn't have come as far as I have without them."

"True enough, but—"

"Is there always going to be a but?"

Jill tried to hold back a laugh. Actually she was en-

joying this, while her tired husband was left to suffer the indignities of her insights.

"Well," he said shortly, "go on, knock down my argument."

"Oh, I agree your intelligence and dedication have played a large role in your success, but others have worked just as hard, been just as determined and shown just as much foresight—and lost everything."

Jordan scowled. "My, you're full of cheer, aren't you?"

"I don't want you to put so much store in this one project. If it falls apart, so what? You're beating yourself to death with this." She didn't mention what it was doing to their marriage.

He considered her words for a few seconds, then his face tightened. "I won't lose. I absolutely, categorically, refuse not to succeed."

"How much longer?" Jill asked when she could disguise the defeat and frustration she was feeling.

He hesitated, then massaged the back of his neck as though to ease away a tiredness that stretched from the top of his head to the bottom of his feet. "A week. It shouldn't be much more than that."

A week. Seven days. She closed her eyes, because looking at him, seeing him this exhausted, this spent, was painful. He needed her support now, not her censure.

"All right," she murmured.

"I don't like this any better than you do." Jordan stood and held her securely in his embrace, burying his face in the curve of her neck. "I'm a newlywed, remember. There's no one I want to spend time with more than my wife."

Jill nodded, because it would have been impossible to speak.

"I wish you hadn't waited up for me," he said, lifting her into his arms and carrying her into their bedroom. Without turning on the light, he settled her on the bed and lay down beside her, placing his head on her chest. Jill's fingers idly stroked his hair.

Words burned in her throat, the need to unburden herself, but she dared not. Jordan was exhausted. This wasn't the right time.

Would it ever be the right time?

There'd been so many lonely evenings, so many empty mornings. Every night Jill went to bed alone, and only when Jordan slipped in beside her did she feel alive. Only when they were together did she feel whole. So she waited night after night for a few precious minutes, knowing they were all he had to spare.

The even sound of Jordan's breathing told her he'd fallen asleep. The weight on her chest was growing uncomfortable, yet she continued to stroke his hair for several minutes, unwilling to disturb his rest.

She'd always known it would come to this; she just hadn't expected it to happen so soon.

A week. He'd promised her it would be over within a week.

And it would be—until the next time.

Jill awoke early the following morning, astonished to find Jordan asleep beside her. At some point during the night he'd rolled away from her and covered them both with a blanket. He hadn't bothered to undress.

Jill wriggled toward him and playfully kissed his ear.

She knew she ought to let him sleep, but she also knew he'd be annoyed if he was late for the office.

Slowly he opened his eyes, looking surprised to see her there with him.

"Morning," she whispered, with a series of tiny, nibbling kisses.

"What time is it?" he asked.

"Almost eight." She looped her arms around his neck and smiled down at him.

"Hmm. An indecent hour."

"Very indecent."

"My favorite time of day." His fingers were busy unfastening the opening of her pajama top and his eyes blazed with unmistakable need.

"Jordan," she said breathlessly, "you'll be late for work."

"I fully intend to be," he said, directing her lips to his.

"It's happening already, isn't it?" Elaine Morrison said bluntly the next Saturday. She stood in Jill's living room, holding a china cup and saucer and staring out the window. The view of the Olympic Mountains was spectacular, the white peaks jutting against a backdrop of bright blue sky as fluffy clouds drifted past.

Jill knew precisely what her mother was saying. She responded the only way she could—truthfully. "Yes."

Elaine turned, her face pale, haunted with the pain of the past, the pain she saw reflected in her daughter's life. "I was afraid of this."

Until recently, Jill had found communicating with her mother difficult. After her husband's death, Elaine had withdrawn from life, hidden herself away in her

grief and regrets. In many ways, Jill had lost her mother at the same time as she had her father.

"Mom, it's all right," Jill said in an attempt to reassure her. "It's only for the next little while. Once this project's under control everything will be different."

Jill knew better. She wasn't fooling herself, and she sincerely doubted she'd be able to fool her mother.

"I warned you," Elaine said, walking to the white leather sofa and sitting tensely on the edge. Setting the cup and saucer on a nearby table, she turned pleading eyes to Jill. "Didn't I tell you? The day of the wedding—"

"Yes, Mother, you warned me."

"Why didn't you listen?"

Jill exhaled slowly, praying for patience. "I'm in love with him, just like you loved Daddy."

It seemed unfair to drag her father into this, her much-grieved father, but it was the only way Jill could explain.

"What are you going to do about it?"

"Mother," Jill sighed. "It's not as though Jordan's having an affair."

"He might as well be," Elaine replied heatedly. "Here it is, Saturday afternoon and he's working. One look at him told me he had the same drive and ambition, the same need for power, as your father."

"Mother, please… It isn't like that with Jordan."

The older woman's eyes were infinitely sad as she gazed at her daughter. "Don't count on that, Jill. Just don't count on it."

Her mother's visit had unsettled Jill. Afterward, she tried to relax with a book, but couldn't concentrate. The

phone rang at six, just as it had every night that week.
One of Jordan's assistants had called to let her know he
wouldn't be home for dinner.

One ring.

Walking over to the phone, Jill stood directly in front
of it, but didn't pick up the receiver.

Two rings.

Drawing in a deep breath, she flexed her fingers.
Twice in the past couple of weeks, Jordan had phoned
himself. Maybe he'd be on the other end of the line, inviting her to join him for dinner. Maybe he was phoning
to tell her he'd unscrambled the entire mess and he'd be
home within the next half hour. Perhaps he was calling
to suggest they take a few days off and vacation somewhere exotic, just the two of them.

Three rings.

Jill could feel her pulse throbbing at the base of her
throat. But she didn't answer.

Four rings.

Five rings.

The phone went silent.

Her entire body was trembling when she turned away
and walked into the bedroom. She sat on the bed and
covered her face with both hands.

The phone began to ring again, the sound reverberat-
ing loudly through the apartment. Jill slapped her hands
over her ears, unable to bear it. Each ring tormented
her, pretending to offer hope when there was none. It
wouldn't be Jordan, but his assistant, and his message
would be the same one he'd relayed every night that
week.

Making a rapid decision, Jill got her jacket and purse

and hurried toward the penthouse elevator, purposely leaving her cell phone behind.

Not having any particular destination, she wandered downtown until she passed a movie theater and decided to go in. The movie wasn't one that really interested her, but she bought a ticket, anyway, willing to subject herself to a B-grade comedy if it meant she could escape for a couple of hours.

The movie actually turned out to be quite entertaining. The plot was ridiculous, but there were enough humorous moments to make her laugh. And if Jill had ever needed some comic relief, it was now.

On impulse she stopped at a deli and picked up a couple of sandwiches, then flagged down a taxi. Before she could change her mind, she gave the driver the address of Jordan's office building.

She had a bit of trouble convincing the security guard to admit her, but eventually, after the guard talked to Jordan, she was allowed inside.

"Jill," he snapped when she stepped off the elevator, "where have you been?"

"It's good to see you, too," she said, ignoring the irritation in his voice. She kissed his cheek, then walked casually past him.

"Where were you?"

"I went out to a movie," she said, strolling into his office. His desk, a large mahogany one, was littered with folders and papers. She noted dryly that he was alone. Everyone else was gone, but he hadn't afforded himself the same luxury.

"You were at a movie?"

She didn't answer. "I thought you might be hungry," she said, neatly stacking a pile of folders in order to

clear one small corner of his desk. "I went to Griffin's and bought us both something to eat."

"I ate earlier."

"Oh." So much for that brilliant idea. "Unfortunately, I didn't." She plopped herself down in the comfortable leather chair and pulled a turkey-on-rye from the sack, along with a cup of coffee, setting both on the space she'd cleared.

Jordan looked as though he wasn't sure what to do with her. He leaned over the desk and shoved several files to one side.

"I'm not interrupting anything, am I?"

"Of course not," he answered dryly. "I was staying late for the fun of it."

"There certainly isn't any reason to hurry home," she returned just as dryly.

Jordan rubbed his eyes, and his shoulders slumped. "I'm sorry, Jill. These past few weeks have been hard on you, haven't they?"

He moved behind her and grasped her shoulders. His touch had always had a calming effect on Jill, but she wanted to fight it, wanted to fight her weakness for him.

"Jill," Jordan whispered. "Let's go home." He bent down and kissed the side of her neck. A shiver raced through her body and Jill breathed deeply, placing her hands over his.

"Home," she repeated softly, as if it was the most beautiful word in the English language.

"Jill!" Shelly's eyes widened when she opened the front door one evening a few weeks later. "What's wrong?"

"Wrong," Jill repeated numbly.

"You look awful."

"How kind of you to point it out."

"I've got it!" Shelly said excitedly. "You're pregnant, too."

"Unfortunately, no," she said, passing Shelly and walking into the kitchen. She took a clean mug from the dishwasher and poured herself a cup of coffee. "How are you feeling, by the way?"

"Rotten," Shelly admitted, then added with a smile, "Wonderful."

Jill pulled out a kitchen chair and sat down. If she spent another evening alone, she was going to go crazy. She probably should have phoned Shelly first rather than dropping in unannounced, but driving over here had given her an excuse to leave the penthouse. This evening she badly needed an excuse. Anything to get away. Anything to escape the loneliness. Funny, she'd lived by herself for years, yet she'd never felt so empty, so alone, as she had in the past two months. Even the conversation with Andrew Howard earlier in the evening had only momentarily lifted her spirits.

"Where's Mark?"

Shelly grinned. "You won't believe it if I tell you."

"Tell me."

"He's taking a carpentry class."

"Carpentry? Mark?"

Shelly's grin broadened. "He wants to make a cradle for the baby. He's so sweet I can hardly stand it. You know Mark, he's absolutely useless when it comes to anything practical. Give him a few numbers and he's a whiz kid, but when he has to change a lightbulb, he needs an instruction manual. I love him dearly, but

when he told me he was going to build a cradle for the baby, I couldn't help it, I laughed."

"Shelly!"

"I know. It was a rotten thing to do, so Mark's out there proving how wrong I am. This is his first night, and I just hope the instructor doesn't kick him out of the class."

Despite her unhappiness, Jill smiled. It felt good to be around Shelly, to laugh again, to have a reason to laugh.

"I haven't talked to you in ages," Shelly remarked. "But then I shouldn't expect to, should I? You and Jordan are still on your honeymoon, aren't you?"

Tears sprang instantly to Jill's eyes, blurring her vision. "Yes," she lied, looking away, praying that Shelly, who was so happy in her own marriage, wouldn't notice how miserable Jill was in hers.

"Oh, before I forget," Shelly said excitedly, "I heard from Aunt Milly."

"What did she have to say?"

"She asked me to thank you for your letter, telling her about meeting Jordan and everything. She loves a good romance. Then she said something odd."

"Oh?"

"She felt the dress was meant to be worn one more time."

"Again? By whom?"

Shelly leaned forward. "You and Jordan were too wrapped up in each other on your wedding day to notice, but your mother and Mr. Howard got along famously. Milly wouldn't have known that, of course, but...it's obviously meant to be."

"My mother." Now that she recalled her conversa-

tion with Andrew at the wedding, it made sense. In the weeks since their return from Hawaii, she'd forgotten about it. He'd phoned Jill twice, but he hadn't mentioned Elaine, nor had her mother mentioned him.

"What do you think?"

"My mother and Mr. Howard?" Jill experienced a feeling of rightness.

"Isn't that incredible?" Shelly positively beamed. Until recently—the arrival of the wedding dress, to be exact—Jill hadn't realized what a complete romantic her friend was.

"But Mom hasn't said a word."

"Did you expect her to?"

Jill shrugged. Shelly was right; Elaine would approach romance and remarriage with extreme caution.

"Wouldn't it be fabulous if your mother ended up wearing the dress?"

Jill nodded and, placing her fingertips to her temples, closed her eyes. "A vision's coming to me now...."

Shelly laughed.

"I think we should call my mom and tell her that we both had a clear vision of her standing in the dress next to a distinguished-looking older man."

Once again, Shelly giggled. "Oh, that's good. That's really good." She sighed contentedly. "The dress definitely belongs with your mother. We'll have to do something about that soon."

Jill pretended her tears were ones of mirth and dashed them away with the back of one hand.

But the amusement slowly faded from Shelly's eyes. "Are you going to tell me what's wrong, or are you going to make me force it out of you?"

"I— I'm fine."

"No, you're not. Don't forget I know you. You've been my best friend for years. You wouldn't be here if something wasn't wrong."

"It's that crazy wedding dress again," Jill confessed.

"The wedding dress?"

"I should never have worn it."

"Jill!" Shelly exclaimed, then frowned. "I don't understand what you're saying."

"It clouded my judgment. I was always the romantic one, remember? Always a sucker for a good love story. When Milly first mailed you the dress, I thought it was the neatest thing to happen since low-fat ice cream."

"Not true! Remember how you persuaded me—"

"I know what I said," Jill interrupted. "But deep down, I could hardly wait to see what happened. When you and Mark decided to marry, I was thrilled. Later, after I arrived in Hawaii and you had the dress delivered to me, I kind of allowed myself to play along with the fantasy. I've wanted to get married for a long time. I'd like to have children."

"Jill," Shelly said, looking puzzled, "I'm not sure I follow you."

"I think I might even have felt a little…jealous that you got married before I did. I was the one who wanted a husband, not you, and yet here you were, so much in love. Somehow it just didn't seem fair." The tears slipped down her cheeks and she absently brushed them away.

"But you're married now and Jordan's crazy about you."

"He was for about a week, but that's worn off."

"He loves you!"

"Yes, I suppose in his own way he does." Jill didn't have the strength to argue. "But not enough."

"Not enough?"

"It's too hard to explain," she said. "I came over to tell you I've made a decision." As hard as she tried, she couldn't keep herself from sobbing, "I've decided to leave Jordan."

Ten

Shelly's eyes narrowed with disbelief. "You can't possibly mean that!"

Leaving Jordan wasn't a decision Jill had made lightly. She'd agonized over it for days. Unable to answer her friend, she pushed back her hair with hands that wouldn't stop shaking. Her stomach was in knots. "It just isn't going to work. I need some time away from him to sort through my feelings. I don't *want* to leave, but I'm afraid I'll just fall apart if I stay."

Shelly had never been one to disguise her feelings. Anger flashed from her eyes. "You haven't given the marriage a decent chance. It hasn't even been two months."

"I know everything I need to know. Jordan isn't married to me, he's married to his company. Shelly, you're my best friend—but there are things you don't know, things I can't explain about what's happening between me and Jordan. Things that go back to my childhood and being raised the way I was."

"You love him."

Jill closed her eyes and nodded. She did love Jordan,

so much her heart was breaking, so much she didn't know if she'd survive leaving him, so much she doubted she'd ever love this deeply again.

"I don't expect you to understand," Jill continued, choking over the words. "I wanted you to know...because I'm going to be living with my mother for a while. Just until I can sort through my feelings and figure out what I'm going to do."

"Have you told him yet?" Shelly's voice sounded less sharp.

"No." Jill had delayed that as long as possible, not knowing what to say or how to say it. This wasn't a game, or an attempt to manipulate Jordan into devoting more time to her and their marriage. She refused to fall into that trap. If she was going to make the break, she wanted it to be clean. Decisive. Not cluttered with threats.

"You *do* plan to tell him?"

"Of course." She could never be so cowardly as to move out while Jordan was at the office. Besides, the sorry truth was that she might be gone for days before he noticed.

Confronting him wasn't a task she relished. She could predict his reaction—he'd be furious with her, more furious than she'd ever seen him. Jill was prepared for that. But in the end he would let her go as if she meant nothing to him. His pride would demand that.

"When do you plan to tell him?" Shelly asked softly, seeming to understand for the first time Jill's torment. A true sign of their friendship was that Shelly didn't ply her with questions, but accepted Jill's less-than-satisfactory explanation.

"Tonight." She hadn't packed yet, but she intended to do that when she got home.

Home.

The word echoed in her mind. Although the penthouse was so distinctly marked with Jordan's personality, it did feel like home. She'd only lived there a short while, but in the lonely weeks following her honeymoon with Jordan, she'd become intimately acquainted with every room. She was going to miss the solace she gained from looking out over Puget Sound and the jagged peaks of the Olympics. And Mrs. Murphy had become a special friend, almost like a second mother, who fretted over her and worried about the long hours Jordan worked. Jill would miss her, too. Although Jill hadn't mentioned it to the cook, she guessed that Mrs. Murphy wouldn't be surprised.

"You're sure this is what you want?" Shelly asked regretfully.

Leaving Jordan was the last thing Jill wanted. Yet it had to be done—and soon, before it was too late, before she found it impossible to go.

"Don't answer that," Shelly whispered. "The pain in your eyes says everything I need to know."

Jill stood and searched in her purse for a tissue. The tears were rolling freely down her cheeks now. She had to compose herself before she encountered Jordan. Had to draw on every bit of inner strength she possessed.

Shelly hugged her, and once again Jill was grateful for their friendship. They were as close as sisters, and Jill had never needed family more than she did right then.

The penthouse echoed with emptiness when she arrived home. Jill stood in the middle of the living room,

then slowly moved around, skimming her hand over each piece of furniture. Her gaze gravitated toward the view, and she walked over to the window, staring into the night. Far below, lights flashed and glowed, but she was far removed from the brilliance. Far removed from the light…

Finally she entered the bedroom she shared with Jordan. Her breath came in shallow, painful gasps as she dragged out her suitcases and set them on the bed. Carefully, she folded her clothes and deposited them inside.

Several times she had to stop, clutching an article of clothing, crushing the fabric, until she composed herself enough to continue. Tears stung her eyes, but she refused to succumb to them.

"Jill?"

She froze. She hadn't expected Jordan to come home for several hours yet. They'd barely seen one another all week.

"Where are you going?" he asked.

Pulling herself together, Jill turned to face him. Jordan stood on the other side of the room, his expression confused.

"My mother's," she eventually said.

"Is she ill?"

"No…" Drawing a deep breath, hoping it would calm her frantic heart, she forged ahead. "I'm leaving for a while. I—I need to sort out my feelings…make some important decisions."

The fire that leapt into his eyes was filled with anger. "You plan to divorce me?" he demanded incredulously.

"No. For now, I'm just moving in with my mother."

"Why?"

Jill could feel her own anger mounting. "That you

even have to ask should be answer enough! Can't you see what's happening? Don't you care? At this rate our marriage isn't going to last another month." She paused to gulp in a much-needed breath. "My instincts told me this would happen, but I was so much in love with you that I chose to ignore what was obvious from the first. You don't need a wife. You never have. I don't understand why you wanted to marry me because—"

"When did all this come on?"

"It's been coming on, as you say, from the minute we got home from our honeymoon. Our marriage has to be one of the shortest on record. One week. That's all the time you allotted to it. I need more than five minutes at the end of the day when you're so exhausted you can hardly speak. I wish I was stronger, but I'm not. I need more from you than you can give me."

"You might have said something to me earlier."

"I did. A hundred times."

"When?" he barked.

"I'm not going to get involved in a shouting match with you, Jordan. I won't sit by and watch you work yourself to death over some stupid project. You'd said ages ago that it'd be finished in a week. I was foolish enough to believe you. If this project is so important to you that you're willing to risk everything to keep it from folding, then fine, it's all yours."

"When did you tell me?" he asked a second time.

"Do you remember our conversation last night?" she asked starkly.

Jordan frowned, then shook his head.

"I didn't think you had."

The previous afternoon, Jill had been so lonely that she'd reached for the phone, planning to call Ralph to

invite him to a movie. She'd nearly dialed his number before she remembered she was married. The incident had had a profound effect on her. She didn't *feel* married. She felt abandoned. Forgotten. Unimportant. If she was going to live her life alone, she could accept that. But she wasn't interested in a one-sided marriage.

This time apart would help her gain perspective, show her what she needed to do. Explaining it to Jordan was impossible. But in time, a week perhaps, she might be able to tell him all that was in her heart.

"What was it you said last night?" Jordan wanted to know, clearly confused.

Jill neatly folded a silk blouse and put it in the suitcase. "I told you how I almost called Ralph to ask him if he wanted to see a movie…and you laughed. Remember? You found it humorous that your wife had forgotten she was a married woman. You didn't bother to understand what had led me to the point of wanting to call an old boyfriend."

"You're not making any sense."

"No, I suppose not. I'm sorry, Jordan. I wish I could explain it better. But as I already told you, I need more from our relationship than you can give me…"

"I've said this project would be settled soon. I'll grant you it's taking longer than I thought, but if you'd just be patient for a little while… Is that so much to ask? You'd think…" He hesitated, then jammed his hands in his pockets and marched across the room. "These past few weeks haven't been a picnic for me, either. You'd think a wife would be willing to lend her husband some support, instead of using threats to bully him into doing what *she* wants."

It didn't surprise Jill that Jordan assumed her leav-

ing was merely a ploy. He didn't realize how serious she was.

"I can't live like this. I just can't!" she cried. "Not now, not ever. I want my children to know their father! My own was a shadow who passed through my life, and I couldn't bear my children to suffer what I did."

"This is a fine time for you to figure it all out," Jordan growled, his hold on his frustration and anger obviously precarious.

"If I could go back and change everything, I would… I would." Hurrying now, she closed her suitcases.

"Are you pregnant?" The question came at her like a bolt of lightning.

"No."

"You're sure?"

"Of course."

A moment of silence followed as she collected her purse and a sweater.

"Nothing I can say is going to change your mind, is it?"

"No." She took the handles of the two suitcases and pulled them off the bed. "If…if there's any reason you need to get hold of me, I'll be at my mother's."

Jordan stood there unmoving, his back toward her. "If you're so set on leaving," he said, "then just go."

"Jill, sweetheart." Her mother knocked lightly, then walked into the darkening bedroom. Jill sat on the padded window seat, her knees tucked under her chin, staring out the bay window to the oak-lined street below. Often as a child she'd sat there and reflected on her problems. But now her problems couldn't be worked

out by staring out her bedroom window or by pounding on a piano for an hour or two.

"How are you feeling?"

"Fine." She wasn't ready to talk yet.

"I've made dinner," Elaine said, her voice sympathetic. There was a radiance about her these days. Andrew Howard had called almost daily since Jill had been living with her mother, although he didn't know about her separation from Jordan. Jill had sworn her mother to secrecy. The last Jill had heard, Andrew planned to fly to the mainland early the next month so he and Elaine could spend some time together. Jill was delighted for her mother and for Andrew. Her own situation, though, was bleak.

"Thanks, Mom, but I'm not hungry."

Her mother didn't argue, but sat on the edge of the cushion and leaned forward to hug Jill. The unexpected display of affection moved Jill to tears.

"You haven't eaten anything to speak of all week."

"I'm fine, Mom." Jill didn't want her mother fussing over her just now, and she was grateful when Elaine seemed to realize it. Elaine lovingly stroked Jill's hair, then got to her feet.

"If you need me…"

"I'm fine, Mom."

Her mother hesitated. "Are you going back to him, Jill?"

Jill didn't answer. Not because she didn't want to, but because she didn't know. She hadn't heard from Jordan even once in the week she'd been gone. A concerned Shelly had dropped by twice, unobtrusively leaving the wedding dress, in its original mailing box, on Jill's

window seat. Even Ralph had called. But she hadn't heard from Jordan.

She shouldn't miss him this much. Shouldn't feel so empty without him, so lost. Jill had hoped their time apart would clear her thoughts. It hadn't. If anything, they were more confused than ever. Her musings were like snagged fishing lines, impossible to untangle.

She hadn't really expected him to get in touch with her, but she'd hoped. Foolishly hoped. Although if he had, Jill didn't know how she would've reacted.

The doorbell chimed in the distance. A minute later Jill heard her mother talking with another woman. The voice wasn't familiar and Jill pressed her forehead to her knees, suddenly weary. Part of her had wanted the visitor to be Jordan. Fool that she was, Jill prayed that he'd be willing to put aside his pride enough to come after her, to convince her they could make their marriage work. She ached for the sight of him. Obviously, though, any move would have to come from her. But Jill wasn't ready. Not when her heart was in such turmoil.

"Jill?" Her mother knocked at her bedroom door again and opened it a crack. "There's someone here to see you. A Suzi Lundquist. She says it's important."

"Suzi Lundquist?" Jill repeated incredulously.

"She's waiting for you in the living room," her mother said.

Jill hadn't the slightest idea why Suzi would want to see her. Jordan had used her to ward off the younger woman's affections. Perhaps Suzi still loved Jordan and intended to rekindle the fire. But in that case, she wasn't likely to announce her plans to Jill.

After quickly changing her clothes, Jill went down-

stairs. Suzi was pacing the living room, her movements tense and agitated, when Jill appeared.

"I hope you're happy."

Jill blinked. "I beg your pardon?"

"He's done it, you know, and it's all because of you."

"Done what?"

"Given up the fight." Suzi was staring at her as though Jill was completely dense.

"I hate to seem ignorant, but I honestly don't know what you're talking about."

"You're married to Jordan, aren't you?"

"Yes." They stood several feet apart from each other, like duelists preparing to choose their weapons.

"Jordan's handed control of the firm to my father and brother," Suzi said impatiently.

"Isn't this rather sudden? When did all this happen?" Surely if Jordan was in a proxy fight, he would've said something to her. Surely he would have let her know. She'd only been away for a week. Nothing could have threatened his hold on the company in that short a time, could it?

"This proxy battle's been going on for months," Suzi snapped. "It all started while you and Jordan were on your honeymoon. He couldn't have chosen a worse time to leave. He knew it, too—that's what was so confusing. When he returned from Hawaii, he had a full-fledged revolt on his hands. Dad used that time against Jordan, buying shares until he controlled as large a percentage of the company as Jordan did. He wanted Jordan out as CEO and my brother in."

"What happened?"

"After months of gathering supporters, of buying and selling stock, of doing whatever he could to avoid a

proxy fight," Suzi continued, "Jordan handed the whole thing over to my father, who'll hand it all to my brother on a silver platter. You met Dean, and we both know he doesn't have the leadership or the maturity to be a CEO. Within five years, he'll wipe out everything Jordan's spent his life building."

Jill didn't know what to say. Her immediate reaction was to argue with Suzi. Jordan would never willingly surrender control of his company. She didn't need the younger woman to tell her that Jordan had worked his entire adult life to build the company; he'd invested everything in it—everything.

Although it seemed a long time ago, she remembered that he'd told her about buying the controlling shares. He'd also said he'd soon be forced to battle to remain in power. Jill remembered what she'd said to him. She'd told him she couldn't imagine him losing.

"Jordan's resigned?" she repeated, breathless with disbelief.

"This morning, effective immediately."

"But why?"

"You should know," Suzi said harshly. "Because he's in love with you."

"What has that got to do with anything?"

"Apparently he felt it was either you or the company. He chose you."

"He sent you here to tell me?" That didn't sound like something Jordan would do. He preferred to do his own talking.

Suzi gave a short, humorless laugh. "You've got to be joking. He'd have my hide if he knew I was within a mile of you."

"Then why are you here?"

"Because I fancied myself in love with him not long ago. He was pretty decent about it. He could have used me to his own advantage if he'd wanted, but he didn't. Beneath that surly exterior is a real heart. You know it, too, otherwise you'd never have married him."

"Yes…" Jill agreed softly.

"He needs you. I don't know why you left him, but I figure that's between you and Jordan. He's not the kind of man who'd be unfaithful, so I doubt there's another woman involved. If anything, he's too honorable. If you don't realize what you've got, you're a fool."

Jill's emotions were playing havoc with her. Jordan had resigned! It was too much to take in.

"Are you going to him?" Suzi demanded.

Jill hesitated. "I, uh…"

Suzi shook her head. "If it's pride that's stopping you, I don't think you have anything to worry about. Eventually Jordan will come to you. It may take a while, though, if you're determined to wait him out."

"I'm going to him." Recovering somewhat, Jill looked at Suzi, struggling to speak. "I can't thank you enough for coming. I owe you so much."

"Don't thank me. I just hope you appreciate what he's done," Suzi muttered as she picked up her purse, tucking it under her arm.

"I do," Jill assured her, leading the way to the front door. No sooner had Suzi left than Jill went looking for her mother.

She found her in the kitchen. "I heard," Elaine said before Jill could explain the purpose of the other woman's visit. "It might not last, you know."

"I'm going to him."

Her mother's eyes searched Jill's face before she nodded. "I knew that, too."

As they embraced briefly, Jill whispered, "There's a box in my room, Mom. Shelly brought it over for you—and for Andrew Howard."

The drive into downtown Seattle seemed to take forever. It was rush hour and the only parking space she could find was in a loading zone. Without a qualm, she took it, then hurried toward Jordan's office. Luck was with her because the building hadn't been locked yet, but she was waylaid by a security guard. Fortunately, he was the same man she'd met earlier, and he let her stay.

"Has Mr. Wilcox left yet?" she asked.

"Not yet."

"Thank you," she said, sighing with relief.

She hurried to the elevator. Jordan's office was on the top floor. When the elevator doors opened, she ran down the wide corridor to the outer office where his assistants worked. No one was there, but the double doors leading into Jordan's massive office were open. He was packing the things from his desk into a cardboard box.

Jill stared at Jordan, unable to move or speak. He looked haggard, as though he hadn't slept at all during the week she'd been gone. Dark stubble shadowed his face, and his hair, ordinarily neat and trim, was rumpled.

He must have sensed her presence because he paused in his task, his eyes slowly meeting hers. His hands went still. The whole world seemed to come to a sudden halt. In that unguarded moment she read his pain and it became hers.

"You can't do it!" she cried, choking on a sob. "You just can't."

Jordan's face hardened and he seemed to clamp down on his emotions. He ignored her and continued packing up the objects from his desk. A smile, one that spoke more of sadness than joy, came into his eyes. "Your husband is unemployed as of five o'clock this afternoon."

"Oh, Jordan, why would you do such a thing? For me? Because I left you? But you never told me... Not once did you explain, even when I pleaded with you. Didn't you trust me enough to tell me what was happening?" That was what hurt most of all, that Jordan had kept everything to himself. Not sharing his burden, carrying it alone.

"It was a mistake not to tell you," he admitted, the regret written clearly across his face. "I realized that the night you left. By nature, I tend to keep my troubles to myself."

"But I'm your *wife*."

He grinned at that, but again his smile was marked with sadness. "I'm new to this marriage business. Obviously I'm not much good at it. The one thing I was hoping to do was keep my business life separate from my personal life. I didn't want to bring my company problems home to you."

"But, Jordan, if I'd known, if you'd explained, I might have been able to help."

"You did, in more ways than you know."

Tears blurred Jill's eyes. She would have given everything she owned for Jordan to take her in his arms, but he stood so far away, so alone.

Jordan picked up a small photograph, one of their wedding day. He stared at it for a moment, then tucked it into the box. "I loved you almost from the day we met. Don't ask me to explain it, because I can't. After

that first night, when we kissed on the beach, I knew my life would never be the same."

"Oh, Jordan."

"Being with you was like standing in the sun. I never knew how lonely I was, how my heart ached for love, how much I longed to share my life with someone...."

Tears ran unashamedly down Jill's face.

"The day we were married," he went on, "I swear I've never seen a more beautiful bride. I couldn't believe you'd actually agreed to be my wife. I vowed then and there that I'd never do anything to risk what I'd found."

"But to resign..." Trembling a little, nervous and unsure, Jill moved across the room to Jordan's side. He tensed at her approach, his expression a blend of undisguised longing and hope.

"I can't lose you," he said.

"But to walk away from your life's work?" What he'd done remained incomprehensible to Jill.

"I have a new life," he said, gently pulling her into his arms. He buried his face in her hair and inhaled deeply. "None of this means anything without you. Not anymore."

"But what are you going to do?"

"I thought we'd take a year off and travel. Would you like that?"

Jill nodded through her tears.

"And after that, I'd like to start our family."

Once again Jill nodded, her heart pounding with love and excitement.

"Then, when the time's right, I'll find something that interests me and start over, but I'll never allow work to control my life again. I can't," he said quietly. "You're my life now."

"You're sure this is what you want?" He'd given up so much.

She felt him smile against her hair. "Without a doubt. I don't need a business to fill up the emptiness in my life. Not when I have you."

"Oh, Jordan," she whispered, her throat tight. "I love you so much." She squeezed her eyes shut and murmured a prayer of thanksgiving for the wonderful man she'd married.

"Shall we go home, my love?" he asked her.

Jill nodded and slipped her hand into his. "Home," she repeated. With her husband. The man she loved. The man she'd married.

* * * * *

BRIDE ON THE LOOSE

To Virginia and Dean,
whose many years of love have inspired me.

One

It was one of those days. Jason Manning scrubbed his hands in the stainless-steel sink, then applied ointment to several scratches. He'd just finished examining and prescribing antibiotics for a feisty Persian cat with a bladder infection. The usually ill-mannered feline had never been his most cooperative patient, but today she'd taken a particular dislike to Jason.

He left the examining room and was greeted by Stella, his receptionist, who steered him toward his office. She wore a suspiciously silly grin, as if to say "this should be interesting."

"There's a young lady who'd like a few minutes with you," was all the information she'd give him. Her cryptic message didn't please him any more than the Persian's blatant distaste for him had.

Curious, Jason moved into his book-lined office. "Hello," he said in the friendliest voice he could muster.

"Hi." A teenage girl who seemed vaguely familiar stood as he entered the room. She glanced nervously in his direction as if he should recognize her. When it was

obvious he didn't, she introduced herself. "I'm Carrie Weston." She paused, waiting expectantly.

"Hello, Carrie," Jason said. He'd seen her around, but for the life of him, couldn't recall where. "How can I help you?"

"You don't remember me, do you?"

"Ah...no." He couldn't see any point in pretending. If a cat could outsmart him, he was fair game for a teenager.

"We're neighbors. My mom and I live in the same apartment complex as you."

He did his best to smile and nod as though he'd immediately placed her, but he hadn't. He racked his brain trying to recall which apartment was hers. Although he owned and managed the building, Jason didn't interact much with his tenants. He was careful to choose renters who cared about their privacy as much as he cared about his. He rarely saw any of them other than to collect the rent, and even then most just slipped their checks under his door around the first of the month.

Carrie sat back down, her hands clenched tightly in her lap. "I—I'm sorry to bother you, but I've been trying to talk to you for some time, and...and this seemed to be the only way I could do it without my mother finding out."

"Your mother?"

"Charlotte Weston. We live in 1-A."

Jason nodded. The Westons had been in the apartment for more than a year. Other than when they'd signed the rental agreement, Jason couldn't recall speaking to either the mother or her daughter.

"Is there a problem?"

"Not a problem...exactly." Carrie stood once again

and opened her purse, taking out a thin wad of bills, which she leafed through and counted slowly. When she'd finished, she looked up at him. "It's my mother," she announced.

"Yes?" Jason prompted. He didn't have a clue where this conversation was leading or how long it would take the girl to get there. Stella knew he had a terrier waiting, yet she'd purposely routed him into his office.

"She needs a man," Carrie said, squaring her shoulders.

"I beg your pardon?" The girl had his attention now.

"My mother needs a man. I'm here to offer you one hundred dollars if you'll take her out on a date. You are single, aren't you?"

"Yes...but..." Jason was so surprised, he answered without thinking. Frankly, he didn't know whether to ask which of his brothers had put her up to this, or simply to laugh outright. He couldn't very well claim he'd never been propositioned before, but this was by far the most original instance he'd encountered in thirty-odd years.

"She's not ugly or anything."

"Ah... I'm not sure what to tell you." The girl was staring at him so candidly, so forthrightly, Jason realized within seconds it was no joke.

"I don't think my mother's happy."

Jason leaned against the side of his oak desk and crossed his arms. "Why would you assume my taking her out will make a difference?"

"I...don't know. I'm just hoping. You see, my mom and dad got divorced when I was little. I don't remember my dad, and apparently he doesn't remember me, either, because I've never heard from him. Mom doesn't

say much about what went wrong, but it must've been bad because she never dates. I didn't care about that before, only now…"

"Only now what?" Jason asked when she hesitated.

"I want to start dating myself, and my mother's going totally weird on me. She says I'm too young. Boy, is she out of it! I'm not allowed to date until I'm sixteen. Can you imagine anything so ridiculous?"

"Uhh…" Jason wasn't interested in getting involved in a mother-daughter squabble. "Not being a father myself, I can't really say."

"The ninth-grade dance is coming up in a few weeks and I want to go."

"Your mother won't allow you to attend the dance?" That sounded a bit harsh to Jason, but as he'd just stated, he wasn't in a position to know.

"Oh, she'll let me go, except she intends to drop me off and pick me up when the dance is over."

"And that's unacceptable?"

"Of course it is! It's—it's the most awful thing she could do to me. I'd be mortified to have my mother waiting in the school parking lot to take me home after the dance. I'd be humiliated in front of my friends. You've just got to help me." A note of desperation raised her voice on the last few words.

"I don't understand what you want me to do," Jason hedged. He couldn't see any connection between Carrie's attending the all-important ninth-grade dance and him wining and dining her mother.

"You need me to spell it out for you?" Carrie's eyes were wide, her gaze scanning the room. "I'm offering you serious money to seduce my mother."

For a wild instant, Jason thought he hadn't heard her right. "Seduce her?"

"My mother's practically a virgin all over again. She needs a man."

"You're sure about this?" Jason was having a hard time keeping a straight face. He could hardly wait to tell his brother Rich. The two of them would have a good laugh over it.

"Absolutely positive." Carrie didn't even flinch. Her expression grew more confident. "Mom's forgotten what it's like to be in love. All she thinks about is work. Don't get me wrong… My mother's an awesome person, but she's so prim and proper…and stubborn. What she really needs is…well, you know."

Jason felt sorry for the kid, but he didn't see how he could help her. Now that he thought about it, he did recall what Charlotte Weston looked like. In fact, he could remember the day she'd moved in. She'd seemed feminine and attractive, more than a little intriguing. But he'd noticed a guardedness, too, that sent an unmistakable signal. He'd walked away with the impression that she was as straitlaced as a nun and about as warm and inviting as an Alaskan winter.

"Why me?" Jason was curious enough to wonder why Carrie had sought *him* out. Apparently his charisma was more alluring than he'd realized.

"Well, because…just because, that's all," Carrie answered with perfect teenage logic. "And I figured I wouldn't have to pay you as much as I would one of those dating services. You seem nice." She gnawed on her lower lip. "Being a veterinarian is good, too."

"How's that?"

"You've probably had lots of experience soothing

injured animals, and I think my mother's going to need some of that—comforting and reassuring, you know?" The girl's voice became fervent. "She's been hurt.... She doesn't talk about it, but she loved my father and I think she must be afraid of falling in love again. I even think she might like another baby someday." This last bit of information was clearly an afterthought. Carrie cast him a speculative glance to be sure she hadn't said something she shouldn't have. "Don't worry about that—she's probably too old anyway," she added quickly.

"She wants a baby?" Jason could feel the hair on the back of his neck rising. This woman-child was leading him toward quicksand, and he was going to put a stop to it right now.

"No—no... I mean, she's never said so, but I saw her the other day holding a friend's newborn and she had that look in her eyes... I thought she was going to cry." She paused. "I shouldn't have said anything."

For one brief, insane moment, Jason had actually considered the challenge of seducing Charlotte Weston, but the mention of a baby brought him solidly back to earth.

"Listen, Carrie," Jason said, "I'm sorry, but this isn't going to work."

"It's got to," she pleaded urgently, "just for one date. Couldn't you ask her out? Just once? If you don't, I'll be humiliated in front of my entire class. I'd rather not even go to the dance if my mother drives me."

Jason hated to disappoint her, but he couldn't see himself in the role of rescuing a fifteen-year-old damsel in distress from her mother's heavy hand, even if Carrie did make a halfway decent case.

"Is it the money?" Carrie asked, her eyes imploring. "I might be able to scrounge up another twenty dollars...but I'm going to need some cash for the dance."

"It isn't the money," Jason assured her.

Wearing a dejected look, Carrie stood. "You sure you don't want to take a couple of days to think it over?"

"I'm sure."

She released a long, frustrated sigh. "I was afraid you were going to say that."

"Good luck." Jason held open the door. He had no intention of asking Charlotte Weston out on a date, but he he did feel sorry for Carrie. Although he hadn't been a teenager in years, he hadn't forgotten how important these things could seem. Things like the ninth-grade dance.

Charlotte let herself into the apartment at six that evening. She slipped off her heels and rubbed the tense muscles at the back of her neck.

"Hi, Mom," Carrie called cheerfully from the kitchen. "How was work?"

"Fine." There was no need to burden her daughter with how terrible her day had been. Her job as an executive assistant at a large insurance agency might have sounded high-powered and influential, but in reality it was neither. Charlotte worked long hours with little appreciation or reward. For six months, ever since Harry Ward had taken over as managing director, she'd been telling herself it was time to change jobs. But she couldn't give up the security of her position, no matter how much she disliked her boss.

"How was school?" she asked.

"Good. Tickets for the dance went on sale today."

Her daughter looked hopefully at Charlotte, as though
expecting her to make some profound comment.

Charlotte chose to ignore the pointed stare. Her stand
on the dance issue was causing a strain in their relationship, but she refused to give in to her daughter's pressure. Carrie wasn't going on an actual *date*. She was
interested in a boy named Brad, but as far as Charlotte
was concerned, Carrie could attend the dance with her
girlfriends and meet him there. Good grief, the girl
was only fifteen!

"Mom, can we *please* talk about the dance?"

"Of course, but…"

"You're not going to change your mind, right?" Carrie guessed, then sighed. "What can I say to prove how
unreasonable you're being? Every girl in my class is
going to the dance with a *boy*. And Brad *asked* me."

Charlotte reached for an apron, tied it about her waist
and opened the refrigerator door. She took out a package of ground turkey for taco salad. She wasn't up to
another round of arguments over the dance.

"Did you buy a dance ticket?" Charlotte asked, forcing an artificial lightness into her voice.

"No. I won't, either. I'd rather sit home for the rest
of my life than have my *mother* drop me off and pick
me up. Brad's father said he'd drive us both… What
am I supposed to tell Brad? That my mother doesn't
trust his father's driving? You're making way too big
a deal out of this."

Ah, the certainty of youth, Charlotte mused.

"Will you think about it?" Carrie implored. "Please?"

"All right," Charlotte promised. She hated to be so
hardheaded, but when it came to her daughter, she found
little room for compromise. To her way of thinking,

Carrie was too young for a real date, even if the boy in question wasn't the one driving.

The meat was simmering in the cast-iron skillet as Charlotte started to wash the lettuce. The faucet came off in her hand, squirting icy water toward the ceiling, and she gasped.

"What's wrong?" Carrie asked, leaping up from the kitchen table where she was doing her homework.

"The faucet broke!" Already Charlotte was down on her knees, her head under the sink, searching for the valve to cut off the water supply.

"There's water everywhere," Carrie shrieked.

"I know." Most of it had landed on Charlotte.

"Are you going to be able to fix it?" Carrie asked anxiously.

Charlotte sat on the floor, her back against the lower cupboards, her knees under her chin. This was all she needed to make her day complete. "I don't know," she muttered, pushing damp hair away from her face with both hands. "But it shouldn't be that hard."

"You should call the apartment manager," Carrie said. "You've had to work all day. If something breaks down, he should be the one to fix it, not you. We don't know anything about faucets. We're helpless."

"Helpless?" Charlotte raised her eyebrows at that. The two of them had dealt with far more difficult problems over the years. By comparison, a broken faucet was nothing. "I think we can handle it."

"Of course we can, but why should we?" Carrie demanded. "We pay our rent on time every month. The least the manager could do is see to minor repairs. He should fix them right away, too." She marched over to

the wall phone and yanked the receiver from the hook. "Here," she said dramatically. "You call him."

"I... I don't know the number." They'd lived in the apartment for well over a year and until now there hadn't been any reason to contact the manager.

"It's around here somewhere," Carrie said, pulling open the top kitchen drawer and riffling through the phone book and some other papers. Within a very brief time, she'd located the phone number. "His name is Jason Manning. He's a veterinarian."

"He's a vet? I didn't realize that." But then, Charlotte had only met the man once, and their entire conversation had been about the apartment. He seemed pleasant enough. She'd seen him in the parking lot a few times and he struck her as an overgrown kid. Frankly, she was surprised to learn he was a veterinarian, since she'd never seen him in anything other than a baseball cap, jeans and a T-shirt. Dressing up for him was a pair of jeans that weren't torn or stained and a sweatshirt.

"Are you going to phone him?" Carrie asked, holding out the receiver.

"I suppose I will." Charlotte rose awkwardly to her feet in her straight skirt. By the time she was upright, her daughter had dialed the number and handed her the receiver.

"Hello," came Jason Manning's voice after the first ring, catching her off guard.

"Oh...hello... This is Charlotte Weston in apartment 1-A. We have a broken faucet. I managed to turn off the valve, but we'd appreciate having it repaired as quickly as possible."

"A broken faucet," he repeated, and although she knew it made no sense, he sounded suspicious to Char-

lotte, as though he thought she'd purposely interrupted his evening. She resented his attitude.

"Yes, a broken faucet," she returned stiffly. "It came off in my hand when I went to wash some lettuce. There's water everywhere." A slight exaggeration, but a necessary one. "If you'd prefer, I can contact a plumber. Naturally there'll be an additional charge for repairs this late in the day."

He muttered something Charlotte couldn't decipher, then said, "I'll be right over." He didn't seem too pleased, but that was his problem. He shouldn't have agreed to manage the apartments if he wasn't willing to deal with the hassles that went along with the job.

"What did he say?" her daughter asked, eyes curious, when Charlotte hung up the phone. "Is he coming?"

"He said he'd be right over."

"Good." Carrie studied her critically. "You might want to change clothes."

"Change clothes? Whatever for?" Surprised at her daughter's concern, Charlotte glanced down at her business suit. She didn't see anything wrong with it other than a little water, and in any event, she couldn't care less about impressing the apartment manager.

"Whatever." Carrie rolled her eyes, returning to her homework. No sooner had she sat down than the doorbell chimed. Her daughter leapt suddenly to her feet as if she expected to find a rock star at the door. "I'll get it!"

Jason considered the whole thing a nuisance call. It didn't take a rocket scientist to figure out what Carrie Weston was doing. The girl had arranged this broken faucet just so he'd have a chance to see Charlotte. The

kid seemed to think that once Jason got a good look at her mother, he'd change his mind about wanting to date her. Well, there wasn't much chance of that.

Apparently the girl thought he was something of a player. Jason might've gotten a kick out of that a few years ago, but not now. Not when he was nearing middle age. These days he was more concerned about his cholesterol level and his weight than with seducing a reluctant woman.

He probably would've ended up getting married if things had worked out between him and Julie, but they hadn't. She'd been with Charlie nearly seven years now, and the last he'd heard, she had three kids. He wished her and her husband well, and suffered no regrets. Sure, it had hurt when they'd broken off their relationship, but in the end it just wasn't meant to be. He was pragmatic enough to accept that and go on with his life.

Jason enjoyed the company of women as much as any man did, but he didn't like the fact that they all wanted to reform him. He was disorganized, slovenly and a sports nut. Women didn't appreciate those qualities in a man. They would smile sweetly, claim they loved him just the way he was and then try to change him. The problem was, Jason didn't want to be refined, reformed or domesticated.

Charlotte Weston was a prime example of the type of woman he particularly avoided. Haughty. Dignified. Proper. She actually washed lettuce. Furthermore, she made a point of letting him know it.

"Hi." Carrie opened the door for him, grinning from ear to ear.

"The faucet broke?" Jason didn't bother to keep the sarcasm out of his voice.

She nodded, her smile as sly as a wink. "Kind of accidentally on purpose," she explained under her breath.

Jason was surprised she'd admit as much. "I thought that might be the case."

She pulled a screw from the small front pocket of her jeans and handed it to him. "It was the only way I could think of to get you here to see my mother up close— only don't be obvious about it, all right?"

"Carrie, is it the apartment manager?" The subject of their discussion walked into the living room, drying her hands on a terry-cloth apron.

Not bad was Jason's first reaction. She'd changed her hair since the last time he'd seen her; it was a cloud of disarrayed brown curls instead of the chignon she'd worn a year earlier. The curls gave her a softer, more feminine appeal. She was good-looking, too, not trying-to-make-an-impression gorgeous, but attractive in a modest sort of way. Her eyes were a deep shade of blue, as blue as his own. They were also intense and... sad, as though she'd withstood more than her share of problems over the years. But then, who hadn't?

Her legs were attractive, too. Long and slender. She was tall—easily five-eight, maybe five-nine.

"She's not bad-looking, is she?" Carrie asked in a whisper.

"Shh." Jason slid back a warning.

"Mom, this is Dr. Jason Manning, remember? Our apartment manager," Carrie said, her arm making a sweeping gesture toward her mother.

"Hello." She stayed where she was, her fingers still clutching the apron.

"Hi. You called about the broken faucet?" He took a couple of steps into the room, carrying his tool kit. He'd

have a talk with Carrie later. If this took more than a few minutes, he might be late for the Lakers play-off game. It was the fifth game in the series, and Jason had no intention of missing it.

"The broken faucet's in the kitchen," Charlotte said, leading the way.

"This shouldn't take long." Jason set his tools on the counter and reached for the disconnected faucet. "Looks like it might be missing a screw." He turned pointedly to Carrie, then made a show of sorting through his tool kit. "My guess is that I have an identical one in here." He pretended to find the screw Carrie had handed him, then held it up so they could all examine it. "Ah, here's one now."

"Don't be so obvious about it," Carrie warned in a heated whisper. "I don't want Mom to know."

Charlotte seemed oblivious to the undercurrents passing between him and Carrie, which was probably just as well. He'd let the kid get away with it this time, but he wasn't coming back for any repeat performances of this handyman routine.

"I should have this fixed in a couple of minutes," he said.

"Take your time," Carrie told him. "No need to rush." She walked up behind Jason and whispered, "Give her a chance, will you?"

True to his word, it took Jason all of thirty seconds to make the necessary repair.

"The bathroom faucet's been leaking, hasn't it, Mom? Don't you think we should have him look at that, too, while he's here?"

Jason glanced at his watch and frowned. If the kid kept this up, he'd miss the start of the basketball game.

But he decided he had little choice: pay now or pay later. He gave Carrie the lead she was hoping for. "Or it'll need fixing tomorrow, right?"

"Probably." There was a clear glint of warning in the fifteen-year-old's eyes.

Charlotte turned around and glanced from one to the other. Crossing her arms, she studied her daughter, then looked at Jason as if seeing him for the first time. Really seeing him. Apparently she didn't like what she saw.

"Is something going on here I don't know about?" she asked.

"What makes you say that?" Carrie said with wide-eyed innocence.

Jason had to hand it to the girl; she had the look down to an art form.

"Just answer the question, Caroline Marie."

The mother wasn't a slacker in "the look" department, either. She had eyes that would flash freeze a pot of boiling water.

The girl held her own for an admirable length of time before caving in to the icy glare. She lifted her shoulders with an expressive sigh and said, "If you must know, I took the screw out of the faucet so we'd have to call Jason over here."

Once again Jason glanced at his watch, hoping to extract himself from their discussion. This was between mother and daughter—not mother, daughter and innocent bystander. He hadn't meant to let Charlotte in on her daughter's scheme, but neither was he willing to become a full-time pawn in Carrie's little games. No telling how many other repair projects the girl might turn up for him.

"Why would you want Dr. Manning here?" Charlotte asked with a frown.

"Because he's a good-looking man and he seems nice and I thought it would be great if you got to know each other."

It was time to make his move, Jason decided. "If you'll excuse me, I'll be leaving now."

"You purposely broke the faucet so we could call him down here?" Charlotte gestured toward Jason.

Carrie sent him an irritated look as though to suggest this was all his fault. "I wanted him to see you. For being thirty-five, you aren't half bad. Once he saw your potential, I was sure he'd ask you out on a date. I tried to talk him into it earlier, but—"

"You *what?*" Charlotte exploded. Color flashed into her cheeks like bright neon lights. Her eyes narrowed. "Tell me you didn't! *Please* tell me you didn't!"

Carrie snapped her mouth shut, about ten seconds too late to suit Jason.

"This is all a big joke, isn't it?" Charlotte turned to Jason for reassurance, which was a mistake, since he was glaring at Carrie, irritated with her for saying far more than necessary.

"I had to do something," Carrie cried, defending herself. "You need a man. I saw the look on your face when you were holding Kathy Crenshaw's baby. You've never said anything, but you want more children. You never date… I don't know what my father did to you, but you've shut yourself off and—and… I was just trying to help."

Charlotte stalked to the far side of the small kitchen. "I can't *believe* this. You actually asked a man to take me out?"

"I did more than ask. I offered him money!"

Charlotte whirled on Jason. "Just what kind of man are you? Agreeing to my daughter's plans... Why... you're detestable!"

Despite himself, Jason smiled, which was no doubt the worst thing he could have done. "So I've been told. Now if you'll both excuse me, I'll leave you to your discussion."

"What kind of man are you?" Charlotte demanded a second time, following him to the door, blocking his exit.

"Mom..."

"Go to your room, young lady. I'll deal with you later." She pointed the way, as if Carrie needed directions.

Jason hadn't imagined things would go like this, and he did feel badly about it, but that didn't help. Charlotte Weston could think harshly of him if she wanted, but now Carrie was in trouble and Jason felt halfway responsible.

"She was just trying to do you a good turn," he said matter-of-factly. "Think of it as an early Mother's Day gift."

Two

With her daughter out of the room, Charlotte scowled at Jason Manning, angrier than she could ever remember being.

"You're…" She couldn't think of anything bad enough to call him.

"*Detestable* is a good word." He was practically laughing at her!

"Detestable," she repeated, clenching her fists. "I'll have you know I'm reporting you to…" The name of the government agency, any government agency, was beyond her.

"Children Protective Services," he supplied.

"Them, too." She jerked the apron from her waist and threw it on the floor. Surprised by her own action, Charlotte tried to steady herself. "According to the terms of our rental agreement, I'm giving you our two-weeks' notice as of this minute. I refuse to live near a man as…"

"Heinous," he offered, looking bored.

"Heinous as you," she stated emphatically. Then with an indignant tilt of her chin, she said as undramatically as she could manage, "Now kindly leave my home."

"As you wish." He opened the door and without a backward glance walked out of her apartment. He'd worn a cocky grin throughout, as if he found her tirade thoroughly amusing.

His attitude infuriated Charlotte. She followed him to the door and loudly turned the lock, hoping the sound of it would echo in his ears for a good long time.

When he'd gone, Charlotte discovered she was shaking so badly she needed to sit down. She sank onto a chair, her knees trembling.

"Mom?" A small voice drifted down from the hallway. "You weren't serious about us moving, were you?"

"You're darn right I'm serious. I'm so serious I'd prefer to live in our car than have anything to do with that...that...apartment manager!"

"But why?" Carrie's voice gained strength as she wandered from her bedroom to the living room, where Charlotte was seated. "Why are we moving?"

Charlotte had clearly failed as a mother. One more layer of guilt to add to all the others. "You mean you honestly don't know?"

"To punish me?" Carrie asked, her eyes brimming with unshed tears. "I'm really sorry, Mom. I didn't mean to embarrass you."

What Carrie had done was bad enough, but Jason Manning was an adult. He should've known better. True, her daughter had played a major role in all this, but Carrie was a child and didn't fully understand what she was suggesting. Her daughter had Charlotte's best interests at heart, misguided though she was.

Jason Manning, on the other hand, had planned to take advantage of them both.

"It isn't you I'm furious with, it's him." Charlotte

pointed after Jason. To think a professional man would actually agree to such an idiotic scheme.

"Dr. Manning?"

"The man's a sleaze! Imagine, taking money from you—"

"He didn't."

Charlotte hesitated, the sick feeling in her stomach intensifying. "Of course he did," she argued, "otherwise he wouldn't have played out this ridiculous game with you."

"I was the one who took the screw out of the faucet, Mom. Jason Manning didn't know anything about it. When I asked him if he'd agree to take you out on a date, he refused. He was really nice about it and everything, but he didn't seem to think it was a good idea. That's when I offered him the babysitting money I've been saving, but he wouldn't take it."

A dizziness replaced Charlotte's nausea. Several of Jason's comments suddenly made sense, especially the hint of sarcasm she'd detected when he'd held up the missing screw. Yet he'd allowed her to rant at him, not even bothering to defend himself.

"But…"

"You really aren't going to make us move, are you?"

Charlotte closed her eyes and groaned. She'd had a rotten day at the office, but misplacing a file and getting yelled at in front of an important client didn't compare with the humiliation that had been awaiting her at home.

"I wonder how many fat grams there are in crow," she muttered under her breath.

"Fat grams in crow? Are you all right, Mom?"

"I'm going to be eating a huge serving of it," Char-

lotte grumbled, and she had the distinct feeling she wasn't going to enjoy the experience.

She gave herself an hour. Sixty minutes to calm her nerves, have dinner and wipe down the counters while Carrie loaded the dishwasher. Sixty minutes to figure out how she was going to take back her two-weeks' notice.

"You're going to talk to him, aren't you?" Carrie prodded her. "Right away."

Charlotte didn't need Carrie to identify *him*. They both had only one *him* on their minds.

"I'll talk to him."

"Thank heaven." Carrie sighed with relief.

"But when I finish with Jason Manning, you and I are going to sit down and have a serious discussion, young lady."

Some of the enthusiasm left Carrie's pretty blue eyes as she nodded reluctantly.

Charlotte would've preferred to delay the apology, but the longer she put it off, the more difficult it would become.

Her steps were hesitant as she approached Jason's apartment. For some reason, she chose to knock instead of pressing the doorbell.

When he didn't answer right away, she assumed, gratefully, that she'd been given a reprieve. Yet, at the same time, she hated letting the situation fester overnight. With reinforced determination, she knocked again.

"Hold your horses," Jason shouted from the other side of the door.

Charlotte took one step in retreat, squared her shoul-

ders and drew in a deep breath. He opened the door. He looked preoccupied and revealed no emotion when he saw her.

"Hello," she said, hating how shaky she sounded. She paused long enough to clear her throat. "Would it be okay if I came inside?"

"Sure." He stepped aside to let her into his apartment. One glance told her he wasn't much of a housekeeper. A week's worth of newspapers were scattered across the carpet. Dirty dishes, presumably from his dinner, sat on the coffee table, along with the remote control, which he picked up. The TV was instantly muted. He walked over to the recliner and removed a pile of clothes, probably things he'd recently taken from the dryer.

"You can sit here," he said, indicating the recliner, his arms full of clothes.

Charlotte smiled and sat down.

"You want a beer?"

"Ah…sure." She didn't normally drink much, but if there was ever a time she needed to fortify her courage, it was now.

Her response seemed to surprise him. It certainly surprised her. He went into the kitchen, returning a moment later with a bottle and a glass. Apparently he found something he didn't like in the glass because he grabbed a dish towel from the stack of clothes he'd dumped on the floor and used it to rub the inside. When he'd finished, he raised the glass to the light for inspection.

"Don't worry about it. I prefer to drink my beer from the bottle."

He nodded, then sat down across from her, leaning back and resting his ankle on his knee. He seemed

completely relaxed, as well he should. *He* wasn't the one who'd have to plead temporary insanity.

"It's about what happened earlier," she began, gripping the beer bottle with both hands. "I talked to Carrie and discovered you hadn't exactly, uh, fallen in with her scheme. I'm afraid I assumed you had."

"Don't worry about it. It was a simple misunderstanding."

"I know. Nevertheless…"

"I'll place an ad in the paper for the apartment tomorrow. Would it be okay if I started showing it right away?"

So, he was going to make this difficult after all. "That's another reason I'm here."

"You've changed your mind about moving?" he asked conversationally, his gaze slipping from her to the television screen and back. Charlotte, however, wasn't fooled. Like any other man, he would enjoy watching her squirm.

His eyes wandered back to the silent TV. He made a fist, then jerked his elbow back in a gesture of satisfaction. Obviously things were going well for whichever team he was rooting for—much better than they were for her.

"I'd prefer not to move… Carrie and I like living where we do. The area suits us and, well…to be honest, I spoke in anger." This was all she was willing to give. If he was vindictive enough to demand she vacate the apartment, then so be it. She wasn't going to beg.

"Fine, then." He shrugged. "You're a good tenant and I'd hate to lose you." His gaze didn't waver from the television.

"Who's playing?"

He seemed surprised by her question, as though she should know something so elementary. "The Lakers and the Denver Nuggets."

"Go ahead and turn up the sound if you want."

He frowned. "You don't mind?"

"Of course not. I interrupted your game. If I'd known you were watching it, I would've waited until it was over." She took a swig of beer so he'd realize she intended to be on her way shortly.

He reached for the remote control with an eagerness he didn't bother to disguise. He pushed the volume button, dropped his leg and scooted forward, immediately absorbed in the game.

Charlotte didn't know that much about sports. Generally they bored her, but perhaps that was because she didn't understand the rules. No one had ever taken the time to explain them to her. Football seemed absolutely senseless, and basketball hardly less so.

As far as she could tell, basketball involved a herd of impossibly tall men racing up and down a polished wooden floor, passing a ball back and forth until one of them forged ahead to the basket to try to score. It seemed that whenever the contest became interesting, the referees would blow their whistles and everything would come to a grinding halt. She couldn't understand why the referees chose to wear zebra-striped shirts, either, since it wasn't likely anyone would confuse the short, balding men with the players.

"Who's winning?" That was innocuous enough, she decided. Such a simple question wouldn't reveal the extent of her ignorance.

"For now, the Lakers. They're up by four, but the lead's been changing the entire game."

"Oh." She watched for several minutes, then asked what she considered to be another harmless question. "Why do some throws count for three points and others only two?"

The thoroughness of his response astonished her, prompting several more questions. By the time he'd answered them all, he must've been aware that she barely knew one end of the court from the other. But if he was shocked by her lack of knowledge, he didn't let it show.

Soon Charlotte found herself actually enjoying the game. Now that it made a bit more sense, she began to understand why Jason liked it so much. The score was tied a minute before halftime and when the Lakers scored at the buzzer to take the lead, Charlotte leapt to her feet and cheered.

Jason raised his eyebrows at her display of enthusiasm, which made Charlotte all the more self-conscious. Slowly she lowered herself back into the chair. "Sorry," she mumbled.

"Don't be. I just didn't expect you'd be the type to appreciate sports."

"Generally I'm not. This is the first time I've had any idea what was going on."

A patronizing smile flashed in and out of his eyes. But that one instant was enough. Charlotte recognized the look; she'd seen other men wear the same expression. Men seemed to assume that because they could change their own oil and hook up a TV by themselves, they were naturally superior to women. Charlotte had run into that attitude most of her life.

Since it was her duty to defend womankind, and because she'd been fortified with a beer, Charlotte jumped

to her feet. "Don't get haughty with me, Jason Manning!" she said.

Trying to recover her dignity, she sat back down, tucking one leg beneath her. "You think just because you happen to know a few sports rules, men are superior to women."

"We are," he returned wholeheartedly, without the least bit of reservation.

Charlotte laughed. "At least you're honest. I'm sick of men who pay lip service to women, then go into the men's room and snicker behind our backs."

"I'm honest to a fault," Jason agreed. "I'm willing to snicker right in front of you."

"Somehow I don't find that much of a compliment."

"Hey, admit it. Men *are* superior, and if you haven't owned up to it by now, you should. Don't forget, God created us first."

"Give me a break," Charlotte said, rolling her eyes.

"All right. If you can, name one thing a woman does better than a man, other than having babies, which is a given."

"I'll improve on that. I'll name…several."

"Several? You won't be able to come up with one."

"Okay, then," Charlotte said, accepting his challenge. "Women are more sensitive than men. Really," she added when he snorted in response.

"Sure, you cry in movies. That negates your whole argument."

"I'm not talking about crying." She frowned at him. "I'm referring to feelings! Women aren't afraid to face their feelings. Men are so terrified of emotion they hold it inside until they're totally bent out of shape."

Jason laughed, although grudgingly. "I suppose you think women are smarter than men, too."

"No," she said sincerely. "I'd say we're about even in that department."

"Go on," he urged, as though he suspected she'd depleted her list.

"Another thing. Women are better at multitasking than men. We're used to juggling all kinds of responsibilities."

Jason snickered.

"I'm serious," she returned. "If you think about it, you'll realize it's true. Women are expected to help support the family financially. Not only that, we're *also* expected to assume the role of emotional caretaker. Responsibility for the family falls on the woman's shoulders, not the man's. Have you ever noticed how rarely men put the needs of others before their own?"

"'Needs,'" Jason echoed. "Good grief, what's *that?* Some pop-psych buzzword."

Charlotte ignored him. "Frankly, I feel sorry for you guys. You've been allowed to remain children most of your lives. You've never been given the chance to grow up."

Jason looked as though he wanted to argue with her, but couldn't come up with an adequate rebuttal.

"Women handle pain better than men, too." Charlotte was on a roll. "I've never seen a bigger baby in my life than a man who's got a minor case of the flu. Most of them act as though we should call in the World Health Organization."

"I suppose you're going to drag the horrors of giving birth into this now—which, I'll remind you, is completely unfair."

"I don't need to. Men have a hard time just dealing with a simple cold. If God had left procreation up to the male of the species, humanity would've died out with Adam."

"That's three," Jason muttered ungraciously. "Three is not several. Three is a *few*."

Charlotte shook her head. "It's enough. You don't have a leg to stand on, but you're too proud to admit it, which is something else a woman's more capable of doing."

"What? Standing on one leg?"

"No, admitting she's wrong. Don't get me started on that one. It happens to be a personal peeve of mine."

"You mean the others weren't?"

"Not particularly. I was just listing a few of the more obvious facts, waiting for you to come up with even one logical defense—which you failed to do."

He didn't seem willing to agree, but it was apparent from the smile he ineffectively struggled to hide that he was aware of his dilemma. He had no option, no argument.

"You realize you've backed me into a corner, don't you? I don't have any choice but to agree with you, otherwise you'll brand me as being smug and insensitive, unaware of my feelings and too childish to accept the truth."

"I suppose you're right." If anyone was wearing a smug look, it was Charlotte. She felt triumphant, better than she had all day. All week. Come to think of it, she couldn't remember when she'd enjoyed herself more.

Conceding defeat, Jason moved into the kitchen and returned with a second cold beer for each of them. Charlotte hesitated. She'd never intended to stay this

long, and Carrie might be concerned. After all the lectures she'd delivered about being gone longer than expected, Charlotte felt she should go home now. But, to her amazement, she discovered she didn't want to leave. Watching the rest of the Lakers game with Jason appealed to her a lot more.

"Thanks, anyway, but I should get back to Carrie," she said.

Although she smiled brightly, some of her reluctance must have shown because Jason said, "So soon?"

"I stayed much longer than I'd planned to."

"But the game's only half over."

"I know, but..."

"Why don't you call her?" Jason suggested, pointing toward the counter where he kept his phone.

It seemed like a reasonable idea. Charlotte smiled and headed for the kitchen. She punched out her number and waited. Carrie answered on the third ring.

"Oh, hi, Mom," she said in an unconcerned voice.

"I'm watching the Lakers game with Jason."

"Okay. We're not going to move, are we?"

"No, Jason was kind enough to let me withdraw my two-weeks' notice."

"Oh, good. He's a great guy, isn't he?"

"Yeah." Charlotte was surprised by how much she meant it. Jason *was* a great guy. She hadn't stumbled on many in the past few—or was that several?—years. It was a treat to encounter a man who was candid, sincere and fun. But Charlotte had been fooled by men before, so she wasn't taking anything for granted.

"Well?" Jason asked when she replaced the receiver. If she needed an excuse, he was handing her one on

a platter. All she needed to do was make some vague reply about Carrie and she'd be on her way.

"Carrie says she'll call if she needs me."

"Excellent."

His smile was definitely charming, Charlotte decided.

"How about some popcorn?" he asked.

Charlotte nodded eagerly. She hadn't eaten much dinner, unnerved as she was by her discovery, knowing she'd need to confront him. Jason's offhand acceptance of her apology endeared him to her even more. If Jason was like her boss, he'd have flayed her alive. Instead, he'd just shrugged it off and given her a beer.

"Let me help," she said, following him into the kitchen.

"There's not much to do," he said, opening his microwave and tossing a bag inside. He set the timer, pushed a button and within a minute the sound of popping kernels filled the kitchen. The smell was heavenly.

When it was ready, Jason poured the popcorn into a large bowl and carried it out to the living room. Charlotte brought paper towels, since she couldn't find any napkins.

He placed the bowl in the middle of the coffee table and Charlotte joined him on the sofa. The game was about to resume. She tucked her feet beneath her as she'd done earlier, leaning forward now and then to scoop up some popcorn. It tasted wonderful, but that might've been because of the company. Or the fact that for the first time all day, she was feeling relaxed.

The Lakers scored twelve straight points and Charlotte rose to her knees, cheering loudly. Normally she was far more reserved, more in control of her emotions.

It was as if someone else had taken charge of her mind. Someone more free-spirited and uninhibited. Someone who'd downed two beers on a near-empty stomach. Apparently, hearing that her daughter was bribing men to date her had that kind of effect on her.

Jason cheered, too, and they turned to smile at each other. Their eyes met and held for the longest time. Flustered and unnerved, Charlotte was the first to glance away.

She hadn't shared such an intense look with a man since college. A look that said, I'm enjoying myself. I'm attracted to you. I'd like to get to know you better...a whole lot better.

Her heart was thumping as she forced her attention back to the TV. She took a deep swallow of beer to hide her discomfort.

Jason went strangely quiet afterward, too. They both made a pretense of being involved in the game. As time went on, however, it wasn't the Lakers who held their attention—it was each other.

"So," Jason said abruptly, "where do you work?"

"Downtown, for a large insurance agency. You might've heard of them. Davidson and Krier. They have a radio commercial that's played a lot." In an effort, weak though it was, to disguise her uneasiness, she sang the all-too-familiar jingle.

"I have heard of them," Jason said, nodding. His rich baritone concluded the song.

They laughed self-consciously. Charlotte wished she'd had the sense to leave at halftime. No, she amended silently, that wasn't true. She was glad she'd stayed. If she regretted anything, it was that she was

so clumsy when it came to dealing with male-female relationships.

Maybe it wasn't so strange that Carrie had tried to bribe someone to ask her on a date. Charlotte hadn't been out with a man in three years. But she hadn't really missed the dating scene. How could she miss something she'd never actually experienced? She'd hardly dated at all since Tom left.

Tom. The accustomed pain she felt whenever she thought of her ex-husband followed on the heels of the unexpected attraction she felt toward Jason. The two didn't mix well. One brought back the pain of the past and reminded her that she had no future. The other tempted her to believe she did.

"I should be going," she announced suddenly, her decision made. She scurried to her feet as if she had a pressing appointment.

"The game's not over," Jason said, frowning. He didn't move for a moment. "Don't go yet."

"I'll watch the rest of it at my place. Thanks so much for the wonderful evening. I enjoyed myself. Really, I did." She picked up the empty popcorn bowl and the two beer bottles and took them into the kitchen.

Jason trailed her, his hands buried deep in his pockets. He nodded at his garbage can, which was overflowing. There was a semicircle of half-filled bags stacked around it.

"I've been meaning to take this out to the Dumpster," he explained, removing the bottles from her hands and throwing them into a plastic recycling bin.

"I appreciate how understanding you've been," Charlotte said as she walked to the door.

"About what?" he asked.

"Carrie and me and...everything."

"No problem," he said a few steps behind. He slipped in front of her and stood by the door.

Charlotte knew she was running away like a frightened rabbit. The trapped feeling had returned and it terrified her as it always had. She'd thought it would be different this time, but that had been the beer. Her fears would never change, never go away. They'd always be there to remind her of her shortcomings, how inadequate she was, how no man could ever be trusted. Tom had proved that. She was anxious to be on her way now, but Jason was blocking her only means of escape.

When she glanced up, some of the fear must have shown in her eyes because he hesitated, studying her.

There was a short silence, too deep to last long, but too intense to ignore. Charlotte held his gaze for as long as she dared before looking away. His eyes were so blue, so serious, so filled with questions. She'd perplexed him, she knew, but she couldn't explain. *Wouldn't* explain.

They'd laughed and teased and joked. But Jason was somber now. Funny, this mood was as appealing as the lightheartedness she'd sensed in him earlier. His mouth, even when he wasn't smiling, was perfectly shaped. Everything about him was perfect. His high cheekbones, his wide brow and straight nose. Too perfect for her.

The paralyzing regret threatened to explode within her, but Charlotte managed to keep it in check. How, she wasn't sure. It must've been her fear, she decided. Fear of what could happen, the happiness a relationship with him could bring—and the disappointment that would inevitably come afterward. The disappoint-

ment he'd feel in her. Then it would be over almost before it had begun.

She looked up one last time, to say goodbye, to thank him, to escape.

In that instant she knew Jason was going to kiss her. But one word, the least bit of resistance, and he wouldn't go through with it. Charlotte was completely confident of that.

Need and curiosity overcame the anxiety, and she watched, mesmerized, as his mouth descended toward her own. His lips, so warm and seductive, barely touched hers.

Charlotte closed her eyes, trembling and afraid. Her body, seemingly of its own accord, moved toward him, turning into his, seeking the security and the strength she felt in him.

He moaned softly and Charlotte did, too, slanting her head to one side, inviting him to deepen the kiss.

Yet Jason held back. The kiss was light. Sweet. More seductive than anything she'd ever known. It felt wonderful. So wonderful...

Charlotte didn't understand why he resisted kissing her completely, the way her body was begging him to. Restraining himself demanded obvious effort. She could tell by the rigid way he held himself, the way his hands curved over her shoulders, keeping her at bay. Keeping himself at bay.

Her head was full of the promise his lips had made and hadn't kept. Full of the possibilities. Full of the surprise and the wonder. She'd never felt like this before.

Once again his mouth brushed over hers, warm and exciting. Moving slowly—so slowly—and so easy, as though he had all the time in the world.

"Jason." It was a battle for her to breathe. Her heart sounded like a frantic drumbeat in her ears, drowning out coherent thought.

He tensed, then kissed her, really kissed her, wrapping himself around her, absorbing her in his size, his strength, his need.

They remained entwined, arms around each other, until Charlotte could no longer stand. She broke away and buried her head in his shoulder, her breathing heavy.

"Charlotte, I didn't mean to frighten you."

"You didn't." It was the truth; any fear she felt had nothing to do with him. "I have to go… Thank you. For everything."

But most of all for that kiss, she added silently. It was unlikely he'd ever know how much that single kiss had meant to her.

Three

He'd kissed her. He'd actually kissed Charlotte. An hour later, Jason still had trouble taking it in.

Oh, he'd kissed plenty of women in his day. But this time, with this woman, it was different. He didn't know how he understood that, but he did. He'd realized it long before he'd touched her. Perhaps because she was so different from what he'd assumed. He'd figured she was dignified, straitlaced, unapproachable. Then, as soon as he'd told her about basketball rules, she'd kicked off her shoes and was cheering as enthusiastically as he was himself. What a contrast he found in her. Prim and proper on the outside, a hellion waiting to break loose on the inside.

She intrigued him. Beguiled him.

At some point during their evening together—exactly when, he couldn't be sure—he'd felt an unfamiliar tug, a stirring deep within. The feeling hadn't gone away. If anything, it had intensified.

What they'd shared wasn't any ordinary kiss, either. Perhaps that explained it. They'd communicated on an entirely different level, one he'd never known before.

It seemed their spirits—the deepest, innermost part of themselves—had somehow touched. He shook his head. He was getting fanciful.

No, this wasn't the kind of kiss he'd had with any other woman. He'd never gone so slowly, been so careful. Although she'd acted blatantly provocative, urging him to deepen the contact, he'd resisted. That same inner voice that had said Charlotte was different had also warned him to proceed with caution. He'd sensed how fragile she was, and the urge to protect her, even from himself, had been overwhelming.

Jason wasn't generally so philosophical. He didn't waste time deliberating on relationships or motivations. He wasn't sure what he was thinking right now. His reaction to Charlotte was unwarranted—wasn't it? Although it'd been a nice kiss, it wasn't so spectacular that his whole world should be turned upside down.

Yet it was—flipped over completely.

Jason felt almost giddy with sensation. These feelings weren't logical. It was as if God had decided to play a world-class trick on him.

Jason considered himself too old for romance. He didn't even know what romance was. Pure foolishness, he thought sarcastically. It was one of the primary reasons he'd never married, and never intended to. He wasn't a romantic kind of guy. A pizza and cold beer while watching a football game interested him far more than staring across a candlelit table at some woman and pretending to be overwhelmed by her beauty. Flattery and small talk weren't for him.

And yet...he remembered how good Charlotte's arms had felt around his neck. She'd held her body so tightly

against his that he could feel her heart beat. It was a closeness that had transcended the physical.

By the time she'd left, Jason felt heady, as if he'd had too much to drink. He didn't understand her rush, either. He hadn't wanted her to leave and had tried to come up with a reason for her to stay. Any reason. But she'd quietly slipped out of his arms and left before he could think of a way to keep her there. If he was witty and romantic he might've thought of something. But he wasn't, so he'd been forced to let her go.

Jason started pacing, the Lakers game forgotten. He needed to clear the cobwebs from his head. He wasn't any good at analyzing situations like this. All he knew was that he'd enjoyed holding Charlotte in his arms, enjoyed kissing her, and he looked forward to doing it again.

He sank down in front of the television, surprised to find the basketball game already over. Stunned, he stared at the credits rolling down the screen. He didn't even know who won. He waited, hoping the camera would scan the scoreboard, but it didn't happen.

He had a bet riding on the outcome of the game. Nothing major, just a friendly wager between brothers. Nevertheless, high stakes or low, it wasn't like Jason Manning to be caught without a final score.

The phone rang and Jason hurried to the kitchen to answer it.

"Hello," he said absently, keeping his eye on the television, still hoping to learn the final outcome.

"I knew I never should've picked the Nuggets," Rich muttered.

"You mean the Lakers won?"

"By eight points. Where have *you* been all evening?"

"Home," Jason returned defensively. "I had company. A tenant stopped in to chat."

"During a play-off game, and you didn't get rid of them?"

Actually Jason hadn't intended to tell his brother even that much, but Rich had a point. Jason wasn't one to sit around and shoot the breeze when he could be watching a game. Any kind of game.

"It was business," he explained, unnecessarily annoyed. He felt mildly guilty for stretching the truth. Charlotte's original intent had been to apologize and tell him she'd changed her mind about moving. That was business. Staying the better part of two hours wasn't.

Ignoring Jason's bad mood, Rich chatted on, replaying the last half of the fourth quarter in which the Lakers had made an "amazing" comeback. While his brother was speaking, Jason glanced at the list of his tenants' phone numbers, which he kept by the phone for easy reference. The way his eyes immediately latched on to Charlotte's name, anyone might think it had been circled in red. He was so distracted by reading her name over and over in his mind that he missed most of what Rich was telling him.

When the conversation with his brother ended, Jason couldn't recall more than a few words of what they'd said. Just enough to regret that he hadn't been watching the game. Just enough to wish he'd thought of something that would've prompted Charlotte to stay.

Without a second's deliberation, he reached for his phone and dialed her number. Carrie answered before the first ring had been completed. She must not have recognized his voice, because she got Charlotte without comment.

"Hello."

"Hi," he said, feeling gauche. "The Lakers won."

"I know."

Apparently their kiss hadn't deranged her the way it had him. She must have gone back to her apartment, plunked herself down and watched the rest of the game, while he'd been walking around in a stupor for the past hour.

"I was thinking," Jason began, "about dinner tomorrow night. That is, if you're free."

"Dinner," she repeated as if this was a foreign concept. "What time?" she asked a moment later.

"Six."

"Sure."

His mood lightened. "Great, I'll pick you up then." He replaced the receiver and glanced around his kitchen, frustrated by how messy it was. He hated housework, hated having to pick up after himself, hated the everyday chores that made life so mundane. Every dish he owned was dirty, except the ones in his dishwasher, which were clean. It didn't make sense to reload it while there were clean dishes he could use in there.

Needing something to occupy his mind, he tackled the task of cleaning up the kitchen with unprecedented enthusiasm.

Jason's eagerness to see Charlotte again had waned by the following afternoon. A good night's sleep and a day at the clinic had sufficiently straightened out his brain. He'd behaved in a manner that was completely out of character. He couldn't even begin to figure out why.

Charlotte was a woman. There wasn't anything special about her. No reason he should be falling all over

himself for the opportunity to take her out. He'd missed the last half of an important basketball game because his thoughts had become so tangled up with her. That would've been devotion enough for any woman in his life—only she wasn't in his life, and he intended to keep it that way.

Furthermore, Jason wasn't that keen on Charlotte's teenage daughter thinking he'd fallen in with her scheme. He could see it now. Carrie would give him a brilliant smile and a high-five when he arrived. The girl was bound to believe she was responsible for Jason asking Charlotte out. She might even try to slip him some of the money she'd offered him earlier. The whole thing had the potential for disaster written all over it.

If a convenient excuse to cancel this date had presented itself, Jason would've grabbed it with both hands.

The way his luck was going, they'd probably run into his parents, and his mother would start hounding him again about getting married. He'd never understood why women considered marriage so important. Frustrated, he'd asked his mother once, and her answer had confused him even more. She'd looked at him serenely without interrupting the task that occupied her hands and had casually said, "It's good to have a partner."

A partner! She'd made it sound like he needed a wife in order to compete in a mixed bowling league.

His parents weren't exactly throwing potential mates his way, but they'd let it be known that they were hoping he'd get married sometime soon. Jason, however, was intelligent enough not to become involved in a lifetime relationship just to satisfy his parents' wishes.

Whatever craziness had prompted him to ask Charlotte out to dinner had passed during the night. He'd

awakened sane and in command of his usual common sense.

As the day went on he found himself actually dreading the date. The two of them had absolutely nothing in common. He'd go through with this, Jason decided grimly, because he was a man of his word. Since he told her he'd be there by six, he would be, but snow would fall at the equator before he gave in to an impulse like this again.

She was dressed completely wrong, Charlotte realized as soon as Jason arrived. Not knowing what to wear, she'd chosen a navy blue suit, not unlike the one she'd worn to the office. She'd attempted to dress it up a bit with a bright turquoise-and-pink scarf and a quarter-size silver pin of a colorful toucan. Jason arrived in jeans, sweatshirt and a baseball cap with a University of Washington Huskies logo on it.

"Hello," she said, forcing herself to smile. A hundred times in the last hour she'd regretted ever agreeing to this date. Jason had caught her off guard when he'd phoned. She hadn't known what to say. Hadn't had time to think of an excuse.

Now she was stuck, but judging by his expression, Jason didn't seem any more pleased than she was. He frowned at her until she was so self-conscious, she suggested changing clothes.

"Don't worry about it," he muttered, tucking the tips of his fingers into his back pockets. They definitely made a pair. He'd dressed like someone visiting the amusement park, and she looked like a student of Emily Post.

Charlotte was grateful that Carrie had gone to the

library with a friend. The other mom was picking them up, but it would give Charlotte a convenient excuse to hurry home.

"Where would you like to eat?" Jason asked once they were outside the apartment.

"Wherever you want."

"Mexican food?" He didn't sound enthusiastic.

"Fine." Especially since there was a restaurant close by. "How about Mr. Tamales on Old Military Road?"

"Sure," he agreed easily enough. He was probably thinking the same thing she was. The sooner they got there, the sooner they'd be finished and could go back to their respective lives instead of dabbling in this nonsense.

For the short time they were together, Charlotte figured she might as well enjoy herself. The restaurant was little more than a greasy spoon, but the food had earned its excellent reputation.

The place apparently did a brisk business on weeknights because there was only one spot available.

"I never would've thought we'd need reservations," Jason said, looking as surprised as Charlotte.

The hostess, wearing an off-the-shoulder peasant blouse and black skirt, smiled and escorted them to the booth. The waitress followed close behind. She handed them each a menu shaped like a cactus and then brought water, tortilla chips and salsa. Charlotte read over the choices, made her selection and scooped up a jalapeño pepper with a chip.

"You aren't going to eat that, are you?" Jason asked, staring at her as if she'd pulled the pin activating a grenade.

Charlotte grinned. "Oh, that's another thing I forgot

to mention last night—women can eat chili peppers better than a man."

"Not this time, sweetheart. I was weaned on hot peppers." He took one, poising it in front of his mouth.

"Me, too," she challenged.

They bit into the peppers simultaneously. The seeds and juice dribbled down Charlotte's chin and she grabbed a paper napkin, dabbing it against her skin.

"You weren't kidding," Jason said, obviously impressed.

"I never kid." A five-alarm fire was blazing in her mouth, but she smiled and reached casually for another chip and some water. The water intensified the burning, but she smiled cheerfully as though nothing was wrong.

"Rich and I used to eat these peppers right out of Dad's garden."

"I take it Rich is your brother?"

"I'm one of five," Jason went on to explain, and she noted that his eyes brightened with pride. "Paul's the oldest, then there's me, followed by Rich. My sisters, Taylor and Christy, round out the family."

"Are any of them married?"

"Everyone but me. I'm beginning to lose track of how many nieces and nephews I've got now, and there doesn't seem to be a lull yet."

Charlotte had never had much of a family. Her father had deserted her and her mother when Charlotte was too young to remember him. Then her mother had died just about the time Charlotte graduated from high school. The insurance money was set up to cover her college expenses. Only the money hadn't been used for her. Instead, Tom had been educated on her inheritance; he'd robbed her of even that.

Charlotte lowered her gaze. It hurt too much to think about Tom and that bleak period of her life when she'd been so lost and vulnerable. So alone, with no family. Her ex-husband had used her and when he'd finished, he'd thrown her aside.

All the time she was growing up, Charlotte had dreamed about being part of a large, loving family. How she envied Jason his brothers and sisters.

"The story of my family tree is less about the roots," he said, grinning as he spoke, "than the sap."

Charlotte's laugh was spontaneous. She picked up her water, warmed by his wit and his willingness to laugh at himself. "I was an only child. I promised myself I'd have a houseful of kids when I got married so my children wouldn't grow up lonely."

"Lonely," Jason echoed. "I would have given anything for some peace and quiet. The girls were the worst."

"Somehow I guessed you'd complain about the women in your family."

"You know," he said, "I never thought I'd say this, but I really miss Taylor and Christy. They're both living in Montana now, raising their families. We get together when we can, which isn't nearly often enough. It's been over a year since we saw each other."

The waitress came for their order. Charlotte asked for the specialty salad, which consisted of beans, rice, cheese, shredded chicken, lettuce and slices of tomato and jalapeño peppers. Jason chose the chicken enchiladas.

"Do your brothers live in the Seattle area?"

Jason nodded. "Paul's a journalist and Rich works as an engineer for Boeing. We see each other frequently."

Their orders arrived and they chatted amicably over their meal. Jason sampled her salad and fed her a bite of his enchiladas; both were delicious. Soon they'd asked the waitress for two additional plates and were unabashedly sharing their meals.

It was only seven-thirty when they'd finished, even though they lingered over coffee. Charlotte couldn't remember time passing more quickly.

All day she'd been worried about this dinner—and for nothing. She'd enjoyed herself even more than she'd hoped, but that was easy to do with Jason. He didn't put on airs or pretend to be something he wasn't. Nor did he feign agreement with her; their differing opinions meant a free and interesting exchange of ideas.

"I should be heading home," Charlotte said, although she could happily have sat there talking. They weren't at a loss for topics, but the restaurant was busy and Carrie would be home soon.

"Yeah, I suppose we should go," he said reluctantly, standing. He left a generous tip and took the tab up to the counter.

After talking nonstop for nearly an hour, both were strangely quiet on the drive home. Charlotte had been determined to enjoy herself from the start, but she'd expected to make the best of a bad situation. Instead she'd had a wonderful time.

She hadn't known how starved she was for adult companionship, hadn't realized how empty she'd felt inside, how deep the void had become.

As they neared the apartment complex, she realized one more thing. She didn't want this evening to end.

"Would you like to come in for coffee?" she asked as he parked his car. For half the ride home, Charlotte

had been engaging in a silent debate. She was sure that if Carrie was home, she'd make a big deal about Jason's presence. But Charlotte would get the third degree from her daughter anyway, so she decided it didn't matter if Jason came in.

"I could use another cup of coffee," Jason told her, although they'd both had large mugs at the restaurant.

As luck would have it, Carrie wasn't home yet. Charlotte had been counting on her teenage daughter to act as a buffer between her and Jason. She half suspected Jason was thinking the same thing.

"Carrie's at the library with a friend," she explained. "But I'm sure she'll be back any minute."

"I wondered what she was up to tonight."

"I'll put on the coffee," she said self-consciously, going directly to the kitchen. "Make yourself at home."

While she scooped up the grounds and poured water into the pot, she saw that Jason had lowered himself onto her sofa. He reached for a magazine and flipped through the pages, then set it back and reached for another. Since it was upside down, his attention was clearly elsewhere. He noted his mistake, righted the magazine, then placed it with the others. Apparently *Seventeen* magazine didn't interest him after all.

There was no reason for him to be so nervous. It was funny; they'd chatted like old friends at the restaurant, but the instant they were alone, they became uncomfortable with each other.

"I thought you might like some cookies," she said, as she carried the tray into the living room. She'd baked chocolate chip cookies that weekend, and there were plenty left over.

Being a single mother left her vulnerable to attacks

of guilt—guilt that often led to an abundance of home-made cookies. There were so many things she didn't know about family, so much she'd missed out on. It bothered her more than she wanted to admit. Whenever Charlotte was feeling anxious or contrite about something, she baked. And with the ninth-grade dance hanging over her head, she'd been doing a lot of baking lately. The cookie jar was full. The freezer was packed, too. Even Carrie was complaining about all the goodies around the house. Too tempting, she said. Her daughter claimed Charlotte was trying to raise her cholesterol and kill her off.

More guilt, more need to bake cookies. It was a vicious circle.

"Homemade cookies," Jason said, sliding forward, far more appreciative than her daughter. "I didn't know anyone but my mother baked these days." He took one and downed it in two bites, nodding vigorously even before he'd finished chewing.

Charlotte smiled at the unspoken compliment and poured their coffee in plain white china cups. "There's plenty more where those came from."

Jason helped himself to a second and then a third.

Charlotte was pleased that he seemed to value her culinary skills. "I guess it's true, then."

He cocked one eyebrow. "What?"

"Never mind," she muttered, sorry she'd brought up the subject.

"If you're thinking the way to a man's heart is through his stomach, forget it. Others before you have tried that route."

"Several dozen, no doubt," she teased, amused by his complete lack of modesty. Not to mention his arrogance.

"I've suffered my share of feminine wiles."

"Feminine wiles," Charlotte repeated, trying hard not to laugh out loud. He acted as though she was setting a trap for him. She was about to reassure him that she had no intention of remarrying, then decided against it. She'd let him assume whatever he wanted. After all, he was helping her get rid of these cookies before they overran the apartment.

She did bring up another topic, though, one she couldn't help being curious about. "Why aren't you married?" She hoped he wouldn't be offended by her directness; based on their previous conversations she didn't expect him to be.

Jason shrugged and swallowed the last bite of the last cookie she'd set out. He seemed to be thinking over his response as he picked up his coffee and relaxed against the back of the sofa. "I learned something recently about the differences between a man and a woman. It's information that's served me well."

They certainly had a routine going with this subject. "Oh, what's that?"

"Tell me, all kidding aside," he said, his blue eyes serious, "what is it women want from a man?"

Charlotte thought about that for a moment. "To be loved."

He nodded approvingly.

"To be needed and respected."

"Exactly." He grinned, clearly pleased by her answer.

He was making this easy, and Charlotte warmed to her ideas. "A woman longs to be held, of course, but more than that, she wants to be treasured, appreciated."

"Perfect," Jason said, smiling benignly. "Now ask me what a man wants."

"All right," she said, crossing her legs, holding the saucer with one hand, her cup in the other. "What is it a man wants?"

"Tickets to the World Series," Jason returned without a pause.

Charlotte nearly choked on her laughter. Fortunately she wasn't swallowing a sip of coffee at the time. "I see what you mean," she said after she'd composed herself. "There does seem to be a basic, shall we say, disconnect here."

He nodded. "It was when Rich gave up two tickets for a Seahawks football game that I knew he'd fallen in love."

"That's sweet," Charlotte said with a sigh, enjoying the romance of it all.

"Don't go all soft on me. It wasn't like it sounds. He gave the tickets to a friend as a bribe. Rich didn't want to date Jamie himself, he wanted someone else to fall in love with her."

"He bribed another guy to take her out?"

"Yup. He was in love with her himself, but like the rest of us, he's useless when it comes to romance. I figured it out before he did, and I know next to nothing about that kind of stuff." Jason grinned. "From that point on, it was all downhill for Rich. He's married and has a couple of kids now. A girl and a boy."

"I don't care what you say. That's sweet."

"Perhaps."

Charlotte was relaxed now. She removed her shoes and propped her feet on the coffee table, crossing her legs at the ankles. "Have *you* ever been in love?" At Jason's hesitation, she hurried to add, "I shouldn't have asked that."

"I don't mind, if you won't take offense at my answer—which is, I don't know. I thought I was once, several years back, but in retrospect I'm not sure. It hurt when we broke up, and I was sorry we hadn't been able to work things out, but I don't have any real regrets."

"What was her name?"

"Julie. She's married now."

Charlotte didn't understand where she found the courage, but she reached forward and brushed her index finger down the side of Jason's face. She wanted to ease the pain she read in his expression, the pain he discounted so casually. A pain she recognized, since she'd walked through this valley herself, with the cold wind of despair howling at her back.

Jason's gaze met hers and she felt immersed in a look so warm, so intense, that her breath caught. She couldn't remember a man ever looking at her that way, as though he wasn't sure she was even real. As if he was afraid she'd vanish if he touched her.

Jason removed the cup and saucer from her hands and set them on the tray next to the empty plate.

He was going to kiss her; she realized it in the same moment she owned up to how much she wanted him to. All night she'd been looking forward to having him do exactly this, only she hadn't been willing to admit it.

His mouth was gentle and sweet with the taste of coffee and chocolate. He kissed her the way he had the night before, and Charlotte could barely take in the sensation that overwhelmed her. She'd never thought she'd feel anything so profound, so exciting, again. She hadn't believed she was capable of such a rush of feeling....

She whimpered and wrapped her arms around his neck, holding on to him in a world that had started to

spin out of control. His hands framed her face and he slanted his mouth over hers, answering her need with his own.

Jason kissed her again and again.

The sound coming from the front door barely registered in her passion-drugged brain.

"Mom… Jason…" was followed by a shocked pause, then, "Wow, this is great."

Charlotte broke away from Jason and leapt to her feet.

"Gee, Mom, there's no need to get embarrassed. People kiss all the time." Carrie floated across the carpet, then threw herself into a chair. "So," she said, smiling broadly, "is there anything either of you want to tell me?"

"Like what?" Charlotte asked.

Carrie shrugged with utter nonchalance. "That you're getting married?"

Four

On his way back to his apartment, Jason had to admit that Charlotte's daughter possessed a knack for the unexpected. Arriving when she did was only the beginning; introducing the subject of marriage had nearly sent him into hysterics.

Him married? It was downright laughable.

Thinking about it, Jason realized Charlotte had brought up the subject herself, wanting to know why he hadn't married, asking him if he'd ever been in love. Typical women questions.

Perhaps mother and daughter were in cahoots, plotting his downfall. No, that was equally laughable.

Jason simply wasn't the marrying kind. Not because he was a womanizer or because he had anything against the opposite sex. He liked women...at times and enjoyed being with them...occasionally. Liked kissing them... definitely. But he relished his freedom too much to sacrifice it to commitment and responsibility.

No, he told himself resolutely, Charlotte wasn't involved in any scheme to drag him to the altar. She'd been so embarrassed and flustered by Carrie's sugges-

tion, her face had gone bright red. The woman's face was too open to hide her feelings. She had chastised Carrie, asked for and received an apology, and looked genuinely grateful when Jason said it was time he left.

Despite the episode with Carrie, Jason had thoroughly enjoyed his evening with Charlotte. He hadn't expected to. In fact he'd originally regretted having asked her out, but in the end their date had been a pleasant success.

Once again he was bewildered by the strong desire he experienced when he kissed her. He had ordained a hands-off policy for the night, but had shelved that idea the minute she'd sat next to him, gazing up at him with those pretty eyes of hers.

Actually, he'd known he was in trouble when he accepted her invitation to come inside for coffee. He'd thought of it as a challenge; he'd wanted to see how far he could push his determination. Not far, he concluded. When she'd looked at him, her eyes soft and inviting, he was lost. His hands-off policy had quickly become a hands-on experiment.

There was something about Charlotte Weston that got to him. Really got to him.

All that outward confidence she worked so hard to display hadn't fooled him. Beneath a paper-thin veneer, she was vulnerable. Any fool with two functional brain cells would have figured that out on the first date.

Only she didn't date.

Carrie had told him it'd been years since her mother had even gone out with a man. Undoubtedly she'd been asked—and if she hadn't been, why not? She was attractive, intelligent and fun. Offhand, he knew a half-

dozen men who'd jump at the chance to meet a woman like Charlotte.

If she'd turned down offers, and surely she had, then there must be a reason. The question that confused Jason was: If she didn't date, then why had she agreed to have dinner with him?

Probably the same reason that had goaded him to ask, Jason concluded. The kiss. That infamous first kiss. It had rocked them both. Taken them by surprise, leaving them excited—and unsure.

As for the other questions that hounded him, Jason didn't have any answers. Nor did he understand everything that was happening between him and Charlotte. One thing he did know—and it terrified him the most— was that they were, in effect, playing with lighted sticks of dynamite, tossing them back and forth. The attraction between them was that explosive. That dangerous.

Carrie's arrival had been more timely than she'd realized.

All right, Jason was willing to own up, albeit grudgingly, that he was fascinated with Charlotte. He suspected she'd confess to feeling the same thing. To his way of thinking, if they were so strongly attracted to each other, they should both be prepared to do something about it.

In other words, they should stop fighting the inevitable and make love. That would get it out of their system—he hoped.

Naw, Jason mused darkly. Charlotte wasn't the kind of woman who'd indulge in an affair. She might wear only straight, dark business suits to work, but deep down she was the romantic type, which made her impractical. Most women seemed to be. If they were going

to make love, they wanted it prettied up with a bunch of flowery words, a declaration of undying love and promises of commitment.

Well, Charlotte, along with every other woman, could forget that, he told himself. As far as he was concerned, romance and commitment were out of the question.

What he wanted in this relationship was honesty. If it were up to him, he'd suggest they do away with the formalities, admit what they wanted and then scratch that itch.

He mulled that over for a few minutes, knowing it was unlikely that Charlotte would see the situation his way. He might not know her well, but Jason readily acknowledged that she wasn't going to be satisfied with so little. Women tended to see lovemaking as more than just the relief of a physical craving.

Well, he, for one, wasn't going to play that game. He liked Charlotte—how much he liked her surprised him—but he knew the rules. Either they dropped everything now, while they still could, or they continued driving each other insane. Sooner or later, one of them would have to give in.

Without a second's hesitation, Jason knew it would be him.

Charlotte affected him deep down. He couldn't bear the thought of hurting her or causing her one second of unhappiness. In the end he'd say all the words she wanted to hear, and he'd do the best job he could, because pleasing her would mean so much to him.

Then he'd get what he wanted; she'd make love to him willingly, with everything in her. He'd give her all

he had, too. The problem was—and he knew it was inevitable—that before he'd quite figured out what was happening, they'd be talking about marriage, which was something he hadn't done since Julie.

Jason stopped right there. If he started thinking along those lines, everything would change. Soon Charlotte would be organizing his life, straightening up his apartment, making suggestions about little things he could do to improve his sorry lot. Women always saw his lot as sorry. He was happy living the way he was, but women couldn't accept that. They didn't believe a man could survive without them constantly fussing over him, dictating his life.

Bit by bit, Charlotte would dominate his world, eroding his independence until he was like every other married man he'd ever known—willing to change his ways for a wife. Picking up his socks, getting hassled about sports games on TV, the whole deal.

No, the domesticated life wasn't for him. Still, Charlotte tempted him more than anyone else had in ages, and he could *almost* imagine their lives together. Not quite, but almost.

He stared at his apartment door, wondering how long he'd been standing there mulling over his thoughts. He was light-years ahead of himself, he realized. Good grief, he was already trying to finagle his way out of marrying her and they'd only gone out on one date. He'd only kissed her twice.

But, oh, those kisses…

Like he'd told himself before, they were playing with explosives, and the best way to avoid getting hurt was to get out now, before they became too involved. Before he lost the strength to walk away from her.

* * *

"Aren't you going to *do* something?" Carrie demanded.

"About what?" Charlotte returned calmly, feigning ignorance. She glanced up from her novel, looking over the rims of her reading glasses with practiced innocence.

"Jason!" Carrie cried. "You haven't heard from him in a whole week."

"Has it been that long?" Seven days, two hours and three minutes, but who was counting? Certainly not her.

"Mom," Carrie insisted, hands on her hips, "you know how long it's been. You jump every time the phone rings. You keep making excuses about checking the mail and getting the newspaper. We both know you're hoping to run into Jason."

It hurt Charlotte's pride to learn she'd been so obvious.

"You like him, don't you?" Carrie asked. Her expression said that if *she* were in charge, this romance would be making far greater progress. Charlotte, however, had no intention of letting her daughter take control of her relationship with Jason Manning.

"I think Jason's wonderful," Charlotte admitted softly. She did like her landlord. Yet, at the same time, she was grateful he hadn't taken the initiative and contacted her again. If he had, she wasn't sure how she would've responded.

"If you're so crazy about him, then do something about it," Carrie said again.

"Like what?" Even if Charlotte had a drawerful of ideas, she doubted she'd ever find the courage to use

any of them. She didn't know how to chase after a man and had no interest in doing so.

"You're asking me?" Carrie asked. "C'mon, who's the kid here?" She launched herself onto the cushion beside Charlotte. "What went wrong?" she asked, looking up at her mother with mournful eyes. "The two of you seemed to be getting along really well when I walked in last week."

Charlotte slid her arm around Carrie's shoulders. Despite her efforts not to, she grinned, remembering when she, too, had been so wise and confident.

"It might've had something to do with the subject of marriage—which *you* brought up. He seemed to get a bit green around the gills at that point."

"You think it frightened him off?" Carrie asked anxiously.

Charlotte shrugged. She'd brought up the subject herself, not quite as directly, but she *had* mentioned it. If ever there was a born bachelor, she decided, it was Jason Manning. Together, mother and daughter had managed to terrify the man. He must think they were sitting in their apartment ready to ambush him, tie him up and drag him in front of the closest preacher.

Charlotte wasn't sure what she wanted anymore. Perhaps she was protecting her ego by convincing herself that she wouldn't have gone out with Jason if he'd asked again. Perhaps it was just her pride. Charlotte didn't know because the opportunity hadn't come up.

She was embarrassed to admit it, but what Carrie had said about her hanging around the mailbox hoping to *accidentally* run into Jason was true. But she wasn't looking for a way to get him to ask her out, she told herself. She only wanted to set things straight. Since they

hadn't met, accidentally or otherwise, Charlotte was content to let it drop. He apparently was, too.

Jason Manning had been a brief but pleasant interlude in her—she had to acknowledge it—humdrum life. She was grateful for their time together. He'd taught her everything she needed to know about basketball. He'd challenged her in a battle of wits about male and female roles in society. Convinced her never again to eat a jalapeño pepper to prove a point. And most important, he'd kissed her in a way that made her believe, for those few minutes, that she was whole and desirable. It'd felt so good to surrender her fears and her doubts. If nothing else, she'd always be grateful for that.

"Maybe he's waiting to hear from you," Carrie said next. "It's your turn to ask him out, isn't it?"

"It doesn't work that way with adults, sweetie." Although Charlotte had no idea if that was even true.

"Then it should. I'm not going to sit home and wait for a man to call me. If I like him, I'll phone him. It's ridiculous to be a slave to such an outdated tradition."

Charlotte agreed with her daughter, but in this instance she planned to do nothing at all. And that included hovering around the mailboxes.

It had been a long day, and Jason was tired when he pulled into the parking lot outside his apartment complex. He scanned the limited spaces, looking for Charlotte's car. The blue PT Cruiser was in the appropriate slot, so he knew she was home.

It wasn't that he was trying to run into her, but he wouldn't mind seeing her, finding out how she was doing—that sort of thing. He didn't intend anything more than a wave and maybe a friendly "I'm-fine-how-

are-you?" exchange. Then he'd go about his business and she could go about hers.

Not calling Charlotte was proving to be more difficult than he'd ever expected. He thought about her even more now. He dreamed about her. Just that morning, the alarm had gone off and he was lying there in bed, trying to force himself to get up, when Charlotte casually sauntered into his mind. He couldn't help thinking how good it would feel to have her there beside him, how soft her body would feel next to his. He'd banished the thought immediately, angry about indulging in such a fantasy.

It had started the night before. When he'd arrived home from work, he'd found himself checking out the rear tire of Charlotte's car. From a distance it looked like it might be low on air. On closer examination, he realized it wasn't. He felt almost disappointed not to have an excuse to speak to her.

This evening he could tell from a distance that there wasn't anything wrong with her tires. Once again he wished there was, so he could talk to her.

Inside his apartment, he reached for the remote control and automatically turned on the television. The six-thirty news crew made for excellent company.

As the forecaster gave dire warnings about the weather, Jason checked out the meager contents of his refrigerator. One of these days he'd have to break down and buy groceries.

As he suspected, nothing interesting presented itself, at least nothing he'd seriously consider eating. An empty cardboard carton from a six-pack of beer. A can of half-eaten pork and beans. A leftover taco, probably harder than cement, wrapped in a napkin, and a jar of

green olives. He opened the jar, stuck his hand inside and fished out the last two, returning the container of liquid to the shelf. Chewing on the olives, he closed the door.

What he was really in the mood for was—he hated to admit it. What he'd really like was chocolate chip cookies. Well, he could forget that. The store-bought ones tasted like lumpy paste, and his mother would keep him on the phone with an endless list of questions if he were to call her and request a batch. Besides, it wasn't his mother's recipe he craved. It was Charlotte's.

Well, you can forget that, ol' boy.

A box of macaroni and cheese was the most interesting prospect his cupboard had to offer. He took it out and checked the freezer compartment of the refrigerator and brought out two frozen wieners wrapped in aluminum foil.

He was adding water to a pan when there was a frantic knocking on his door. Whoever it was pounded again before he had time to cross the apartment.

He saw Charlotte, pale and stricken, her lavender cardigan covered in blood. Her eyes were panicky. "A dog…someone ran over a dog…they didn't even stop. Please…can you come?"

"Of course." He kept a black bag at the house for just such emergencies. He grabbed that and hurried after her.

Charlotte was waiting for him, her eyes bright with tears. "He's unconscious."

"You moved him?"

"Only to get him out of the street."

"Did you see it happen?" he asked, trotting along behind her.

"No. I heard tires screech and a yelp, and that was it. By the time I got outside, a few kids had gathered around, but no one knew what to do."

Her pace slowed as they approached the injured animal. A group of neighborhood children had gathered around. Jason knelt beside the small, black dog. He was a mixed breed, mostly spaniel, Jason guessed. He was badly hurt and in shock. Probably a stray, since he wasn't wearing a collar, and the poor thing looked mangy and thin.

"Does anyone know who he belongs to?" Jason asked.

"I don't think he belongs to anyone," a boy on a bicycle answered. "He's been around the last couple of days. I never saw him before that."

"I'm going to take him to my office," Jason said after a preliminary examination. He didn't feel too positive about the dog's chances.

"Is he going to live?" Charlotte alone voiced the question, but she seemed to be the spokesperson for the small gathering—each one wanted, indeed needed, to know. The children and Charlotte stared down at Jason, waiting for his response.

"I'm not sure," Jason answered honestly. "He's got a broken leg and internal injuries."

"I'll pay for his medical expenses," Charlotte offered, using her index finger to wipe a tear from her eye.

Jason wasn't even thinking about the expenses. Frankly, he didn't think the dog would last the night. "Give me your sweater," he told Charlotte. Since it was already stained with blood, he figured they'd save time by using it to transport the injured dog.

She did as he asked, and he spread it out on the pave-

ment, then placed the wounded dog on it. Jason carefully lifted him, using the sweater sleeves, and walked toward his car.

"I'll go with you," Charlotte said, while Jason placed the now-unconscious dog in the backseat.

"You're sure?" he asked. "This could take some time."

"I'm sure." Carrie came running up to the car. The girl had tears in her eyes, too. Mother and daughter briefly hugged before Carrie stepped away. She looked so mournful it was all Jason could do not to stop and reassure her. But he had no reassurances to offer.

His veterinary clinic was only a few blocks from the apartment complex. Charlotte followed him in. He set the injured dog on the stainless-steel examination table and turned on the lights above it. Charlotte's sweater was soaked with blood beyond the point of salvaging it, but she didn't seem concerned.

Jason examined the dog's injuries and it was as he'd feared: surgery would be required.

He told Charlotte and she nodded bravely. "Can I do anything? I'm not a nurse, but I'd like to assist—that is, if you think I'd be any help?"

Jason hesitated, uncertain, then decided. "You can if you really want to."

She nodded. "Please."

"You don't have to," he said. This wasn't going to be pretty and if she was the least bit squeamish, it would be better to sit out in the waiting room. He told her as much.

"I want to," she said confidently. "I can handle it."

Jason didn't take long to set up everything he needed for the surgery. They both scrubbed down and he gave

her a green surgical cap and gown. He smiled at her before administering the anesthesia, taking pains to explain what he was doing and why.

The procedure didn't last more than an hour. When he'd finished, he transferred the dog to the hospital portion of his facility. There was a night-time staff member who'd watch over the spaniel and the other pets who required continuous care.

"What do you think?" she asked hopefully when he returned.

"It doesn't look promising," Jason told her. He didn't want to give her any false hopes or mislead her. "But he might surprise us. He's only a couple of years old and he's got a strong heart. The next twenty-four hours will be critical. If he survives until tomorrow night, then he should do okay. But he's going to need a lot of attention and love afterward."

"Carrie and I will make sure he gets it. Can we come see him?" She paused. "Do veterinary hospitals have visiting hours?"

"You can come anytime you like." He sighed and rubbed his hand along the back of his neck. He was tired and hungry.

"You were wonderful...." She seemed to sense his worry and exhaustion.

"Let's decide that in the morning."

"If Higgins lives, we'll owe everything to you."

"Higgins?"

"I thought it was a good name. Do you like it?"

He shrugged. He was too tired and too hungry to have much of an opinion on anything at the moment.

"You haven't had dinner, have you?" she surprised him by asking.

"No. How'd you know that?"

"You look hungry."

"That's because I am. You want to grab something?" he asked as if it were the most natural thing in the world.

She smiled. "Only this time I'll treat."

"Charlotte…"

"I insist. Please don't argue."

He didn't have the energy to protest, so he simply agreed. Since she was buying, he let her choose the restaurant. She decided on a nearby sandwich shop. He breathed in the scent of freshly baked bread as soon as he walked in the door.

It was the type of place where customers seated themselves and the silverware was wrapped in a red checkered napkin. The waitress, who looked all of sixteen, took their order, and promptly brought coffee. She came back a few minutes later with six-inch-high sandwiches, layered with sliced turkey, ham, roast beef, lettuce, tomato slices and onion.

"How have you been?" he asked casually after wolfing down the first half of his sandwich.

"Until the accident tonight I was just fine," Charlotte told him, her eyes flitting away from his. "I don't know what came over me. I'm usually not so emotional, but seeing that poor little dog on the road bleeding and hurt like that really got to me."

"It gets to me, too." The sight of an innocent animal suffering never failed to disturb Jason, although he saw it time and time again. The helplessness of the situation, the complete disregard for life that a hit-and-run accident revealed, angered him.

"I'm so glad you were home," Charlotte said, keep-

ing her gaze lowered. "I don't know what I would have done otherwise."

"I'm glad I was there, too." He reached across the table, taking her hand, linking their fingers. Her skin was smooth and soft, just the way he remembered.

His eyes sought hers. He smiled and she smiled back. Jason felt ridiculously, unreasonably pleased that they were together. For days he'd been fighting it, and now that they were together, he felt foolish for having put up such a struggle. He should quit worrying about the future, he told himself. Live for the moment. Wasn't that what all the self-help books said? One day at a time. One kiss at a time.

After what seemed like an eternity, Charlotte dragged her eyes from his.

"How about dessert?" he asked.

Charlotte picked up the menu and read over the limited selection.

"I was thinking more along the lines of homemade chocolate chip cookies," Jason said.

"They don't seem to have... Oh, you mean *mine?*" She raised eyes as blue as a summer sky.

He nodded enthusiastically. "I've reconsidered. It's true." His voice sounded slightly hoarse and, if he didn't know better, seductive.

"What is?"

"The way to my heart takes a direct route through my stomach."

"Oh." She blinked as if he'd caught her off guard. She was beautiful, he realized all over again. So gentle and caring. He'd missed her, yet he'd tried to convince himself otherwise, and had been doing a good job of it, too—too good, in fact.

The world seemed to stop. Jason knew his breathing did. He felt as if he were drowning in her eyes. He would've liked to blame it on how tired he was, but he'd only be lying to himself.

"You like softball?" he found himself asking next.

She nodded, obviously trying to keep her eyes averted from his. Apparently she was having a difficult time of it, because whenever their eyes met, it would be several moments before she looked away.

"I understand softball, more than basketball at any rate," she said, sounding slightly breathless.

"My brothers and I play on a team Saturday mornings. Do you and Carrie want to come and watch this weekend?"

Charlotte nodded.

"Good."

They were both silent on the way home. Jason knew he was going to kiss her again. He couldn't imagine *not* kissing her again.

Charlotte must have read his intentions, because her hand was on the car door the minute he shut off the engine. She reminded him of a trapped bird, eager to escape, and yet she didn't move.

His hand on her shoulder turned her toward him. His heart tripped wildly as she leaned toward him. He felt sure her heart was pounding as furiously as his.

Slowly, so slowly he wondered if he was dreaming it, Charlotte swayed closer. He lowered his mouth to hers. Jason wanted this kiss, wanted it more than he could remember wanting anything. It'd been over a week since he'd seen her and it felt like a lifetime. A thousand lifetimes.

Charlotte's hands were braced against his chest as he kissed her again, deeper, more fully. Again he kissed her, and again. Finally she broke away.

"Stop," she pleaded. The words were breathless and he could feel her shudder.

Reluctantly, Jason pulled back. Their eyes met again, and for the second time that night, Jason had the feeling she was frightened, although he didn't understand why. Wanting to comfort her, he traced a knuckle down the curve of her cheek.

"Carrie will be worried," she said.

He said nothing.

"I can't thank you enough. For saving Higgins. The dog."

Again Jason said nothing.

"Jason," she whispered. "Don't look at me like that."

"Like what?"

"Like you want to kiss me again."

"I do." He wasn't going to lie about it.

He saw that her hand was shaking as she opened the car door and climbed out. She seemed eager to make her escape now.

"Good night," she said with obvious false cheer.

"Little coward," Jason muttered under his breath, amused. "Saturday morning!" he shouted after her.

"What time?" She turned to face him again.

"Nine-thirty. Is that too early?"

"I'll be ready."

"I'll call you in the morning about Higgins."

"Please," she said, her eyes widening as though she'd momentarily forgotten the dog. "Oh, please do." She snapped open her purse and withdrew a business card,

walking toward him now. "This is my number at the office. I'll be there after nine."

"Then I'll phone at nine."

"'Night."

"'Night," he echoed, returning to his apartment.

He wasn't there more than five minutes when his doorbell chimed. He certainly wasn't in the mood for company, but as the building owner and manager, he couldn't very well ignore a visitor.

He opened his door to discover Carrie standing on the other side, a covered plastic bowl in her hand. "These are for you."

He accepted the container with a puzzled frown.

"Mom asked me to bring you some chocolate chip cookies," she said, grinning broadly.

Five

"Mom, you look fine."

"I don't look fine... I look wretched," Charlotte insisted, viewing her backside in the hallway mirror. She must've been mad to let Carrie talk her into buying jeans. Fashionably faded jeans, no less. Not only had she plunked down ninety bucks for the pair, they looked as if they'd spent the past ten years in someone's attic.

"You're acting like a little kid," Carrie said, slapping her hands against her sides in disgust. "We're going to a softball game, not the senior prom."

"Why didn't you tell me my thighs are so...round?" Charlotte cried in despair. "No woman wants to be seen in pants that make her legs look like hot dogs. I'm not going anywhere."

Carrie just rolled her eyes.

"Call Jason," Charlotte told her daughter. "Tell him...anything. Make up some excuse."

"You can't be serious."

"Please do as I say."

"Mom?"

"We're meeting his *family*," Charlotte cried. "I can't meet his brothers and sisters-in-law looking like this."

"Change clothes, then, if you're so self-conscious."

As though she had anything to change into. Charlotte's wardrobe was limited to business suits and sweatpants. There was no in-between. She couldn't afford to clothe both of them in expensive jeans. But after Jason had invited her out for today, she'd allowed Carrie to talk her into a shopping spree. Thank heaven for Visa. And thank heaven for Jason's generosity; he'd refused to accept any payment for the dog's care.

"I'm not calling Jason!" Carrie crossed her arms righteously. The girl had a streak of stubbornness a mile wide, and Charlotte had collided with it more than once.

Defeated, Charlotte muttered under her breath and fled to her room, sitting on the end of her bed. Before the shopping trip, she'd managed to put today's plans out of her mind and focus her attention on Higgins. Then the softball game had turned into the better part of a day, including a picnic, involving most of his family.

"Mom," Carrie said, approaching her carefully. "What's wrong?"

Charlotte shrugged, not sure how to explain her nervousness. "I wish I'd never agreed to this."

"But why?" Carrie wanted to know. "I've been looking forward to it all week. Just think of all the babysitting prospects. Jason's family is a potential gold mine for me." Carrie sat on the bed beside Charlotte. "We're going, aren't we?"

Charlotte nodded. She was overreacting, and she knew it. After shelling out ninety bucks she was wearing those jeans, no matter how they made her look.

"Good," Carrie said, leaping excitedly to her feet.

"I've got the picnic basket packed. Honestly, Mom, we're bringing so much food, we could open a concession stand."

"I didn't want to run short." Charlotte didn't bother denying that she'd packed enough to feed Jason's entire family. A fruit-and-cheese plate, sandwiches, potato salad, a batch of chocolate chip cookies and a variety of other goodies she'd thrown in at the last minute.

Jason had casually mentioned the picnic the day before, when she'd gone to the hospital to visit Higgins. The dog was just beginning to respond to them. He was recovering slowly, but according to Jason, they'd be able to bring him home within a week. Charlotte soon discovered that visiting her new dog was a dual-edged sword. Every time she was at the veterinary hospital, she ran into Jason. Usually they had a cup of coffee together and talked; once he'd suggested dinner and Charlotte hadn't been able to dredge up a single excuse not to join him. He'd even taken her and Carrie to a movie. Now she was meeting his family, and it terrified her.

Ten minutes later, as Charlotte was rearranging their picnic basket to find room for a tablecloth and paper napkins, Jason arrived.

Carrie answered the door and directed him to the kitchen.

"Jason's here," she said unnecessarily.

"Hi." Charlotte greeted him nervously, turning around, a tense smile on her face. She was watching him carefully, wanting to read his expression when he saw her in the tight jeans.

"Hi, I was just—" He stopped abruptly, letting whatever he meant to say fade into nothingness. He stood

before her, his mouth dangling open. Slowly his eyes widened.

With appreciation.

At least she thought it was appreciation. She prayed that was what it was, and not disgust or shock or any of the emotions she'd endured that morning.

"I… I've got everything ready." She rubbed her suddenly damp hands down her thighs. "Carrie says I've packed too much food, but I don't think so. I hope you like cantaloupe, because I just added one." She knew she was chattering aimlessly, but couldn't seem to stop.

"You look…fabulous."

"I do?" Charlotte hated how uncertain she sounded.

Jason nodded as though he wouldn't be able to take his eyes off her long enough to play ball, which had to be the nicest compliment he'd ever paid her.

"Carrie talked me into buying the jeans," she mumbled, tossing the napkins on top of the heap and closing the lid as far as it would go.

"Remind me to thank her."

He didn't say any more, just reached for the basket and brought it out to the car. Charlotte was so relieved, she wanted to weep with gratitude. Her spirits lifted— more than lifted—they soared as she and Carrie followed him. Carrie climbed in the backseat as Charlotte got in the front, hoping her jeans wouldn't split.

The ball field was several miles away, near the Southcenter shopping mall. Charlotte was grateful to Carrie for carrying the conversation. Thrilled with the outing, the girl had plenty to say.

Charlotte had never been to this park before, and when she saw it she was astonished she hadn't heard of it. It had several baseball diamonds, and an equal

number of soccer fields. The Green River intersected the park, with several footbridges spanning its banks.

"I didn't mention I was bringing anyone," Jason told her after he'd parked the car. "Everyone's going to ask you a bunch of embarrassing questions. Do you mind?"

"No," she answered, having trouble meeting his eyes. "Don't worry about it." She was a big girl—she could deal with a bit of curiosity.

"I don't usually bring someone."

Charlotte stiffened, not because she was timid or dreaded the questions, but because it confirmed something she'd rather not deal with right then. Jason was attracted to her. As attracted as she was to him.

What did bring fear to her heart was that he might be taking their time together seriously—that he might really start to care for her. That would be disastrous. *You care for him,* her heart reminded her. Yes, but that was different.

Kissing was all they'd done; it was all Charlotte had allowed. A few innocent kisses didn't amount to much. Or did they?

"Uncle Jase!" Two boys—Charlotte guessed they were seven or eight—raced across the green lawn toward Jason. One glance told her the pair were identical twins.

"Hello, boys," Jason said with a wide smile.

They stopped abruptly when they noticed Charlotte and Carrie, their eyes huge and questioning. Suspicious.

"These are my friends, Charlotte and Carrie," Jason said, motioning toward them.

"They're *girls,*" one of the pair muttered.

"I noticed that myself," a tall, athletic man said as he strode toward them. He was wearing the same uni-

form as Jason. Charlotte didn't need an introduction to know this was his brother.

"This is Paul, my oldest brother," Jason said, tucking a couple of baseball bats under his arm, along with his mitt. The task appeared to demand a great deal of attention.

In the next five minutes, Charlotte was introduced to Leah, Paul's wife, who was five months pregnant and chasing after a toddler named Kelsey. Jason's younger brother, Rich, his wife, Jamie, and their two children, Bethany and Jeremy, arrived shortly afterward, and there was another series of introductions.

Charlotte's head was spinning with all the names and faces. Everyone was friendly and helpful. Openly curious, too. Carrie, who loved children, was delighted when Rich's daughter wanted to sit in the bleachers with her.

The men were on the diamond warming up when Jamie sat next to Charlotte. Leah joined them, sitting on her other side. Charlotte smiled from one to the other. Their curiosity was almost visible. As the silence lengthened Charlotte frantically sorted through a number of possible topics, but try as she might, the most inventive thing she could think of was the weather.

Oh, what the heck, she decided. "I imagine you're curious about me," she said. After the morning she'd had, she wasn't up to a game of Twenty Questions.

"We didn't mean to be so blatant about it," Leah, the shorter of the two, murmured. She had one of the nicest smiles Charlotte had ever seen.

"You weren't," Charlotte lied.

"Yes, we were," Jamie said with a laugh. "We can't help it."

"Ask away," Charlotte invited.

"How long have you known Jason?" Rich's wife asked without hesitation.

Charlotte found Jamie Manning to be a study in contrasts. Rich, Jamie's husband, was probably one of the best-looking men she'd ever seen. Definitely *GQ* material. Yet, at first glance, his wife seemed rather plain. Charlotte soon learned how misleading first impressions could be. Five minutes with Jamie, and Charlotte was awed by her radiance. She had an inner glow that touched those around her.

"I met Jason about a year ago," Charlotte answered, when she realized both women were staring at her, waiting for her response. "My daughter and I live in one of his apartments."

"A year," Jamie repeated, leaning forward so she could exchange a wide-eyed look with Leah. "Did you hear that? He's known her a whole year."

Charlotte felt she should explain further. "Actually, I met him a year ago, but we've only recently started to, uh, know each other."

"I see." Once again it was Leah who spoke, wearing a subtle smile as though she was amused and trying to disguise it.

"You'll have to forgive us for acting so surprised, but Jason doesn't usually bring anyone with him on Saturdays," Leah elaborated.

"Or any other day for that matter," Jamie added.

"So I understand. I… I take it he doesn't date often?" Charlotte asked. In some ways she was hoping they'd tell her he went through women like water. But in her heart she knew it wasn't true. If anything, it was just the opposite. Charlotte didn't want to hear that, either,

didn't want to know she was special, because it made everything so much more difficult.

"Let's put it this way," Jamie answered, crossing her legs and resting her elbows on her knees. "We've been coming out here for what, two, three summers now, and this is the first time Jason's ever brought a woman."

Charlotte drew in a slow, deep breath.

"I don't remember Jason bringing a woman to any family function, ever," Leah said, looking positively delighted. Her eyes sparkled. "I'd say it was about time, wouldn't you, Jamie?"

"About time, indeed," Leah's sister-in-law said with a grin.

From his position on the diamond, Jason could see his two sisters-in-law on either side of Charlotte. No doubt they were pumping her for information, wanting to know every minute detail of their relationship. The distance was too great for him to be able to read Charlotte's expression.

If he had half a brain, he would've realized what he was doing before he invited her to join him. Why had he asked Charlotte to this game? Clearly he needed his head examined. Only an idiot would thrust a lamb like Charlotte into a pack of hounds without warning.

He'd told her his family would probably be curious about her, but he'd said it casually in the parking lot after they'd arrived. It wasn't like he'd given her much advance warning.

His family was far too nosy. By the end of the afternoon, Charlotte would be so sick of answering questions, she'd never want to go out with him again.

He pitched the ball to Paul with enough force to make

his oldest brother remove his mitt, shake his hand and cast Jason an odd look.

Jason was angry. But it wasn't the way Leah and Jamie had surrounded Charlotte that had set him off. He'd had no business inviting Charlotte and Carrie to this game. For one thing, they were playing the league leaders and likely to be soundly defeated. If he was going to ask someone to come and watch them play ball, it should be against a team that'd make him look good, not like a bunch of fools. The outcome could prove to be downright embarrassing.

Not only were they likely to get their butts kicked, but Charlotte was going to spend the entire time being interrogated. First by Jamie and Leah, and then, when the game was over, by his brothers. They wouldn't be subtle about it, either. The first woman he'd cared about in years was going to come away thinking his family had been trained by the CIA.

Even now, Jason wasn't sure what had prompted him to ask Charlotte to come. But he certainly remembered the night he'd done it....

They'd been sitting in the car outside the apartment the night of Higgins's surgery. She'd been shaken by the accident, struggling to hide how much. He had known when he dropped her off that he was going to kiss her again. She'd known it, too. His lips had brushed hers. Lightly. Briefly. He had sensed she was still frightened—of him? Of their mutual passion? Of her own desires? Until she was at ease with him, he was content to proceed slowly. He'd never indulged in any kisses more sensual or seductive than those he'd shared with Charlotte.

He could tell she was a novice when it came to love-

making. That surprised him because she'd been married. He'd never asked about her ex-husband, preferring to wait until she was comfortable enough to talk about it on her own. But from what Carrie had told him the day she'd come to his office, the marriage had been short and disastrous.

Jason was convinced Charlotte hadn't realized how much he enjoyed their kissing sessions. How much holding her satisfied him. How she left him feeling dizzy with need.

The same magic that had made him kiss her that night had encouraged him to risk inviting her to the ball game. Only now did he understand what he'd done. He'd dragged Charlotte into an impossible situation. Carrie, too. He was glad they were with him, but he wished he'd thought of some other way of introducing Charlotte and her daughter to his family. Some other time, when he'd be at her side to ward off their curiosity.

"Jase!" Rich's voice shot past his ear two seconds after a ball nearly creamed the side of his head.

Stunned, Jason took two steps backward.

"What's wrong with you?" Rich demanded furiously.

"You mean you don't know?" Paul shouted from the shortstop position. He looked pointedly toward the stands. "It seems to me that he's met his Waterloo."

After nearly getting his head knocked off by a fly ball, Jason focused his concentration on the game, which to his surprise wasn't going badly. Every now and then he could hear a high-pitched shout, which he'd like to think came from Charlotte. By the end of the seventh inning the score was tied.

Jason came to bat at the bottom of the ninth. The all-important ninth inning. The score remained tied and

there were already two outs. Either he pulled off a hit or they were going into extra innings.

Charlotte was sitting in the stands almost directly behind him. He set the bat over his shoulder and eyed the pitcher. The first pitch was a fast ball and Jason swung, determined to hit it out of the field. More to the point, he was hoping not to be embarrassed in front of Charlotte.

He heard the cracking of the wood against the ball and he dropped the bat, then started running as though his life depended on making it to first base. It wasn't until he got there that he realized he'd hit a home run. He felt jubilant as he rounded the bases.

He cast his eyes toward the bleachers to find Charlotte on her feet, cheering and clapping. Her face was bright with excitement. In all his life, Jason had never felt such elation.

He crossed home plate and didn't stop. His brothers, his whole team, stared at him as he trotted behind the protective barrier between home plate and the viewing stands and headed straight for Charlotte. Excitedly, she launched herself into his arms.

Jason grabbed her around her waist, lifted her from the bleachers and swung her down. Her eyes shone with happiness and Jason thought he'd never seen a more beautiful woman.

Charlotte threw back her head and laughed. It wasn't for several minutes that Jason was even aware of the crowd that had gathered around them.

A bit self-conscious now, he lowered Charlotte to the ground, but kept his arm around her. Paul and Rich were the first to congratulate him, followed by several other teammates, who slapped him heartily on the back.

One suggested Jason bring Charlotte again, since she was definitely his good-luck charm.

"You were wonderful," Charlotte said, smiling at him proudly. Jason found it difficult to pull his gaze away. The urge to kiss her was so strong, he had to fight to restrain himself. He would've done it, too, would've kissed her in front of everyone and ignored the consequences, if only his brothers hadn't been present. He held back more to protect Charlotte from embarrassment than to ward off any razzing he'd get from his family.

"I'm hungry," Ryan, one of the twins, announced once the excitement had died down. "When are we gonna eat?"

"Soon," Leah promised. Paul headed toward the parking lot.

"I'll be right back," Jason said and, without thinking, did the very thing he'd decided against. He kissed Charlotte briefly, before trailing after his brother to get the picnic basket in the trunk of his car.

Jason couldn't believe he'd done that. Neither could Charlotte, judging by the look of surprise that flashed in her blue eyes.

"Are you going to fess up?" Paul asked, holding a heavy cooler with both hands, studying Jason.

"To what?" he demanded, narrowing his eyes, hoping his brother would take the hint.

"Charlotte."

"What about her?"

"Don't go all defensive on me. I was just wondering how you met."

Jason relaxed a little. He was being too touchy. "She lives in the complex." He didn't think it would sound

good if he admitted Carrie had offered him money to take her mother out.

"She seems nice."

"She is. Lay off her, though, will you?"

Paul's eyes went solemn, as if he was offended by Jason's remark. Then he nodded. "Whatever you want."

Paul must've said something to Rich, too, because when they sat down to eat, after pushing three picnic tables together, no one gave Charlotte more than a glance. It was as though she'd been part of the family for years. Which was just the way Jason wanted everyone to treat her. Heaven forbid she figure out how special she was to him. He'd already made a big enough fool of himself, simply by inviting her and Carrie to this outing.

Charlotte's daughter had won a few hearts all on her own, Jason saw, secretly pleased. Ryan and Ronnie had clamored to sit next to her at lunch, beating out Bethany, who cried with disappointment until Carrie agreed to hold the little girl on her lap.

"I think Carrie's made a conquest," Jason said to Charlotte, munching on a chocolate chip cookie. His fourth, and he was ready for another.

"She loves children. She's the type of kid who'd prefer to be the oldest of ten."

Jason watched as a sadness, however brief, flashed in Charlotte's eyes. It told him she wasn't speaking only for Carrie, but herself, as well. She must've wanted so much more from her marriage than she'd gotten. He remembered something else then, something Carrie had told him about Charlotte wanting more children. At the time he'd decided to stay away. A woman with marriage and children on her mind was someone he

planned to avoid. Strangely, the thought didn't terrify him nearly as much now.

Still, he had to admit that the fleeting look of pain got to him. He'd experienced the desire to protect her in the past, to guard her from hurt, but only when she was in his arms. Only when he feared *he* might hurt her. Now, the need to keep her safe burned in his chest. He wanted to block out anything that would cause her pain. Most of all, he wanted to meet the ex-husband who'd walked away from his family, and he'd prefer it be in a dark alley some night.

Although he didn't know any details of the divorce, Carrie had told him she never heard from her father. What kind of man would desert his family? What kind of man would turn a warm, vivacious woman like Charlotte into a near-recluse?

"I like your family," Charlotte said, smiling up at him, distracting him from his thoughts.

"Did Leah and Jamie bombard you with questions?"

"A few, but they're so nice, I didn't mind."

"What did you tell them?" Jason was eager to know, partially because it might clear up a few questions he had himself. Maybe Charlotte could put into perspective what he was feeling and was unable to define.

She laughed, causing the others to momentarily look their way. "Are you worried?"

"No." The question surprised him.

"For a moment there, you looked as if you were afraid I might've told them something you'd rather I didn't."

"You can tell them anything you want," he said decisively, meaning it. If she chose to imply that they were madly in love, then fine, he'd deal with it. On the other

hand, if she'd chosen to let his family believe they'd only just met, which wasn't so far from the truth, then he'd live with that, too.

"I told them we're friends...special friends."

Jason approved. He couldn't have said it better.

"Uncle Jase," Ronnie shouted, clutching a Frisbee. "Are we ready to play?"

"Play?" Jason didn't need to be invited twice. His favorite part of these family get-togethers was the time after lunch that he spent with his nieces and nephews. Chasing after Ronnie and Ryan and a Frisbee kept him young at heart, he told himself. Though he didn't care to admit out loud just how much he liked running around with a pair of eight-year-olds. The boys enjoyed it, too, and before the afternoon was over Rich and Paul invariably joined in.

As they did now. The two brothers against Jason and a handful of youngsters in a game of Frisbee football. A few minutes into the competition, Jason dived to catch a wild throw, catapulting himself into the air and latching triumphantly on to the disk.

Ronnie and Ryan cheered, and Jason felt as pleased with his small feat as he'd been with the home run. After an hour, the two teams took a break. Breathless, he reached for a cold soda, pulled back the tab and guzzled it down.

He turned, looking for Charlotte. The last time he'd seen her she was with Leah and Jamie cleaning up the remains of their picnic. He saw her sitting on a blanket under a madrona tree, bouncing Jeremy on her knee. Bethany and Kelsey were sprawled out, napping, beside her. She was playing a game with the baby, nuzzling

his neck and making cooing sounds. Her eyes radiated a happiness he'd never seen. A joy that transfixed him.

"Jason, are you in or out?"

Jason barely heard the words, his gaze on Charlotte.

"In," he decided, tossing the empty can in the garbage and heading back to the field. A couple of minutes later he was completely engrossed in the game. Carrie had sided with his brothers against him and was proving to be a worthy opponent. Ronnie caught the Frisbee and lobbed it to his twin. Jason glanced toward Charlotte again and saw her lift Jeremy above her head and laugh up at him.

Jason's heart constricted. Watching Charlotte with his brother's child did funny things to his chest. She was smiling, happy. A powerful emotion seized his heart in a way that was almost painful.

One pain was followed almost immediately by another as the Frisbee hit him hard. The wind momentarily knocked out of him, he doubled over.

"Uncle Jase!"

"Jason!"

Paul and Ronnie were the first to reach him.

"You all right?" Paul asked.

Jason's eyes moved toward Charlotte and he shook his head. "No," he muttered, "I don't think I am."

Six

So this was what it meant to be part of a family, Charlotte mused, as Jason drove her and Carrie home from the ball field. This profound sense of belonging, of acceptance. She'd never experienced anything like it before. It was as though Jason's family had known and loved her for years. As though they genuinely cared for her. Charlotte couldn't recall a time when she'd felt anything as uplifting as she had that afternoon.

After the game they'd gathered together for a picnic. Charlotte didn't think she'd ever laughed more. There'd been good-natured teasing, jokes, games. Even now, driving home, laughter echoed in her ears. The cousins were as close as brothers and sisters, the older ones watching out for the smaller children. They fought like brothers and sisters, too, mostly over Carrie, each wanting her attention.

Carrie had beamed, loving every minute of it.

After the initial round of questions, Leah and Jamie had treated Charlotte like...well, like family. The women were obviously good friends, yet included Charlotte in all their conversations. Jason's brothers, too,

had tried to make her feel comfortable. Neither Paul nor Rich had asked a single question about her relationship with Jason, probably content to have their wives fill in the gaps later.

"You're very quiet," Jason said, taking his eyes off the road for a second. "Anything wrong? My brothers didn't—"

"No," she assured him with a smile.

The only sound was the hum of the road. Carrie, usually filled with boundless energy, was exhausted after chasing the children around for most of the afternoon. She'd enjoyed herself as much as Charlotte had.

And perhaps her daughter was thinking the same thing Charlotte was—that she'd missed out on something important because they only had each other.

Jason parked the car, then carried the near-empty picnic basket into her kitchen. He hesitated after setting it on the counter. "You're *sure* nothing's wrong?"

Charlotte nodded. "Positive. I had a wonderful time. A fabulous time. Thank you for asking Carrie and me."

He didn't seem to believe her. "Did Leah and Jamie hound you with questions?" he asked for the second time that day, a pensive frown on his face.

"Jason," she murmured, resting her hands on his forearms and gazing up at him. "I meant it. Every word. This day with you and your brothers and their families was one of the happiest of my life. If I'm being introspective it's because…well, because I've never realized until now how much I've missed in life." Jason's questioning eyes sought hers, as if he wasn't sure he understood.

She managed to meet his eyes. She felt close to Jason just then, closer than she had to anyone, and that con-

fused her. She was falling in love with this man and that was something she couldn't allow. Was it Jason she loved, or his family?

"Charlotte, look at me."

She ignored the request. "I was an only child, too," she told him, "like Carrie." She wanted to explain. "There were never outings that included aunts and uncles or cousins. This is a new experience for Carrie *and* me."

"Look at me," he said again, his voice low and commanding.

Slowly her gaze traveled the length of him, up his chest, over the width of his shoulders, to his eyes. She stared into them and felt a sudden sense of connection. It was a powerful sensation, powerful and exciting.

"Where's Carrie?" Jason asked, glancing over his shoulder.

"She's on the phone in her room. Why?"

"Because I'm going to kiss you."

Charlotte's heart tripped into double time. She was tempted to make some excuse, anything that would put an end to the craziness that overcame her with Jason, but she didn't trust her voice, let alone her heart.

Whatever she might've said was never meant to be. Jason's kiss saw to that. He gathered her in his arms, and lowered his mouth to hers. His lips were there, warm and moist, reminding her of sunshine. The kiss was chaste, yet curiously sensual.

Of her own accord she deepened their kiss. Jason responded quickly.

He moaned, or perhaps it was her own voice making those soft sounds. She melted into him, her body responding instinctively, naturally, to his.

"Charlotte." He brought her even closer, and their kiss went on and on. She grew hot, and hotter, then hotter still...until...

"No more..." she cried, breaking away, panting. "Please...no more."

Jason trembled with restraint, closing his eyes. "You're right," he murmured. "Carrie's in the other room."

"Carrie," Charlotte repeated, grateful for the excuse.

Jason drew in several deep breaths, then said, "I should be leaving."

Charlotte nodded, but she didn't want him to go. Her body was on fire. She wondered if he was experiencing the same kind of torment himself—and if he was angry with her for sending him away.

"Would you like to come with me again next Saturday?" The question was offhanded, as though he'd just thought of it.

Charlotte's heart soared at the prospect. "If you're sure you want me."

Laughter leapt into his eyes, melding with the fire that was already there. "Trust me, Charlotte, I want you."

With that, he was out the door.

No sooner had Jason left than Carrie appeared in the kitchen. "Did Jason leave?"

Charlotte nodded, too preoccupied to answer outright. She was trembling, and all because of a few words. *He wanted her.* He'd been honest and forthright as she'd come to expect.

"Mom, we need to talk."

"Go ahead," Charlotte said, as she unloaded the picnic basket. There was surprisingly little food left over.

Ryan and Ronnie had discovered her chocolate chip cookies, thanks to Jason, and the three dozen she'd brought had disappeared in no time. She'd set out the fresh fruit-and-cheese platter and that had disappeared, too. There were a couple of sandwiches still wrapped, but they'd keep for her and Carrie to eat the following day.

"It's about the ninth-grade dance," Carrie said stiffly from behind her.

Charlotte froze. This wasn't a subject she wanted to discuss, not again. "I've said everything I'm going to say about it, Carrie. The subject is closed."

"I hope you realize you're ruining my entire life," Carrie announced theatrically.

"Dropping you off at the dance and picking you up myself is a reasonable compromise, I think."

"Then you think wrong. I'd…rather walk to school naked than have you drive me to the dance as if…as if there wasn't a single boy in the entire class who wanted to be seen with me."

She sighed. "I'll be happy to pick up Brad, too, if that'll help." That was more than she was really in favor of, but she supposed she could live with it.

"Then everyone will think I asked Brad to the dance. I mean, I know girls do that, but it's important to me that a certain girl find out that Brad asked *me*. How can you do this, Mom? Can't you see how important this is?" Her eyes were imploring, a look designed to melt any mother's heart.

Charlotte steeled herself. "You're too young, Carrie, and that's the end of it."

"You don't understand what you're doing to me!" Carried wailed.

"The subject is closed."

"Fine, ruin my life. See if I care." She stalked out of the kitchen, arms swinging.

With a heavy sigh, Charlotte watched her go. This argument was getting old. She'd been under the impression that her daughter had accepted her decision. But now it was apparent Carrie had only been regrouping, altering her tactics. Cool reason had evolved into implied guilt. Her fifteen-year-old made it sound as though Charlotte had done untold psychological damage by not letting her go on an actual date. Well, so be it, Charlotte decided. This issue was one she didn't intend to back down on any more than she already had.

Pulling out a kitchen chair, Charlotte sank tiredly into it, resting her face in her hands. She sighed again. She had trouble enough raising one child; she was insane to even contemplate having another.

A baby.

But she *did* want another child, so badly she ached with it. Holding Jeremy, Jamie and Rich's little boy, had stirred to life a craving buried deep within her heart. She attempted to push the desire away, rebury it, anything but acknowledge it. She'd had to repress this desire several times over the years.

A baby now was out of the question, she stubbornly reminded herself. She was too old; there were dangers for a woman on the other side of thirty-five. But age was the least of her concerns.

Getting pregnant required a man. Even more problematic, it required making love.

The sadness that weighed down Charlotte's heart felt impossible to carry alone. Tears blurred her eyes. If ever there was a man she could love, it was Jason Man-

ning. But the thought of falling in love again terrified her. Charlotte was afraid of love. Afraid of all the feelings and desires Jason had stirred to life. He was wonderful. His family was wonderful. But it was a painful kind of wonderful, taunting her with all that was never meant to be in her life.

Charlotte had dealt with her share of problems. Finances. Isolation. Low self-esteem. Everything had been a struggle for her. She didn't know how to react to *wonderful*.

For the first time since her divorce, Charlotte felt the protective walls she'd erected around her heart being threatened. Those barriers were fortified by years of disappointment, years of resentment and pain. Now they seemed to be crumbling and all because of a man she'd never even seen without a baseball cap.

For now, Jason was attracted to her, but in her heart she believed his interest in her wouldn't last. It couldn't. The time was fast approaching when she wouldn't be able to put him off, and he'd know. That very afternoon, she'd seen the way he'd trembled in an effort to restrain himself. She'd watched as he'd closed his eyes and drawn in several deep breaths.

Soon kissing wouldn't be enough for him. Soon he'd discover how inadequate she was when it came to making love. She had never satisfied Tom, no matter how hard she'd tried. In the end he'd taunted her, claiming the day would come when she'd realize all the ugly things he'd said about her were true. She didn't have what it took to satisfy a man.

When Jason learned that, he'd start to make excuses not to see her again. He'd regret ever having met her, and worse, he'd regret having introduced her to his family.

She never should've accepted his invitation. It would make everything so much more awkward later....

The tears slipped from her eyes before she was aware she was crying. The soul-deep insecurity, awakened by the memories of her marriage, returned to haunt her. The doubts, the fear and dread, were back, taking up residence in her mind.

Covering her face with her hands, Charlotte swallowed the sobs beginning to spill out in huge swells of emotion. In an effort to gain control, she held her breath so long her lungs ached.

She heard her ex-husband's words—*you aren't woman enough*—inflicting injury all over again until she covered her ears and closed her eyes, wanting to blot them out forever.

Why should Jason fall in love with her when the world was full of whole, sexual women who'd gladly satisfy his needs? Passionate women who'd blossom in his arms and sigh with pleasure and fulfillment. She was incapable of giving a man what he needed. Tom had repeatedly told her so. She was inept as a woman, inept at lovemaking.

"Mom," Carrie said coolly from behind her. "I'm going to Amanda's house." She waited as though she expected Charlotte to object.

Charlotte nodded, then stood and resumed unpacking the picnic basket, not wanting Carrie to see her tears. "Okay, honey. Just don't be late."

"I may never come home again," Carrie said dramatically.

"Dinner's at six."

"All right," Carrie muttered and walked out the door.

* * *

It wasn't until later, much later, while she was in bed finding it impossible to sleep, that Charlotte's thoughts returned to Jason. She'd allowed things to go further than she should have. It was a mistake. One she had to correct at the earliest possible moment. She must've been crazy to let their relationship reach this point.

Crazy or desperate? Charlotte didn't know which. It had all started weeks earlier when she'd held a friend's baby. Funny how she could remember the precise moment with such accuracy. The longing for a child had escalated within her, gaining momentum, refusing to be ignored. She'd gone home and wept and although the tears had finally dried, inside she hadn't stopped weeping.

Shortly after the incident with Kathy Crenshaw and her baby, Charlotte had met Jason. He'd kissed her that first night and it had been... She hadn't tensed or frozen up and that had given her hope. Her confidence continued to grow when he kissed her again and again; he'd always been gentle and undemanding. He was special that way, and she'd be forever grateful for the uncanny gift he had of understanding her needs.

But Jason was a man of raw sensuality. He wouldn't be satisfied with a few chaste kisses for much longer. He had no idea how terrified she was of him, of any man.

No, it was only a matter of time before the best thing that had happened to her in years came abruptly to an end.

On Sunday, Jason wasn't in the mood to cook. Micro-wave popcorn for dinner suited him better than a fro-

zen entrée. He popped a batch and sat down in front of the television to watch a bowling tournament. Not his favorite sport, but there wasn't much to choose from.

When his phone rang, he stood on the sofa and reached across to grab it from the kitchen counter. He was half hoping it was Charlotte.

It wasn't.

"Jase, I don't suppose you've got Charlotte's phone number, do you?" Paul asked cordially enough, only Jason wasn't fooled. As the oldest, his brother sometimes got the notion that he needed to oversee family matters. That didn't include Charlotte, and Jason intended to make sure Paul understood that.

"Jase?"

Of course he had Charlotte's number. "Yeah. What do you want it for?" Suspicions multiplied in his brain. Being a newspaper reporter, Paul was used to getting information out of people.

"Don't get all bent out of shape, little brother. Leah and I want to go to a movie."

"So?"

"So, we'd like Carrie to babysit. She was a real hit with the boys yesterday. You don't mind, do you? The girl's a natural with kids."

"Of course I don't mind." The fact was, Jason felt downright pleased. If Paul and Leah wanted Carrie to babysit, then Charlotte would be at home alone. He could come up with an excuse—Higgins would do— and casually drop in on her.

They needed to talk, and the sooner the better, although it wasn't talking that interested him.

He tossed what remained of his popcorn in the garbage, brushed his teeth and shaved. He even slapped on

some cologne. He wasn't accustomed to using anything more than aftershave, but this evening was an exception.

He was whistling when he'd finished, his spirits high.

On the pretense of asking about next Saturday's ball game, he phoned his brother to be certain Paul had managed to get hold of Carrie. He had. In fact, he'd be picking her up in the next half hour. Allowing ten minutes for Paul to whisk Carrie out of the apartment, that left him with forty minutes to kill.

Forty minutes would go fast, Jason mused, as he sat back down and turned on the TV. But his mind wasn't on the bowling match. A far more intriguing match was playing in his mind. One between Charlotte and him.

Tonight was the night, he decided, determined to take Charlotte beyond the kissing stage. He didn't mean to be calculating and devious about it... Well, yes, he did, Jason thought with a grin.

He'd be gentle with her, he promised himself. Patient and reassuring. For years he'd been treating terrified animals. One stubborn woman shouldn't be any more difficult. He had no intention of pressuring her into anything. Nor would he coerce her if she was at all uncomfortable. He'd lead into lovemaking naturally, spontaneously.

He glanced at his watch, eager now, and was disappointed to see that only ten minutes had passed. Half an hour wasn't *really* very long, but it seemed to feel that way to Jason.

"I'm leaving now, Mom," Carrie called out.

Charlotte walked out of the kitchen, drying her hands on a terry-cloth towel. She smiled at Paul, then looked at her daughter. "Do you know what time you'll be home?"

"Before ten. Don't worry, I know it's a school night."

"I'll have her back closer to nine," Paul assured Charlotte.

"Okay." She nodded. "Have fun."

"I will," Carrie said as they left, offering her first smile of the day. Actually, Charlotte had been talking to Paul, but she let it pass. Carrie was still upset about the school dance and had been cool toward Charlotte all afternoon.

Charlotte had just settled down with a book when there was a knock at the door. *Please, God, don't let it be Jason,* she prayed, but apparently God was occupied elsewhere. Just as she'd feared, she opened the door and came face-to-face with Jason, boyishly handsome in his baseball cap.

"Hi," he said, charming her with his smile. It wasn't fair that a man should be able to wreak such havoc on a woman's heart with a mere movement of the lips.

"Hello." She'd been dreading this moment all day. "I was going to phone you later." A slight exaggeration; she'd been planning to delay calling for as long as possible.

"Oh?"

"Yes… I won't be able to go to the ball game with you next Saturday after all."

"Don't worry about it," he said, making himself comfortable on her sofa. He anchored his ankle on the opposite knee and grinned up at her. "There'll be plenty of other Saturdays. The summer is filled with Saturdays."

It was awkward for her to be standing, while he seemed completely at home. So Charlotte sat, too— as far away from him as she could while still being on the same sofa. She angled her legs sideways, her hands

clasped. "I'm afraid I won't be able to make it any other Saturday, either."

A pause followed her announcement. "Why not?"

"I... I..." She couldn't look at him. "I don't think it's a good idea for us to see each other anymore."

"Uh-huh." He didn't reveal his reactions one way or another.

Emotion seemed to thicken the air. He might not be *saying* anything, but he was feeling it. Charlotte was, too.

"Is it something I said?"

She lowered her eyes farther and shook her head.

"Something I did?"

"No... Oh, please, Jason, just accept this. Don't make it any more difficult than it already is." Her voice, which had remained steady until then, cracked.

"Charlotte," Jason said, moving next to her with startling agility. "For heaven's sake, what's wrong?"

She covered her mouth with one hand and closed her eyes.

"I'm not leaving until you tell me," he said.

"I can't."

"Why can't you?"

"Because!" she cried, leaping to her feet. "Everything would've been all right if you hadn't been so... so nice." She was angry now, unreasonably angry, and not quite sure why.

Jason stood, too, his gaze holding hers. "I'm not sorry I kissed you. Nothing would make me regret that."

His words made it all so difficult. She wasn't sorry, either.

Her expression must have told him as much. He relaxed visibly and reached for her, gently holding her

shoulders. Slowly, he drew her forward. Charlotte had no resistance left, and walked right into his embrace.

She sobbed once, then hid her face in his chest and wept openly.

Jason stroked her hair and whispered reassurances in her ear, as if she were a small child needing comforting. In some ways, she was exactly that.

After several minutes he lifted her face upward to meet his mouth. Over and over again he kissed her, lightly, softly, gently. Her breathing grew shallow.

"Jason…"

"Yes?" He raised his head, his eyes meeting hers.

"You're doing it again."

His mouth curved into a deliberate smile. "I know."

Her hands were against his chest when he sought her mouth again. He was still gentle, but the kisses changed in texture and intensity. Their lips were fused together, the heat between them burning so fierce, she thought it might scorch her. Charlotte found it difficult to breathe, but she didn't care. Breathing wasn't important. She held on, her hands clutching his upper arms.

Jason led her back to the sofa, and without protest, Charlotte followed. He sat down and brought her into his lap. He didn't give her the opportunity to protest before he directed her lips back to his. When her mouth opened in exultant welcome, he moaned. He kissed her again and again, until she was panting. Until her heart seemed to stop beating. Until there was nothing in her world but him.

His hands were opening the front of her blouse even before she realized his intent.

"Jason, no," she said in a panic. "Please, no."

"All right." Jason twisted around and turned off the

light. The room dimmed and shadows danced across the walls. "Is this better?" he asked.

Charlotte clamped her eyes shut. "I... I'm not very good at this," she whispered, close to tears. "I'm not... sexy enough." The only thing that kept her from springing free of his hold was fear. It held her immobile.

"You're beautiful," he whispered. "Charlotte, do you hear me? You're perfect."

She buried her hands in his hair. His cap was gone, but she didn't remember when he'd removed it. Or if he had. She sighed.

He kissed her again, his mouth hard and hungry. Charlotte understood his hunger, but she wasn't capable of satisfying it. "No," she whispered when she could.

"No?" How disappointed he sounded.

"No," she said a second time.

"You're sure of that?" he asked, sounding regretful.

"Y-yes."

He nodded, kissed her once more, then inhaled sharply. "I just wanted to check."

Seven

"Who told you that you aren't sexy?" Jason asked, relaxing on her sofa.

Charlotte's hands stilled as she poured coffee into two mugs.

How do you expect a man to get excited when his wife's such a cold fish? No wonder you're a failure at lovemaking. Are you sure you're even a woman?

Charlotte's heart reeled as Tom's words returned to haunt her. She'd laid to rest as much of his vindictiveness as she could, bound her wounds and gone on with her life. Pulling away the bandage, examining the damage now, just seemed pointless.

"Charlotte?" he probed gently.

"My ex-husband," she muttered.

"He's wrong, you know."

She nodded, rather than argue with Jason. For the moment he was infatuated with her, but his fascination wouldn't last, and eventually he'd feel the same way as Tom.

"You never mention your ex-husband."

"There's not much to say." She carried the two mugs

into the living room. "Carrie was excited about baby-sitting Paul and Leah's children," she said, pointedly changing the subject.

Jason stood and took a cup from her hands, then sat next to her on the sofa, sliding his arm around her shoulders. His touch was warm against her chilled skin.

"You're perfect," he whispered and kissed her cheek. "You're lovely and sensuous and beautiful. Don't ever let anyone tell you differently. I'm not going to force you to discuss your marriage. Not now, but I want you to know I'll be ready to listen whenever you're ready to talk."

She smiled wanly, determined to steer the conversation away from the past.

Jason drank his coffee and left soon afterward, when it was apparent Charlotte wasn't in the mood to talk. She wasn't sure *what* her mood was, but she lacked the strength to analyze it.

Before leaving, Jason asked if she'd changed her mind again about the ball game on Saturday, and after a short hesitation, she nodded. Yes, she'd go, she told him. Jason smiled, obviously pleased, and headed out the door.

Something was happening to her, Charlotte thought, trembling. And it was happening against her will.

She'd made the decision earlier—she wasn't going to see him again. After careful deliberation she'd decided it was best to end everything now before one or both of them ended up hurt. It was a simple, cut-and-dried conclusion.

Yet…yet when she'd tried to talk to him about it, regret and doubt had consumed her until she'd dissolved in tears and pain.

Heaven help her, she didn't want it to end! Jason

must've sensed that because he hadn't appeared too concerned when she'd told him.

His confidence was well-founded. Within minutes, he'd broken through her resolve and was kissing her senseless. And Charlotte hadn't raised a single objection.

It was too late. Too late to walk away from him. Too late to go back to the way her life had been before Jason. She was trapped by her own weakness and would continue to be until Jason discovered the truth for himself.

Carrie arrived home soon afterward, full of tales about the twins and Kelsey. Seconds later, it seemed, she was in her room and on the phone. Her thoughts heavy, Charlotte appreciated the privacy.

It wasn't as though this was the first time Jason had kissed her. The impact he had on her senses wasn't startling or new. The man had the uncanny knack of stirring awake the part of her she'd thought had died the day Tom asked for a divorce.

She felt reborn, alive with hope. And yet she was more frightened than she'd ever been before. Everything was different with Jason. In his arms she experienced an excitement she'd never even known was possible. His tenderness, the loving gentle way in which he touched her, had given her cause to wonder, for the first time, if what Tom had said was true.

What if it wasn't? Could that be possible? With Jason she felt none of the dread she'd felt when Tom had kissed her. His lovemaking had always been so hurried, so raw, as if he were in a rush to complete the act so he could turn away from her. She couldn't imagine Jason being anything but compassionate and tender.

But what if all the things Tom had said *were* true? Her heart slowed with uneasiness. Jason Manning was

an attractive, sensual man. A passionate man. And he'd expect—no, he'd need—a passionate woman.

Thinking of her years with Tom conjured up such ugly images in her mind. His taunts echoed like the constant sound of waves in a seashell, never stopping, never fading, always there to remind her of what a failure she was.

At ten, Charlotte turned out the lights, made sure Carrie was off the phone and went to bed. She should've guessed that sleep would escape her that night.

You're perfect, Jason had said.

Only she wasn't—Tom had made certain she knew as much. The need to weep welled up within her, tightening her throat.

She had loved Tom. She'd hated him.

He had stripped her of her pride when he left.

Her life had ended that day. Yet, in other ways, her life had begun.

She'd known for weeks, months, that Tom was involved with another woman, and she'd said nothing because she was afraid. Because she feared life alone. Because she was willing to do whatever she could to save her marriage, even if that meant denying the truth. So she'd chosen to believe his lies.

When he'd forced her to face reality, he'd come at her in anger and guilt...and hate. She hadn't cried. Not a single tear, not even when the divorce was decreed final. It wasn't until years later that she gave herself permission to grieve for the marriage, the fantasy she'd built in her mind of what might have been.

In the beginning she'd been too numb with shock, too dazed by that last horrible scene, to experience any emotion. Gradually, as time passed, Charlotte began to

feel again, a little at a time. It was like an anesthetic wearing off. As the years went by, as the numbness faded, she had to deal with the pain. A throbbing, savage pain.

Her grief came in waves. Regret struck first, reminding her of all the might-have-beens; one fantasy led to another. By now they would've had more children, she'd told herself. Tom would be established in his career and she'd be living the life she'd been cheated of as a child.

Anger followed regret. How could she have given her heart to a man who'd ravaged her self-respect? How could she have loved him when he'd treated her so poorly? But love him she had, so much that she still ached at losing the life she'd dreamed they'd share.

But mostly, as the years went on, Charlotte felt an overwhelming sense of guilt. She knew it was unreasonable. After all, it was Tom who'd cheated on her, Tom who'd walked out on his family, abandoned his wife and child. It was Tom who'd forsaken their vows. Yet *she* was the one who accepted responsibility.

Sometimes the guilt was so overpowering, Charlotte found it intolerable. If she'd been a better wife, Tom wouldn't have sought another woman. He'd said so himself. If she'd been more enticing, more sexual, more attractive, more satisfying, he wouldn't have done it. She was too thin, too flat, too cold. The list was endless.

After years of telling herself that Tom had used her inadequacies as an excuse for adultery, years of struggling to repair her self-esteem, Charlotte gave up. Surrendered. She bought it all. The reassurances she tried to offer herself were empty. Null and void.

Everything Tom had said was true. She was a failure as a woman. A failure as a wife. No man would ever be

satisfied with her. Not for long. Tom hadn't been and Jason wouldn't be, either. She might as well accept that now and stop fighting the inevitable.

The doorbell chimed just as Jason finished reading the latest issue of one of the veterinary periodicals he subscribed to.

"Yeah?" he said, opening the door, half expecting one of his tenants.

"Hi," Carrie said, striding purposefully into his apartment. "Have you got a minute to talk?"

"Sure." Jason led the way into the living room and sat down. Carrie started to pace in front of his television, hands behind her back. Walking in his apartment was dangerous with the week's worth of newspapers spread across the carpet.

"Is it Higgins?" he prompted, when she didn't speak right away.

She shook her head, eyes lighting up. "Higgins is doing great. He's eating and everything. I think he likes it with Mom and me."

"I'm sure he does." They'd lavished the dog with love and attention from the moment Jason had carried him into their apartment on Monday afternoon. One would've thought the mutt was some kind of hero. In a way he was, Jason decided. If it hadn't been for the dog, Jason didn't know how long it would have taken him and Charlotte to connect.

"What can I do for you?"

"It's Mom," Carrie said.

"What about your mother?" He saw that tears had pooled in Carrie's eyes, and she wasn't trying to hide the fact. Like most men, Jason was uncomfortable when

a woman started to cry. No matter what the cause, he felt personally responsible. And he felt an overpowering urge to do whatever he could to rectify the problem.

He certainly felt that way with Charlotte—even more so. She'd look at him with her beautiful blue eyes and the instant he saw the slightest hint of tears, he'd be putty in her hands. He was putty in her hands, anyway, tears or not, but that was because it was Charlotte.

"My mother's ruining my life," Carrie was saying.

Jason was no psychiatrist, but he wasn't completely obtuse. "Does this have something to do with that dance?"

Carrie nodded. "There's this boy…his name's Brad. He's the cutest boy in class and the star of the track team. Every girl in school's crazy about him and he asked *me*. Me," she emphasized again, bringing her hand to her heart. "He asked me to the ninth-grade dance. When I talked to Mom, she said I could go, but when I said Brad's father was picking us up and…and driving us there, she went totally weird on me."

"I'm sure your mother has a good reason for feeling the way she does."

"She won't even talk about it."

"Carrie, listen. I'd like to help, but this is between you and your mother. I can't interfere with a parenting decision."

Carrie nodded, her throat working as she struggled not to cry. "I don't expect you to interfere… I was hoping that you'd help me—tell me what to say to make Mom understand how old-fashioned she's being. I haven't said anything to Brad about my mom not wanting me to be in the same car as him and his dad and… and the dance is next Friday night. There isn't much time left."

Jason rubbed the side of his face. "What's your mother's primary objection?"

"She thinks driving with him makes it a real date. And I'm not allowed to *date* until next year."

"I see. What if she drove you and Brad to the dance?"

"That won't work, either.... Everyone will think I asked him and...it might be silly, but I want Suzie Jennings to know otherwise." She wiped her eyes and took a moment to regain her composure.

"How about if Brad's dad drops you off and your mother picks the two of you up after the dance?"

Carrie dropped her hands to her side. "Picks us up?" she repeated thoughtfully.

"It wouldn't be considered a date then, would it? The two of you obviously need to be driven to and from the dance and this would simply be a means of transporting you."

"There's a party at Amanda Emerich's house right afterward, but it's directly across the street from the school and everyone's invited."

"I have an even better idea," Jason said enthusiastically. At Carrie's blank stare, he explained. "How about if your mother offered to chaperone the dance?"

Judging by the look Carrie gave him, she didn't share his enthusiasm. "That wouldn't work because she'd need a date. Chaperones at our school dances are always couples."

"I'll go with her," Jason said casually. As soon as he made the suggestion, he wanted to jerk it back. Him dancing? The last dance he'd attended had been his sister's engagement party. He'd rented a tuxedo and been miserable most of the night. Before then, his only other experience on the dance floor had been as a high-

school junior. He didn't know how to dance then and he hadn't learned since.

"You'd do that?" Carrie asked, her voice rising. For the first time since she'd entered his home, her eyes sparkled with hope.

"Ah..." Oh, what the heck, he'd do it if it would help the kid. "Sure," he answered. "I'd volunteer to be a chaperone."

Carrie let out a cry of glee and raced across the room to throw her arms around his neck.

"Your mother might not be willing—"

"She will," Carrie said confidently. "Mom's crazy about you."

"Yes, but will she be crazy about the idea of Brad's dad driving you there and the two of us taking you home?"

Carrie mulled that over for a moment. "Of course she will," she said, revealing no doubt. "Why shouldn't she be? It's a wonderful compromise. We'll both be satisfied.... I mean, this plan isn't perfect—no one wants their mother chaperoning a school dance—but it'll work because Mom's going to agree when she knows you suggested it."

Jason was suffering from second thoughts when he rang Charlotte's doorbell an hour later. Carrie had devised a plan for approaching Charlotte with his idea. At the appropriate point, he was to suggest the two of them chaperone the dance and make it sound like a spur-of-the-moment idea.

He was rather proud of his compromise—not the part about chaperoning the dance, but the shared-driving idea. By the time Carrie had left his apartment, he felt

like an expert. Raising children wasn't so difficult if you applied a bit of common sense.

Now, though, he wasn't entirely sure he should get involved. The dance was an issue between Charlotte and Carrie, and his instincts told him he was trespassing.

It would've been different if Charlotte had come to him for advice, but she hadn't and he doubted she would. There wasn't any reason for her to, at least not with regard to Carrie. Charlotte was the one with parenting experience, not him.

Despite his second thoughts over his role in this drama, he'd agreed to help Carrie—even though his instincts now told him he was going to regret this.

Carrie answered the doorbell and smiled brightly when she saw him.

Charlotte looked pleased to see him, too, but she also looked like she'd rather not be. Jason was learning to read her quite well, and that skill was coming in handy.

"Hello, Jason," she said softly.

"Hi. I stopped by to see how Higgins is doing." A weak excuse, and one she was bound to see through in the next couple of minutes.

The black dog trotted toward him, his tail wagging slowly. Jason squatted beside him and affectionately rubbed his ears. "How do you like your new home, fellow?" he asked.

"Do you want a cup of coffee?" Carrie called out from the kitchen. Her voice was enthusiastic. The kid wasn't any better at disguising her emotions than her mother was.

"Please." Jason glanced up at Charlotte. He didn't know what was going on with her lately. She'd been avoiding him—that much he understood—but he was

willing to give her the space she needed. For now. He was a patient man. She was attracted to him, fighting it as hard as she could, but her resistance wasn't strong enough to defeat him.

For the first time in his life, Jason had met a woman who needed him. Unfortunately she was too self-sufficient and proud to admit it. Charlotte Weston brought out all his protective urges. And his intuition told him he'd begun to bring out qualities in her—a sensual confidence and an ability to laugh, have fun—that she'd been repressing for years.

The woman was a puzzle, but slowly, surely, he was putting together the various pieces she revealed. Once he had the whole picture, he'd be able to scale those defensive walls of hers.

He strongly suspected Charlotte's problems revolved around her ex-husband and her marriage. She'd been badly hurt, and gaining her trust and her love would require time and patience. Where Charlotte was concerned, Jason had an abundant supply of both. Carrie brought him a cup of coffee, and Jason pulled out a kitchen chair, then nonchalantly sat down. Carrie did the same. Higgins ambled over and settled at his feet.

Charlotte glanced at the two of them and frowned. "Is something going on here that I should know about?"

The kid couldn't have been more obvious, Jason mused again. "Carrie came to me earlier this afternoon," he announced, deciding honesty was the best policy, after all. The way he figured, if they were forthright about *what* they'd discussed, then Charlotte might be willing to forgive them for discussing it behind her back.

"Jason," Carrie muttered a warning under her breath.

"Carrie came to you?" Charlotte demanded. "About what?"

"The dance," Carrie admitted sheepishly.

"You went to Jason about an issue that's strictly between you and me?"

"I needed to talk to someone," Carrie cried, pushing back the chair when she stood. She faced her mother, feet braced apart, hands on her hips. "You're being completely unreasonable and Jason agrees with me. He came up with—"

"Carrie." Jason could see he'd been wrong. In this case, honesty might not have been the best policy. "I didn't ever say I thought your mother was unreasonable."

His defense came too late. Charlotte whirled on him, her face red and growing redder. Her eyes, the eyes he'd always found so intriguing, were filled with disdain.

"Who gave you the right to intrude in my life?" she flared.

"Charlotte, it's not what you think." Jason could feel himself sinking waist-deep in the quicksand of regret.

"You're undermining my authority."

"Mom...please, hear me out."

"Charlotte, give me a chance to explain." Jason didn't have much of an argument; he should've listened to his instincts and stayed out of this.

"You may think because...because I've let you get close to Carrie and me that you have the right to express your opinion on how she should be raised, but you're wrong. What goes on between my daughter and me is none of your business. Do I make myself clear?"

Feeling all the more chagrined, Jason nodded. The

best thing to do now was make a hasty retreat. "I can see I've—"

"Just go." Charlotte's voice trembled as she pointed to her door.

"Mom," Carrie shouted. "The least you can do is listen to him."

Charlotte ignored her daughter while Jason, calling himself every kind of fool, made his way out of the apartment. He paused long enough to cast an apologetic glance at Carrie, but he agreed with Charlotte. He'd butted in where he didn't belong.

After Jason's departure, Carrie went to her room, slamming her door with such force Higgins scrambled across the living room, frantically looking for a place to hide.

Charlotte was so angry, it was all she could do not to follow Jason and tell him she never wanted to see him again. She would have done it, too, if she didn't know she'd regret it later. And if she didn't need to coax Higgins out from behind the couch and comfort him.

The man had some nerve! If Carrie thought she was going to manipulate her into giving in by getting Jason to side with her, then her daughter was wrong.

"I hope you realize what you've just done!" Carrie shouted as she opened her door.

Still stroking Higgins, Charlotte ignored her.

"You've insulted Jason."

"He deserved it."

"Like hell."

"Watch your language, young lady."

Thirty silent minutes passed while Charlotte cooled her temper. Carrie was apparently doing the same thing.

A short while later, her bedroom door opened again and she walked out. She was pale and her eyes showed evidence of crying, but she appeared to have composed herself.

The same didn't hold true for Charlotte. She was still furious. How dare Jason involve himself in her affairs!

"I've called Brad," Carrie announced, opening the refrigerator. She stared at the contents, took out a cold pop and pulled back the tab. After taking one long drink, she turned to face Charlotte. "Brad said he'd tell his dad you'd be driving us to and from the dance."

Of all the things Charlotte might have expected, this wasn't one. "Good," she said, feeling only a little better.

"I...was hoping you'd be willing to split the duties. Let Brad's father drive us there and you pick us up."

Charlotte mulled it over. That didn't sound so unreasonable. She'd have a chance to meet the boy's father when he came to get Carrie, and it wasn't as if the two kids would be alone in the car—or at the dance.

"I... I'd be willing to agree to that."

Charlotte thought Carrie would be grateful or relieved; instead she broke into giant hiccuping sobs. Her daughter slumped in a kitchen chair and buried her face in her arms and wept as if she'd lost her best friend.

"Carrie." Charlotte placed her hand on Carrie's shoulder. "What's wrong?"

She raised her head and brushed the tears from her face, her shoulders heaving with the effort to stop crying. "You should never have said those things to Jason."

"Carrie, he intruded in my affairs."

"But I was the one who asked him to talk to you. If you're going to be angry with anyone, it should be me, not him."

Charlotte realized Carrie didn't understand the nu-
ances of a male-female relationship. Frankly, she wasn't
that well acquainted with them herself. She'd admit that
she'd reacted in anger, but it was justified. Jason had
simply assumed too much.

"But Jason didn't want to interfere," Carrie sobbed.
"It took me forever to get him to agree and…and he
only did it because I was desperate."

"He overstepped the bounds." Charlotte tried to remain adamant.

"You made him leave without even bothering to listen."

Charlotte said nothing.

"I like Jason—and you do, too," Carrie added unnecessarily. "He's the best thing that's ever happened
to us. Higgins is alive because of him and…and he took
us to meet his family. Saturday was the most fun day
I've ever had. It…it was like we belonged with Jason
and his brothers."

Charlotte had felt the same way.

"Jason wasn't minding your business, Mom, at least
not the way you think. He…he was helping a friend.
Me. And you hated him for that."

"I don't hate Jason." Far from it. She was falling in
love with him.

"He's the one who came up with the idea of Brad's
father driving one way and you driving the other. He…
he suggested you chaperone the dance just so you'd feel
comfortable about everything." She drew in a shaky
breath. "When I told him you'd need a date for the dance
if you were going to be a chaperone, he said *he'd* take
you. I mean, Jason isn't the kind of man who dances…
but he'd be willing to do it, for me, because he's my

friend. And for you, too, so you'd be comfortable at the dance. And what did he get for being so nice?"

"My anger," Charlotte whispered, feeling wretched.

"You kicked him out of the house, and I don't think he'll ever want to come back. I know I wouldn't."

Charlotte sat down next to her daughter, feeling strangely like weeping herself.

"I wanted to go to the dance with Brad more than anything," Carrie admitted, "but now I don't care if I do or not."

"Carrie, this isn't the end of the world."

"I *really* like Jason," she said emphatically. "When I asked him if he'd ask you out, I did it for selfish reasons, and I apologize for that…but I'm glad I did it. You're happier when you're with him, Mom. You don't think I notice, but I do. Jason makes you smile and laugh and forget how much you don't like your job."

Charlotte folded her arms around her middle. What Carrie said was true. It was as if her life had started all over again when Jason first kissed her.

"I don't care about the dance anymore," Carrie murmured. "But I care what happens with you and Jason. Go to him, Mom. Tell him you're sorry. Please."

Her daughter's entreaty affected Charlotte more than any regrets she might feel about what she'd said and done. For one thing, she hadn't realized how fond Carrie was of Jason.

"Will you do it, Mom?"

It didn't take Charlotte long to decide. "Yes," she said. She would apologize, for not giving him the benefit of the doubt, for not being willing to listen to him and Carrie, but mostly for the rude way in which she'd told him to leave her apartment.

It was the second time she'd had to apologize to this man.

"When?" Carrie asked.

"Soon," Charlotte promised.

The opportunity came the following morning. After walking Higgins, Charlotte was on her way to the office, crossing the parking lot. She'd spent a sleepless night composing what she intended to say to Jason. She'd wait until that evening, go to his apartment and say what needed to be said.

She was halfway to her car when she heard her name. Her heart filled with dread when she saw Jason jogging toward her.

"Hello," she said, feeling wretched.

"I won't keep you." His eyes bored into hers. "I want you to know I'm sorry for what happened yesterday. I should never have gotten involved. This is between you and Carrie, and I was out of line."

"I should never have spoken to you the way I did."

"You were angry and you had every right to be."

"But you… Oh, Jason, I feel terrible."

He frowned. "Why should you?"

"Carrie told me how you were willing to help chaperone the dance and…and I didn't have the common decency to hear you out."

"It's probably for the best. I'm not much of a dancer."

Charlotte smiled up at him, knowing her heart shone in her eyes, and not caring. "Why don't you let me find that out for myself Friday night?"

Eight

"You need to borrow a suit?" Rich asked, looking smugly amused as he led Jason to the walk-in closet in the huge master bedroom. The home had been built several years earlier, when Jamie was pregnant with Bethany. Rich himself had designed the sprawling L-shaped rambler that overlooked Puget Sound, and he was justifiably proud.

"Yes, I need to borrow a suit," Jason muttered, not giving his brother the satisfaction of explaining. Already he regretted having volunteered to be a chaperone for this dance. No matter how hard he tried, he wasn't going to be whirling around a dance floor as if he knew what he was doing. He'd probably make a fool of himself in front of Charlotte and a bunch of smart-aleck ninth-graders.

As an engineer, Rich was required to dress more formally on the job than Jason was. Jason owned a suit, but it was outdated. Maybe if he waited a few more years it would become fashionable again.

If the truth be known, he wasn't even sure when he'd last worn it. Sometime in college, he guessed. He'd buy

another one if he thought he'd get any use out of it, but that didn't seem likely.

"What do you need a suit for?" Rich asked outright.

"I wouldn't be borrowing one if I'd known I was going to face an inquisition."

Rich chuckled, clearly enjoying Jason's discomfort. "I just want to be sure you aren't going to run off and marry Charlotte. Mom would kill you if you pulled a stunt like that."

Jason snickered, hoping to give the impression that marriage was the furthest thing from his mind, which it was. Wasn't it?

"Hey, don't act like it couldn't happen," Rich said, pushing hangers aside as he sorted through several tailored jackets. "With our family's history, it wouldn't be unheard-of for you to elope."

Jason couldn't argue with that. It had all started with Taylor. A few years back, his sister had moved to Montana and within three months had married Russ Palmer. The decision to marry had apparently been impulsive— and it happened while they were chaperoning the high-school drill team in Reno. The deed was done by the time they bothered to contact any family.

Jason frowned. Taylor had been a chaperone, too, and look where it had led. This high-school dance was beginning to sound more and more dangerous.

Christy had married on the sly, too, again without telling anyone in the family. There were extenuating circumstances in her case, however. Well, sort of. His youngest sister had actually been engaged—to a lawyer, James Wilkens—when she'd gone to Idaho with Cody Franklin and married him. Their marriage had caused quite a ruckus in the family, but eventually everything

had been smoothed over. Anyway, Christy was much better suited to Cody than to James, although the attorney had remained a good family friend.

Rich had followed suit, marrying Jamie with some idiotic idea of being a sperm donor for her baby. Jason had stood up for his brother, but he'd known from the beginning that the two of them were in love. He'd predicted that this sperm donor business wouldn't pan out, and he'd been right. Jamie had gotten pregnant, sooner than either of them had expected, and the process hadn't involved any artificial insemination, either.

Paul had been next. Diane, Paul's first wife, had died tragically, shortly after giving birth to Kelsey. Her loss had sent the family reeling. For six months, Paul had shunned his family's offers of help, attempting to balance his duties at home with his job and at the same time comfort his grieving children, all preschoolers. He'd been proud and angry. Leah, Diane's sister, had convinced him he couldn't continue alone. She'd given up her teaching position at the college and moved in with Paul and the children. Shortly afterward, they were married. But once again, no one in the family was informed of the ceremony.

The only single Manning left was Jason, and he didn't plan to get married. He'd decided that years before. It was unfortunate that his parents had been cheated out of putting on a large wedding, but those were the breaks. He wasn't marching down any aisle just to satisfy his mother's need to work with caterers and some florist friend she'd known for years.

"So, Jase," Rich said casually, breaking into his thoughts. "How are things with you and Charlotte?"

"Fine."

"Fine?" Rich repeated, with that smug look Jason found so irritating.

"You don't need to concern yourself with my affairs," Jason said, resenting the way Rich and Paul made his love life their business.

"Are you going to ask her to marry you?" Almost in afterthought, Rich held up a well-cut gray suit coat. The tailoring was excellent and the material was top of the line.

Jason ignored the question and reached for the jacket, trying it on over his black T-shirt with *Seattle at Night* silk-screened across the front.

"What are your intentions toward Charlotte?" Rich asked with a pensive frown. He sounded oddly formal— and unusually serious.

"My intentions are my own, but since you asked," Jason said, turning around to admire his profile in the full-length mirror, "I'll tell you…. They're dishonor-able, as always." He tried to make a joke of it, laugh off the attraction he'd been battling from the moment he'd met Charlotte Weston over a leaky faucet.

His joke, however, fell decidedly flat.

"Not this time, big brother."

"What do you mean by that?" Jason demanded. He didn't like his brother sticking his nose where it didn't belong, but he couldn't help being curious about Rich's remark.

"You're in love with her."

"Is that right?" Jason returned flippantly.

"It's the first time you've ever invited a woman to watch you play softball."

Rich made it sound as if that alone was enough to force him into a shotgun wedding. Jason refused to get

into an argument with his younger brother. It wouldn't do him any good. Just because Rich and Jamie were so happy together, his brother seemed to think he was an expert on the subject of love and marriage. Jason didn't want to be the one to disillusion him.

Perhaps he did have some deep affection for Charlotte, Jason told himself. He'd be the first to admit he was strongly attracted to her, but marriage? Out of the question.

This was a familiar argument, one he'd worked through early in their relationship. It had worried him then, but he'd been so fascinated with her that he'd pushed his apprehensions to the back of his mind, deciding to take one day at a time.

He'd face one hurdle, he decided, before he confronted another. For now, the obstacle was their physical relationship. When she trusted him enough to put aside her fears and allow him to make love to her, it would be time to reevaluate what was happening between them. But not yet.

"Are you going to let me borrow the suit or not?" Jason asked stiffly. "If I have to stand here and listen to a lecture, too, I'd rather go to the rental shop."

He half expected Rich to jerk the coat off his shoulders and send him on his way. Instead, his youngest brother grinned, as if he knew something Jason didn't. It was another irritating habit of his.

"You're welcome to keep the suit as long as you like," Rich assured him. "You never know when you're suddenly going to need one."

Friday evening came, and it took Jason a full half hour to knot his tie correctly. He was out of practice,

and getting it just right frustrated him. He should've borrowed the clip-on variety, but he hadn't thought of asking for one. No doubt Rich had plenty of each type.

Surveying his reflection in the mirror, he barely recognized himself. He was tall, besting his brothers by an inch or more, his shoulders were wide and, if he had anything to be proud of physically, it was that his stomach had remained flat. Haphazard meals and baseball did that for a man.

Charlotte probably wouldn't recognize him, either. If memory served, it was the first time she'd gone anywhere with him when he wasn't wearing a baseball cap. He brushed his hand along the side of his head, making sure his hair stayed flat. He carefully examined himself to see if he could find any gray hairs for a more distinguished look. When he didn't, he was actually disappointed.

He checked his watch. If everything had gone according to schedule, Carrie would have been picked up fifteen minutes ago for a pre-dance buffet. Since the dance didn't start for another two hours, Jason had suggested taking Charlotte out to dinner.

He didn't know what had gotten into him lately. He'd made reservations at an expensive restaurant, and ordered a fancy corsage to give her when they arrived.

Normally, his idea of a night on the town included pizza, beer and a Mariners' game. Drag an irresistible woman into his life, and before he knew it, he was forking out major bucks for dinner and flowers. The thing was, he'd come up with the idea on his own and was even excited about it, knowing how pleased Charlotte would be.

He'd seen this happen with his friends—his broth-

ers, too—but he would never have believed *he'd* fall such willing prey to a woman's charms. It wouldn't have happened with anyone but Charlotte. Of that, he was certain.

At exactly seven, he walked over to Charlotte's apartment and rang the bell. She kept him waiting for several minutes before she opened the door—not a promising sign.

When she finally did come, Jason was about to complain. He was going to a lot of trouble for this blasted dance; the least she could do was be ready on time.

Whatever he'd intended to say, however, flew out of his mind when he saw Charlotte. For the longest moment of his life, he stood there immobile.

This was Charlotte! She was…stunning.

"I'm…sorry," she said, sounding flustered. "I didn't mean to keep you standing out here, but I'm having a problem with this dress."

She was beautiful.

The word didn't begin to describe how breathtaking she looked. Her hair was done in a way he'd never seen before, swirled to one side, exposing the smooth skin of her cheek and her long, slender neck. Dangling gold earrings swung from her ears. Her eyes were a brighter blue than ever before, the color of the sky washed clean by a summer squall. Her dress was a paler shade of blue… Her dress… Jason's gaze slid over the sleeveless dress with its tight bodice and flared skirt, and an invisible hand seemed to appear out of thin air and knock him senseless.

"Jason." Her eyes implored him as she held one hand behind her back. "Is something wrong? I look terrible,

don't I? Don't worry about hurting my feelings... This dress is too fancy, isn't it?"

It was all he could do to close his mouth. "You look... fabulous." Which was the understatement of the century. Jason felt sorry that he wasn't more sophisticated and urbane.

If he had been, he might have told her how exquisite she was. He might have found the words to say he'd gladly rework the knot in his tie for another hour if it meant he could spend the evening with her. For the first time since he'd donned the suit jacket, he felt no remorse for volunteering to escort Charlotte to her daughter's dance.

"I can't get the zipper all the way up," Charlotte explained. "I was so busy helping Carrie get ready before Brad and his father arrived that I... I didn't get dressed myself, and now I can't reach the zipper. Would you mind?"

She presented him with her back and it was all Jason could do to pull the tab up instead of down. If he went on instinct he'd have had her out of that dress, in his arms and on the way to the bedroom. He couldn't recall a time he'd wanted a woman more than he did Charlotte Weston right then and there.

"Jason?" She glanced over her shoulder when he delayed.

His hand felt clammy, and at first his fingers refused to cooperate, but with some effort he managed to do as she asked, sliding the zipper up her back.

"Thank you," she said. "You can't imagine what a madhouse it's been around here," she went on. "Carrie was so nervous. She looked so grown-up. I can't believe my baby isn't a baby anymore."

Jason returned her smile. "My mother felt the same way when Christy—my sister—attended her first big dance."

Even now, Jason was having trouble forming coherent sentences.

"The dress isn't mine," she told him as she searched for her evening bag, wandering from one room to the next until she located it. "I borrowed it from one of my friends at the office... It's too close to the end of the month to go out and buy one." She sighed, sounding breathless. "Even if I'd had the extra money, I doubt I would've been able to find one at the last minute. I'd feel dreadful if something happened to Cheryl's dress."

"I borrowed the suit from my brother." Maintaining an intelligible conversation, he discovered, wasn't as much of a problem as keeping his eyes off her.

Charlotte drew in a deep, steadying breath. "I know it's silly, but I'm as nervous as Carrie."

He smiled, trying to reassure her.

"The last dance I attended was in college," she said. "I... I don't know if I can dance anymore."

"I'm not exactly light on my feet, Charlotte," Jason felt obliged to remind her. He'd warned her earlier, but he doubted she'd taken him seriously.

"Do you think we should practice?" she asked.

She was gazing up at him with wide eyes. Jason would've given everything he owned to find out if she was feeling anything close to the emotional havoc he was.

"Practice?" he echoed. "That's an idea." He swallowed, wondering exactly what he was inviting. Trouble with a capital *T,* considering the way his body was reacting.

Charlotte set aside her evening bag and walked into his embrace. "I'm afraid I'm not going to be very good at this," she murmured.

"Don't worry. Hey, as far as I'm concerned, those ninth-graders are going to dance circles around us anyway."

Charlotte's laugh sounded sweet and soft, and Jason's heart constricted. Could this be love? This pleasure he felt in doing small things for her—like the dinner and flowers? This need to hold her in his arms? This desire to be with her and her alone?

The feel of Charlotte's body against his was the purest form of torture he'd ever experienced. She fit in his arms as though she belonged there. Had always belonged there. He tried to ignore how right it felt.

And couldn't.

He tried to ignore the fragrance of wildflowers that whispered through her hair whenever she moved her head.

And didn't.

He tried, but failed.

Everything went fairly well for the first few minutes. At least he wasn't stepping on her feet. Then Jason realized their feet weren't moving and they were staring at each other more than they were dancing. Gazing at each other with starry-eyed wonder.

He shifted his hand upward, wanting to lessen the feeling of intimacy, but his fingers inadvertently grazed the skin of her upper back.

Either he kissed her now or he'd regret it the rest of the night. Either he continued the pretense or confessed openly to how vulnerable she made him feel.

He brought her closer to him. He could feel her heart

racing, echoing his own. Once he kissed her, he knew there'd be no stopping. Not this time.

He lowered his head ever so slightly and waited.

Charlotte sighed, closed her eyes and lifted her mouth enticingly to his. He suspected she was unconscious of what she was doing, what she was seeking.

Frankly, Jason didn't care. He was so hungry for the taste of her, nothing mattered. His mouth found hers and he groaned. Charlotte did, too.

He hadn't touched her in days, wanting to give her time, give himself time to define the boundaries of their relationship. It had been too long. He felt so needy he trembled.

The kiss was long, slow, deliberate.

Slowly, reluctantly dragging his mouth from hers, he created a small distance between them. Her eyes slowly fluttered open and met his.

"Jason?"

"I want you, Charlotte." He couldn't be any plainer than that. "I need you."

Emotion flickered in her gaze. Was it fear? Pain? Jason found it impossible to tell.

"Do you want to stop?" His hands were in her hair. By the time she lifted her mouth from his, Jason was melting with a need so powerful it throbbed within him.

Charlotte sighed into the hollow of his throat. "Jason, will you be angry with me?"

He saw the emotions assailing her, but noted the dignified way in which she tilted her chin and the proud squaring of her shoulders.

"No, I won't be angry."

She relaxed. Visibly. "Didn't you tell me you made dinner reservations for seven-thirty?"

"Yes." He recognized her fear and tried to ignore his own disappointment.

Self-conscious now, Charlotte broke away, quietly adjusting her clothes, then retrieved her evening bag. It wasn't until she looked up at him that he saw the anguish in her eyes.

He didn't know what her ex-husband—he assumed it was her ex-husband—had done. Her gaze linked with his, regret and misery so evident it was all he could do not to reach for her again. To comfort, not to kiss. To offer her solace, not passion.

Now, more than ever, Jason was determined to discover how her ex-husband had hurt her so badly. Determined to help her recover and teach her how beautiful love could be.

Charlotte was shaken to her very core. The intensity of their kisses had grown fervent and passionate, near the point of no return. If she'd given him the least bit of encouragement, he would have carried her into the bedroom.

For one wild moment, she'd been tempted to let him. Then the haze of desire had faded enough for sanity to return.

She felt grateful that Jason had allowed her to regain her senses, had given her the option to stop or proceed. Not like Tom…

Charlotte was jarred by this latest exchange even more than the other times Jason had held her and kissed her.

He'd almost made her forget.

Since her divorce, Charlotte had been content in her own small, secure world. The world she'd so carefully

constructed for herself and Carrie. It had been the two of them, prevailing against all odds, forging a life together. The borders of her world had been narrow and confining, but Charlotte had made peace with that, had accepted its limitations.

Then a series of events had thrown her into confusion. It had all started at the baby shower for her friend Kathy Crenshaw. Charlotte had held the newborn in her arms and the longing she'd managed to ignore all these years had struck her full-force.

Shortly afterward she'd met Jason, and her life hadn't been the same since.

Because of Jason, she'd recognized how restricted her world had become. How limited. If that wasn't enough, he'd shown her glimpses of a life she'd never dared hope existed. He'd taught her to dream, to believe in the impossible.

Almost.

After a protracted farewell to Higgins, they went out to the parking lot. Jason opened the car door and helped her inside, then stood in the fresh air for several minutes, hands in his coat pockets. He closed his eyes and turned his face toward the night sky.

Charlotte knew it was difficult for a man to cut the lovemaking off as abruptly as they'd done. He needed a few minutes to compose himself.

She watched him as he climbed into the car. He hesitated after inserting the key into the ignition and smiled over at her. "Ready?"

Charlotte nodded. "Are you...all right?"

"Never finer," he assured her, then clasped her hand to kiss her knuckles.

Nine

Jason Manning was a romantic. Beneath that I-don't-give-a-damn attitude was a tenderness and warmth that left Charlotte feeling like a starry-eyed adolescent. The candlelight dinner at an elegant cliffside restaurant had been wonderful. There he'd given her a fragrant rose-bud corsage that was so lovely, it had brought tears to her eyes.

The dance had been the best part of their evening. They'd had a delightful time, despite being surrounded by ninth-graders and forced to endure an earsplitting mixture of songs.

Jason and Charlotte had discovered early on that they weren't going to be able to dance to rap music. After a number of hilarious attempts, they'd given up. Several of their efforts had left Charlotte laughing so hard, her ribs ached.

Jason had been equally amused, and after their un-successful attempts to blend in with the kids, he'd reached for Charlotte, guiding her into his arms. She'd draped her wrists loosely around his neck and he placed

his hands on her hips. Then they'd invented their own dance....

Although Charlotte knew Carrie had risked her "cool" status, her daughter had come to her, eyes bright with excitement, to confess it wasn't so bad having her mother chaperone a dance, after all.

After the dance, while Carrie and Brad attended the nearby party, Charlotte and Jason sat outside in the schoolyard, gazing at the stars, laughing and kissing. Not the passionate, soul-deep kisses of earlier, but tender, sweet ones. By the end of the evening the barriers surrounding her heart had started to crumble.

Charlotte and Carrie came home at a respectable hour, their heads filled with romance. With barely a word, they wandered off to bed, passing each other like sleepwalkers in the hall.

Several hours later, Charlotte, unable to sleep, wrapped her memories around her like a cloak. Not since her own schooldays had she been more at ease with a man. In the space of one evening, she'd come to realize—without doubt, fear or regret—that she was deeply in love with Jason Manning.

After an hour of savoring every moment, she found she could finally sleep, knowing she'd be with him the next morning when he picked her up for the game.

"You ready, Mom?" Carrie called happily from the kitchen. It was shortly after ten. "Jason'll be here any minute."

Charlotte sucked in her stomach and zipped up her skinny jeans. Then she reached for a clean sweatshirt and tossed it over her head. Jason was already in the kitchen, checking the contents of the picnic basket,

when she sauntered in from her bedroom. Her heart did a little dance when she saw him.

"Good morning." She felt shy, and couldn't explain it.

He turned around and their eyes met before he sent her a wide smile. "'Morning."

Charlotte opened the refrigerator and withdrew a six-pack of diet soda to add to the cooler.

"Is that all I get—just a friendly 'good morning'?" he asked, keeping his voice low so Carrie wouldn't hear.

"What else do you want?"

"You should know the answer to that. I swear, Charlotte, leaving you last night was one of the hardest things I've ever done." He slipped his arms around her waist and nuzzled his face in the slope of her neck.

Charlotte twisted around and stared up at him. "It was?"

"The only thing that got me through it was knowing I'd be with you again this morning." He lowered his mouth to hers, and she parted her lips. The kiss was slow and deep and hot.

"Honestly, you two are getting ridiculous," Carrie said from behind Charlotte. "Even Higgins thinks so." At the last minute, Carrie had convinced her they should bring the dog. Charlotte wasn't sure he was healed enough to run around the park, but Carrie had phoned Jason and he'd felt it would be all right.

"You ready?" Jason asked, picking up the wicker basket, his hand around Charlotte's waist as though, even now, it was difficult to let her go.

"*I've* been ready for the last ten minutes," Carrie said pointedly, holding Higgins's leash and leading him to Jason's car.

On the ride across town, Jason put on a CD and

the three of them sang along with Bon Jovi. But as they pulled into the massive parking lot, Jason's voice stopped abruptly.

"What's wrong?" Charlotte asked.

"Nothing for you to worry about." He tried to reassure her with a smile, but she wasn't so easily fooled. She glanced around, wondering what could possibly be amiss. She couldn't imagine, unless it was a vehicle he happened to recognize.

"I'm going to take Higgins for a walk," Carrie announced as soon as she'd climbed out of the backseat. Charlotte knew her daughter was eager to show off the dog to Ryan, Ronnie and the other children.

When Jason was opening the trunk of his car and removing his softball equipment, Charlotte spoke.

"Is there someone here you'd rather I not meet? An old girlfriend, a former lover?"

He turned and his gaze met hers. He smiled, a smile that started with his eyes and worked its way down to his mouth. "Nothing quite so dramatic. My parents are here."

"I see," she said. "You'd rather I wasn't with you."

"No," he said vehemently, and she realized he wanted her with him as much as she wanted to be. A rugged sigh followed his response. "I don't like the idea of you having to endure another inquisition."

"I'm a big girl."

"You don't know my mother."

"I'd like to, though," Charlotte assured him. She couldn't help thinking Jason's parents must be exceptional people, to have raised such a wonderful family. Before meeting the Manning clan, she'd known so little of what it meant to be part of a family, one in which ev-

eryone supported and encouraged one another. Where joys were shared and grief divided. All her life, Charlotte had been on the outside looking in, yearning for that special bond.

"They're going to drive you crazy with questions," he said grimly.

"Don't worry about it. I know how to be evasive. You forget, I'm the mother of a teenage daughter."

Jason's laugh was automatic. He grinned over at her, tossed a baseball bat over one shoulder and reached for her hand, linking their fingers. Linking them in a way that would dissolve any doubts.

Charlotte's heart sang with a joy that radiated from her heart.

They strolled casually, hand in hand, across the freshly mowed lawn. Jason's steps slowed as they approached the playing field.

Charlotte glanced up to find his eyes on her. "I just pray I can keep from hitting a home run," he whispered.

Charlotte laughed as they walked toward the older couple talking with Paul and Rich. Jason made the introductions and Charlotte smiled warmly and held her hand out to his parents.

"I've been looking forward to meeting you," she said confidently. "After getting to know Jason and his brothers, I can't help thinking you two must be very special people."

Jason waited a restless twenty-four hours for the summons. It arrived Sunday morning, disguised as an invitation to dinner at his parents' house that same evening. Jason, however, wasn't fooled. His mother in-

tended to feed him, but he knew he'd be obliged to sing for his supper.

He showed up promptly at six and was pleased to see that his mother had gone to the trouble of preparing all his favorites. Homemade rolls hot from the oven. Crispy fried chicken, mashed potatoes and gravy, fresh-picked peas. A molded gelatin salad rested in the center of the dining-room table.

Jason had always been a meat-and-potatoes man, unless he had to cook for himself, which unfortunately he did most evenings. His eating habits were atrocious and he knew it. A homemade dinner like this was a rare treat.

"We don't see nearly enough of you," his mother said, as the three of them sat down at the table.

Jason noted that she'd set out her best china and silverware, as well as linen napkins and a matching tablecloth. This was going to be a heavy-duty interrogation. And it didn't look as if he had much chance of escaping before his mother ferreted out the information she wanted.

His father handed him the platter of chicken and Jason thought he might have read sympathy in his eyes.

"Generally, when your brothers are here for dinner, I get so involved with the grandchildren," his mother said conversationally. "You and I don't have much of a chance to talk."

"We talk," Jason said, reaching for the rolls and adding three to his plate, along with a thick slab of butter and a spoonful of strawberry preserves. His mother would have to wait for her information while he enjoyed his dinner.

"Gravy, son?"

"Thanks, Dad." A look of understanding passed between them.

"I hardly know what's going on in your life these days," his mother continued, undaunted. "I haven't seen you in a month of Sundays."

"That's not true, Elizabeth. Jason was over two weeks ago. Now, let the boy eat. You can drill him about Charlotte later."

His father was nothing if not direct. His mother didn't even pretend to be affronted; she simply sighed and nodded. "If you insist."

"I do," his father muttered, ladling gravy over a modest pile of mashed potatoes. He set the gravy boat aside and shook his head. "I don't understand you, Elizabeth. You've been half starving me for months, claiming we've got to start eating healthier. I've been eating salads and fish and broiled chicken. Now *this*. I'm beginning to feel like it's my last dinner before facing the executioner."

"This is Jason's favorite dinner!" Elizabeth declared righteously.

"Don't be fooled, son," Eric Manning said, his elbows on the table. "Your mother's after something big this time."

"Eric!"

"Sorry, dear," Jason's father said contritely, then winked at him.

If his mouth hadn't been full of homemade bread, Jason would have laughed. His mother was in quite a mood. His father, too, but he was well aware of the love they shared. They had the kind of relationship he'd always hoped to have with a woman himself. For the first time in his life, he felt that might be possible.

They ate in relative silence with short discourses from Jason as he answered their questions about the veterinary hospital and his practice. He noticed how carefully his mother steered away from the subject of Charlotte and his social life.

No sooner had Jason and his father cleared the table than his mother brought out a deep-dish apple pie. Even the dessert was Jason's favorite.

While she dished up heaping bowlfuls and added ice cream, his father poured coffee.

"Now, Eric?" she asked, looking expectantly toward her husband.

"If you insist."

Jason glanced from his mother to his father, realizing his reprieve was about to end.

"I most certainly do. Jason," she said, shifting her attention to him, "as you probably know, your father and I are curious about you and Charlotte. *Very* curious."

"Yeah, I had that impression."

"We both liked her very much."

"She's a likable person," Jason said.

"How'd you meet her?"

He finished his pie, tipping the bowl on its side and spooning up the last of the melted ice cream. When he was convinced he'd gotten every drop, he wiped his mouth with the napkin, set it aside and reached for his coffee.

"She lives in the apartment complex."

"Widowed?"

"Divorced." He wasn't going to volunteer any more information than necessary.

"Are you in love with her?"

His mother was going for the jugular. Jason sup-

posed she was entitled to the truth, since she'd gone to so much trouble with this dinner.

"Yes." The reaction he received was definitely satisfying. His mother's eyes grew huge, and she glanced excitedly at his father.

"I thought as much," she murmured.

"It's obvious the boy's in love, Elizabeth. I told you so, didn't I?"

"But it makes all the difference in the world that he's willing to admit it himself."

"Charlotte means a lot to me," Jason added without hesitation.

"Are you going to marry her?" His mother's voice had a breathless, hopeful quality.

Jason sipped his coffee. He was in love with Charlotte, no question. He woke in the morning and his first thoughts were of her. When he went to bed at night, she was there in his mind, following him into sleep. His whole day was focused on when he'd see her again. Kiss her again.

"Jason?" his mother urged.

"Yes, I'm sure I'll eventually marry Charlotte."

"Hot damn." His father slapped the table.

"Oh, Jason, I couldn't be happier." His mother dabbed the corners of her eyes with a napkin. "I'm so pleased," she said with a sniffle, reaching for her husband's hand.

"I'm happy you two are so happy." Jason hadn't talked about marriage with Charlotte yet, but he'd do that in due course. They were still beginning to know each other, feel comfortable together. By next summer at just about this time, they'd be ready to take such a monumental step.

"Now this is important, son," his father said, his eyes serious. "Your mother and I want your word that you're not going to do what your sisters and Rich and Paul did. In other words, don't marry Charlotte without the family being there."

Elizabeth backed her husband up. "I've waited all these years for a family wedding and I refuse to be cheated out of my last chance. Do you understand me, Jason?"

"Don't worry," Jason said calmly. "When Charlotte and I get married, we'll do it up big, just for you. The whole nine yards."

"A reception, with a dinner and dance?" His mother's eyes implored him.

"As long as Charlotte agrees, and I'm sure she will. She enjoys that sort of thing."

"But will she mind…my helping with the arrangements?"

Jason shrugged. "My guess is she'd welcome it. She doesn't have any family of her own, you know."

"Personally, I don't care if your mother has her hand in the arrangements or not," his father muttered. "I just want to be sure you aren't going to marry Charlotte behind our backs."

"I already promised I wouldn't." Still, given their family's history, Jason could understand his parents' skepticism.

"So I have your word on this?" his mother asked anxiously.

"My word of honor. Only…"

"Only what?" His mother looked concerned.

"Nothing, Mom. Don't worry about it."

"What is it?" she demanded.

"Well, I was wondering… Once Charlotte and I decide to marry, would you show her how to make fried chicken like yours?"

It wasn't fair to bother Jason with her problems, but there wasn't anyone she trusted more, anyone's opinion she valued as much. Her day at the office had been one of the worst ever. Her boss, Mr. Ward, had been unreasonable and demanding in the past, but his abuse that afternoon had reached an all-time high. He'd shouted at her, called her incompetent, belittled her. And it had been over something that was completely out of her control. A client had left the agency due to a problem with accounting, not anything Charlotte had done, yet she'd taken the brunt of Mr. Ward's anger. Unfortunately the insurance agency wasn't large enough to have a Human Resources department, so there was no one to complain to, no recourse to speak of.

It wasn't the first time and it wouldn't be the last. For three years she'd been employed as an executive assistant at the insurance agency. In the beginning she'd enjoyed her job and thrived on the challenge. Then, six months ago, Mr. Beatty, her original boss, had retired, and she'd found his replacement to be the worst kind of supervisor.

She'd made her decision earlier that afternoon, prepared her letter of resignation and placed it on Mr. Ward's desk before leaving the office. Although she'd felt confident when she left work, she was vacillating now, uncertain that she'd made the right decision.

It always seemed to be like this. She'd become indignant, decide to leave, and later, after her anger had cooled, she'd change her mind. Mr. Ward would seem

repentant, try to convince her that his outbursts weren't personal; they were just his way. She'd start to believe him, at least until the next time.

Then it occurred to her.

What kind of woman would allow a man to verbally abuse her like that? What kind of woman allowed herself to be swayed by cheap talk and empty promises? The kind of woman who'd stayed married to Tom Weston for as long as she had, that was who.

She needed a sounding board, someone who'd listen to her frustration and doubts without casting judgment, without anger. Someone whose self-esteem was strong enough to accept her decisions whether she took his advice or not. Someone like Jason Manning.

Jason answered the phone immediately, sounding delighted to hear from her.

"I… I had a crummy day," she said when he asked. "Do you…would you go for a walk with me?" She considered bringing Higgins, but he was curled up with Carrie on the sofa.

"I'll be right over."

As Charlotte left, Carrie was talking on the phone with Brad. She hadn't told her daughter about quitting her job, although she was sure Carrie would cheer her decision.

"Hello," Jason said, kissing her lightly on the lips when she stepped out the door.

Charlotte closed her eyes. They joined hands and walked in the direction of the community park several blocks over.

The evening was beautiful. The fragrance of rhododendrons filled the evening air, mingling with the scent

of blooming azaleas. Birds chirped and several people were getting a start on their yard work.

"I...did something I'm not positive I should have done," she said, keeping her eyes lowered.

"Was it illegal?"

The question made her smile. "No."

"Then why look so grave?"

"Well..."

"Do you want to tell me about it?"

She nodded, grateful they'd arrived at the park. Jason steered her toward an unoccupied bench and they sat down, his hand still holding hers.

"I... I don't get along with my boss. I'm good at my job—at least I used to be. But now... Mr. Ward makes unreasonable demands and takes out his frustration on whoever's close at hand. Unfortunately most of the time that's me."

"It doesn't seem like a healthy atmosphere to be working in."

"It isn't." Charlotte wasn't the only employee who felt unhappy. Cheryl was on the verge of giving her notice, too, and so were a couple of the others. It wouldn't surprise Charlotte if half the office staff left with her.

"Then you should quit."

He made it sound so straightforward.

"I've never been a quitter. It's one of the reasons the divorce was so difficult for me. I—" She stopped abruptly. She hadn't meant to drag her marriage into this, lay it out for Jason to examine...yet, perhaps it was time.

"Go on," he urged.

Charlotte inhaled deeply, gathering her resolve. "I wrote my two-weeks' notice this afternoon and left it

on Mr. Ward's desk and now…now I'm having second thoughts."

"Why? Do you want to continue working at the agency?"

"No."

"Are you afraid you won't be able to find another job?"

"Not particularly—there's always a high demand for executive assistants. It's just… I know what's going to happen in the morning. Mr. Ward will arrive and read my letter and call me into his office. He'll apologize the way he always does. He seems to know exactly what to say, and when he's through with the apology, he'll offer me a token raise."

"It'd be nice if he threw in a bouquet of flowers."

"He might. He has before."

"Are you going to be swayed by that?"

"No-o." Her voice trembled and she shut her eyes to hold back the tears that burned. "It's so much like my marriage."

"Having to deal with an angry unreasonable man?"

"Yes…but more than that. Mr. Ward treats me the same way Tom did, and I swore… I promised myself I'd never allow another human being to do the things he did to me. And yet I take it, day after day, and I hate myself for it."

Jason's arm was around her now, hugging her close as if he wanted to absorb her pain. She was thankful he wasn't kissing her; she couldn't have endured that just then.

"I feel so angry when I let someone manipulate me. I want so badly to believe that things will change…that they'll get better. But they never do. Sooner or later Mr. Ward will go back to doing exactly what he's al-

ways done…and I'll realize I've let myself be controlled again. I can't seem to deal with the truth…. I guess it's easier to deny everything than face the reality. Why is truth so painful?"

Jason waited a few minutes, his arm about her calm and comforting. "Is it your boss you're talking about or your ex-husband?"

"Both." Charlotte raised her head and wiped the tears from her eyes before they had a chance to fall. "Tom… had an affair. I knew it for months but… I pretended I didn't. I made believe we were happy and in love, while doing everything I could to win him back. But it wasn't enough… Now I know nothing would have been enough."

Jason didn't interrupt her with questions; once again she was grateful. The effort not to weep had produced a lump in her throat, and talking was almost painful. She hesitated, head still lowered.

Jason's mouth brushed her hair. "Your husband was a fool, Charlotte."

She didn't respond; she couldn't. Jason didn't know the full story, didn't understand that there'd been a reason Tom had turned to another woman. Any healthy male would have, or so her ex-husband had vehemently assured her time and again.

"I'm stubborn and hardheaded," she said, her voice cracking. "I don't know when to let go and…so I hold on, no matter how painful…or damaging."

"I can't tell you what to do," Jason said after a thoughtful moment, "but don't judge yourself so harshly. Some people know exactly what to say to get what they want. Everyone needs to hear they're important, that they're loved and appreciated. But those are

only words, and talk is cheap. You got out of your marriage at the right time and—"

"No," she sobbed, "I didn't…. I didn't *want* out of the marriage, don't you see? It was Tom who asked for the divorce, Tom who forced everything into the open. I would've gone on pretending forever if he hadn't. I won't do it again. I won't! I'm quitting my job, Jason. I'm walking out two weeks from now and I won't look back. I swear to you, I won't look back."

There was a message from his mother when he returned to his apartment. His mind was heavy with everything he'd learned about Charlotte's marriage and he contemplated waiting to return his mother's call, but she'd sounded so excited.

Sighing, he reached for the phone. His mother answered on the first ring.

"Jason, I'm so glad you called! I have so much to tell you. I talked to Taylor and Christy and they've both agreed to come."

"Come?"

"You can't imagine what a day I've had," his mother continued, her voice animated. "I called Barbara Johnson, you remember Barbara, my friend who owns the floral shop, don't you? We went to high school together a thousand years ago."

"Mom…"

"Let me finish." With barely a pause to breathe, she went on, "Barbara was the one who got things started. She suggested we contact the yacht club right away and book a date for the reception. They're booked at least a year in advance. A year, I told myself. I know you, Jason, and when you're ready to do something, you

don't want to wait an entire year. Barbara was right. The earliest date was August the year after next. I can tell you, I was shocked. I had no idea we'd need to book the reception so early."

"Reception? What reception?" Jason was starting to get a frightening premonition.

His mother ignored his question. "That's when I learned there'd been a cancellation in July. This July! I couldn't believe our luck. Naturally I booked it that very instant. Then I contacted the caterers and, as luck would have it, they agreed to do the dinner, although it's only three weeks' notice. *Three weeks,* Jason. Three weeks. It sounds crazy to even attempt something of this magnitude, but we're going to pull it off without a hitch."

Jason's vague premonition was beginning to solidify. "Mom, what are you talking about?" he asked with growing anxiety.

Once again his mother disregarded his question. "That's when I phoned Taylor and Christy. They both called back to say they're coming. They've already made their plane reservations. Russ is coming, and Mandy, too. Remember Mandy, Russ's sister? She's in college now, you know."

"Coming? To *what,* Mother?" Jason demanded.

"Why, Jason, I've spent the day making the arrangements for your wedding to Charlotte. What else would I be talking about, for heaven's sake?"

Ten

"Mother, have you gone stark, raving mad?" Jason had difficulty keeping a rein on his anger. "How can you set a wedding date and hire caterers when I haven't even *mentioned* it to Charlotte? This is insane." He rubbed his face, wondering if he'd imagined this entire fiasco.

"Your father warned me you'd be angry, but, Jason, I know you. Once you and Charlotte decide to marry, you won't want to wait two years."

"Mom, I don't suppose it dawned on you that there are other places we could have a wedding reception— *if* we were actually having one. The yacht club isn't the only venue in this town."

"Frankly, no, it didn't occur to me," his mother returned calmly. "Since we're just going to have one formal wedding in this family, we're doing it up big, and the yacht club's the best alternative."

Jason could see he was losing ground. "Let me talk to Dad."

"But, Jason—"

"Mother!"

"All right, just a minute."

That minute seemed to take an hour. By the time he had his father on the line, Jason was as angry as he'd ever been. The instant he heard Eric pick up the receiver, he shouted, "Has Mother gone crazy? Have you? How could you let things go this far?"

His father chuckled, apparently amused, something Jason most definitely wasn't. "I agree with you," his father said breezily, "your mother has gone a little crazy."

"Dad, listen, I know you and Mom mean well, but I refuse to let you run my life. Scheduling the reception, talking to florists, I can't believe you'd allow Mom to do all this without talking to me first."

"Don't forget, she's involved Taylor and Christy, as well. That's when I thought she'd stepped over the line. You haven't even asked Charlotte to marry you, and Elizabeth's got your sisters choosing bridesmaids' dresses. By the way, I don't suppose she told you about the honeymoon? Two weeks in Hawaii—it's our wedding gift to you."

Jason clenched his fist at his side and closed his eyes, trying to calm himself. It didn't work. The situation was absurd. And he was beginning to see that his father was in on this nonsense. "Two weeks in Hawaii... Taylor and Christy choosing bridesmaids' dresses. You've both gone off the deep end."

"To your mother's credit, she didn't intend for this to happen. It just did. I know you're upset now, and to be honest, I don't blame you, but once you get used to the idea, it doesn't sound so ludicrous."

Get used to the idea, Jason mused. He felt like he was in the middle of a nightmare. "You honestly think I should agree to this...this outrageousness?" He could barely speak.

"Answer me this. Are you in love with Charlotte?"

"Yes." That much was a given—he'd already told his parents so.

"Do you intend to ask her to marry you?"

His dad knew the answer to that, too. "Yes…eventually, in my own time and my own way."

"If you're planning to marry the girl anyway, then what's the problem?"

"I wasn't going to do it in three weeks!"

"Three weeks, three months, what's the difference?"

Jason couldn't believe it. His father was talking pure craziness.

"I realize your mother and I went about this wrong, but after what happened with your brothers and sisters, all I ask is that you cut us a little slack."

"A little slack," he snorted. "Marriage is a serious step. A man doesn't make that kind of decision one minute and march up the aisle the next."

"I used to feel that way myself, but it's pretty much what happened with Taylor and Russ, as well as Christy and Cody. They made up their minds, then went right ahead and did it."

"All right, all right," Jason muttered, willing to concede the point. Their weddings were spontaneous, to say the least. Same for Rich and Paul.

"I agree, marriage is a serious step," his father went on calmly, "but if you're in love with Charlotte and intend to marry her anyway, I don't see the harm in your mother getting the ball rolling."

The ball rolling. She'd started an avalanche. "Don't you think Mom's just a tad premature?"

"Perhaps," his father agreed amicably enough. "But you can't really blame her for that. She got caught up in

the excitement of the moment. Once she talked to the yacht club, everything sort of fell into place. It makes sense once you analyze it. You've been a bachelor a long time, Jason. If you're as serious about marrying Charlotte as you claim, my advice is, just do it. If you wait, you might talk yourself out of it."

"Do it," Jason echoed. "You make marriage sound like taking up an exercise program." He could see he wasn't going to make any more headway with his father than he had his mother.

"Think about it, all right? That's all I ask."

"Aren't you forgetting something?"

"What?"

"Charlotte might say no."

His father laughed. "Charlotte's as much in love with you as you are with her. She'll marry you in a New York minute and we both know it."

"But, Dad…"

"Just think about it overnight. That's all your mother and I are asking. If you decide you'd rather not go through with this, then phone us in the morning and we'll put a stop to everything."

"I don't need to sleep on this," Jason argued. "I can tell you right now that I'm not going to agree. I've never heard anything more absurd in my life. A wedding in a few weeks! I was thinking more along the lines of two or three years!"

A heavy silence followed his words. "Then you must not be as much in love as your mother and I assumed. Give us a call in the morning," his father said and hung up the phone.

Jason was too furious to stand still. He paced his living room, jerked his baseball cap off his head and

slapped it against his thigh. He tried to smooth out the crease in the bill, realized he couldn't and tossed the hat on top of the television.

Earlier that evening, he'd been talking to Charlotte about this very thing—people manipulating and controlling others. Well, he wasn't about to fall prey to it now. Especially not with his parents.

If he allowed his mother to schedule his wedding, there was no telling where she'd stop. The next thing he knew she'd be meddling in *all* his personal affairs. She'd be deciding when it was time for him and Charlotte to have a family.

He drew in a deep, calming breath to clear his head.

His assessment of his mother was unfair, he told himself a few minutes later. His parents hadn't interfered in his brothers' or sisters' marriages. From what he understood, they'd suggested Leah and Paul get married, but that was common sense. Leah and Paul should have seen it themselves. He knew his parents had debated long and hard about confronting them and had done so reluctantly, after much soul-searching.

But arranging his marriage to Charlotte was an entirely different matter. They'd stepped over the boundary there—although…although he did understand how easy it must have been to get caught up in the heat of the moment. Getting the date at the yacht club had set everything in motion, and before either of his parents were aware of it, they'd planned the whole wedding.

As he recalled from his dinner conversation the day before, Jason had told his mother that Charlotte would welcome her assistance in planning the wedding. She'd done a bit more than suggest what type of flowers to use in the bridal bouquet, however.

No, it was out of the question.

Jason flatly refused to be a pawn. When he was ready to marry Charlotte he'd...

Married. He and Charlotte.

He needed at least a year just to get used to the idea. A man his age didn't surrender his freedom without plenty of serious thought.

Then he remembered the phenomenon of holding Charlotte in his arms, of loving her, and the simple pleasure he found in spending time with her. He tried to imagine what his life would be like without her and discovered he couldn't. So his belief that he wasn't ready flew out the window.

But marriage, he told himself, would take away his freedom. He'd never watch another game on TV again without feeling guilty—a wife would make sure of that. Women nagged and controlled, didn't they?

Charlotte was a woman, but she wasn't like the others he'd known. She'd been controlled and manipulated herself; she'd fought against it. Jason couldn't in all honesty believe she'd try the same tactics on him.

Once again his argument wouldn't hold.

All right, maybe there were more things to consider besides his freedom. But here, too, he was losing ground. He'd found freedom in Charlotte, freedom to be himself, freedom to look toward the future.

Charlotte wanted children.

Another contentious issue. Children. Carrie had said as much the day she'd stopped by his office to bribe him to take out her mother. If he married Charlotte, he might as well accept that a year or so down the road they'd have a baby.

So? Wasn't that what he wanted?

He hadn't thought much about a family until recently. He vividly remembered the sensations that had overwhelmed him the first time he'd seen Charlotte holding Jeremy. Watching her play with his brother's son had left him breathless. Of course, being hit by a fast-moving Frisbee might have contributed to that.

Okay, so he wanted children. A man didn't marry a woman without giving the prospect some consideration. Since he was well past thirty, and fast approaching forty, he should start thinking along those lines soon. Charlotte was nearly thirty-six herself, and he knew it was safer for a woman to give birth before the age of forty.

Which meant he had to throw out his idea of waiting two or three years to get married. If he was serious, and he was, they should do it soon.

But three weeks was *too* soon....

He'd sleep on it, Jason decided, take his father's advice and give this whole wedding business some thought. But he could say right now, that on general principles alone, he was against it.

An hour later, after tossing and turning and wreaking havoc with his bedsheets, Jason knew. Knew it from the way he couldn't keep his hands from clenching. Knew it from the way his stomach tensed.

He was going to marry Charlotte Weston. The wedding was already scheduled.

Charlotte didn't know what was wrong with him. Jason had fidgeted all through dinner, although dinner had been his idea. He'd called her early that morning, before she'd left for work, and invited her out.

The invitation had sounded offhand, spur of the mo-

ment. Or that was how he'd apparently intended it to sound. But Charlotte wasn't fooled. His voice had tensed as though he wasn't sure she'd say yes—which was ridiculous. Surely he knew how crazy she was about him. Yet, when she assured him she'd be happy to join him for dinner, he hadn't seemed the least bit relieved.

She'd suggested Mr. Tamales, but he'd disagreed. Instead he'd chosen a fancy seafood restaurant near the harbor. She'd been looking forward to chicken enchiladas, but certainly wasn't disappointed with her shrimp Louis.

Charlotte could have sworn, however, that Jason hadn't eaten more than three bites of his wine-sautéed scallops. "Jason," she said after a long silence. "Is something bothering you?"

"No," he replied abruptly.

"You haven't said a word in the last five minutes. Aren't you feeling well?"

"My stomach's in knots." His reply was quick and short-tempered. He reached for his water glass, emptying ice chips into his mouth, then chewed on them fiercely.

"Do you want to leave?"

His eyes met hers and for an all-too-brief moment the tension eased from around his mouth. "Not yet."

"Okay," she said, wondering at his strange mood.

"How did everything go with your boss?" he asked, seeming to want to change the subject.

She'd already told him, but apparently he hadn't been paying attention. "He's angry, especially since two other people also gave their notice when they learned I wasn't changing my mind."

"Did he try to make staying worth your while?"

Charlotte nodded. "He offered me and the others a raise." Mr. Ward had called all three of them into his office, smugly claimed he was willing to overlook this small mutiny and offered them each a raise if they'd withdraw their resignations.

"You didn't take his bride—I mean bribe—did you?"

"No." Charlotte was still basking in the satisfaction she'd felt when she told Mr. Ward she wasn't interested in withdrawing her notice. Cheryl and Janice hadn't changed their minds, either. Mr. Ward had been stunned, but she knew that would soon pass.

Before the end of the two weeks, he'd try every manipulative tactic in the book. When she didn't give in, he'd try anger, his least effective tool.

She was through with a boss who was so angry and unreasonable. Through with guilt and regret and abuse. She already had a line on another job, although she would've enjoyed taking the summer off.

Unfortunately, she couldn't afford it. As it was, she only had two months' budget in her savings account, and it had taken her a year to accumulate that much. She called it her "attitude money." It was a whole lot easier to walk away from her position at the agency, knowing she had some cash to fall back on if she didn't get a job right away.

"How about dessert?" Jason suggested after the waitress had taken their dinner dishes away.

She shook her head. "No, thanks. I'm stuffed."

He looked disappointed at her response.

"You go ahead, though," she urged.

Jason immediately rejected the idea, proving her initial impression wrong. But if he *wasn't* craving dessert,

what did he want? He seemed restless, yet obviously wasn't inclined to leave.

Whatever was bothering Jason wasn't trivial, Charlotte realized. Jason Manning wasn't a man easily unnerved. She wondered if it was something she'd done, something she'd said. She didn't know what to make of his behavior. Throughout dinner, she'd considered various explanations, none of which seemed all that logical.

The silence between them lingered as they sipped their after-dinner coffee. From the moment he'd picked her up, she'd been surprised that Jason was wearing a suit, the same attractive gray one he'd had on the night of the dance. His brother's suit. She knew very well that he didn't dress formally unless it was some important occasion. His entire wardrobe consisted of jeans and T-shirts.

He hated wearing a suit. Five minutes after they'd arrived at the dance, he'd loosened his tie, and had completely discarded it by the end of the evening. Why he'd worn one this evening remained a mystery.

Charlotte frowned, trying to analyze what was wrong. Waiting for Jason to tell her was making her nervous. He looked miserable, which made *her* increasingly miserable.

She felt close to Jason, closer than she'd felt to any man since Tom. She hadn't meant that to happen, and she didn't think Jason had, either. Their relationship had grown steadily more intense in the past weeks. She'd fallen in love—it was that simple—and thought he had, too.

But perhaps falling in love wasn't what Jason wanted. Perhaps he was trying to find a way to tell her they were in too deep, that he wanted out.

It made sense.

The fancy dinner, the hesitation and even regret. The fact that his eyes kept avoiding hers. The silence. That was the worst. The awkward silence, as though he couldn't bear to speak those final words.

"I'm ready to leave, if you are," she said with false enthusiasm.

He looked over at her, his expression uncertain. Perhaps he planned to tell her in the restaurant, in order to avoid a scene. She'd heard that was a popular tactic. All Charlotte wanted to do was leave, before she made a fool of herself by breaking into tears.

He was going to break up with her; she was sure of it. A hundred explanations crowded her mind. They'd gotten too close, too fast. It wasn't as if she was...unencumbered. True, she was single, but she had a child, and if a man was going to get serious with a woman, he'd prefer that she didn't bring along excess baggage. That was common knowledge. She'd heard it often enough from friends and acquaintances.

Jason's parents might have disapproved of her, too. It wasn't as if she came from a fine, upstanding family. His mother had asked her a number of questions Saturday morning about her parents and grandparents. Charlotte had found it difficult to explain that she had no idea where her father was, or even if he was still alive. Neither of the elder Mannings had seemed to disapprove of her openly. If anything, they'd been warm and gracious. But although they might have accepted her, even liked her, they might also think she was the wrong kind of woman for their son.

Jason paid the bill while Charlotte excused herself

for a visit to the ladies' room, hoping to regain her composure.

He was waiting for her by the door when she returned.

Silence accompanied them into the parking lot.

Jason opened her door. By the time he'd walked around the front of his car, Charlotte's hold on her poise was tenuous. When he glanced in her direction, though, she managed a smile. Her pride demanded it.

Charlotte expected Jason to drive her directly to the apartment, since he hadn't been able to break the news to her at the restaurant. At least when he delivered the blow, it would be in the comfort of familiar surroundings.

But he drove to a deserted stretch of beach, then pulled off the road, climbed out of the car and came around to her side.

"It's late," she said, frowning at her watch. "I should be getting home. Carrie's by herself."

"In a minute." He wore a pensive frown, the same expression she'd seen all evening.

She gazed past him to the shoreline. Small breakers rolled onto the sand, their motion soothing. Charlotte wasn't soothed, however, and she looked away to the wide expanse of darkening sky. The scent of the sea hung in the air.

"Just say it," she muttered. Her patience had evaporated and she couldn't bear the painful silence anymore.

"You know?"

"Of course I know." She walked onto the sand, removed her shoes and purposefully forged ahead, stopping at a thick log that was charred at one end.

Swallowing a mouthful of self-pity, she looked over

her shoulder to discover that Jason had followed her onto the beach. She almost wished he'd driven away, left her behind. It would've been easier that way.

Her legs didn't feel as if they'd support her much longer, so she sat on the log and stared sightlessly out at the horizon, waiting for him to begin his litany of excuses and stumbling explanations.

"Charlotte... I'm not very good at this sort of thing."

"Who is? Listen, it's been great." She strove to sound flippant and knew she'd failed. She lowered her gaze to her hands, forcing herself to continue. "I'll always be grateful for this time with you." Tears rolled down her cheeks and she brushed them aside, not daring to look at Jason. "But as we both know, all good things must come to an end...."

Jason said nothing. Not one word, and that made everything even more difficult.

His hands were buried in his pants pockets and when she glanced up at his face, she saw that his jaw was tightly clenched. She didn't understand his anger, not when she'd made it so easy for him.

"So you had me sit through that whole miserable dinner," he said with barely controlled antagonism. "Did you enjoy watching me squirm?"

"No."

"You know, Charlotte, if you weren't interested in marrying me in the first place you could have—"

"Marrying you!" Charlotte's head snapped up. "You planned on asking me to *marry* you?" For one wild second she was paralyzed with shock, unable to move or think. There must've been a mistake. It was a joke. Jason Manning was a confirmed bachelor, wasn't he? Despite her feelings for him, Charlotte had accepted that.

"Don't pretend you didn't know," he said.

"But I thought… I thought you wanted to stop seeing me."

He snickered as though he didn't believe her and turned away. "Why would I take you to a fancy restaurant if I wanted to say something as ridiculous as that?" He turned back, glaring at her.

"To let me down easy. What did you expect me to think, when you were in such a bad mood?"

"I already told you I'm no good at this sort of thing. If you want romance and a bunch of pretty words, you're going to have to marry someone else."

She was on her feet and not quite sure how she got there. "You honestly want to marry me?" she repeated as her eyes brimmed with tears. They were tears of relief. Tears of joy.

"Sit down," he said gruffly. "If I'm going to do this, I want to do it right."

Charlotte complied and was shocked when Jason got down on one knee directly in front of her. He cleared his throat. "I love you, Charlotte. I wasn't planning to fall in love with you, but I knew it was happening, and I let it happen because—well, I don't really know. It happened and I'm glad it did. I can't think of spending a day without you at my side. I can't imagine playing softball without you there. I love you. I love the chocolate chip cookies you bake. I admire you for the wonderful job you've done raising Carrie. I'm deeply impressed by your wisdom and courage."

"Oh, Jase." She blinked back her tears and brought her fingertips to her lips.

"You're the first woman I ever dated who let me be myself. You didn't feel obligated to clean up after me.

You don't act as if my refrigerator's some kind of scary science experiment." He grinned, apparently pleased with his own wit. "You even like sports."

The lump in her throat made it impossible to speak. Tears ran unrestrained down her face. With all her heart she wanted to shout, "Yes, I'll marry you," and throw her arms around him. But she was afraid to believe Jason would continue to love her once he learned how inadequate she was, how worthless she was as a lover. She didn't know if she could bear to disappoint him.

"If it helps," he said in a low voice, "I talked to Carrie, and she's all for us getting married."

Charlotte sniffed tearfully. "You mean my daughter's given you her seal of approval?"

"Yup."

There was another silence. Then he said, "I don't mean to rush you, but I have this sore knee. I slid into first base last week and I've been in pain ever since. So, if you don't mind, I'd prefer a quick answer."

Before she could stop herself, before she could listen to her head instead of her heart, she nodded. It wasn't a very enthusiastic nod, perhaps, but Jason didn't seem to have any objections.

"Thank God," he murmured, awkwardly rising to his feet.

"You idiot. You didn't have to get down on your knee," she whispered through her tears.

"Yes, I did," he said, but he sounded grateful to be off it as he sat down on the log beside her. A deep sigh rumbled through his chest. "It wasn't the most romantic proposal, was it?"

"Oh, Jase, it was perfect," she said, touching the side of his face and gazing into his eyes. Her throat was tight

and constricted. "What you said about not being able to live without me…that's how I feel about you. Sharing cookies, going to ball games, walking the dog together—it all sounds wonderful. I guess I'm not much of a romantic, either," she said with a shy laugh.

"I didn't buy a diamond ring. I figured you'd want to pick a setting yourself."

A ring. Charlotte froze. Soon he'd want to discuss a wedding date. A chill worked its way through her, the same cold feeling she'd experienced whenever Tom wanted to make love. A sick sensation would build in the pit of her stomach and by the time they went to bed she'd feel encased in ice. All Tom had to do was kiss her and he'd know. Then the tirades would begin, the accusations, the ugliness.

Jason was going to kiss her, too. Now. His lips grazed hers. Briefly. Lightly. The cold fear melted as if it had never been. Charlotte groaned and slipped her arms around his neck.

He kissed her again, but this time the kiss blossomed into something wild and erotic that left Charlotte panting, seeking more.

They drew apart, and she rested her forehead against his. When he spoke, his voice was husky and warm, as warm as heated brandy and just as intoxicating.

"We're going to be very good in bed," he whispered.

Charlotte tensed, panic a heartbeat away, but she forced it down, focusing instead on how gentle he'd always been with her. How patient. With Jason, she'd felt a level of pleasure she'd never realized she was capable of reaching. When he kissed her she felt hot and quivery from the inside out. Maybe it would be different this time, with this man. Maybe. She prayed that was true.

"You're worried about making love, aren't you?"

She nodded.

"I'd never hurt you, Charlotte. I hope you understand that. Whatever the problem is, we'll work it out together."

"I'm grateful…for that." Despite the excitement she felt at his kisses, she had to fight back the fear that threatened to choke her every time he mentioned the physical aspects of their relationship.

Her only recourse was to insist on a long engagement. That way she could slowly, gradually, feel comfortable with their sexual relationship. After they made love… She hesitated. There'd been a time she wouldn't have thought that was possible, but Jason had given her hope.

"Do you want to set the wedding date?" she asked, deciding to broach the subject now.

"Yes, but…" He shrugged. "There's one small problem."

"What's that?"

"I'm going to let my parents tell you. It's only fair. They're at home, waiting for us now."

Eleven

"I don't believe this!" Jason muttered under his breath as they pulled into his parents' driveway.

"What are all these cars doing here?" Carrie asked from the backseat. Jason had insisted on going back to the apartment to pick her up.

"You'll see," he said grimly.

Either his parents owned a car dealership or they were entertaining a houseful of company.

"This is going to be a real circus." He sighed as he helped Charlotte out of the front seat. Carrie bounded out from the back.

Charlotte's nervousness, already heightened by the prospect of an audience, grew exponentially.

The door opened and Elizabeth Manning stepped out of the house. Jason's father and brothers, sisters-in-law and several children all crowded on the front porch behind her. The porch light revealed a variety of expressions, from amusement to elation.

"Well?" his mother asked as she walked toward them.

Jason slid his arm around Charlotte's waist and

slowly, sweetly smiled down at her. In those brief seconds, Charlotte was comforted and reassured by his love. Her senses sang and her heart fluttered wildly.

Jason lowered his head. Charlotte wasn't sure that kissing in front of his parents, his whole family, was the best thing to do. Oh, what the heck. She was marrying Jason. They were in love, so a simple kiss shouldn't offend anyone.

Their lips met and she moaned a little with surprise and wonder at the ready response he never failed to evoke from her. Her hand crept up his chest and gripped the lapel of his suit jacket as his mouth made love to hers.

When he broke away, he was breathless. For that matter, so was Charlotte. She marveled that he was able to speak at all. "Does that answer your question, Mother?"

"Charlotte's agreed to marry you?"

"In a heartbeat," she answered for herself.

"Isn't it great!" Carrie shouted.

Spontaneous applause broke out from the porch, followed by several earsplitting whistles. Ryan and Ronnie were pounding their feet but she doubted the little boys understood exactly what the family was celebrating.

The evening was lovely; honeysuckle and roses scented the air. The sun had almost set, casting—literally—a rosy glow over the scene.

Jason bowed as though he were a knight and she his lady, accepting his family's enthusiasm.

"I hope you realize you're getting the runt of the litter," Paul told her, laughing.

"Hey," Rich put in. "Just be grateful that Charlotte's

willing to put Jason out of his misery. He's been walking around like a lovesick puppy for weeks."

Jason glowered at his brothers, but she could tell he wasn't angry. He took their teasing in stride. From the time he'd brought her to that first softball game, Charlotte had envied him his family, especially the close relationship he shared with his brothers. The three were more than brothers; they were best friends. They looked out for one another and, just as important, they laughed together.

Leah and Jamie were best friends, too. Yet they seemed eager to extend that camaraderie to Charlotte. They'd gone out of their way to include her, to make her feel welcome, a part of the family. One of them.

Jason's mother came forward, tears in her eyes as she hugged Charlotte. "I couldn't be more pleased. Jason couldn't have chosen better."

"Thank you," Charlotte said, blushing. Doubt bobbed like a cork to the surface of her mind. Not that she didn't love Jason. She did, with all her heart, but she still wasn't sure whether she was the right woman for him.

"I'm so happy for you—and for us," Jamie said, hugging her next. "The two of you are perfect for each other. Leah and I agreed on that the minute we saw you together."

A warmth permeated Charlotte's heart. She wanted so badly to believe it was true.

"We'll be sisters now," Leah whispered, taking Charlotte's hands and lightly squeezing her fingers.

"I couldn't be marrying into a more wonderful family," Charlotte said to Jason as they made their way into the house. Carrie followed, carrying Jeremy, while the other children raced excitedly ahead.

His brothers congratulated Jason, slapping him on the back.

Once inside, Jason and Charlotte sat on the couch and the family gathered around them, making them the center of attention. Every eye was on Charlotte, smiling and happy, yet expectant. Puzzled, she glanced up at Jason, wondering if they wanted her to say something, to make some speech or pronouncement.

"Does she know yet?" Paul asked.

"No," Jason murmured. "I'm leaving the explanation up to Mom and Dad."

"Smart boy," Rich said, sitting on the armrest of the couch. He leaned forward eagerly, as though waiting for the opening act of an award-winning play.

"What's everyone talking about?" she asked.

"Mom?" Jason gestured eloquently toward his mother.

Elizabeth hesitated and turned to her husband. Eric Manning grinned and gave his wife a reassuring nod, which only compounded Charlotte's curiosity.

"As I said, I'm delighted that you've agreed to marry Jason," Elizabeth began. "He's waited all this time to meet the right woman and, frankly, Eric and I were beginning to wonder if that was ever going to happen. Now that we've met you, Charlotte, we're glad he waited so long. We understood the moment we saw you together how special you were to him."

A low murmuring chorus of assent brought a sheen of tears to Charlotte's eyes. If anyone should be grateful, it was her. Jason had changed her world, opened her mind to everything she'd believed was closed off to her. Love. Family. Joy. Partnership.

The room went strangely quiet. Charlotte looked

around and, although everyone seemed genuinely pleased, there was a tension here, too.

"Just tell her, Mother," Jason advised. "No need to drag this out."

By now, Charlotte was more than curious. "Tell me what?"

"Don't rush me," Elizabeth said, chiding her son. "Charlotte," she began, "when Jason told us he'd fallen in love with you, his father and I naturally wondered about his intentions. Then he told us he intended to ask you to marry him, so we decided to do a bit of checking in regard to the arrangements. Weddings need to be planned."

Jason's fingers entwined with hers, his hold on her hand tightening.

Elizabeth paused as though she expected a response. "Well, yes," Charlotte said, since everyone was staring at her. "That's a practical thing to do."

"I learned some distressing news," his mother continued. "The yacht club, which we feel is the best place for the reception, is booked solid for the next twenty-three months."

Once again, like clockwork, all eyes in the room swiveled to Charlotte, awaiting her response. "I hope you put our name on a waiting list, then," she murmured.

Elizabeth brightened, and some of the tension lines on her forehead seemed to relax. "I did better than that. You see," she went on, her voice growing more confident, "there happened to be a cancellation, and so I asked they reserve that day for you and Jason."

"Wonderful."

"You're leaving out the most important part," Jason said, his lips barely moving.

"The date is July fourteenth," Elizabeth announced, folding her hands and nodding sagely. "Don't you think that's excellent timing?"

"That sounds fine," Charlotte agreed, when it was apparent once again that everyone was waiting for her to respond. A little more than a year would give her and Jason ample time to discover if a marriage between them was viable. By then, they'd certainly know if a sexual relationship was possible. A year gave them both an opportunity to adjust.

"It's not July fourteenth of *next* year," Jason filled in, his gaze locking with hers. "Mother meant July fourteenth of *this* year."

Charlotte was too stunned to respond, other than with a gasp. Her mouth fell open in shock.

"What's the problem, Mom?" Carrie asked, looking surprised.

"But...but no one can plan a wedding of any size in that length of time," Charlotte managed after a moment. "It's...impossible."

"Not for Elizabeth," Leah said, her eyes sparkling with excitement. "Mom's been working on this since Jason mentioned the word *marriage*."

"But..."

"I've seen to everything," Elizabeth said confidently. "And it *is* possible, very possible—if you'll agree to such a quick wedding. I realize we're being unfair to you, and I do hope you'll find it in your heart to forgive me for taking over like this. The thing is, I know my son, and once he makes up his mind, that's the end

of it. Jason wouldn't have been willing to wait almost two years."

"But…there are other places. Besides the yacht club, I mean."

"Yes, but none of them are as special."

"Charlotte," Jason said, raising her hand to his lips and kissing it. "I know it sounds crazy, but Mom's right. I wouldn't have wanted to wait just so my mother could put on a fancy wedding. At first I thought she'd gone berserk. The idea's preposterous, but the more I thought about it, the more I liked it."

"Leah and I will do anything we can to help," Jamie inserted. "If you want the truth, we're both thrilled."

"Taylor and Christy and their families are flying out. They've already made their reservations," Elizabeth added.

"But they can change them," Jason told her, frowning at his mother as if to say Charlotte was under enough pressure as it was.

And he was right. She felt as if a giant hammer was poised above her head, ready to smash down on her at any second. The entire family was waiting. Happy. Excited. Thrilled. Carrie's eyes begged her to say yes.

"Of course, Taylor and Christy can change their reservations, if necessary," someone said. That was Paul, and Charlotte wanted to thank him.

"Personally, I think it's wildly romantic," Leah added. She was sitting in the recliner, her hand resting on her swollen abdomen. Paul was sitting on the armrest, his arm wrapped around his wife's shoulders, his eyes filled with love as he gazed down on her.

"Naturally I haven't made any final decisions—that would be up to you," Elizabeth said.

"I...don't know what to say."

"You must think I'm a domineering old woman, and I suppose I am, but nothing's been finalized. I don't generally meddle in my children's lives, but—"

"Actually, if you want to be angry with anyone, it should be with the rest of us," Jamie told her. "Jason is the family's last chance for Mom to put on a big wedding. She'd been looking forward to it for years and we all disappointed her. She's always done a fabulous job with the receptions, though."

"We've had our hearts set on a formal wedding for so long," Eric said.

"But in three weeks?" Charlotte murmured.

"We'll all need to work together, of course, but we can do it." Jason's mother sounded utterly convinced of that. Her eyes sought out Charlotte's and, in their beautiful blue depths, Charlotte saw how much Elizabeth wanted this. How much the entire family did. They all looked forward to contributing.

"Charlotte," Jason said softly, "would you like more time to decide?"

She glanced around; everyone was waiting. The room had gone completely silent; even the children were quiet. Charlotte didn't know how she could refuse. She closed her eyes and tried to think. If she postponed the wedding, the elder Mannings might hold it against her. It could taint their future relationship. The others were just as eager for this to happen. Each one felt guilty for cheating Eric and Elizabeth out of the family wedding they wanted.

Her whole future with the Manning family could be at stake, Charlotte thought.

"Do I...need to decide now?" she asked after an awkward moment.

"There's so little time," Elizabeth warned.

Charlotte glanced from one to the other and knew she couldn't refuse. She loved Jason and wanted to marry him more than she'd wanted anything in her life. She could be happy with him, happy in ways she'd hardly imagined before. And for the first time she and Carrie had the chance to be part of a real family.

If she were to marry Jason there was the possibility of her having another child. *If* she conquered her fear of sex. The hollow ache inside her intensified as she studied the soft swell of Leah's abdomen.

She turned to Jason, needing some kind of confirmation, some indication of what he was thinking. His eyes, so like his mother's, blue and intense, reflected his love for her. His faith in her. The desire to be part of *her* life. He believed their love was enough to overcome any obstacle. Their love was all that was necessary.

For now, because she wanted to believe it, too, that was enough for her, too.

"We have a lot to do, then, don't we?" she said, reluctantly dragging her gaze away from Jason and back to his mother.

"Does that mean you agree?"

She nodded and the entire family broke into cheers.

The excitement and the enthusiasm carried Charlotte for a full two weeks. Two of the busiest weeks of her life. When she wasn't putting in her final days at work, she was with Jason's mother.

During their first afternoon together, it became apparent that Elizabeth was a gifted organizer. She'd have

to be in order to pull off a full-scale wedding in less than a month.

Ignorance had been bliss. Had Charlotte realized the sheer magnitude of what they needed to accomplish in such a short time, she would have refused.

Not a day passed that she didn't have some kind of appointment, some place to be, someone to meet, some decision to make. There were dressmakers, florists, photographers, caterers and printers. And countless decisions, all of which had to be dealt with right that minute. There wasn't time to ponder or reflect. As soon as one task was completed, Elizabeth steered her toward the next.

Carrie was delighted to be her mother's maid of honor. Charlotte's four soon-to-be sisters-in-law were to be her bridesmaids, and that meant frequent conference calls between Montana and Seattle.

When Charlotte somehow found time to see Jason, it was for a few moments, and then only in passing. He, too, was exceptionally busy.

Just when it looked like everything was falling neatly into place, and Charlotte would finally be able to return to a life of her own, a series of showers and parties began. Every night was busy with one event or another. Even the women in the office held a bridal shower for her on her last day with the agency.

The Mannings were a well-established, well-liked family. Three of Elizabeth's closest friends decided to honor Charlotte with a shower the Monday before the wedding.

"I can't believe how generous everyone is," Charlotte said to Carrie, who had just attended the shower with

her. They were carrying the wide array of gifts from the car into the apartment.

"Those old ladies don't even know you," Carrie remarked, her voice filled with astonishment. "All these gifts! You don't suppose they'd throw a birthday party for me sometime, do you?"

"Carrie!"

"Just joking, Mom." She hurried past Charlotte and brought in a gaily decorated box that was still unopened. Charlotte had been told the gift was for Jason, therefore he should be the one to open it. The giver was his godmother, a spry older woman named Donna Bondi.

"You want me to see if Jason's home?" Carrie asked eagerly.

Charlotte, too, was curious to see what was inside. "Go ahead." It was almost ten, and under normal circumstances Charlotte would've been more concerned about getting to bed so she'd be ready for work in the morning, but her two-weeks' notice was up and she was officially among the unemployed.

She had the entire week free, or as free as any bride's time could be five days before her wedding.

Carrie returned a few minutes later with Jason in tow. He smiled when he saw her and kissed her lightly on the lips, then bent to stroke an ecstatic Higgins. "What's this I hear about Mrs. Bondi sending me a gift?"

"She insisted you open it yourself."

Jason's look was skeptical. "Is it a gag gift?"

"I don't know. Why don't you find out?" Charlotte leaned against the kitchen counter and crossed her arms. "When you're finished, I'll show you all the loot we collected. I had no idea everyone would be so extravagant."

"Don't get any ideas about spending our honeymoon writing thank-you notes," he warned. He was grinning but she caught a serious undertone.

The honeymoon.

She wanted to talk to Jason about that, *needed* to talk to him about it, but there'd been so little time. They'd each been caught up in a whirlwind of activity. Since the evening he'd taken her to dinner and proposed, she hadn't spent any uninterrupted time with him. Now wasn't good, either. He was tired and so was she. Perhaps they could arrange to have lunch one day later this week.

Jason tore at the paper.

"You wouldn't believe Mom," Carrie said, her hands on the back of a kitchen chair as she looked on excitedly. "She doesn't tear a single piece of wrapping paper."

"It's all so pretty," Charlotte defended herself. "And I can use it again."

"It takes her forever to unwrap anything. I had to help her tonight, or we'd still be there."

Jason paused when he uncovered a plain white box. He raised his eyes to Charlotte.

"Don't look at me. I have no idea what Mrs. Bondi sent you."

Carefully he raised the lid and folded back the white tissue paper, but Charlotte couldn't see what was inside with Carrie bending over the table.

"All right, Mrs. Bondi," Jason said, emitting a low whistle.

Carrie covered her mouth and giggled before glancing at her mother.

"What is it?" Charlotte asked.

"Wait until you see this, Mom."

Using both hands, holding on to the thin straps, Jason lifted the sheerest, slinkiest, blackest nightie Charlotte had ever seen.

Charlotte forced a smile but she felt as though the older woman had slapped her in the face.

Charlotte knew better than to even try to sleep.

The next morning she'd walk down the church aisle and pledge her life to Jason Manning. She would vow to love and honor this man who'd come to mean so much to her.

To love him....

What would happen if she couldn't love him properly? What would happen when he realized she was incapable of satisfying him sexually? Would he claim he'd been cheated the way Tom had? Would he seek out another woman who'd give him the gratification she couldn't?

Oh, please, not that, not again—she couldn't bear it.

Charlotte didn't know how Jason would react, but she knew she'd find out soon.

She stared at the bright green numbers on her clock radio as one in the morning became two and then three.

The alarm was set for six. Charlotte's stomach tightened and a cold sweat broke out on her forehead. Her happiness had been supplanted by her fears, her anxieties and the certainty that her heart would be broken once again.

She'd made an effort to talk to Jason several times, she reasoned. It wasn't like she'd *planned* it this way. In the past week alone she'd called him three times, but he'd been so busy with his practice, tying up the loose

ends so he'd have two uninterrupted weeks for their honeymoon in Hawaii.

The honeymoon terrified her even more than the wedding.

What was she supposed to do? Wait for Jason to say "I do," before she whispered in his ear that she wasn't sure she could satisfy him? Or should she say something before he slipped the ring on her finger?

It seemed cruel to wait until they got to their honeymoon suite. How could she possibly tell him something like that wearing the sheer black nightie Mrs. Bondi had sent?

The tightening in her stomach grew worse, until she thought she might actually throw up.

She shouldn't have left it to the last minute like this, but she'd had no other options.

She'd tried to spend time alone with Jason, to talk to him, but they hadn't connected all week. Whenever she saw him, there were other people around. She'd decided to demand time with him after the wedding rehearsal. They had to talk.

Only that hadn't worked, either.

They'd sat next to each other at the rehearsal dinner, but before she could say more than a few words, his brothers had spirited him away for a bachelor party.

Although she hadn't been in any mood to socialize, Charlotte had pretended to have a good time with Leah, Jamie, Jason's two sisters from Montana and her future mother-in-law. If any of them noticed how distracted she was, they must have attributed it to nerves.

By now the bachelor party would be over, probably had been for hours.

What was she going to do?

Her dinner, what little she'd eaten, soured in her stomach and she thought she might be sick. Tossing back the sheets, she climbed out of bed, waiting for the nausea to subside, then wandered aimlessly into the living room.

Dragging the afghan from the back of the sofa, she wrapped it around her shoulders and huddled in the recliner, the dog at her feet. Carrie and Mandy, Russ Palmer's half sister, were in the bedroom down the hall sleeping soundly, unaware of her torment.

Jason knew so little about her first marriage. He hadn't asked for information, and she'd volunteered even less. Instead, he'd cautiously tried to learn the details, but she'd put off explaining, afraid she'd lose him.

Soon, within less than twenty-four hours, Jason would know for himself why Tom had gone to another woman. Charlotte would have to face her inadequacies all over again.

As she sat in the dark, the shadows from the street danced against the walls, taunting her, jeering, shouting that she was a fool to believe she could ever satisfy a man.

Another hour passed and still the trapped, restless feeling refused to leave her; if anything, it became more intense. If only she could sleep. If only she could disappear. Vanish. Go someplace where no one would find her.

Squeezing her eyes shut, she tried to force her body to relax, but closing her eyes was just one more mistake. In her mind, Tom rose, scorn engraved on his handsome features. A cocky smile lifted the edges of his mouth, as if to tell her this was exactly what he'd been waiting for. As soon as she tried to make love with

another man, she'd know everything he'd told her was true. *He* wasn't the one to blame for the failure of their marriage; she was. Charlotte—a woman too cold, too stiff, too lacking in sensuality.

Her eyes shot open and hot tears dripped down her face. A series of sobs racked her shoulders and took control of her body until she was trembling from head to foot.

She couldn't bear it, couldn't deal with it. Tom was right, he'd always been right. She was a fool to believe that a sexual relationship between her and Jason would be any different, any better. They could kiss without a problem, but after the wedding, he was going to expect a lot more than a few kisses.

Panic filled her lungs, and it was all she could do not to scream in sheer terror.

Jason was wrapped in a warm cocoon of blankets, but the irritating noise refused to go away. He reached out his hand to turn off the alarm, fumbling with the dials before he realized it wasn't his alarm.

Opening one eye, he read the digital readout and discovered it was only four. He was entitled to another couple of hours' sleep. His head throbbed. Who'd come up with the bright idea of a morning wedding, anyway? No one had asked *him* about it.

The noise increased. It was now a steady pounding.

Someone was at his door. If this was one of his brothers' idea of a joke, he wasn't amused. He'd only gotten a few hours' sleep so far. If anyone in his family was involved in this, he'd make his displeasure clear in no uncertain terms.

Apparently whoever was at his door wasn't leaving.

Jason struggled out of bed, pulled on a pair of pants and walked blindly through his apartment.

"Who is it?" he demanded irritably, wiping a hand down his face.

"Carrie."

"And Mandy."

The two vaulted into the room as he opened the door.

"You've got to do something!" Carrie cried.

Although his vision was a bit fuzzy, he could tell that she'd been crying.

"We didn't know what to do," Mandy wailed.

"About what?"

"This." Carrie handed him an envelope with his name written across the front. He recognized the hand-writing as Charlotte's, but her usually smooth script was jerky and uneven.

Puzzled that she'd resort to writing a letter and having it delivered in the wee hours of the morning by two worried teenagers, he removed the single piece of paper.

He read it quickly.

Jason,
I'm sorry *seems so inadequate, but I can't go through with the wedding. Please, if you can, find it in your heart to forgive me.*

She'd signed it with her name.

It was a joke. Not a very good one, but he'd laugh over it in a few minutes.

"Who put you two up to this?" he asked, using his sternest voice.

"No one!" Carrie sobbed. "It's true. I got up to go to the bathroom and Mom's bedroom light was on, so

I went in to see what was wrong and she wasn't there. She wasn't anywhere."

"The car's gone, too," Mandy added.

The words galvanized Jason into action. He shook the hair out of his face.

"What are we going to do?" Carrie asked, still crying softly.

"*We* aren't doing anything," Jason answered firmly.

"But someone has to do something!"

"I'll take care of it," he assured them. "Don't breathe a word of this to anyone, understand?"

"But…"

"Just do as I say. There isn't time to argue. If I'm not back with Charlotte before the car comes to take her to the church, tell everyone she's with me."

"What are you going to do?" Mandy asked, her eyes following him as he trotted back to his bedroom. He turned back and grinned. "Do?" he repeated. "Find her, of course. She's got a wedding to attend."

Twelve

Jason couldn't even guess where Charlotte was. He finished dressing, grabbed his car keys and took off, determined to find her.

He drove around for an hour, considering various possibilities. He tried to think like she would. If he were a bride running away from a wedding, where would he go? But that didn't work; he'd never run away from anything in his life, certainly not a wedding.

Darned if he knew what Charlotte was thinking. He had difficulty enough understanding women under normal circumstances. Still, he'd thought Charlotte was different. He'd thought—he'd assumed, erroneously it seemed—that Charlotte was as eager for their wedding as he was. He was shocked that he'd been so blind to her doubts. She must be terrified to have run away like this. Terrified and alone.

He should've known something like this would happen. He'd backed her into a corner, pushed her into this wedding. He'd allowed his own needs, his own desires, to overrule hers.

As dawn streaked the horizon with lavender and pink, he found himself growing ever more concerned.

Where could she be?

His driving became increasingly reckless, his speed gaining as he raced desperately from one possible location to the next. Checking the time, he was nearly swallowed by panic.

There wasn't much time left. They were both supposed to be at the church in a couple of hours. The thought of hurrying back to his family and having to announce that Charlotte had run away filled him with a sick kind of dread. He wouldn't return, he decided, until he'd found her. Until he'd done whatever he could to calm her fears, to reassure her, convince her how much he loved her.

Jason wasn't sure what led him to the beach where he'd proposed to her.

When he saw her car parked haphazardly along the side of the road, he nearly collapsed in relief. A calmness took hold of him and his pulse slowed to an even, steady pace.

He parked behind her and rushed out of his car. The sound of the door closing must have been carried away with the wind, because she didn't turn around or give any indication that she realized he was there.

He paused for a few seconds, looking at her, his heart swelling with gratitude at finding her safe.

Charlotte sat on a log, facing the water. The same log he'd knelt in front of to ask her to marry him. He felt a stab of pain as he remembered that night and how ecstatic he'd been when she accepted his proposal. He didn't expect to feel that good again until they shared in the birth of a child.

Charlotte's shoulders were slumped forward and she seemed mesmerized by the gentle lapping of the water. The wind whipped her hair, which flew wildly about, but she didn't appear to notice. She wasn't wearing a sweater. She must be half freezing, Jason thought, peeling off his jacket.

He watched her for another moment, wondering exactly what he'd say. He'd had hours to prepare for this, hours to come up with the words to tell her how much he loved her and how sorry he was for the way everything had gone. Now he found himself speechless.

She didn't see him until he was almost upon her. When she happened to look up, he saw that her face, ravaged by tears, was as pale as moonlight. She blinked, then frowned as though she couldn't quite believe he was really there.

"Jason?"

"Funny meeting you here," he said, placing his jacket around her shoulders.

"I… How did you find me?"

"It took some effort. If you had any doubts, Charlotte, I wish you'd talked them over with me."

She frowned again. "There wasn't any time… I tried, honestly I did, but you were always so busy and the time went so fast, and now…" The rest of her words faded into nothingness, her gaze avoiding his.

"There's time now," he said, sitting down on the log beside her.

Her eyes widened. "I…can't go through with it."

"Why not?" he asked calmly.

She answered him with a wrenching sob. "Please… I can't. I don't love you…"

Jason tensed. "I don't believe that, Charlotte. There's something else."

"There is… I realize now that it's your family I love. I never had one of my own and it came to me that I was marrying you for all the wrong reasons. I…can't go through with the wedding… I just can't."

Jason felt as if someone had punched him. Hard. "My…family?"

"Yes," she cried. "They're all so wonderful and I… got carried away, thinking that if I married you… Carrie and I would be part of a large, loving family. Then I saw how unfair I was being to *you*…marrying you when I didn't love you."

A cold anger took hold of Jason. An anger rooted in pain and disillusionment.

"It's too bad you didn't think of that sooner, because all this soul-searching is a little too late." He grasped her arm and pulled her to her feet. She sagged against him, but he tugged at her and she straightened.

"Jason, please…"

"Shut up, Charlotte. Just shut up before I say something I'll regret." It was no comfort realizing she was the only woman who'd ever brought him willingly to his knees. He'd gone to her in love, a love so strong it had swept away his loneliness. Charlotte was throwing it all back at him now, rejecting his love, betraying him with her last-minute revelations.

Walking out on him at the eleventh hour like this couldn't be considered anything less. Nothing she could've done would have humiliated him more than to leave him standing at the altar.

"I can't be your wife… Don't you understand?"

Her voice was so weak he wasn't sure he'd heard her

correctly. Not that it mattered; nothing she could have said would've had any effect on him after her confession. It didn't matter if he could hear her or not. She was mumbling, pleading with him, but he closed off his heart the same way he had his ears.

When they reached his car, he opened the passenger door and deposited her inside. He ran around to the driver's side, not knowing if he could trust her to stay put. He was mildly surprised that she didn't try to escape.

He started the engine and turned on the heater. A blast of warm air filled the car. She didn't seem to notice.

Neither spoke until they were close to the freeway entrance.

"Why are you doing this?" she demanded.

"I don't know," he answered. "But I do know you're going through with this wedding, if it's the last thing either of us ever does."

"But how can you force me to marry you, knowing what you do?"

"It must have something to do with saving my entire family from humiliation," he continued with the same chilly irony. "That family you claim to love so much. Maybe it's because I don't want my mother—who's worked day and night on this wedding for the past three weeks, who's looked forward to this day for years—to become an object of pity among her friends. Maybe it's because I'd have trouble looking my two sisters and their husbands in the eye, knowing they rearranged their entire summer, gave up their vacations, to fly out here for our wedding. Just maybe it's because I have an aversion to being ridiculed myself. I can't really tell you what else would reduce a man to drag a woman

who's rejected him to the altar. But make no mistake, Charlotte, you will marry me."

"It isn't that I don't care for you," she whispered through her tears.

"Right. You care so deeply that you decided to go into hiding on our wedding day."

"I know you're angry..."

"You're damn right I'm angry."

"We can't go through with the wedding, Jason! We just can't."

"Oh, but we are, Charlotte."

"What will we do afterward? I mean, once we're married and—"

"Somehow we'll find a way to miss our flight to Hawaii, then, first thing Monday morning, I'll file for an annulment."

"But it doesn't make sense to go through with the wedding—"

"Yes, my darling Charlotte, it does. It makes a whole lot of sense."

Charlotte was determined to survive the day, although she wasn't sure how she'd manage. She'd been a fool to run off the way she had. A fool and a coward. She was an even bigger fool to think she'd appease Jason's anger by lying.

When she'd left, she hadn't thought about what she was doing to Jason or his family. She hadn't been thinking at all, overpowered instead by her own fears.

On the way back, she tried to tell Jason she was sorry, to apologize for the hurt and humiliation she'd caused, but each time he cut her off, saying he didn't want to hear it.

The ride back to her apartment was like living through the worst nightmare of her life. Jason was so cold, so furiously angry.

He dropped her off at her apartment, took her arm, leveled his steely blue eyes on her and said, "I'll be by to pick you up in forty minutes."

"I can't possibly be ready by then."

"You can and you will. And, Charlotte, don't even think about running away again. Do you understand me?"

Charlotte nodded and almost told him it was bad luck for the groom to see the bride before the wedding. Then she remembered the whole wedding was a farce, anyway.

"Fine. I'll be ready," she assured him calmly.

She showered, brushed her hair and dressed, but she wasn't conscious of doing any of those things. Carrie was with her, and Mandy, too, both silent and pale. Worried. What she'd done to them was terrible, Charlotte realized. They were both too young to carry this secret, too young to bear the burden of her foolishness.

Neither girl asked her any questions, and for that, Charlotte was grateful. She didn't know what she would've told them if they had.

Leah and Jamie had arrived within minutes of Jason's bringing her home. They were both happy and excited. If her complete lack of emotion bewildered them, they didn't let it show. They chatted excitedly, recalling events at their own weddings, bubbling over with enthusiasm. Charlotte tried to smile, tried to pretend this was the happiest moment of her life. Leah and Jamie seemed to believe it, even if the girls had their doubts.

Jason arrived to escort her to the church, and her fu-

ture sisters-in-law shooed him away. She wore the beautiful off-white dress Elizabeth Manning had insisted on buying her, and Leah had woven flowers in her hair.

Before she knew it, Charlotte was at the church. The number of guests surprised her. Tears clogged her throat when she reminded herself that she was playing a role. Tomorrow morning she'd go back to what her life had been before she met Jason Manning. Back to the emptiness. The loneliness.

At the appropriate moment, with organ music swirling around her, she walked dutifully down the aisle, aware every second of Jason standing at the front of the church. His eyes held hers as effectively as a vise, as though he suspected she might try to run even now. And if she tried, she didn't doubt for a second that he'd go after her.

With her morning little more than a vague memory, Charlotte found it ironic that the actual wedding ceremony was so clear to her.

Jason stood at her side, revealing no emotion, and calmly repeated his vows. Charlotte wondered why the minister didn't stop him. It was all too evident from the clipped, angry tone of his voice that he didn't mean what he was saying. He had no intention of loving her, of cherishing her, of allowing her ever to be important in his life. Not after what she'd done. Not after she'd led him to believe her motives were so deceitful. Not after she'd made him think she planned to ridicule him and his family. Whatever love he'd once felt for her was dead. He'd practically told her so himself.

When it was her turn to say her vows, Charlotte's voice was surprisingly strong. She would always love Jason, and she'd always treasure the months they'd

shared. The sincerity in her voice must have caught his attention, because he looked at her for the first time since they'd approached the altar. His eyes narrowed scornfully. For a moment she nearly faltered, but decided she wouldn't let him intimidate her.

His eyes seemed to be laughing at her—a mocking laugh that told her she was the biggest hypocrite who'd ever lived. He could think what he wanted, but in her heart she knew the truth.

After the ceremony, they were whisked from the church to the reception at the yacht club.

For Charlotte, the lengthy reception was a thousand times worse than the ceremony. They stood, for what seemed like hours, with the members of their wedding party, while an endless line of guests paraded past.

Everyone was so thrilled for them, so happy, everyone except the two of them. From the moment they'd arrived at the reception, Charlotte was a heartbeat away from dissolving into tears. Heaven knew how she survived the ordeal.

Later they had to cut the cake. The photographer took picture after picture.

"Resist the urge to shove the cake in my face," Jason whispered behind a smile, when she went to feed him a small piece for the camera, "and I'll do the same."

They ate, they danced, they opened gifts. Outwardly they were the perfect couple. Madly in love, solicitous of each other, eager to be alone. Eager to start their lives together.

Only Charlotte and Jason knew the reality beneath the pretense.

Despite herself, Charlotte was impressed by what a brilliant actor Jason was. He refrained from touching

her, but when it was unavoidable, his arms were gentle, his look as tender as he could make it, although she knew that he seethed with outrage. She could feel his anger, hidden below the surface, out of everyone's sight but hers. At times Charlotte felt as if that anger would devour her whole.

"Just a few minutes longer," Jason whispered harshly while they were on the dance floor. "Then we can leave."

She relaxed. "Where are we going?"

"Not the airport, so don't worry about it."

"We need to talk."

"No, we don't. Everything's been said. I'll drop you off at your apartment and you can forget this day ever happened."

"But—"

"Like I said, don't worry about it. I'll arrange everything. Once this is over, we won't ever have to see each other again. Needless to say, I'll expect you to find a new place as soon as possible."

She nodded, knowing she'd brought this on herself. But when it was time to go, there was a surprise awaiting both of them. Jason's brothers and brothers-in-law had rented two limousines. The first to take them to the airport, Rich explained, grinning proudly. And the second limousine was so the entire wedding party could follow them and see them off with as much fanfare and enthusiasm as was allowed.

Jason's eyes sought out Charlotte's when she returned from changing her clothes. His gaze assured her not to worry. He wasn't any more willing to spend two weeks in her company than she'd been about going through

with the wedding. She was sure he'd find some way to miss the flight.

Except that he didn't.

His mother waited with them at the airline counter, wiping the tears from her eyes as she hugged her son. Carrie was there, too, more relaxed now, excited that she and Higgins would be spending two weeks with Leah and Paul.

Charlotte hugged Jason's mother farewell, tears brimming in her eyes. "No woman ever had a more beautiful wedding," she whispered. "Thank you."

Her father-in-law was waiting when she'd finished, holding out his arms to her as though she were a small child needing reassurance. Nothing could be closer to the truth.

"Eric, thank you," she murmured, as she slipped into his embrace. This might well be the only opportunity she'd have to express her gratitude. Soon enough Jason's parents would know. She wouldn't be able to face them.

"You call me Dad," Eric said, hugging her close. "We already love you like a daughter, Charlotte."

Tears blurred her vision and when she turned, she nearly collided with Jason. He took her by the elbow, his fingers pinching her skin. "You're laying it on a bit thick, aren't you?"

She didn't answer him, couldn't have said a word if she'd tried. They got their boarding passes as everyone watched. They were going to Hawaii, like it or not.

Charlotte realized there was no escape for them, unless they owned up to the truth immediately. Jason didn't look any more pleased than she did, but obviously didn't want to disillusion the family quite so soon.

As he led her into the security area, away from his family, he muttered, "I didn't plan this."

"I know," she said with a helpless sigh. "Oh—my car. I left it at the beach."

"Mandy's getting it for you."

His thoughtfulness surprised her. "Thank you."

"Don't mention it," he said sarcastically. "I wanted it back in the apartment lot so you wouldn't have any trouble leaving again. Next time you can go with my blessing."

Their seats were in business class and they were quickly served glasses of champagne that neither of them drank.

As the plane taxied away from the jetway and toward the airstrip, he closed his eyes, heaved a massive sigh and said, "Don't worry, I'll get us out of this yet."

Charlotte nodded and lowered her gaze. "I'll do everything I can to stay out of your way."

"That would be appreciated."

The flight was five hours, but it seemed closer to fifty. Jason didn't exchange one unnecessary word with Charlotte. At this rate, she didn't know how they'd be able to spend two weeks in each other's company.

Jason must have been thinking the same thing. "I'll see what I can do about arranging a flight back to Seattle as soon as we land," he told her briskly, without a shred of emotion. No regret, no disappointment, nothing.

Charlotte bit her lip. "I... I didn't pack much of anything...since the suitcase was just for show."

He didn't respond. By the time they landed and collected their luggage, Charlotte was falling asleep on her feet. Apparently Jason suspected as much, since he

made some excuse about contacting the airlines from the hotel instead of rushing her onto a return flight. But she wasn't sure if this small kindness was for her benefit or his own, since he couldn't have had much more sleep than she had.

She barely noticed the scenery as the taxi carried them through town. Their hotel was on Waikiki Beach, built on white sands and surrounded by swaying palms.

When they went to check in at the front desk, Charlotte stepped back, letting Jason take care of the necessary paperwork. He was obviously upset about something, but she couldn't tell what.

"Is everything all right?" she asked, as they moved toward the elevator.

"I thought we could get a double room, but…" Jason rubbed a hand across his face, looking weary and defeated. "My parents booked us into the bridal suite."

"Oh." Charlotte didn't fully realize the implications of that until the bellman ushered them, with much fanfare, into the corner suite. There was one bed. A king-size bed that loomed before her.

Charlotte's startled gaze sought out Jason's as he paid the attendant and closed the door. The fear she'd managed to bury for hours spilled over now, but before she could say a word, he turned to her.

"Don't look so shocked. It isn't as if I intend to make love to you."

"But where will…we sleep?"

He laughed, the sound abrupt. "If you want to call down to the front desk and order a rollaway for the bridal suite, then by all means, be my guest. Frankly, I feel enough of a fool for one day, so I'll leave that option to you."

With no real alternative, she showered, put on an old T-shirt and crawled between the crisp sheets of the bed, making sure she was as far on her side as possible.

She was drifting off to sleep when Jason finished his shower and returned to the bedroom. He stood for several minutes looking down at her. Her heart roared like a crazed animal as she wondered about his intentions. He could force her. Tom had often enough, using her body, leaving her feeling sick and abused afterward. She'd curl up tightly while he shouted how incompetent she was, how unattractive, how lacking. She'd lie there silently as the ugly, demeaning words rained down on her. When he was done with his tirade he'd leave.

The memories made her shiver with revulsion and fear.

"Charlotte."

She didn't answer, pretending to be asleep. Jason was angry with her, angrier than she'd ever seen him. Eyes closed, she lay still, her heart pounding with dread.

She heard Jason dressing, heard him pause and then, after a moment, heard him turn off the light and leave the room.

Abruptly Charlotte sat up. He'd left her, walked away just like Tom had, as though he couldn't bear to be in the same room with her. Like Tom, he couldn't wait to be rid of her.

He'd left without a word.

Wasn't that what she wanted? Then why did she feel so alone, so deserted and unloved, so empty inside?

The tears that had threatened most of the day broke free with a low, eerie wail. She tucked her knees against her chest as the sobs overtook her.

She wept for all she'd lost. Jason's love. Any chance

of sharing their lives. The dream of having another child. The family she'd never had. It was gone now, crushed by her own hand.

It was too late to try and get any of it back. Jason hated her. She could never recapture what she'd destroyed with her fear. Never rebuild the trust she'd demolished when she'd run away.

She sobbed until the well of grief was emptied. Even that wasn't enough. She tore at the sheets, pulling the blankets from the bed and beating the pillows.

It didn't take long to exhaust what little energy she had, and she fell across the bed sobbing, then fell into a deep, troubled sleep.

Jason came back to the room an hour later, moving as silently as possible, not wanting to wake Charlotte. He wished he could hate his wife, punish her for what she'd done. She deserved to suffer, didn't she?

But if that was really the case, then why was *he* the one in pain? He saw her climb into bed and curl up, and it was all he could do not to dash across the room and take her in his arms. This woman had betrayed him, and yet he wanted to comfort her.

It was either leave the room or beg her forgiveness for forcing her to endure this day. She wasn't entitled to his forgiveness, he reminded himself, which meant there was only one option. He'd left.

He'd gone for a walk on the beach, which wasn't exactly how he'd expected to spend his wedding night. Not that he was any great shakes as a husband. A hundred times or more he'd gone over his own part in this fiasco. He'd rushed Charlotte into marriage and so had his family, not giving her a chance for second thoughts.

Looking back, he understood now that it was the urgency of his mother's idea that he'd found so appealing. Now he understood why.

He'd rushed into marriage with Charlotte because, deep down, he'd been afraid that if she'd had the chance to change her mind, she would. And he'd been right.

Jason didn't know what lunacy had prompted him to make her go through with the ceremony. To avoid embarrassment? Having their marriage annulled the following week would still embarrass him and his family. There was the problem, too, of returning all the wedding gifts. Eventually he'd have to face people. Make explanations.

He'd taken the easy way out, delaying the inevitable because of his pride.

Charlotte had wanted to cancel the wedding and he'd perversely refused to release her. So now they were stuck in Hawaii on a two-week honeymoon neither of them wanted. Stuck in each other's company, in the bridal suite no less, until he could find a flight back to Seattle.

Once his eyes had adjusted to the dark, Jason made his way across the elegant room. Charlotte was still curled up on the bed, but the sheets and blankets were strewn about as though a storm had raged through.

He discovered a second and a third pillow hurled across the room. One was on the floor, the other dangling from a chair. It looked as if his bride had thrown a temper tantrum.

So she hadn't liked it that he'd left. A smile played across his lips. It was the first time since he'd found her on the beach that she'd displayed any emotion.

The thought of Charlotte losing her temper pleased

him, until he remembered she wasn't given to bouts of anger. He felt a pang of concern but brushed it aside—it belonged to the past, to the old Charlotte, the one he'd loved.

Exhausted and depressed, he gazed about the room and noted that the bed was all she'd bothered to disarrange. Everything else in the room remained untouched.

Not knowing what to think, and too tired to care, he quietly stripped off his clothes and slipped beneath a rumpled sheet. It didn't take him long to fall asleep, but his dreams were disturbing and he woke several times before morning.

Not once during the night did Charlotte move. She stayed on her side, facing away from him, never changing her position.

He woke in the morning, the bright sunshine slashing through the bedroom curtains. Charlotte was on her back, already awake. She shifted her head and stared at him with eyes so filled with pain that he hurt just looking at her.

"I lied when I said I didn't love you, Jason," she whispered and a tear rolled down the side of her face. "I do… so very much. I'm sorry…for everything I've done."

He nodded, his throat thick. "I'm sorry, too, Charlotte."

Thirteen

Charlotte closed her eyes because looking at Jason was so painful, knowing he hated her, knowing he'd never really forgive her for what she'd done.

"I lied when I said I wanted to marry you because of your family. I...ran away because I was afraid."

"Of me?"

Her pulse scampered. She should've told him the truth weeks earlier. She'd agreed to be his wife; he had a right to know. But the truth was so easy to put off, so easy to deny. So hard to explain.

There'd been opportunities to tell him, plenty of them, although she'd tried to convince herself otherwise. She'd been too much of a coward to present Jason with the truth. And then, when time ran out, she'd panicked.

"Charlotte?" Jason said in a low voice. "What are you afraid of?"

She couldn't explain that she was, to put it bluntly, afraid of sex. Of intimacy. That wasn't what a man wanted to hear. Not just Jason, but any man.

He deserved so much more than she was capable of giving him. He deserved a woman who was emotion-

ally whole and healthy. A woman who was physically responsive. Not someone scared and battle-weary and all but dead to her own sexuality.

"I owe you an explanation…."

"I'd say so," he agreed, but his voice was devoid of the previous day's sarcasm, without a trace of anger.

"I meant to tell you sooner. To give you the choice of going through with the wedding or not. But as time went on I—I couldn't…and then it was too late."

"Tell me now."

Charlotte thought back to an age when she'd been innocent, vulnerable and naive. "My mother died while I was in high school. My father had abandoned us years earlier and I don't think my mother ever recovered. If he contacted her at any point after he left, I didn't know about it. She was different after he was gone. It was like she'd given up on life. She loved me, though—I know she did— and she'd been insightful enough to plan for my future."

Jason's hand reached across the bed for hers. Their fingers entwined and Charlotte was grateful for his touch.

"I met Tom my first year of college. He came from another state and was attending classes on a limited scholarship. He was intelligent and good-looking. When he asked me out, I was thrilled. He seemed to like me…. Later I realized it wasn't me that attracted him, but the insurance money I'd received when my mother died. After a few months, we made love and…and he asked me to marry him. I didn't have any family and… I desperately needed someone. I was too stupid to know why Tom really wanted to marry me. He saw marriage as a way of paying for his education without having to work for it.

"I dropped out of school after one semester and we

got married. The money that was meant for my education went toward Tom's while I got a full-time job to pay our living expenses."

Jason's hand flinched, tightening around hers.

"I should've gotten out of the marriage as soon as I figured out he was using me. Instead, I compounded my mistake. I thought if I got pregnant it would make everything better. If Tom didn't love me, surely he'd love the baby."

"You've been so hard on yourself."

"I'll never regret having Carrie. She's been the best thing in my life…but Tom wasn't happy." She hesitated, reliving the terrible scene, so many years past, when she'd told Tom she was pregnant. He'd wanted her to have an abortion, even given her the money. She'd lied and told him she'd done it, hiding her pregnancy until it was too late. He'd been so furious that he'd hit her. The blow had been so hard, it had loosened three of her teeth.

"Go on," Jason prompted.

"I had Carrie and for a while I thought the marriage might work. Tom liked his little girl and was proud of her."

"You told me Tom was having an affair. When did this happen?"

"It started while I was pregnant. Tom enjoyed sex… and after a while he said I was too fat and ugly to make love to, and everything came to a stop." Charlotte remembered how relieved she was, how grateful because she no longer had to give in to his rough physical demands. She was working a forty-hour week, waiting tables, and was too exhausted at night to satisfy him. He'd been telling her for months that a man needed en-

thusiasm from his wife during sex, but Charlotte had never seemed able to rouse any. It was like making love to a corpse, he told her.

"I... I never was very good at sex," she continued in a tight voice. "And after Carrie was born, I lost all interest." Actually any pleasure in the physical aspects of their marriage had died months earlier, when Tom had demanded she have an abortion. After Carrie was born, she found herself unwilling to make any effort to please him physically.

"That was when the really bad fights began," she said as evenly as the remembered emotions would allow. "Tom claimed it was his right to make love to me whenever he wanted and...and..." Her throat closed up, forcing her to stop.

"Did he rape you, Charlotte?"

Biting her lower lip, she nodded. Only Tom hadn't called it rape; he'd said it was his right. He'd married her, hadn't he? That meant she'd given him the right to do whatever he wanted with her body the moment she'd signed the marriage document.

Jason moved closer and brought her into his arms, cradling her head against his shoulder, stroking her hair. His chest was heaving and Charlotte knew he was fighting his own anger.

Her eyes glazed over with tears as she struggled to hold back the fear, the memory of the violence, the feeling of powerlessness, the revulsion of those terror-filled episodes. Her breathing became labored.

"I...couldn't satisfy Tom," she admitted in a breathless whisper.

"That has everything to do with Tom—not with

you." He paused. "Are you afraid you won't be able to satisfy me?"

She nodded through her tears.

"But, Charlotte," he said, raising himself on one elbow and gazing down at her, "how can you think that? Everything between us has always been so good. Or am I wrong? Haven't you enjoyed the times we kissed?"

She lowered her lashes. "Yes...but they've frightened me."

"I never forced you."

"I... I know that. You've been so patient and gentle. I almost convinced myself I could make love again... that I could erase those nightmare years with Tom and start all over...but I can't. That's why I ran away...that's the real reason, not what I told you earlier."

"Why couldn't you tell me this before?"

She wiped the tears from her face, and swallowed the bittersweet agony of the moment. "Because I love you so much."

Her words were met with a puzzled hesitation. "You wouldn't tell me because you love me?"

She nodded, and hiccuped a sobbing laugh. "It sounds ludicrous, I know, but it's true. Because I couldn't stand to lose you—not that way. Because if we ever did make love, you'd see—you wouldn't want me anymore."

"How could you think that?" Jason asked.

This was the moment she'd dreaded. The moment of truth. She turned her head away, unwilling to look at him, unwilling to let him see her face. A tightness gripped her chest, crushing her, the pressure so intense she could hardly breathe.

"Charlotte?"

It would've been easier if he hadn't been so gentle. She could deal with his anger and frustration, but not his tenderness. She didn't know how to respond to that in a man.

Shoving aside the blanket and sheet, she sat on the edge of the bed. When he caressed her back, she stood, unable to deal with being touched just then. Her arms were locked around her middle and the aching pressure in her chest rose, settling in her throat. Tears burned her eyes.

"Tell me," he demanded, not unkindly. "Just say it."

"I can't be your wife."

"It's too late for that," he murmured. "You already are."

"I'm not…not in the ways that matter to a man."

"Oh?"

"Don't you understand what I'm saying?" she cried. "Do I have to spell out every degrading detail? Is that what you want? Then fine, I'll say it. I can't be your wife because I can't make love." She gulped in a deep breath. "I'm frigid, Jason. The term might be out of fashion but it still applies."

There was a brief, shocked silence. Then Jason started to laugh.

"Don't you dare laugh at me! Don't you dare laugh." A fury rose inside Charlotte, one that had been years in the making, one so strong there was no holding back. She threw herself at him, arms swinging, feet kicking, fingers clawing, before he had a chance to react.

He caught her by the wrists. "Charlotte… I wasn't laughing at *you*."

She barely heard his words, not that it mattered. She twisted and bucked in his hold. He twisted, too, and with the momentum of his weight they fell together on

the bed. He was sprawled over her upper body, his thigh across her legs, holding her down.

Her chest was heaving, her shoulders jerking upward in an effort to escape.

"Charlotte, for heaven's sake, I wasn't laughing at you," he said again.

She gritted her teeth, refusing to answer him.

"Stop struggling, before you destroy any chance of my fathering our future child."

She went still, although the fight hadn't completely left her.

"Now let me explain."

There were too many years of agony inside her, too many insecurities to be soothed away with a few simple words. "No. Just let me go."

"In a minute. Then if you still want me to release you I will. You owe me this much. All right?"

She twisted her head away from him, still refusing to answer.

"I love you, Charlotte. I realized when we first started seeing each other that you'd been badly hurt by your ex-husband. I didn't understand the extent of it until now, but in some ways I think not knowing was for the best. It would have intimidated me in the beginning."

A sob tore through her throat.

"The first time we kissed… I wish I knew how to explain it, but I knew you were different. That moment was different than any I'd ever known before. Kissing you was so good."

Charlotte didn't respond, but she knew he was right. Their kisses *had* been good. Very good.

"It got even better, didn't it?"

She nodded, although only slightly.

"You're not frigid, or whatever term the psychologists prefer now. Not even close. What you are, my love, is afraid, and for a very legitimate reason. You've been sexually abused."

"I'm sexually…damaged. Forever."

"No, not forever. In time you'll heal. We'll heal together." He said it with such conviction, as though they faced only a small problem, when to her it was bigger than both of them. Bigger than even their love.

"But it isn't *you* who…can't make love," she sobbed. "It's me. You're not the one who has to heal…and I don't know if I can."

"We're in this together, Charlotte. Whatever it takes."

"There isn't any reason you should—"

"We can't heal," he interrupted, "unless we try. We can't sweep this under the carpet and ignore it. I'm not so stupid as to believe that all the pain and all the memories will go away simply because we make love and it's as good as our kisses have been."

"I…don't know if I'll ever be able to forget."

Jason rolled away from her, freeing her arms and legs. He stood and raked his hand through his hair. "The decision is yours, and I'll abide by whatever you want. I'm not going to force you to be my wife. I've made some mistakes in this relationship and just now was one of them. I'm sure I'll make more. You should know that."

"I don't understand what you're saying." She sat up and wiped the tears from her burning cheeks, her hands trembling. Jason had moved away from her and was staring out the window.

"Like I said, the decision is yours. If you want me to

file for an annulment, then I will. I'll make the arrangements to get us off this island as quickly as possible. As soon as I can, I'll take care of all the legalities. In a few days there won't be anything to bind us together—if that's what you want."

"I see." Her heart filled with mourning.

"But there's something you should understand, Charlotte. If you decide you want to give this marriage a try, there'll be no turning back."

She did understand, and the thought filled her with panic.

"I'm willing to devote myself to you and the marriage, but I'll need the same kind of commitment from you. In other words, you're going to have to *want* to heal. It may mean counseling for you, for us both. We both have to be willing to do whatever it takes."

"I don't know if I could...ever tell anyone else about my marriage to Tom."

"That's your decision, too. If you want to stay my wife, you have to realize that the time will come when we *will* make love—but only when you're ready. And when we do, it'll be good, Charlotte... I promise you that."

"How often?" It was probably a stupid question, but one she needed to know. She might be able to bear it if Jason wanted to make love occasionally. She might be able to overcome the terror if he wasn't too demanding.

"I can't answer that because I don't know."

"More than once a month?"

He turned away from her, but not before she saw his smile. "Yes, Charlotte, more than once a month."

"I see."

"It seems to me that you have some serious think-

ing to do. Perhaps it would be best if I left for a while. When I come back, you can tell me your thoughts. Does that sound fair?"

She waited until he turned to look at her before she nodded.

So this was what it meant to love someone, Jason thought as he left the hotel and headed for the beach. He felt as though a hole had been carved through the center of his life, and nothing—besides Charlotte—was capable of filling it. He wanted to believe she'd realize he wasn't another Tom. That didn't seem to be the case, however.

He'd felt a glimmer of hope when he'd first started talking, trying to get through to her, soothe her fears. The anger had drained from her eyes as she'd studied him, seeming to measure his words. He'd seen trust gradually replace that anger.

He hoped she'd be willing to give their marriage a chance. He loved her, but he wasn't naive or arrogant enough to believe his feelings for her could, on their own, heal the horror of her experience. She was going to need more than his love, more than his gentleness. Being tender and patient with her wasn't going to wipe out the trauma of having been raped by her own husband. No wonder she was so terrified.

Jason sensed that other things, maybe even worse than those he knew, had happened in her marriage. Things she hadn't told him yet.

Her marriage had been so ugly, so abusive. He marveled that she'd even considered remarrying. Knowing what he did now, it didn't surprise him that she'd run

away at the eleventh hour. It wouldn't surprise him if she decided to go through with the annulment, either.

He'd given her the option, laid everything out on the table for her to examine. His love, his commitment, his willingness to do whatever he could to help her overcome her fears. But in light of what he'd learned, it seemed so little....

A couple of hours later, Jason returned to the hotel to confront Charlotte again. Two hours didn't seem like much time to come to such a monumental decision, but he wanted to be with her.

Perhaps it would be best if he waited for her to come to him, but he quickly rejected that idea as impractical. If he was going to waste precious time debating with himself, he should do it over something important, like how was he going to live without Charlotte. How was he going to let her go, the only woman he'd ever truly loved? Those were the questions he should be asking himself.

Charlotte sat in the darkened room, the drapes pulled against the brightness of the sun, waiting for Jason. Having carefully considered her husband's words, she knew with a clarity that defied explanation what she was meant to do. She *should* remain his wife. *Should* share his bed. *Should* share his life.

The heavy ache in her chest intensified. Fresh tears moistened her eyes. Jason had offered her his love, his devotion, and his wholehearted commitment. He'd done so with a courage that left her humbled. He was willing to help her heal, but Charlotte didn't know if it would be enough.

There was no guarantee the pain would ever end. No guarantee she'd ever feel whole again. Healing demanded courage. It meant reaching back into the past, into the pain, and reliving the nightmare. Wasn't enduring it *once* enough? Healing meant risking whatever serenity she'd found in the years since her divorce. Healing meant trusting a man again, trusting him enough to freely share her body.

Charlotte closed her eyes, wanting to blot everything out. She was such a coward. A world-class wimp. She knew what she *should* do, but it was so frightening. She wanted to run away, bury her feelings. Hide, the way she'd been doing for years. There was something so comfortable in denial.

There had to be more to life than this choking anger. More than this grief and fear.

With Jason's love there *was* more.

There was hope.

Charlotte must have fallen asleep. When she stirred she saw that the drapes were open and Jason was sitting on the lanai, sipping a glass of orange juice.

"Hello," he said with a smile.

"Hi." She felt a little shy as she slipped out of bed and rubbed her eyes. "What time is it?"

"Afternoon. I imagine you're starved."

Now that he mentioned it, she realized she was hungry. The last food she'd eaten had been at their wedding dinner, and that had been the day before.

"I took the liberty of ordering you lunch."

She smiled and joined him on the lanai. "I slept for so long."

"You needed the rest." He looked so familiar and

handsome, sitting there in the sunlight with his baseball cap shading his eyes. His skin was bronzed, and his eyes, as blue as the Hawaiian sky, roamed over her with undisguised love and tenderness. "Listen, Charlotte, I was wrong."

"Wrong?"

"I shouldn't have given you an ultimatum. You're going to need more than a few hours to decide what you want. I made the same mistake earlier by rushing you into a marriage you didn't want and…"

"But I did want this marriage, very badly."

"Did," he repeated in a husky, regretful voice.

"Do," she corrected firmly.

For several minutes, he said nothing. "Even now, knowing what it'll mean?"

"Even now," she said, holding out her hand to him.

Jason held it fast. "I love you, Charlotte Manning."

"I know." Her voice broke, and she struggled not to break down and weep. Someday she'd tell him how close she'd come to walking away from the brightest promise of her life. She'd tell him how she'd finally decided that loving Jason, being his wife, sharing his life wasn't just something she *should* do, but something she *wanted* to do. *Ached* to do, with all her heart. Someday she'd tell him all of this.

"I don't want to live without you."

He reached for her, bringing her onto his lap, his mouth instinctively finding hers. Everything she'd planned to say was caught between two hungry mouths. Trapped between two pounding hearts.

Fourteen

Several months later a storm, a Seattle cloudburst, woke Charlotte. Dawn was on the horizon, but very little light filtered through the gray clouds. The wind beat hard against the windows, rattling them until Charlotte feared they might break.

Gently setting aside the covers, she climbed out of bed and crept into the living room. Higgins was sleeping there, looking worried. She patted his head and offered him reassurances.

She opened the living-room drapes just in time to watch a bolt of lightning rip apart the night. For an hour or so afterward, smiling contentedly, she watched morning creep across the sky. Her life, inside and out, was everything she wanted it to be. Jason had moved into her apartment; they planned to buy a house in the spring. She was taking a break from work, enrolled in an advanced accounting course. Eventually she'd handle all of his bookkeeping and maybe look for a few other clients, too. Yes, life was full of new possibilities.

"Charlotte?" Jason murmured when she returned to

bed. He reached for her and without a second's hesitation she slipped into his embrace.

"There's a storm," she whispered.

His smile was lazy, sleepy. "So I hear. Are you frightened?"

"Not anymore." There'd been a time when she would've been terrified, but that time was long past. She felt intensely alive, completely calm. The dangerous storms were gone from her life. She'd survived the raging wind, the drenching rain, the booming thunder. That was all in the past. Her future was holding her in his arms.

She sighed, cuddling close to her husband, suffused with a feeling of profound joy.

"I love you," she whispered.

"I know," he said without opening his eyes. "Believe me, I know."

She slid her arms up his shoulders and brought her mouth to his. He welcomed her kiss, which was slow and deep. Hot excitement poured into her blood. Soon the kiss was no longer slow, but hungry, needy.

Charlotte felt Jason's chest lift with a shuddering intake of breath.

"I want to make love," she said against his lips.

Jason went still. His hand, which was sliding up her thigh, stopped at her hip.

"You're sure?"

It was the first time she'd ever made the request, the first time she'd ever initiated their lovemaking.

"Yes."

Lightning briefly brightened the room, shadows frolicked and danced against the walls, followed by the roar of thunder. The bedroom vibrated with sound.

Jason, ever-sensitive to her moods, paused, but she refused to allow any hesitation. She drew his mouth down to hers and they kissed, until Charlotte's whole body seemed to throb with excitement.

Gently Jason removed her nightgown, pulling it over her head. He'd awakened her to an entire world of sensual pleasure in the months since their marriage, a world she wanted to explore *now.*

He hungrily covered her mouth with his own and her head spun, her nails digging into his back. Abruptly she broke off the kiss, her shoulders heaving. "Jason, please... I want you."

He didn't need any further encouragement....

"Okay, so far?" he asked sometime later.

"Oh, yes," she whispered, smiling her assurance. The pleasure was so keen it was almost beyond bearing.

Lightning flashed and thunder rolled, punctuating their lovemaking. "Jason...oh, Jase," she cried out, her voice a trembling wail of pleasure as her senses caught fire, exploding into a mindless madness. Her body shuddered as she gave herself to the storm, to her husband, to the night.

Afterward, when he, too, had reached completion, they were both panting. Jason gathered her in his arms, and they were silent, words between them unnecessary.

Eventually their breathing steadied.

"I still have trouble believing how good this is," Charlotte whispered. "Making love, I mean."

Jason kissed the crown of her head. "It always has been."

"Not in the beginning."

"It was," he said. "Because you let me try to prove how much I love you."

Charlotte was quiet for a moment as she absorbed his words. Their first attempts at making love, on their honeymoon, had left her frustrated and in tears. She was convinced Jason had made a terrible mistake in marrying her. He wouldn't allow her to criticize herself, though. His patience astonished her and gave her the courage to keep trying.

She'd struggled with her inadequacies, silently condemning herself, but on the seventh night of their stay, they'd broken through the restraints and made beautiful, intoxicating love. Charlotte had wanted everything to be magically different from then on, but that would have been unrealistic. Her fears were unpredictable and continued to be for weeks. But now, four months after their wedding, loving Jason was the most incredible experience of her life.

Tears slipped down Charlotte's cheeks as she recalled the first weeks of their marriage—his gentleness, his unwillingness to give up, his *love*.

"You're crying," he whispered, his lips against her hair.

"You're not supposed to notice."

"But I have. Are you going to tell me why?"

Emotion clogged her throat as she struggled to hold back the tears. "In a minute."

Jason's brow creased with a thoughtful frown. "Is it something that came from your meeting with Bill?"

Bill was her counselor; she saw him twice a week. She shook her head. "You promise you won't laugh?"

"I'll try."

"I'm crying because I'm so happy."

"Happy," Jason repeated slowly. "But if you cry when you're happy, what do you do when you're sad?"

"Cry," she returned with irrefutable logic. "Now aren't you going to ask me *why* I'm so happy?"

"I don't need to. It's obvious."

"It is?"

"Of course. You're married to me."

Charlotte laughed at his mock arrogance. "Carrie cried, too."

"Carrie's *that* happy?"

"It's the reason she's spending the night with a friend. I wanted the evening alone with you."

Jason snickered. "If that's the case, why'd you go to bed at six-thirty?"

"I didn't plan that," she murmured, "but I think it's going to be pretty much the norm for the next few months. I couldn't seem to get enough sleep when I was pregnant with Carrie, either."

"Cute, Charlotte, very cute. You couldn't possibly be—" He stopped cold, his eyes widening.

"It's true," she said, pressing her head to his chest. She smiled as the erratic beat of his heart sounded in her ear.

"How far…?"

"A month."

He shook his head as though in a trance.

"It was inevitable, you know," she told him, happiness spilling from her heart. "How could I not be pregnant? We've been making love for months. And we decided not to use birth control for this very reason."

"Yes, but…"

"When the lovemaking's this good, doesn't it make sense that the result will be equally beautiful?"

Jason kissed her again, his mouth worshipping hers. "I love you so much."

Charlotte sighed and closed her eyes, utterly content. She'd conquered her fears, begun to heal her pain. She'd survived the memories and triumphed over her past.

The future stretched before her, filled with bright promise. She wasn't going to miss a single moment.

* * * * *